COFFIN FOR A HOOD

The two hired killers arriv W9-CPH-128 plane to the little coastal town of Arroyos in the Florida Keys. But why? Could they be here to settle an old debt with Socks Schroeder, the basketball jock who didn't throw the game and turned state's evidence instead? Or did Helen's ex hire them to kill her new husband, Nick? Or possibly they were here for Doc Martins, to settle an old score? Or for Deputy Flack, who used to run with the mob before he'd killed a rival and was forced to hide out. Richard Fullbright is sure they're after *him*, hired by his ex-partners after they found out he'd swindled them. All they know is that two professionals are in town, and they must be here for a reason. While just offshore, Hurricane Bettina is ready to strike…

OPERATION—MURDER

Tina marries Frank so quickly, she really doesn't know much about him. She meets him in the hospital where she is a nurse, and he a patient. But now she is on a bus headed toward Twin Valley to join him so that they can finally celebrate their honeymoon in a lodge up in the Rockies. When she gets there, there's no Frank. Joe the Indian is there to meet her instead. And when she gets to the lodge, nothing seems right. Tina discovers she will be sharing the lodge not only with Joe, but with two other men she doesn't know. Because Frank has a plan, and a belated honeymoon is only a small part of it. He intends to rob the Denver mint train. And nothing Tina can do is going to stop him.

LIONEL WHITE BIBLIOGRAPHY (1905-1985)

The Snatchers (1953)
To Find a Killer (1954; reprinted as Before I Die, 1964)
Clean Break (1955; reprinted as The Killing, 1956)
Flight Into Terror (1955)
Love Trap (1955)
The Big Caper (1955)
Operation—Murder (1956)
The House Next Door (1956)
Right for Murder (1957)
Hostage to a Hood (1957)
Death Takes the Bus (1957)
Invitation to Violence (1958)
Too Young to Die (1958)
Coffin for a Hood (1958)
Rafferty (1959)
Run, Killer, Run! (1959; orig mag version as Seven Hungry Men, 1952)
The Merriweather File (1959)
Lament for a Virgin (1960)
Marilyn K. (1960)
Steal Big (1960)
The Time of Terror (1960)
A Death at Sea (1961)
A Grave Undertaking (1961)
Obsession (1962) [screenplay pub as Pierrot le Fou: A Film, 1969]
The Money Trap (1963)
The Ransomed Madonna (1964)
The House on K Street (1965)
A Party to Murder (1966)
The Mind Poisoners (1966; as Nick Carter, written with Valerie Moolman)
The Crimshaw Memorandum (1967)
The Night of the Rape (1967; reprinted as Death of a City, 1970)

Hijack (1969)
A Rich and Dangerous Game (1974)
Mexico Run (1974)
Jailbreak (1976; reprinted as The Walled Yard, 1978)

As L. W. Blanco
Spykill (1966)

Short Stories
Purely Personal (*Bluebook*, May 1953)
Night Riders of the Florida Swamps (*Bluebook*, Jan 1954)
"Sorry—Your Party Doesn't Answer" (*Bluebook*, July 1954)
The Picture Window Murder (*Cosmopolitan*, Aug 1956; condensed version of *The House Next Door*)
To Kill a Wife (*Murder*, Sept 1956)
Invitation to Violence (*Alfred Hitchcock's Mystery Magazine*, May 1957; condensed version of novel)
Death of a City (*Argosy*, Jan 1971; condensed version of novel)

Non-Fiction
Sports Aren't for Sissies! (*Bluebook*, May 1953; article)
Stocks: America's Fastest Growing Sport (*Bluebook*, Nov 1952; article)
Protect Yourself, Your Family, and Your Property in an Unsafe World (1974)

COFFIN FOR A HOOD
OPERATION—MURDER
Lionel White
Introduction by
Ben Boulden

Stark House Press • Eureka California

COFFIN FOR A HOOD / OPERATION—MURDER

Published by Stark House Press
1315 H Street
Eureka, CA 95501, USA
griffinskye3@sbcglobal.net
www.starkhousepress.com

COFFIN FOR A HOOD
Originally published by Gold Medal Books, Greenwich, and copyright ©
1958 by Fawcett Publications, Inc. Copyright renewed August 8, 1986, by
Hedy White.

OPERATION—MURDER
Originally published by Gold Medal Books, Greenwich, and copyright ©
1956 by Fawcett Publications, Inc. Copyright renewed June 5, 1984, by
Lionel White.

Reprinted by permission of the Estate of Lionel White. All rights
reserved under International and Pan-American Copyright Conventions.

"Lionel White – The Caper King" copyright © 2019 by Ben Boulden

ISBN: 978-1-944520-83-0

Book design by Mark Shepard, shepgraphics.com
Proofreading by Bill Kelly
Cover art by James Heimer

First Stark House Press Edition: November 2019

LIONEL WHITE - THE CAPER KING
Ben Boulden

Lionel White is an enigma.

As crime fiction readers we should know White's writing since he is considered the king of the caper tale. A story type that details a high concept heist from the planning to the execution to its aftermath. Bill Crider wrote in the *St. James Guide to Crime and Mystery Writers*, "If [White] did not invent the caper story [he] is certainly one of the ablest practitioners in the field." Donald E. Westlake acknowledged a debt to White for his most famous character, the hard-as-nails professional thief Parker, published under the pseudonym Richard Stark, and his proficient, but luckless Dortmunder, too. Westlake's caper story is different than White's. His Dortmunder novels are laced with humor and the Parker's are hardboiled, but far removed from Lionel White's noir.

White's novel *Clean Break* (1955) was translated into film by a young Stanley Kubrick with a new title, *The Killing*. The film's title refers to a slang term for a lucrative job—"we're going to make a killing on this deal"—rather than a murder. The movie has become a classic of film noir in the decades since it disappeared from the silver screen in 1956. The script was written by Kubrick (lifted scene-by-scene from White's novel) and the dialogue was written by noir specialist Jim Thompson. Thompson was expecting a co-writer credit, but like everything else in his sad life (a life closer to his bleak tales than anyone should have to suffer), his film credit was simply, "dialogue by."

The film is good, but the novel is better. Kubrick relied on a tired gimmick for an ending that depended on an old woman, her dog and bad luck, while White's ending was perfectly bleak. An ending where everyone gets what they deserve. An ending the reader knows is coming from the first page, but hopes the characters—Johnny Clay and a few others—will somehow dodge its inevitability. It is the essence of noir.

And the irony in its last line, a newspaper headline, is crazy:

"RACE TRACK BANDIT MAKES CLEAN BREAK WITH TWO MILLION"

Another thing Kubrick did was weaken White's female characters. He made Johnny Clay's fiancée Fay a whimpering fool, while White's version of Fay is strong and in control, but fully in love with a doomed criminal. The femme fatale—played nicely in the film by the expressive Marie Windsor—is a sharper knife with plain motivations and a hard cunning that the film doesn't capture. Hollywood made other movies from White's work, too. And most are familiar to film buffs, including *The Big Caper*—starring Rory Calhoun, Mary Costa, and James Gregory. *The Money Trap*—starring Glenn Ford, Elke Sommer, Rita Hayworth, Joseph Cotton, and Ricardo Montalban. *The Night of the Following Day*—based on the novel, *The Snatchers* (1953), and starring Marlon Brando, Richard Boone, and Rita Moreno. A French film, *Pierrot le Fou*, and a Norwegian film, *The Hair*, were odd—the films are odd, I mean—and loosely based on his novel, *Obsession* (1962). And a piece of trivia, his novel, *Rafferty* (1958), was made into a Soviet television movie.

Now that's cool.

So we know Lionel White's work, even if it's through the work of other writers and the films it inspired, but there's almost no information about Lionel White, the man. His biography is shrouded by time and what must have been, and I'm speculating here, hesitancy on his part for publicity. An internet search for Lionel White is empty of any detailed information. There's no obituary and nothing other than generalities about what White did before becoming a fiction writer, where he lived or even where he was born.

I've wondered if White's life story was known, the way Jim Thompson's and Cornell Woolrich's bleak lives are known, if his work would be talked about in hushed voices by the important people? I've wondered this because his stuff is good. His prose isn't fancy, pretty standard stuff, really, but his plots are sharp and relentless. Every scene leads to the next. He never relies on coincidence or other cheap gimmicks to make his stories work. His characters are rich, often developed with exposition in a manner similar to Stephen King (without King's unique shine). Many of his early novels were published by the standard of the paperback era, Fawcett Gold Medal. He started an impressive run of hardcover novels with E. P. Dutton starting with his 1952 novel, *To Find a Killer*, and ending with the 1967 novel, *The Crimshaw Memorandum*.

White was appreciated in his own time, but now, 41 years after his last novel appeared, he and his work are mostly forgotten.

So I did some genealogical research. I found a few things, none are anything more than signposts, but it's something to build on.

Lionel Earle White was born July 9, 1905 in Buffalo, Erie County, New York. His father was Harold Charles White and his mother was Lena (Ostrander) White. Lionel had a twin brother named Harold Jr., an older brother named Donald and a younger sister named Elizabeth. The 1910 census listed Lionel, and Harold Jr. both as four years old and Lionel's name as "Earl L." The 1915 New York census identified Lionel's father as a superintendent in the auto assembly industry and his mother, Lena, as a housekeeper.

There were big changes between 1915 and 1920. The family moved from Buffalo to San Joaquin, California and Harold, Sr. became president of an iron foundry company. Lionel was a 14 year old student. He never graduated, like many of his generation, making it only through the second year of high school. In 1930, at the age of 24, Lionel was married and back in New York. He lived in the Bronx with his first wife, Julia (Yakovleff) White. According to their New York State Marriage License (No. 6749), the two were married March 14, 1927. Julia was born in New York to immigrant parents from Russia. The young couple had a radio, which was probably an uncommon luxury at the time, and Lionel's occupation was listed as "copy reader" and the industry "NY Papers."

In 1940 Julia Yakovleff was gone from his house (although I was unable to identify divorce proceedings or a death certificate). In her place was a woman, listed as "partner" rather than spouse, named Anna Maher. Lionel was 34 and working as an editor of a literary magazine. White's income was an impressive $4,000 per year. Considering inflation, $4,000 would be around $75,000 today, but if you looked at the purchasing power of that $4,000 in New York City in 1940 it would be much greater than $75,000 would be today.

In May 1943, at nearly 38 years old, Lionel enlisted in the United States Army:

"Enlistment for the duration of the war or other emergency, plus six months, subject to the discretion of the president or otherwise according to law[.]"

The Department of Veteran Affairs BIRLS death index shows that White was released from duty five months later on October 11, 1943. His enlistment paperwork identified him as married, but there is no record of White being married unless he was still legally married to Julia Yakovleff or, I suppose, if Anna Maher was considered a common-law spouse. His next documented marriage was to Helaine Levy in 1947. The couple had a single child, a boy named January, and somewhere between 1950 and 1970 White moved from New York to California. He married his third wife, Hedy Bergida in Las Vegas, Nevada on December 18, 1970. The Nevada State Marriage License identifies Hedy as a resident of New Mexico. Lionel and Hedy were married until Lionel's death on December 26, 1985. At the time of White's death, he and Hedy lived in Cullowhee, North Carolina. He died at a hospital in Asheville, North Carolina and he's buried at the Fairview Memorial Gardens Cemetery in Sylva, North Carolina.

That's all I know about Lionel White. Almost everything, anyway, because *Contemporary Authors Online* has a brief biography, but I'm suspicious since there is no mention of his first wife, Julia, and he is quoted as saying, "I am afraid that anything I say may very well be fiction and certainly shouldn't be believed in any case."

The biography does fill in the blanks of his working history, and it jives with the census entries I saw, as a journalist (a crime beat writer) in Ohio between 1923 and 1925, and as a newspaper copy editor in New York from 1925 to 1933, and later as an editor for several true confession magazines until he became a fulltime fiction writer in 1951. But it woefully lacks any tangible personal information. I want to know what happened to his first wife. Why was his World War II military enlistment so short? Who was Anna Maher and what happened to her?

Like I said, Lionel White is an enigma.

But one thing I know about Lionel Earle White. His fiction is pretty damn good, and while he was far from a brilliant stylist—his prose reads more like a facts based newspaper account than fiction—his work is as enthralling today as it must have been when it first appeared because his characters are well-drawn, their motivations explained, the violence, and there isn't as much as one would think, is ugly and realistic, and his plotting is almost perfect.

The two novels in this omnibus, *Coffin for a Hood* and *Operation – Murder*, are no exception. *Coffin for a Hood* is a sun-bleached crime story that was first published by Gold Medal in 1958. The setting is the tiny Florida Keys town of Arroyos during the dreadful heat of the late summer off-season. The tourists and part-time residents have gone back north for cooler weather and the town's few dozen full-time residents, mostly fishermen, a few merchants, a doctor and his daughter, a shamed college basketball star and an artist, are bracing for a hurricane. But everything changes when a pair of thugs, obvious hit-men to anyone who ever met them—"professionals in a rare and highly specialized field…. murderers."—come to Arroyos with the promise of violence. And everyone in Arroyos is hiding from something and almost every resident has reason to think the two hit-men have come to settle a score from their past.

Coffin for a Hood isn't White's regular caper novel. There is a heist, two actually, but the plot focuses on the aftermath rather than on the planning and execution. It's a character study with the perspective skimming from character to character, made brilliant by White's methodical revelations about his characters and their motives. Not one of them is what they appear to be and a few are miserable bastards that deserve what they get. The hurricane, the harsh tropical-like setting, and even the character play, are similar to John Huston's brilliant film, *Key Largo*, but unlike the film nobody finds redemption. *Coffin* is noir with an ironic ending that leaves little doubt about what happens to anyone, no matter how well they plan, who tries to get something for nothing.

Operation – Murder, published by Gold Medal in 1956, is as cold as *Coffin* is hot. We switch from the Florida Keys' blistering heat to Colorado's icy and snow-covered Rocky Mountains. It is a return to White's standard caper plot with a small twist. This novel begins with the murder of a police officer during a bank robbery; a job that is the beginning of an audacious gold train heist. The leader and brains is Frank Scudder, a World War II veteran with bad lungs, a young wife named Tina, and a grudge against the world. The job is planned (without Tina knowing anything about it) to take place during the couple's honeymoon. Tina is confused when three other men arrive at their rented mountain cabin and Frank is less than forthcoming about the true nature of his plans.

Operation—Murder is an adept work of ironic noir with a caveat; one of the characters finds redemption. As in all of White's novels, the reader gets to spend time in each of the characters' heads, from the kind and naïve Tina to Frank to Dave, a nasty drunk with bad intentions. The train heist has an inevitable feel to it and the suspense is built around Tina. As the narrative plays, she becomes suspicious of Frank, she is terrified of the other men staying in the cabin, and she is ultimately forced into action. The violence is threatened—rather than actual—until it blows open in an ugly and gruesome manner across a couple of pages. And the ending...

Wait for it. You won't be disappointed.

What we don't know about Lionel White as a man would likely fill a dozen books, but what he left us—his novels—should be enough.

Unless you're a gossip, like me.

Salt Lake City, Utah
July 2019

References:
United States Census data—1910, 1920, 1930, 1940—was accessed via Ancestry.com
New York Census data, 1915, was accessed via Acenstry.com
"Crime a la White" by Rick Ollerman. *Hardboiled, Noir & Gold Medals: Essays on crime fiction writers from the '50s through the '90s*. Stark House Press, 2017.
"Lionel White." *Contemporary Authors Online*, Gale, 2001.

Ben Boulden is a regular contributor to *Mystery Scene Magazine* where he writes the "Short & Sweet: Short Stories Considered" review column. His short fiction has been published in *Down & Out: The Magazine*, *Paul Bishop Presents... Pattern of Behavior*, and elsewhere.

COFFIN FOR A HOOD
Lionel White

This book is for
Gus Refowich

Chapter One

1

Seeing them step out of Phil Hardin's four-wheeled jeep and turn toward the unpainted screen door of the café, no one in Arroyos could have guessed who they were or what they were.

They were an odd-looking pair, the tall, younger one in his wide gray Stetson, neat white Dacron suit and high-heeled cowboy boots. Despite the intense heat and the dead, fetid air, his sheer silk shirt was unsweated and he wore a black string tie holding the long tabbed collar tight to his neck. He had the clean angular face of a boy in his early twenties, dark expressionless eyes and a fine jawline. His stomach lay flat beneath the ornate silver belt buckle.

He was apparently in no hurry and he looked neither to right nor to left as he entered the restaurant.

His companion was actually the taller of the two, standing almost six feet, but because of his girth, he seemed shorter. He was a man who could have been anywhere from thirty to fifty, heavy-set and barrel-chested. His complexion was saffron yellow and there were dark circles under his large brown eyes, which were magnified by the dark-rimmed, thick glasses. His face was Semitic in cast and he needed a shave. The half bald head, circled by a fringe of curly jet hair, was bare and he was dressed in a soiled white shirt, wrinkled under a blue serge business suit. His brown shoes were beautifully polished and the pink nails on his baby hands had been recently manicured.

They were indeed an odd pair, odd even for the Keys, a location with a long established reputation for attracting eccentrics and strange characters.

They were professionals; professionals in a rare and highly specialized field. They were murderers.

No one was visible in the place when they entered, a fact observed by each of them as they moved past the cash register and ignored the long linoleum counter to take one of the booths which lined the side of the room.

Two old-fashioned, wooden-bladed fans, the type used in ice cream parlors some thirty or forty years ago, slowly turned overhead. A few random flies lazily crawled on the walls and counters and next to the cash register a small portable radio encased in a broken plastic box had been left turned on. An announcer was completing his routine newscast, giving the latest word on Hurricane Bettina.

Neither man paid the slightest attention to it as the pair quietly seated themselves on opposite benches in the booth. They didn't look at each other; they didn't speak. They sat there waiting.

2

Now it is an established fact that the United States Weather Bureau is one of the most conscientious branches of the Federal Government. It rarely gets caught, so to speak, with its pants down. However, no agency is perfect and this is particularly so when it must deal with variable factors which are prone to change and reverse themselves without warning.

Certainly this was the case in the matter of Hurricane Bettina. The Bureau, by which we mean specifically its branches in Miami and in New Orleans, can in no way be blamed for the capricious behavior of this specific disaster. Despite the fact that Hurricane Bettina caused widespread damage and loss of life and property over a vast area of the southeastern section of the country, had it not been for the Bureau and its highly efficient warning system, the hurricane might have gone down in history as one of the major storm tragedies of all time.

This is, of course, of little solace to those persons who lost life and property during the course of the holocaust. On the other hand, a great many lives were saved as a result of the efficiency of the warning system and it was only by the sheerest caprice that the direction of the great winds changed at the last moment and cut in from the Gulf to sweep through the Keys, severing all communications from the mainland of Florida and creating tremendous havoc.

For more than forty-eight hours all contact between the Keys and the mainland was cut off and the psychological effect was severe on those people who had failed to take refuge in protected sectors in time. That the town of Key West itself suffered little damage was a lucky coincidence, based largely on the fact that the eye of the storm passed over the Keys some thirty miles to the east, around the area of Big Pine Key.

This had the effect of separating a segment some fifteen miles in distance, on both sides of the eye of the storm, from all habitation both east and west.

It was that type of hurricane; narrow and terribly devastating in its wild and erratic path.

The damage to the Keys themselves was relatively minor, largely because the area affected is sparsely settled and the storm itself hit during an off season, when few but the natives of the section are in residence. What Hurricane Bettina did after leaving the Keys and striking the mainland is something else again. But that is a matter of record and there are few persons who will fail to remember the gruesome details carried in newspapers and over the air waves.

A number of very small communities and settlements in the Keys themselves were wiped out. However a few of the luckier ones survived the hurricane, a little the worse for its effect. Among those was the tiny village of Arroyos, on Key Arroyos, which itself is quite small, being no more than a mile wide and a couple of miles long.

The Overseas Highway, some ten miles west of Key Arroyos, was destroyed for a matter of some seven hundred yards and one span of the Overseas Bridge to the east was carried away. But the town of Arroyos is situated on a comparatively high point of land and escaped the worst of the disaster, which was caused more by tidal waves than by the tremendous force of the winds.

Along with other fortunate circumstances so far as Arroyos is concerned, is the fact that almost all of its small fleet of fishing boats were at sea at the time the first warnings of the storm were released. The boats were fishing for king mackerel, far off to the southwest, and they received the initial warnings of the approaching hurricane. Being more vulnerable than those on land, and as a result more cautious, these vessels did not wait to find out which way the winds might come, but headed at once for the nearest port, which was Key West. As a result they suffered little damage and no loss of life. In view of the fact that the men crewing these boats made up the majority of the male population of Arroyos, the town was largely depopulated when the storm struck.

It was one of those fortunate inconsistencies which now and then occur during a national disaster.

What is a lot less fortunate, however, is the thing which took place in Arroyos simultaneously with the arrival of Hurricane Bettina. A thing which, in essence, had nothing whatsoever to do with the hurricane itself.

3

The plane, a four-place Cessna, flying charter out of Miami, arrived over Key Arroyos late Thursday afternoon, on August third, approximately one half hour before the weather station reversed itself and put its warning over the air. Up until that point it was believed that Hurricane Bettina would pass well to the west and strike the mainland somewhere in the neighborhood of Bay St. Louis or possibly New Orleans. As a result, there was considerable more interest in the plane than there might have been had it arrived somewhat later.

There is no landing strip on Key Arroyos and the fact that the plane buzzed the town two or three times and then circled and started to come in to land on the long stretch of sandy beach just east of the village proper, created a certain amount of excitement in the town.

Arroyos is so small that it has been missed by the makers of road maps. With the exception of the great concrete block fish house just west of the docks, there is no building of more than two stories in the entire town. The Overseas Highway itself crossed the key with but a single cutoff, which leads off at the ocean side and disappears in a collection of small single-story frame buildings. There is a garage, a general store (closed during the off season) which sells groceries and hardware; a restaurant, a movie theatre, open one day a week, and two motels, occupied only in the winter months.

The residents, for the most part, are fishermen. A few drifters and odd balls, each in his own way having discovered some personal enchantment about Arroyos, have also permanently settled there.

There is a schoolhouse, and a combination fire department and police station. There is no policeman, however, although at the time involved in this story, Deputy Sheriff Tilden Flack, who usually works out of Marathon, was paying his weekly visit. The fire department is volunteer and is headed by Dr. Carter Martins, one of the comparatively reliable men of the place who, with his daughter Sarah, is a permanent resident.

Beyond the center of the village a few sandy streets stretch out, mostly meandering off in the direction of the beach. These are inhabited by the fishermen, the permanent residents of the town. To the west, almost on the beach, are the winter homes of several fairly wealthy, part-time residents who come down each year from the north. In view of recent real estate development in the Keys and the great influx of speculators and operators, Arroyos may be considered slightly backwater and provincial.

This is partly the result of its smallness and partly the result of the character of the land itself, which, although high for those parts, is treeless and barren and prone to breed vast hordes of sand flies and mosquitoes. It is not a spot to attract the casual off-season visitor, but conversely, the few persons who have stopped by have found it peculiarly entrancing and the urge to stay on is often irresistible.

It wasn't the first time that a plane had made a landing on the wide sandy beach of Arroyos. Sports fishermen have come in by air during the season, several times in the past. But it was of sufficient occasion to cause considerable excitement. Very few persons arrived on the island even during the season and the landing of an aircraft in the late summer is highly unusual.

Once it was determined that the small monoplane was actually going to come in, Phil Hardin, who runs the garage, drove his jeep down to the beach to observe the event. The wind had been rising steadily, coming in strong gusts from the southwest and the pilot would have to show considerable skill in setting down his machine.

Fortunately Arroyos has a smooth, hard beach, unencumbered by driftwood, and the tide was at ebb.

The Cessna dropped in with flaps down and bounced only once or twice before straightening out and coming to a gradual stop.

Leaning forward to flip the ignition switch to cut out the engine, Duke Flager experienced a subtle sense of relief. Thirty years of flying, most of which had been spent barnstorming around the tropics, had made him extremely sensitive to weather and geography. It wasn't that he'd had any question in his mind about finding Arroyos, although he had never landed at that particular spot before. He knew exactly where the Key lay and was aware of the fact that the beach would make a fair emergency landing field.

Duke knew the Keys and the islands of the coast and in fact of the entire Caribbean, like he knew the back of his hand. He was a fine navigator and an excellent pilot. At fifty, Duke was fully aware that there were few men in the business who could hold a candle to him. It wasn't his piloting which had held him back, which kept him from working for one of the big airlines. It wasn't his drinking or his willingness to take wild gambles on weather and strange terrain.

Duke's record was clean and although he had been investigated a dozen times by one branch of the government or another, they'd never really pinned anything on him. But even if they couldn't prove anything, the U.S. Coast Guard knew and the Civil Aeronautical Authority people knew and the Treasury people knew—knew the sort of passengers Duke had been moving around the islands and in and out of Cuba and Puerto Rico and Jamaica. They knew the sort of business he handled and although they were never able to get anything on him, they watched him like a hawk.

A word or two must have been dropped into the right ears because, on the three or four occasions when Duke had applied to one of the big outfits, Pan-Am, or TWA or Eastern, for a job when things in his own field became slow, he'd been turned down. Duke had understood. And so he had gone back to the charter work, asking no questions and giving no answers, but being careful. Always being very careful.

The relief he felt as he cut the switch wasn't because he had found the Key and made a safe landing. It wasn't caused, either, because of the weather warnings. Duke only knew that there was a hurricane moving in from the southwest, but at that time the warning that the winds would strike the Keys had not yet been released by the weather stations in Miami and in New Orleans. At that time Duke believed there was an ample margin of time for him to reach his ultimate destination.

He was very sensitive to the barometer and knowing that there was dirty weather ahead, even though it wasn't expected to hit the Keys, would have been enough to have made him turn around and head back to his home port, irrespective of the desires of his two charter passengers.

The trouble was his sensitive ears had detected the slight miss in the motor and Duke was not a man to ignore even the slightest hint of trouble. He would take a few minutes to check the machine over before once more taking off.

But it wasn't even this, this possibility of engine trouble, which was responsible for Duke's sense of worry as he switched off the engine of the plane. It was a much more subtle and indefinite sort of thing.

Duke was worried because of his two passengers.

Although he didn't know their names, had never seen them before they boarded the plane at the airfield on the outskirts of Miami, and had no idea who they were, Duke Flager knew exactly what his two passengers were. He couldn't have been around the islands, taking the sort of charters he'd taken, doing the sort of things he had been doing all of these years, without knowing.

No, there was no outward sign to tell him, but he knew. He'd flown other men to other places who were in the same line of work. Wiry, dark, too well-dressed little men into obscure Caribbean towns; hard-spoken, heavy-set blond men into other places. No two of them ever looked alike or spoke alike. But he knew. Knew as well as though they had engraved the names of their professions on their luggage.

Yes, Duke Flager would be relieved to see the last of his passengers. He didn't mind flying them and taking their money. But Duke knew professional killers when he saw them and he wanted to keep as far away from them as possible once he had delivered them to their destination. He just wanted to be rid of them.

Ten minutes later the matter had completely been erased from his mind. By this time he had learned that his instincts had been right and that the engine of the plane would need attention before he either continued on or returned to Miami. It wasn't a complicated job and would only take a matter of an hour or an hour and a half. Fortunately, he had the spare parts necessary to make the repairs.

He was stripped to the waist and preparing to set to work when he noticed that the wind had changed in direction and sharply risen.

4

Among the several persons who watched as Duke Flager's two passengers climbed down from the plane and walked over to Phil Hardin's jeep for the short ride into the town, only one of those who was to be most involved and affected by their arrival was present to witness it.

Tilden Flack, the deputy from Marathon, was in the small, built-on shanty in back of Nick Cosmos' restaurant, which Nick used as a kitchen. He was with Helen, Nick's wife.

Nick himself was paying a highly unusual visit to the home of Richard Fullbright, one of the wealthy northerners who heretofore only came down to open his home during the winter season but had recently become a permanent resident.

Fullbright, banker, financier and speculator, was at home and was, in a sense, entertaining Nick. At least he was rather impatiently listening to Nick's very attractive proposition.

Dr. Carter Martins was over in the poorer section of the village assisting in the delivery of a new baby, which would make it nine for Mrs. Juan Cantios, whose husband was at the moment somewhere offshore on a sponge boat. The doctor's daughter, Sarah, or Sally as she was called by everyone except her father, was in her small, very neat bedroom, lying stomach down across the studio couch on which she usually slept. She was crying.

Downstairs, in the doctor's living room, Socks Schroeder's six feet three inches of brawn and muscle slumped on the broken leather couch, and he was nursing the bruised knuckles of his hamlike right hand as his blue eyes furiously stared into the floor at his feet.

A half mile away in a very small, weather-beaten shanty on the Gulf side of the island, Charles Anthony Mason III stood in the exact center of the single room which was his living room, bedroom, kitchen and studio. His dark moody eyes, or that is to say the one eye out of which he was able to see at the moment, was riveted on the slashed oil painting which lay in its broken frame on the wide board floor.

In spite of the deep slashes in the canvas it was easy to see that the painting was that of a nude and the model must have been a very beautiful girl with an equally beautiful body. The face itself had been destroyed by the blade which had ravaged the picture, but anyone who knew Sally Martins would have recognized the glitter of her titian hair, which the artist had captured in all of its natural beauty.

Although Tony Mason himself had painted the picture, and although the model which he had used was a girl who meant a great deal to him, Tony was thinking neither of the ravaged canvas nor of the girl. He was thinking solely and exclusively of himself. And they were not pleasant thoughts.

Tony, for the first time in his life, was admitting to himself that it was completely true. Those things he had been telling people for years. It was no longer an idle gesture, a supercilious boast, an artistic pose.

Charles Anthony Mason III was a coward. He was afraid of people and he was afraid of life. He was a fake and a failure. It wasn't an affectation, an excuse to avoid the realities and the responsibilities of existence. It was the cold, bitter, unadorned truth.

Chapter Two

1

When Dr. Carter Martins woke up that Tuesday morning, he knew it was going to be another one of those days. The restless, dream-ridden sleep seemed to have done him no good at all and he had that old familiar taste in his mouth. The taste left by too much rum and too many cigarettes.

He shouldn't smoke at all and no one knew it better than he did. Of course, he shouldn't drink either, as far as that went, but he knew he would never give that up. Sooner or later the smoking would kill him; he'd already had his second heart attack and it was merely a matter of time. The drinking was different. In a sense the drinking kept him alive. It gave him the courage to go on living. Pulling himself out of bed he didn't bother to put his lean, slender feet into the sandals before walking across the room to the bathroom. He coughed several times and cleared his throat, feeling the pain as usual around the area of his heart. He wondered just how many more of these mornings he would be able to take.

The mouthwash burned his mouth and throat and he swore almost silently under his breath as he reached for his toothbrush.

He was a fool; he knew better, knew what he was doing to himself. But somehow or other he was unable to stop it. Unable to control the habits which he knew were destroying him. He'd never been able to exert self-control, that was his trouble. Always he'd taken the easy way out.

He was drying his lean, emaciated body with a Turkish towel after stepping out of the tin Sears,Roebuck shower, when he heard Sarah moving about beyond the thin partition which separated the bathroom from his daughter's small bedroom. Mentally he determined that, today, he would wait at least until the cocktail hour before he had his first rum and cola. He could do it if he tried. At least that way he'd last longer and he'd be sober when they dined.

He was coughing again as he reached into the pocket of his torn and faded bathrobe and took out the crumpled pack of cigarettes. Yes, today he could use self-control. Today he wanted to have a long talk with Sarah. The time had come when he could procrastinate no longer. Unpleasant as it would be, he must speak to her. They must reach an understanding.

Dr. Martins may have cared little about his own life and his own destiny, but Sarah meant everything to him. He might not be able to make the effort for himself, but when it came to Sarah, well ...

She was in the tiny kitchen off the living room when he went downstairs some twenty minutes later. He couldn't see her, but he could hear the dishes rattling around as she prepared their breakfast. He didn't have to see her, of course. He knew just how she would look. She would look exactly the same as her mother had looked, twenty years before.

Long, beautifully fine titian hair hanging in loose waves down to her shoulders, dark, brown-flecked eyes still not quite open. Her lovely, fresh face clean and sparkling and small, square white teeth showing as she grinned a good morning when he walked in.

He was moving toward the kitchen when he suddenly stopped. Sarah was singing softly under her breath, a sort of singing without words, just as her mother had used to sing. It was almost uncanny how much alike they were. Sarah's mother had also sung while she was making breakfast and the doctor knew what it meant. She hadn't sung when she was happy; it was only when she was unhappy that she would accompany herself in whatever small task she was performing with those strange, odd little tunes which were neither quite words nor were yet humming sounds.

"I'm going across the street and get the newspaper, baby," Dr. Martins called. "Be right back."

He could hear her stop for a moment as he spoke, but she didn't answer him. Then he turned and stepped out through the unlocked screen door and moved across the porch and down the three broken steps of the bungalow.

The newspapers were left a half block down the street, at Nick Cosmos' restaurant, by the four A.M. bus driver who turned off the Overseas Highway each day to deliver them. Nick wasn't open yet when Dr. Martins arrived, but the papers were lying on the steps.

Reaching down to pick one up, he heard the sound of the car coming along the sandy road and he turned and looked over his shoulder for a moment as it passed. He didn't nod to the driver, but quickly retrieved his newspaper and returned to the house.

The table was set up as usual on the porch and Dr. Martins dropped his lean, stringy frame into the big rattan chair. He didn't bother to open the newspaper. He had plenty of time for it. All the time in the world.

When his daughter came out on the porch a moment or two later, she was carrying two glasses of freshly squeezed orange juice on a tray, along with a pot of coffee and a stack of buttered toast. She smiled as her father looked up.

"Morning, Dad," she said.

"Good morning, Sarah," Dr. Martins said. "Going to be a hot one again, looks like."

"Sally," his daughter said. "Please call me Sally, Dad, everyone else does, you know."

Dr. Martins nodded absently.

"Certainly, baby," he said. "Anything you say, darling!"

Sally Martins sighed and put the tray on the table. They'd gone through the same routine a thousand times, ten thousand times. But it was meaningless. The next time he used her name he'd call her Sarah.

She sat down opposite her father, her eyes darkening with worry as she noticed how pale he was under his tan and how his hands shook as he laid the folded-up paper next to his plate.

"Saw Tilden Flack driving into town when I went over for the paper," he said. "Wonder what he's doing around."

"Well," Sally said, "He's the deputy sheriff and this is his territory."

Dr. Martins nodded absently.

"Nothing ever happens here to bring the law," he said.

Sally looked at her father and frowned slightly.

"You know why he's here, Dad," she said. "He's here sniffing around Helen, Nick's wife."

Dr. Martins looked up quickly at his daughter.

"Sarah!" he said, his voice suddenly sharp. "That's hardly a nice way to put it. Where in the world do you ever pick up such expressions. Lord, did they teach you that sort of thing at the University? Anyway, no matter how you choose to express yourself, the idea is certainly offensive in itself. The man has a perfect right to be in town and you shouldn't listen to rumor."

"Oh Dad, for Lord's sake," Sally said. "I'm a big girl now, you know. Twenty years old and I know all about the birds and the bees. It's no secret what's going on. Flack's been making passes at Helen Cosmos for months now. Everybody in town knows it. It's no secret, except possibly to Nick. There's no use avoiding the truth."

Dr. Martins slowly shook his head and looked away from his daughter.

"This town," he said. "This town!"

"Drink your juice," Sally said. "There's nothing wrong with the town that hasn't always been wrong with it."

Dr. Martins started to reach for the glass and then dropped his hand to his lap, where it lay thin and almost transparent in the morning sun.

"That's just the point, Sarah," he said. "Just what I want to talk to you about. This town is wrong. All wrong for you. I want you to leave, go back north to school again. This is no place for a young girl. There's nothing here for you, nothing."

Sally Martins leaned back and lifted one browned, slender hand.

"Dad, please," she said. "We've been through it so many times.

There's nothing for you either, but you stay."

"There's my practice," Dr. Martins said.

Sally laughed, a little bitterly.

"Practice?" she said. "What practice, Dad? A fisherman with a hook in his thumb once every couple of months? A new baby once or twice a year? A winter visitor with a cold? Dad, I'm grown up now, I tell you. I know what's going on. There's no use trying to kid me; no use trying to kid yourself. There's no practice in Arroyos. Why, I went over your books and you didn't take in a hundred and fifty—"

Once more Dr. Martins interrupted his daughter. "Please Sarah," he said in a tired voice. "Please, we aren't discussing me. We're discussing you. I don't want you here, don't want you in this dead, forgotten place. You're young and lovely and your life is—"

"I stay where you stay, Dad," Sally said. "Why do you stay here? What is there that attracts you to Arroyos? You're a good doctor, a fine doctor. I know. I talked to people up at the University who remembered you, remembered the work you did. What is there that keeps you here? Why must you stay here and slowly drink yourself—"

She stopped suddenly then, seeing the stricken look in his face as he dropped his eyes.

"Oh Dad," she said, getting up quickly and running around the table to kneel at his side. "Dad, I didn't mean it."

"It's all right, baby," he said, his hand reaching out to stroke her soft hair. "It's all right. It's the truth, I guess. Only don't you see, it's you I am thinking of. There's nothing here for you. Nothing. Who can you meet, who can you see to talk to? You should be around young people."

"Well, there's always Socks," Sally said, laughing. "After all, it isn't every girl who can have the exclusive rights to the time of a legitimate college basketball hero."

Her father looked at her with distaste. "That ape," he said.

"People do come down here, now and then," Sally said, serious this time. "There are the winter people and then every once in a while men like Tony Mason...."

Her father quickly looked at her and she hesitated, suddenly blushing.

"There's nothing wrong with Tony," she said quickly. "Even if he is an artist."

"I didn't say there was anything wrong with him," Dr. Martins said. "But Sarah, you have to listen to me. I'm a good many years older than you are and I've known a good many people. I've known men like

Tony. He's a fine, sensitive boy. He may, some day, be a great artist. I wouldn't know, not being an expert about such things. But, even assuming he will be, he isn't right for you. You see, I understand Tony. It's easy for me to understand him. Tony is very much like I was at his age. Young, idealistic, filled with dreams. Sarah, men like Tony, and men like myself, don't make good husbands. Your mother found that out. I don't want the same thing to happen to you."

Quickly she stood up, standing next to him and looking down into his upturned face.

"What's wrong with you?" she said fiercely. "What's wrong with men like you, Dad? Nobody in the world is better."

"Do you really have to ask," he said in a low, barely audible voice. "Do you really have to?"

"Yes!" she said. "Yes, I do have to ask."

He sighed then and looked away for a long moment.

"The thing that's wrong with me is that I am not only sensitive, I am also weak. Weak and unable to face life. I don't have to remind you of what happened to your mother. You know about that. But what you don't know is what happened to me. Why I did come down here. Why I ran away."

"Was it something about your work, Dad? Something that happened?"

He looked at her and smiled slightly.

"I wasn't running an abortion mill," he said, "if that's what you had in mind. I didn't peddle dope on the side, or anything like that. In a sense, though, what I did could even be considered worse. I did it because I was weak. I don't want to tell you exactly what...."

"You don't have to tell me, Dad," Sally interrupted him. "You don't have to tell me anything. It doesn't matter any longer what you did. All I want you to do is take care of yourself."

"The trouble is," Dr. Martins said, "the things you do, don't go away. They come back to haunt you. Sooner or later ..."

Quickly she reached down and covered his mouth with her hands.

"Not another word," she said, forcing a smile. "Not another word until we've had our breakfast, at least. Now you just forget everything and drink up that juice and get some coffee and toast into your stomach. It's going to be a hot, scorching day again. There's a funny feeling in the air this morning and you're going to need your strength today. This is one day that you do have a patient. Mrs. Cantios' oldest boy was around last night to remind me that his mother is expecting again and today's the day."

Dr. Martins reached for the glass of juice.

"And what's on your schedule this morning, young lady?" he asked.

For a moment Sally looked thoughtful, frowning slightly. "I'm seeing Tony," she said. "He's hoping to finish the picture today."

"How is it coming?" Dr. Martins asked her perfunctorily.

Sally looked over at her father and smiled almost slyly. "You're going to be very surprised when you see it," she said. "Very surprised."

Dr. Martins nodded, without actually hearing her words at all. He was thinking that perhaps, in view of the extreme heat, it might be just as well to have a cool drink around noon rather than wait until four or four-thirty.

They didn't speak again until after finishing their breakfast.

Sally was taking the dishes from the table when Dr. Martins finally unfolded the *Miami Herald*. She hesitated a moment, looking over his shoulder.

"What's the latest on Hurricane Bettina?"

The doctor spoke to his daughter's back as she left the room. "Coming in fast," he said. "Still heading for somewhere around the Mississippi Delta. Guess we may get a little wind, but that will be about all."

"We can stand the breeze," Sally said.

2

Deputy Sheriff Tilden Flack saw Dr. Martins as he was stooping to pick up his morning newspaper. For a moment, as the doctor looked up over his shoulder at him, the deputy started to nod his head in greeting. He caught himself just in time. He knew that the doctor would ignore him.

Swinging the wheel of the car viciously as he cut around the corner, Flack swore aloud.

"The son of a bitch," he said. "Who the hell does he think he is, anyway. Lousy, drunken bum."

He smiled then, secretly, to himself. Hell, he thought, he should know that I know what I do about him. All he, Flack, would have to do is spread that story around and old Martins wouldn't be half so damned cocky. Yes, if he, Tilden Flack, should let out what he had discovered about Dr. Martins and Dr. Martins' past, it would be enough to drive him right out of the Keys. He and that snot-nosed kid of his.

What right did this broken-down old bum have putting on airs anyway? A retired surgeon from Chicago, eh? Sure, sure, he'd been a surgeon and he'd practiced in Chicago. Flack had verified that all right. But he'd also verified a lot more. He'd had the information now for several weeks and he was keeping it to himself. That is the sort of man Tilden Flack was. He never let go of anything until he could find a reason. A profitable reason.

One of the nice things about working out of the sheriff's office was the fact that he was able to come by so much little known and useful information. Information that very frequently came in handy. After all, they don't pay a deputy sheriff a very fancy salary down this way and Flack was always able to find uses for an extra dollar or so.

Of course what he had discovered about Dr. Martins might not actually be worth much in actual cash. It was a pretty sure bet that the doctor himself didn't have a dime; he and that kid of his were poor as church mice. They lived just like those damned conch fishermen. Drank like them too, or at least the old man did.

But the information might very well be useful in some other way. Tilden Flack had been keeping his eye on that Martins kid ever since she'd returned home from that fancy university up north. So far he'd been staying away from her. That was the one thing he'd learned about his job; it might be all right to mess around with the Portuguese girls and the trash, or make a play for some of the local stuff now and then just so long as the sheriff didn't know about it. But it wasn't all right to cross the lines. And there was a very definite social line, even in the Keys. Dr. Martins and his daughter very definitely belonged on one side of that line. The side with the rich northerners, the "good whites." Poor or not, that's where they belonged.

Until Flack had learned what he now knew about Dr. Martins, he'd merely looked at Sally Martins and lusted silently. But now things were different. Now, well, he'd just wait and see.

But he did have to laugh. Dr. Carter Martins high-hatting him, Deputy Sheriff Tilden Flack.

As his mind reached this point, Flack's face suddenly assumed that worried, half-frightened look which he had been trying hard these last years to permanently erase.

That was one thing he wanted to forget, forget forever. Those years when he'd been in with the mob, when he'd been one of the trusted ones. God, he'd been a fool. He'd had the world in his lap. Women, booze, money, anything he'd wanted. And then ...

Well, it hadn't been his fault. How the hell was he to know which faction was going to come out ahead. It had just been his damned bad luck that he'd listened to Paddy and taken Paddy's advice. If it hadn't been for Paddy, he'd never have knocked off Cicero's brother, and if he hadn't knocked off Cicero's brother, he would still be making it. He wouldn't be hiding out here in this godforsaken hole, waiting for the day he'd pick up a newspaper and see that Cicero had finally been chilled.

Flack shuddered in spite of the heat and forced himself to take his mind off Cicero. That was one guy he never wanted to think about. Just remembering him, and remembering what he had done to him, was enough to bring the sweat out on the back of his red neck.

It had been more than four years now and he was finally beginning to feel secure. He'd changed his name, changed his address and changed just about everything else. He'd done everything he could do. But he still would never feel completely safe until he read that obituary in the newspaper.

Once more he shuddered and this time he was successful in getting his mind off it. He started thinking about Nick Cosmos' wife, Helen. Just thinking about her, visualizing her lush rounded breasts, her long, slender, beautiful legs, the round column of her neck and her wanton's lips, took his mind off everything else.

It was nice to think about her. Nice to know that in another hour or so, as soon as Nick left the restaurant, he'd be seeing her. And this time there was going to be no God-damned nonsense about it. No fooling around, and no stalling. This time she was going to give; she was going to give, by God, if he had to knock her down and take it. She was going to give if he had to go to Nick and tell him exactly what kind of a hooker it was he had married. The kind of woman he worshiped as though she were some sort of second edition of the Virgin Mary.

Once more Flack smiled, his thick-lipped, wide mouth opening to expose broken, uneven teeth.

Those years before he had settled down in the Keys were certainly beginning to pay off with a vengeance. He'd never known Helen personally, of course, but once he'd suspected that she'd been a pro and once he'd had her fingerprints checked, the rest had been easy. It hadn't taken him long to make the contact and find out about her. Not long at all.

Helen was going to pay off in more ways than one. She wasn't going to get away just giving him what he wanted from her personally. Oh no, not by a long shot. Nick must have plenty of dough put away some place. All those Greeks had dough.

Flack swung the car down the road past the fishing shanties and pulled up alongside of the new big concrete fish storage house. He was quick to notice the old blue sedan sitting in the lee of the building. Socks Schroeder would be inside, icing down and cleaning up. Getting ready for the fleet which should be coming in soon now, what with the storms kicking up out in the gulf.

Socks Schroeder was the manager of the place, although the title was more of a joke than anything else. Actually, he was a sort of janitor and general caretaker, having worked for the packing firm for a couple of years now. He'd started out on one of the shrimp boats, but a predilection to seasickness had caused him to be transferred to a shore job.

Well, Flack thought, the work certainly fitted him. It was the sort of job that took a guy like Schroeder. A guy who was all muscle and bone and built like a brick backhouse. In spite of the crew cut and the college boy sweat shirt and shorts, Flack knew that Schroeder was all man.

It was partly because of Schroeder that Flack was stopping by in Arroyos. Because of what he had recently learned about Schroeder.

The funny thing was that it was the old sheriff himself who had tipped off Flack.

"That fellow down in Arroyos," the old man had said. "Schroeder. Ernest Schroeder. Think he goes by the name Spock or maybe Sock."

"I've met him," Flack had said, wondering what was coming.

"Well, I happened to hear something about him the other day," the sheriff said. "One of the boys out checking over some real estate ran across him and remembered him. Seems he was something of a basketball player a couple of years back."

Flack had nodded, disinterested. "That so?"

"Yeah. Real by-God hero. Played up north somewhere for one of the universities."

"What's he doing down here then if he's so great?" Flack asked.

"Well, this real estate fellow told me that Schroeder was mixed up in those basketball scandals. You probably remember reading about them. Seems some mobsters got in and bought off a lot of those kids and had 'em throw games. The kids cleaned up—or at least they were supposed to have, until they got caught. Of course it was the professional gamblers who were buying them that really made it big."

"Was Socks one of the ones who got caught up?" Flack asked, suddenly interested.

"That's the funny part of it," the sheriff said. "From what this guy told me, this Socks Schroeder was never actually involved. But his name came out after the thing broke wide open. Some of the boys said that he was one of the key guys in the ring; others said different. The one gambler they did arrest, and who was convicted, said that our boy Socks had been paid off plenty to throw one of the crucial games, but had double-crossed the gamblers and was responsible for winning the game he was supposed to throw. Maybe he was betting the other way—the right way."

"He couldn't have kept the money then," Flack said. "Hell, he's over there in Arroyos working like a slave in the fish plant. Anyway, if he'd crossed up those guys up north, he'd probably be dead by now."

"Working in that fish plant is just about the same thing," the sheriff said sardonically. "Anyway, that's what I heard. You might stop by sometime and have a chat with him. I like to keep an eye on these queer ones we get down this way."

"I'll talk to him," Flack said.

"Don't make him no trouble," the sheriff said. "Just check around and be sure he's keeping his nose clean."

"His nose can't be clean after smelling them God-damned fish all day," Flack said and laughed.

Chapter Three

1

Socks Schroeder checked the gauge on the ice machine and nodded in satisfaction. He reached down with one long brawny arm and lifted the last crate, tossing it with ease on the pile next to the machine. Then he walked across the empty concrete floor and found the half-filled bottle of coke which he had been drinking. He was putting it to his lips when the door opened and Tilden Flack entered.

Looking up, Socks' agate blue eyes, set wide apart under the low, tanned brow, narrowed slightly. His great bare shoulders hunched a trifle and he finished his drink. He didn't move until the other man had walked over and stood leaning against the bench.

"What do you say, boy," Flack greeted him.

Schroeder looked up and frowned. He'd only met the deputy once or twice and he hadn't been impressed with him. He didn't answer.

Flack took a colored bandana handkerchief from his rear pocket and wiped the perspiration from his red, beefy face. He was a big man himself, standing a good six feet, but next to Schroeder he looked like a midget. He sensed the antagonism in the other man, but it failed to perturb him.

"Have a butt," he invited, holding out a crumpled pack of cigarettes. Schroeder shook his head.

"Don't use 'em," he said. "Bad for the wind."

"You know, you're right about that," Flack, said, deadpan. "A guy should watch out for his wind. Gotta keep the old health up. Nothing like it—clean, proper living."

Schroeder moved a little to one side, once more looking at the deputy and frowning.

"There's nothing wrong with clean living," he said, defensively. "You want something?" he asked. "I'm pretty busy."

"Oh, I just stopped in for a chat," Flack, said. "Nothing wrong with that, is there, fellow? Just a sort of friendly visit. Must get a little lonely around this mackerel factory, doesn't it?"

Schroeder grunted.

"I like it," he said, a trifle more friendly, but still on guard. "You want a coke?" he asked.

"Makes a good chaser," Flack said. "Maybe you got—"

"I don't drink," Socks said.

"What's that bad for?"

"Well, anyone knows," Schroeder began, and then stopped, once more frowning. "Say, you trying to kid me or something?" he asked.

Flack could see him suddenly tense, muscles rippling across the great shoulders and hairless chest.

"Look, don't get touchy, kid," Flack said. "There's no reason you have to get touchy. I'm just being friendly. Ain't nobody much in this dump to talk to and I just thought I'd stop by and shoot the breeze. No reason to be unfriendly, you know."

"I'm not unfriendly," Schroeder said shortly. "Just busy."

"Well, take it easy," Flack said. "You got all day. All the time in the world."

"The fleet's due in," Schroeder said, "and I have to have things ready."

Flack nodded. "Say," he said, "they tell me you used to be something of a basketball player. That right?"

Socks shrugged, but looked more friendly.

"Used to play some," he said, modestly.

Flack nodded sagely. "Understand you were really great," he said. "You must have cleaned up."

Schroeder, serious, shook his head.

"I played with LIU," he said. "Guard. We didn't get paid. It was for the school."

Flack smiled knowingly.

"Yeah, yeah," he said. "I know. Just for dear old Siwash. Didn't get paid, just straight amateur." He winked. "But I guess they found ways to see that you—"

"Listen here," Schroeder said. "You got it wrong, Mister. Amateurs don't get paid. No decent university man—"

"I heard all about those big college games," he said. "Sure, you guys didn't get paid, but I bet you made plenty—maybe made it for losing as well as winning, eh?"

Schroeder moved fast, reaching dawn and grabbing Flack by the front of his shirt. He pulled the other man close to him.

"Say, what are you trying to pull, Mister," he said.

Flack looked frightened.

"Listen," he said, "What's wrong with you anyway? Can't you take a joke, fella? I was just kiddin', for God's sake. It's just that I read about those basketball scandals and I thought maybe ..."

"Don't think nothing," Socks Schroeder said, relaxing his grasp slightly but not letting go completely. "Don't think nothing. I don't care if you are the law. I was clean. Clean as a whistle. You just ask the D.A. up in New York. Ask him. Ask him about Socks Schroeder. Why if it hadn't been for me, for my testimony in front of the Grand Jury, they'd have never cracked ..."

He stopped talking then, as suddenly as he had started, and released his hold.

"Anyway, I don't want to talk about it," he said. "But just remember this, I was one of the greatest, and I never took a buck, dishonest or otherwise. Not a buck."

Flack brushed off the front of his shirt. His voice was serious, then, when he spoke.

"You were one of the greatest," he said. "I remember reading about you. One of the really greatest."

Socks looked pleased.

"Sure," Flack said. "I believe you when you say you were on the up and up. After all, I'm a law man and I can tell when a guy's on the square."

Socks pushed a hamlike hand through his short, blond crew cut and nodded.

"They tried to reach me, those gambling fellows," he said. "But I showed 'em. I showed 'em they couldn't make a crook out of me. Just ask the D.A. about my turning 'em in. Ask him."

Flack nodded sympathetically.

"I know," he said. He hesitated a moment and took out another cigarette and lighted it. "Yeah, I know how it is. There's always some God-damned crook around trying to louse up decent people. They have 'em up north and we even got 'em down this way."

For a moment Socks stared at the other man, and then slowly nodded his head.

"There's plenty of strange fish around," he said. "Yeah, plenty." He hesitated for a moment again, and then went on.

"Say," he said, "you know that artist fellow, Mason. The guy with the shanty over on the gulf side?"

Flack nodded, suddenly interested.

"I've seen him around," he said.

Schroeder leaned closer and spoke in a sudden half whisper.

"Maybe you should investigate that character," he said. "Yeah, maybe you should look into him."

Flack looked up at the other man curiously. "Yes? Why? Hell, the guy's nothing but some kind of nut or something. Spends all his time either painting or sitting around with a fishing pole in his hand. Lives like a damned conch. No harm in him that I can see."

Schroeder looked at him and narrowed his eyes.

"No?" he said. "No? Well let me tell you something. You can't trust those artist guys. They're deep. Yeah, you never know what they may be up to. Half of 'em are God-damned Commies anyway. This guy Mason. Well, I happen to know he's got a lot of dirty pictures around. Naked women. Right out in the open too. And that ain't all of it."

Once more he reached out and his heavy hand took the other man by the shoulder as he pulled him closer.

"You know something else?" he said. "You know that he's been getting decent, honest girls—white girls—to come up to that shack of his and take off all their clothes while he paints them? Did you know that?"

Flack whistled, looking serious.

"Go on," he said. "Go on, you ain't telling me—"

"I am telling you," Socks said, indignation and anger blended in his voice. His hand tightened cruelly on the other man's shoulder and Flack winced. "I am telling you. And by God, if the law won't do something about it, I'm going to. No red-blooded, decent American man is going to stand around ..."

Flack squirmed and got out from under the big man's hand.

"I'll stop by and have a talk with him," he said. "You may be right, yes sir, you may be right. Maybe we should sort of check up ..."

Socks nodded emphatically. He looked at the other man darkly.

"Damned degenerate artist," he said. "Nothing but a bum, a beach comber. I don't know why Doc Martins lets Sally go over there."

"You mean to tell me that Dr. Martins' daughter is one of his—"

"Sally Martins is a fine, decent girl," Socks interrupted him, his voice ugly. "Don't you say a word against Sally. But Doc should have better sense."

Flack nodded. "Guess someone should warn her."

Socks shook his head angrily.

"I told her," he said. "I told her all about what kind of fellow that Mason is. But she just don't listen. Don't hear a word I say. Her Dad should take a horsewhip and go over and see him."

"Well, I'll stop by and check on Mason," Flack said. "After all, I am the law around here and if he's doing anything—well, you can be sure we won't stand for no God-damned Commies around these parts."

"Naked girls," Schroeder said. "Standing there without a stitch ..."

"I'll stop by," Flack said. He started to turn away and then stopped.

"Say, I will take you up on one of those cokes," he said. "Got a little time to kill."

"Sure enough," Socks said. "Right away."

2

From where he lay propped up on the extra-wide bed, Richard Fullbright was able to look out through the opened French doors of the large room, through the glass-enclosed terrace and across the sands to where the ocean gently broke on the white beach in front of the house. The room, like the entire house, was air-conditioned, but the architect had been clever, and, although it was closed and protected from the hot outside air, the effect was the same as though the place were completely open. Fullbright saw to it that Sam kept the windows spotless; he didn't wish to be reminded that they existed at all.

The windows were like most of the things he had arranged in his life; if there had to be a necessary evil, he didn't want to be made aware of it.

A small, slight man with white hair and thin, muscular arms and legs, the upper part of his narrow-chested body was completely bare. He wore only the trunks of his sheer pongee pajamas. The top sheet had been thrown off and lay on the floor; the bottom sheet was smooth and unwrinkled, a vast expanse of sheer fine silk.

The room itself was painted in soft pastel colors and the fine rattan furniture, tipped with solid brass fittings, had been sent down from New York by Sloane's. There were several water colors on the walls, in excellent taste, and the floor was covered by a thick white carpet. It was a beautiful room.

Fullbright was a man who loved and appreciated beauty.

Beside the bed was a rectangular end table and on it were the remains of a breakfast. The morning newspaper was unopened, lying next to the breakfast tray.

Looking out toward the ocean, Fullbright sighed contentedly and closed his eyes. He felt marvelous. He knew that pretty soon he would have to get up, have to make the phone call, but he couldn't help procrastinating. Without checking the platinum wrist watch lying on the table next to the bed, he knew that it was already past ten o'clock. He just wanted to lie there with his eyes closed and wallow in his feeling of utter contentment.

My God, he had it made. Yes sir, he, Richard Fullbright, had it made. It had taken a long time, a lot of work and a good many bitter years of fighting and struggle, but at last he had it made. He was sixty years old, but he was in excellent health and he still had a good many years left. They were going to be perfect years.

His thin-lipped mouth smiled with satisfaction. He had it made and he deserved it. Every bit of it. He'd worked hard and he'd taken chances. Taken gambles that most men would never have dreamed of taking. But in the long run it had paid off.

Thinking of the others he had known, the ones who were still in the rat race, the ones who had died and the ones who had fallen by the wayside, he had to congratulate himself. He'd played his cards smoothly and well. He had accomplished what he had set out to accomplish.

He hadn't been greedy, hadn't been impatient, hadn't been a fool. None of this running off to some godforsaken South American country for him. None of this ducking around Europe for the rest of his life. And none of this business of staying on and dying in harness the way most of them had to do.

He opened his eyes slowly and yawned.

He'd been very clever. When the time had come to quit, he'd arranged it so that he could get out. So that he could just turn in his hand and leave. It is true that he'd had to walk away from a million-dollar deal.

Better than a million. He'd had to turn the Casino over to his partners and just take off, giving them his share of the place. They'd been satisfied and hadn't squawked. They'd been more than satisfied. They figured that they were stealing it from him.

They were smart operators and they were sure they were getting all of the best of the deal. In a sense they were.

He really had to laugh about that. About the way Manny and Sal and Knocky had acted when he'd told them what the doctor said. The phony, insincere way they had sympathized with him. Promised to see that he was taken care of once he left and they took the business over. Their phony promises about seeing that he'd always get his cut. His cut, hell. They'd never send him a dime and he knew it and they knew it and they knew that he knew they knew it.

But what they didn't know was that he already had his cut. Had a lot more than his cut. That he'd been taking it out of the kitty for more than five years and putting it away while he prepared for the day when he'd quit for good.

They were smart boys all right, but they hadn't been smart enough. Not by a long shot.

He'd been a small-town banker when he'd gone in with them on the casino deal. They were nothing. Scum. But he'd always been a respectable business man, a man with a reputation and with integrity. They had needed a fellow like Richard Fullbright to front for them. And he'd gone along. He had the front, the respectability. He had the brains. From the very beginning, he'd known what he would eventually do. Known just how he'd handle the thing.

Well, it was all over and done with now. All through. It had taken him a long time to find this place, longer to clear the land and build the bungalow and get the thing set up. During the last years or so, after he'd found Sam, he'd only come down once or twice to check up. Sam was a gold mine. Sam could be trusted to see to everything. And then, four months ago he'd made the break. Cut clean.

For those last four months, he'd been living here. Living alone with no one but Sam, as he always wanted to live, in this perfect house, in this perfect spot. The loveliest spot in the world. Nothing to disturb him; nothing to bother him.

Key Arroyos was the sort of place he'd always dreamed about. Unspoiled, and it would never be spoiled. Just the dozen or so homes and they were only occupied during the few brief months in the winter. No hotels, no tourists. Just the few natives of the town and the fishermen. An island of perpetual sunshine and soft tropical breezes and peace. A place to while away the hours and the days and the years.

He was yawning again when Sam, the Negro from Jamaica, poked his head into the room.

"Time for your phone call to Miami, Mr. Fullbright," Sam said, speaking with an oddly soft British accent.

Fullbright looked up.

"Sam, you call the boatyard and check up," he said. "See if she's ready and when they expect to bring her down."

Sam nodded and silently turned and left.

It was funny how much he was looking forward to delivery of the yacht. Not funny, actually, because it was something he'd been dreaming about for a long time and he was terribly anxious to see her now that she was about ready to be delivered. He had been waiting for weeks, while they installed the big twin diesel engines, the controls on the flying bridge and cleaned up the final details. He himself had been calling the broker and the yard in Miami several times a day, impatient and barely able to wait. But now that it was ready, now that at last they were actually going to bring the boat down, it amused him somehow or other to have Sam make the call.

It was a beautiful boat. It should be. It was costing him seventy thousand dollars, and seventy thousand dollars is a lot of money. But it was going to be worth every cent of it. The yacht was like the house, not large, not ostentatious, but the very best that money could buy.

He looked forward to the long lazy days while he cruised the islands and the Keys, the bays and the coves, sometimes fishing and sometimes doing nothing but lying out on the teak deck in a chair and just letting the tropical sun beat down as the gulf breezes brushed his face and body.

He didn't need people, he didn't need anything but peace and time and luxury. And Sam, of course, to look after him.

Once more he thought of Manny and Sol and Knocky, back there at the Casino sitting around and congratulating themselves that they had gotten rid of him; had stolen the business. This time he laughed out loud.

He stretched and got off the bed, moving slowly and carefully. He suddenly remembered what it was he had to do today. He'd promised that Greek who owned the little restaurant in town that he would see him. He didn't know what it could possibly be about, but the man had asked if he could come in and talk for a minute or two.

Richard Fullbright smiled indulgently. Hell, why not? He wanted to remain on friendly terms with the natives of the town. In fact it rather pleased him to be treated something like a village patron. Just so that the winter people didn't bother him, of course. He wasn't going to bother with them, not going to mingle with them at all. The townsfolk were different. They were like himself, they liked it here all the year round.

Well, thank God it was still summer and none of the northerners had shown up yet and wouldn't show up. Not at least until the hurricane season was over, anyway.

Fools, they were missing the very best part of the year. Well, thank God for the hurricanes; it kept the tourists and part-time residents away.

Fullbright was out on the glassed-in porch, fooling around with the knobs on the big Capehart, when Sam returned.

"Man says boat's ready," Sam said. "Says he wants to talk to you. Doesn't want to have it come down until after the storm blows over."

"Storm?" Fullbright said. "What storm? My God man, it's beautiful outside. Just a nice breeze."

"There's a hurricane warning up in the Gulf," Sam said. "They don't think it is coming this way, but the man said they don't want to take any chances."

"Damned nonsense," Fullbright said, reaching for one of the long slender cigars he had imported from Cuba and which he chewed but never lighted. "The man is a fool. Bring me the phone extension."

Sam nodded, his mahogany face blank as usual.

"Right away, Mr. Fullbright," he said.

Chapter Four

1

Helen Cosmos lay flat on her back and stared up at the fly-speckled ceiling, her large blue eyes wide and unblinking. Tiny dots of perspiration covered her forehead and her face was white and moist. Aside from the red lipstick which outlined her sensuous mouth, she wore no make-up. Her blonde hair was combed and neatly pinned back as it had been when she'd retired several hours earlier. She wore a brassiere and panties and lay on top of the sheet in the dead air of the small room. Her long, beautifully rounded body was completely still but her right hand, lying at her side, moved ever so slightly so that the back of it rubbed against the hand of her husband.

She didn't change her expression when she spoke and the words came out in a dead, colorless monotone.

"He wasn't kidding, Nick," she said. "He wasn't kidding at all."

Nick turned his head on the pillow so that he could look at her, and then quickly turned away. He opened his hand and put his fingers around hers, squeezing them ever so slightly.

"Don't worry, keed," he said. "Don't worry so much about it."

Nick himself was stark naked, lying next to her and half on his side so that he partially faced her. His heavy body made great dents in the bed and he was perspiring all over. He always sweated a great deal and the tiny rivulets of perspiration ran down from his face and neck into the black curly hair of his deep chest.

"You don't know him, Nick," Helen said. "You don't know what kind of a man he is. You don't understand what he can do. He isn't human."

Nick sighed deeply.

"Listen," he said. "It's been years. Years now. My God, what can he care? What does it matter to him. Look what he did to you when you were with him. Jesus. Made a God-damned whore outta ..."

She shuddered and closed her mouth tight on the half sob and he quickly stopped talking. He put one arm across her slender body, resting it very gently on her breasts.

"I'm sorry, keed," he said quickly. "I'm sorry. I shouldn't a said that. Forgive me. But you gotta understand. You can't be afraid of him any longer. You're Mrs. Cosmos now. All nice and legal and right. Mrs. Nick Cosmos."

"Sure," she said. "I'm Mrs. Cosmos. I've changed and thank God for that." She turned and looked into his face and her eyes were soft suddenly and moist. "Thank God, and thank you, Nick."

She leaned forward and lifted his hand and brought it to her lips and kissed it.

"But Nick," she said, "he hasn't changed. He hasn't changed one bit. He's still the same mad, insane, jealous bastard."

"How could he be jealous," Nick asked, honest curiosity in his voice. "How could he be jealous when he did what he did to you? When he brought in other men, when he put you out on the—"

"Nick," Helen said, "Oh, Nick, don't say it."

"I gotta say it," Nick said. "My God, I gotta say it, what with you here worrying yourself to death because of seeing him and what he said and all."

"I'm worried about what he can do. What he will do," she said. "Oh, don't you see, Nick! Don't you see? It isn't really me he cares about or ever did care about. I was nothing to him but a way of making money. Like his slot machines or his punch boards or his dice game. Just something he owned. And Paul isn't a guy who'd ever give up anything that was once his. That's what you have to understand. It wasn't that I was his girl—I was his property. I made money for him."

"For Christ sake," Nick said. "What the hell does he think you are? Ain't you supposed to be human? What the hell you mean he owned you? Nobody owns anybody. This is a free country."

"Not with Paul," she said, her voice listless. "Not with him. Nobody's got any rights with him."

Nick moved suddenly, shifting his weight and sitting up on the edge of the bed. He reached for the package of cigarettes and held it toward her and she shook her head. His hand was shaking as he lighted one for himself.

"God damn it," he said. "You're Mrs. Nick Cosmos. My wife. I don't care what you were or who you were but now you're Mrs. Cosmos. And nobody, nobody at all, is going to change that. See, nobody!"

She reached over and pulled him back down beside her.

"Listen, Nick," she said. "He just walked into the restaurant there in Miami, while I was waiting to be served, and he saw me and the minute he did he came over and he sat down."

"So he sat down," Nick said. "So—"

She put her hand over his mouth.

"Listen to me, Nick. He saw me and he came over and he sat down. He didn't take off his hat. Just sat down. He said, 'How are you, Helen.' Nice and soft and polite. Oh, he's always polite. And that's when he's the most dangerous. When he's polite."

She hesitated and then took the cigarette from her husband's mouth and took a long puff and handed it back.

"Well, he didn't say anything for a minute and then he looked right into my face and his lips curled and he used that word. Called me the name. Then he said, 'So you married the Greek, did you Helen? A nice happy little love nest, eh, kid?' Well, I started to deny it, started to say anything to throw him off but he didn't let me get a word in.

"He went right on. He said, 'I got a message for the Greek, Helen,' he said. 'I want you to go back to that little island love nest, back to that hash house, and tell him he's a dead man. Get it—a dead man!'"

"How could he know where—" Nick started, but again she interrupted him.

"I don't know how he knew, but he did. I could tell that he did. He knew, the same way he knew your name. He said it and then he got up and he tipped his hat and he said, 'Give my regards to Mr. Cosmos, the dead man.' And then he left."

For several minutes neither of them spoke. Finally Nick reached over and butted out the cigarette.

"It's been over a week now," he said, "and nothing's happened yet. Maybe he was just bluffing, just trying to scare you. After all, what could he really do, especially down here. Hell, I got a gun. We got police protection."

Helen laughed without amusement.

"A gun? A gun wouldn't help you with Paul," she said, "You won't even know who it is when they come. You won't know until it's all over. And as far as police protection is concerned, don't make me laugh. Are you referring to that half-witted deputy who's been around making a pest out of himself? Do you think a jerk like him could protect anyone? No, Nick. No, there's only one thing to do. We've got to leave. We've got to get out of here and get out just as soon as we can."

Nick stared at her for several moments and then turned his eyes away.

"Sell the restaurant?" he said. "It won't be easy."

"It doesn't matter. What's a restaurant? We can always get another restaurant. You can turn it over to a real estate agency and sooner or later they'll unload it and send you the money."

"It isn't the money," Nick said. "It isn't that. I don't care about the money. It's just that—"

"It's just that I don't want anything to happen to you," Helen said, turning on her side and putting her arms around him. "I don't want anything to happen to us. Oh Nick, don't you see? For the first time I'm happy. We're happy, or at least I hope that you are as happy as I have been. I don't want anything to happen to it. Anything to happen to us. If we leave, get out of here and find some other place, some place that no one will know about, why then everything will be all right. We won't have to worry and he'll never know where we are."

Nick patted her bare shoulder and gently caressed the side of her face. He held her close for a moment and then released her and stood up.

"I don't like to run," he said. "I don't like to run from nothing. But kid, if it will make you feel better, if it's going to make you stop worrying, why what the hell. I don't care what I gotta do to make you feel good. The restaurant? The hell with the restaurant. As you say, I can always have a restaurant. But I can't always have a girl like you."

Quickly she stood up then and put her arms around him and held him tight, saying nothing.

"Sure," he said. "Don't worry. In fact, I didn't want to say anything, but I knew how you been feeling about it. I knew you been upset. So I already made arrangements."

She leaned back to look up at him.

"Arrangements?"

"Well," he said, "I am seeing Mr. Fullbright today. I got two lots next to his place and I'm going to try and sell them to him. He could use them for protection, so nobody builds next to his place. It will give us getaway money. The restaurant—well, we can sell that later. It will be a little harder to move."

This time when Helen put her arms around him, she was sobbing under her breath. She held him very tight, burying her face in his neck. She didn't let him go as they fell back on the bed together.

2

The letter had been lying unopened on the cluttered top of the long trestle table for three days, but it wasn't until that morning, shortly after he had finished his meagre breakfast, that Tony Mason got around to opening it. The fact that he waited so long before breaking the seal and extracting the single sheet of typewritten paper was not a result of indifference.

Tony Mason wasn't sure, but he had a very good idea of the contents of this particular letter. One look at the return address was enough. The letter was from his father and bore the name of his father's law firm up in Boston.

One thing Tony was sure about: whatever the letter said, it was bound to be unpleasant. Tony had a strong distaste for facing unpleasantness and so, when he had received the letter, he had brought it back to the shanty and tossed it on the table, unopened.

It was because of the breakfast that he'd finally gotten around to it on this particular morning. The breakfast consisted of a can of warmed-up tomato soup and a dry, unbuttered half loaf of Italian bread.

There were other breakfasts which he would have preferred, but a search of his cupboard had turned up nothing else. He had not bothered to go through his pockets and see if he had enough money to go down to the Greek's and eat. He knew, without making the search, that there would be no money. Lunch would present no great problem as he would be able to catch a fish off the back porch of the shanty. But dinner was something else. One can become awfully tired of eating fish.

It was while he was thinking about this, and looking around the place for a stray cigarette, that Tony decided to open the letter.

He didn't find a cigarette, but compromised on a short butt which he retrieved from an overflowing ashtray which lay on the edge of the easel shelf next to the table. He smoked the butt as he read the letter.

"Dear Tony," his father wrote, "I am depositing one hundred dollars in your checking account.

"What I am about to write will not, I believe, come as any great surprise to you. This will be the last money which you can expect from me until such a time as you are prepared to give up this idiotic and adolescent obsession of yours and return home to take your rightful place in society and face life as a grown man; to assume the responsibilities of an adult. After all, you are twenty-five years old and it is time you realized it.

"It has been two years since you graduated from college and, although I have never insisted that you go ahead with your law career with thoughts of eventually coming into the firm, the time has come when I am tired of supporting you and encouraging you on a road which can lead to nothing but failure. Against my advice you have insisted about a career as an artist. For two years now I have been sending you money, agreeing to let you pursue such a career, although it has been against my better judgment.

"My recent visit to you in Key Arroyos, however, has finally convinced me of one thing. Instead of pursuing an artistic career through normal channels of study and work, you have preferred to live the life of an idler and an outcast in a backwater of civilization, where you seem to have spent most of your time in turning yourself into a combination beachcomber and remittance man. You refused to show me what you have been doing and I found you living in a condition of filth and dirt which appalled me. Apparently you have spent the last two years in utter idleness.

"It is difficult for me to understand how any son of mine could voluntarily prefer the type of life you seem to have chosen for yourself.

"As you have said, it is quite true that I do not understand you. On the other hand there is one thing I do understand. Sending you more money will merely encourage you to continue to lead the life you have been living and will procrastinate the time when you regain your senses and return to a normal existence. And so, this will be the last money you will receive from me and I strongly suggest that you use it to arrange for transportation back home.

"In case you decide to do so, you may either return to school for postgraduate work or, if you still find the thought of a law career distasteful, I will try and find you a place in some other respectable business or profession.

"In closing let me add that I hope you will come to your senses before you have completely broken your mother's heart. My own feelings no longer count. Sincerely, Dad."

Tony shifted his lean, bony six-foot frame in the broken rocking chair and stretched his legs out, scratching one bare foot with the large toe of his other foot. He wore nothing but a faded and torn pair of khaki trousers held above his hips by a knotted rope instead of a belt. His body was as brown as a nut. He needed a shave badly and his long, black hair was uncombed. Well-spaced dark eyes were shadowed by heavy lashes and he had a thin, aquiline nose above a generous mouth.

Finishing the letter, he tossed it aside on the littered table and shrugged. What his father had to say came as no surprise. The surprise was the hundred dollars. Quickly he made a mental calculation. Fifteen dollars would pay another month's rent on the shanty. Thirty dollars would go for paints and canvasses. And the other fifty would keep him in groceries and cigarettes for at least thirty days.

And at the end of thirty days? Well, he guessed there was nothing else to do but face the fact that he would be broke again.

For a brief moment he thought of the canvasses he had stacked up against the wall; remembered the dealer from Miami who had dropped by and offered to take a few of them on consignment. But as quickly he dismissed the idea.

In the first place he doubted if the man could actually sell anything and secondly he, Charles Anthony Mason III, wasn't ready to sell. He didn't even want his stuff seen until it was ready and it wouldn't be ready until he, himself, thought it was. No one, no one at all was going to force him to exhibit until he was painting the way he wanted to paint.

There was only one answer, but his father didn't have that answer. He'd take a job on one of the fishing boats. It was hard work and the pay wasn't much. But three months on the boat would mean three free months ashore and three more months of painting.

He hated the thought of it, but there was nothing else to do. In the meantime, hell, he had a month's grace, thanks to that hundred dollars.

Standing up he stretched and yawned. He was still hungry and he would have liked to have had a pack of cigarettes. But he looked over at the old alarm clock on the card table next to the bed and saw that it was almost noon. Sally was due at twelve and he wanted to be there when she arrived.

One more session and the picture would be done. It would only be a matter of an hour or so, and then he could go in and cash a check at the Greek's and pick up what he needed.

He pulled the tall easel out into the center of the room and reversed the canvas which was on it. Crossing over to the north wall, he pulled the blinds aside so that the light flooded the room. Then he yawned again and started searching for another respectably sized cigarette butt.

He remembered the last paragraph of his father's letter and smiled. Breaking his mother's heart? His mother was as happy as a clam; she was honeymooning on Cape Cod with her newest husband, who was twenty years her junior, and nothing could have upset her more than having her grown son in the vicinity.

3

Sally took her time walking the half mile between her house and the shanty over on the edge of the island bordering the Gulf. A large, droopy straw hat protected her from the midday sun, but the heat was terrific.

It's hot, she thought, too hot. It struck her as strange that it could be so hot while the wind was blowing so.

Not like me, Sally thought. I'm too calm. I know what's going to happen when I see him; I've been planning it for days now. And I'm much too calm.

This was to be the last day. After today the painting would be finished and there would no longer be the excuse to go to the shanty each morning. No more excuse for seeing him. Of course he'd still be around, still be living less than a mile away. But it would be like it had been before; before he'd asked her to pose for him. They'd meet, casually, once or twice a week and have a few polite words and that would be that. He'd ignore her and go on living his hermit's life, minding his own business and staying away from everyone.

Whatever had to be done, had to be done this day. And she, Sally Martins, was going to see to it that something was done. It was time that Charles Anthony Mason III became aware of the fact that she was something besides a casual piece of clay; some mechanical doll to be told to stand this way or that way, not to twitch and please stop nodding and so forth. He must learn that she was a real live girl; made out of flesh and blood and with feelings. Physical and emotional feelings.

And it was time that she straightened Charles Anthony Mason out a little about himself. It was all very fine and good to be a dedicated artist and to have high and lofty ideals. But that was no excuse for him living like a castaway on a desert island. It was no reason for him going around half-fed and not taking care of himself. What he needed ...

She was mumbling under her breath as she came in sight of the weather-beaten shanty. She saw at once that the blinds had been raised and that he was up and about.

Well, at least it was one morning that she wouldn't have to pull him out of bed to get him to work. Mostly, when she would arrive, he was either still sleeping or he was fishing. There was another thing that she would take up; his lazy, indolent life when he wasn't working. Her jaw was set with determination as she stepped up to the porch and opened the screen door and entered the studio.

Tony looked up from a pile of newspapers and nodded.

"Got a cigarette?" he asked.

Instinctively she started to reach into her straw bag for the pack and then she hesitated.

"Don't you ever—" she began, but he interrupted.

"Almost never," he said. "And I don't have any pride, if that was going to be your next question. Anyway, we'll be through today and you won't have to have me scrounging from you, so be gracious about it."

She sighed and shook her head.

"You look terrible," she said. "Did you have breakfast?"

"I always have breakfast," Tony said. "Sometimes it's a little late, of course. Maybe a day or so late, but I always have it."

"Well you don't look like you had it this morning," Sally said. "You don't even look as though you have washed and brushed your teeth."

Tony grinned, exposing two rows of beautifully white teeth.

"Never wash," he said. "Bad for the complexion. Now just be a good girl and let me have that cigarette. And then we can get to work." Sally handed over the pack and turned and pulled the broken rocker around and sat down in it.

"Tony," she said, "I want to talk to you. I think that it's about time...."

He held up his hand and shook his head, frowning. "Later—later," he said. "Work first and then the social life. I just have a few more touches."

Sally shook her head and stood up.

"All right, Tony," she said, "work first, if you wish. But don't think you are going to get out of it today. We are going to have a talk. Whether you like it or not, we're going to have a talk. I'll get ready now."

Crossing the room, she started to unbutton the light cotton dress she was wearing.

"You can keep your clothes on," Tony said. "I just want to check some of the shadows on the head and the shoulders. I'm satisfied with the rest of it. I finished in the background last night," he added, turning toward the canvas.

"At night?" Sally said. "I should have thought that you would need daylight."

"The background is supposed to be at dusk," Tony said. "So that's the best time to work on it. Anyway, I'm just about through. Tell me what you think of it."

Sally walked over and stood in front of the easel, cocking her head to one side. She stepped back a pace or two and squinted her eyes, frowning slightly.

"Naturally I'm a little prejudiced," she said at last. "With a model as beautiful ..." she looked up, half smiling, and saw the frown in his face.

"Seriously, Tony," she said quickly, "I think it's fine. Of course I'm completely ignorant, but I think it's fine."

"I don't know," Tony said. "I can't tell myself. But, if I look at it in a week or two and it still looks the way it does to me now, I'll send it up to Ginsburg and see what he says. Maybe it is all right."

"Of course it's all right," Sally said. "It's a lot better than just all right. And so are your other pictures, Tony. Oh why," she said, her voice exasperated, "why can't you just have a little more confidence in yourself? Don't you see, if you don't show your—"

"When I show, I want them to be more than just all right," he interrupted her. "Let's not go into that again. I know what I'm doing and I'm going to do it my way. Now just stand over there, against the wall and we'll get started."

He leaned down and picked up a brush and stepped in front of the canvas.

At ten minutes after two, Tony finally stepped back from the easel and putting the end of the camel hair brush between his teeth, shoved his hands in his pockets and stared for several moments at the picture. He grunted and slowly nodded his head.

"Well," he said, removing the brush, "that's it. It's as done as it ever will be."

Sally stretched and moved her head around on her neck. "I can stand a break," she said. "My neck is so stiff."

"No break," Tony said. "Finished."

She walked over and stood beside him. "It's fine, Tony, really fine."

She turned suddenly and went over to where she had dropped her large, bulging bag. Reaching in she took out a paper sack and opening it, removed a bottle of wine.

"I brought this along to celebrate," she said gaily. "You get the glasses."

He looked at her with approval.

"An excellent idea," he said. "An excellent idea and an excellent lunch."

He found two empty jelly glasses on the table and rinsed them out, wiping them with a piece of torn newspaper. Sally handed him the bottle and he pulled the cork and filled the glasses. They lifted them together, touching rims.

"To the picture," Sally said, looking up into his face.

"To the prettiest model in the world, who made it possible," Tony said.

They drank and Tony reached again for the bottle.

Sally put her hand out. "Later," she said. "Right now we talk."

Tony shrugged and walked over to the couch and sprawled on it. Sally followed him, sitting next to him and half turning toward him.

"My dad," Sally said, "doesn't approve of you."

"Your dad is right," Tony said, not looking at her. "He's absolutely right."

"That isn't the point," Sally said. "I do approve of you. I think you should do what you want to do. I think that if you want to be an artist, you should. I think that no sacrifice is too great, no matter what you have to give up. And I think that you are going to be a great artist. That you are a great artist right now."

Tony shifted uncomfortably, saying nothing.

"The only thing is," Sally went on, "you just aren't being sensible about it. You can't go on living from hand to mouth, living on nothing and just hoping from day to day."

"Oh, I get by."

"You don't get by," Sally said. "Just look at you. You're twenty pounds underweight, you haven't eaten a decent meal in days, you don't take any care—"

He reached over and took both of her hands in one of his and with the other he covered her mouth.

"Now listen," he began. "Don't start ..."

Quickly she pulled her head away.

"I'm serious, Tony," she said. "You have to listen to me."

He hunched his shoulders and dropped her hands. "Well, just what do you want me to do?"

"I'll tell you what," Sally said, her voice determined. "I'll tell you what. The trouble is, you need time. Time to establish yourself. Living down here like this, working against every possible handicap—well, it just doesn't make sense. What you need is enough money to give you a year or so to get on your feet."

"You couldn't be more right," Tony said, half laughing. "And just where do you think I'm going to get it?"

She moved closer to him and took his hand in hers. She avoided his eyes when she next spoke.

"I have over four thousand dollars," she said quietly. "It was money put away to see me through my last two years in college. But I'm not going back to college. That's been definitely decided. I don't want to and even if I did, I wouldn't leave Dad. I want you to take the money."

He jumped up before she had finished and stood off staring at her.

"You want *me* to take *your* money?"

She nodded.

"Yes," she said. "Don't you see, Tony, it's the one thing you need? The money isn't doing me any good and you could pay it back later."

"You mean," he said, interrupting her, "you mean you are offering to loan me four thousand dollars?" His voice was incredulous.

"That's just what I mean, Tony."

For a moment more he stared at her, unbelievingly. He shook his head slightly.

"And just why," he asked, almost coldly, "just why are you offering to give me this money?"

She stood up and faced him, blushing slightly.

"Tony," she said, "you have talent. Real talent. Not," she said hurriedly, "because I say so or know anything about art. But you yourself have said so. Often. You have a real talent and you need the chance.

You need to get out of here; to get away from this place. Go back up north where you can really work. Where people can see what you are doing. You need an opportunity. Well, I have the money to give you that opportunity. I'm not being patronizing or making you a gift or anything like that."

He reached out then suddenly and took her by the arms and pulled her close to him, looking down into her upturned face. For a moment he just stared at her, his eyes wide. And then suddenly he pulled her close and leaned down and his lips found hers.

For a second she was taut in his arms, her mouth cold and unyielding. And then, all in a second, she melted and her lips and her own arms went around his lean body and she clutched him tightly.

At last she pulled away from him and stood back and he still stood there, staring at her. Unconsciously his arms lifted and he half wiped his lips with the back of his hand.

"Why you darling," he said. "You absolute, complete and—"

"Then you'll take it?" she asked, breathless.

For another second or so he stared at her. And then he laughed. He turned away and when he spoke he was facing the wide north window.

"Take it? Take it?" he turned back toward her, looking almost angry. "Of course I won't take it. What do you think I am, anyway? Do you think—"

She cut in, her voice baffled and a little hurt.

"But why?" she asked. "Why? You take money from your father, don't you? And haven't you always said that money doesn't matter? That it's just another necessary evil? That only fools attach importance to it?"

"My father's different," Tony said. "My father has about half a million dollars."

"Money is money," Sally said, the bewilderment in her voice turning to stubborn anger. "You've said so yourself a hundred times. It doesn't make any difference."

"It makes all of the difference," he said. "All the difference in the world."

"You're nothing but a hypocrite," she said. "I thought that you were a realist, that you were sophisticated. That you were serious. If you are really honest, it wouldn't matter where the money came from. The important thing would be that which you want to do. I guess, after all, you're just another conventional ..."

He stepped back across the room and once more took her arms in his long slender hands. He shook her, not gently.

"Now you listen to me," he said. "Just listen to me. You are a darling," he said, almost shouting the words. "A generous, sweet, innocent darling. But you've got to listen to me. Why I couldn't possibly take your money. Don't you see, the one important thing, the most important thing, about what I am trying to do is that I reserve my pride? That I do it in my way and make my own sacrifices? Why do you think I'm living in this dump, living like a damned pig? Why do you think that I won't go back home? Won't even take a job until I have to? It's because I won't compromise. Maybe I'll end up a good painter and maybe I won't. But I have to find out in my own way. I can't have obligations, can't have—"

He saw the sudden hurt expression on her face and stopped.

"There wouldn't be any obligations," she said.

Quickly he shook his head.

"You still don't understand," he said. "Don't you see, if you were some casual millionaire, if you were some rich old bag who didn't mean a thing to me—"

"What do I mean to you, Tony?" Sally interrupted, her eyes wide. "Just what do I mean to you?"

They stared at each other breathlessly and his arms again circled her. He opened his mouth, starting to speak and then slowly closed it. Her own hands met in back of his waist.

"Sally," he said, "Sally ..."

It was then that the screen door crashed open and Socks Schroeder burst into the room. Both of them turned quickly to see him standing there, legs apart and hamlike hands on his hips as he stared at them with fury in his almost colorless blue eyes.

Chapter Five

1

Sam brought Nick Cosmos out to the flagstone patio, built alongside the private slip which Richard Fullbright had dredged to accommodate the blue cruiser he'd ordered from Miami. The patio was completely screened in and was furnished with chromed deck chairs and glass-topped tables. It was bordered, inside the screening, with beds of tropical plants and flowers and large concealed fans blew a constant stream of cooling air across it.

Fullbright lay back on one of the deck chairs, a Panama hat pulled half over his face. He didn't get up as Sam announced Nick.

"Hot," he said, "even here. Take a seat."

Nick said good morning, although it was well along in mid-afternoon, and half bowed, although the other man had not lifted his eyes.

"Something to drink?" Fullbright asked. "Cocktail, or maybe a little rum?"

Nick shook his head.

"No thank you, Mr. Fullbright," he said stiffly. "I never drink before evening. I—"

"Excellent idea," Fullbright, said disinterestedly. "And how is Mrs. Cosmos?"

Nick looked at the other man. "Why, fine," he said.

Fullbright shifted in his seat and lifted the hat so that he could peer out from under the brim at the other man.

"Funny day," he said. "Windy. Sky looks odd, too."

Nick nodded. "Very hot," he said.

"But I like it," Fullbright said. "It can't get too hot for me. I manage to keep cool somehow. Yes, I manage." He stopped talking and for several moments neither spoke.

Fullbright knew that Nick wanted to see him for some particular reason. It was probably going to be a request of some kind or other. Some sort of favor he would want. Fullbright didn't know what it could be, but when people came to him, they always wanted something. He was in no hurry to find out what. Let the fellow stew for a bit.

Nick played nervously with his hat, making it go round and round in circles in his nervous hands. He sat on the very edge of his seat. He didn't quite know where to start. Finally he took a long breath and coughed.

"I'm thinking of leaving Arroyos," he said at last.

Fullbright looked up at him again, noncommittal. "Indeed?"

"Yeah," Nick said. "Me and Mrs. Cosmos."

"Giving up the business, eh?" Fullbright said. "Well, I can't say that I blame you. There can't be a lot of trade—"

"Mrs. Cosmos doesn't take to this climate," Nick interrupted. "We've decided to go north."

"Be sorry to see you go," Fullbright said, his voice bored.

"I'll be sorry to go," Nick said. He hesitated again for a moment or two and then quickly spoke, his words running a little together in his nervousness.

"It's on account of that I have to see you," he said. "I got those two lots on the other side of the canal." He lifted his hand to point across the terrace. "Had them some time now. They're pretty valuable property. Make a fine site for a home."

Fullbright turned to look at him then, his expression one of mock surprise.

"Oh, you mean you are thinking of putting up a winter home then?" he asked. "Something to come back to after you move north?"

"Not exactly," Nick said, not catching the sarcasm in the other man's voice. "No, once we pull out, we pull out."

"A shame," Fullbright said. "It would make such a nice plot for a winter place."

Nick nodded.

"Sure," he said. "It sure would. That's why I thought maybe you'd be interested."

"But I have a home," Fullbright said, speaking as though he were talking to a slightly idiotic child. "I already have my home here. I certainly wouldn't want two houses, charming as I find this lovely tropical paradise. No, I think that two houses would be overdoing it just a trifle."

He smiled with an almost charming simplicity and Nick stared at him and for the first time frowned.

"I don't expect you'd want two houses," he said. "I just thought that because the lots were right next door to you, maybe you'd like to buy them for protection."

"Protection from what, Mr. Cosmos?"

Fullbright was thoroughly enjoying himself. The fact is, he'd been wanting to get his hands on that particular piece of property for a long time now. He'd made overtures to the Greek, indirectly, several times through real estate representatives, but Nick had never been willing to sell. And now, fortunately, for some reason he wanted to leave Key Arroyos and he was anxious to sell. It was a lucky break. Fullbright's instinct told him that he would be able to get the land at a considerable saving.

He couldn't resist egging the other man on a little, pretending ignorance and baiting him just the least bit. But he didn't want to overdo it; didn't want to antagonize him too much.

"What should I protect myself from?" he asked. "Certainly, in this beautiful, serene spot ..."

"You got the nicest place on the island," Nick said. "A beautiful place. I just thought that you wouldn't want someone should come and build some dump next door."

"Now who would do that?" Fullbright asked. "After all, you own the land, Mr. Cosmos, and you are moving away and not going to build there."

"I'm selling the land," Nick said. "We have to raise money."

"There are so few buyers," Fullbright said. "So very few. Fortunately, of course—"

"I've had offers," Nick said shortly.

Fullbright jerked his thin neck around and looked at Nick closely. Mentally he cursed himself for not having waited, having put out those tentative feelers through the real estate agents.

"Just what would you value the land at?" he asked.

"Well, I got two lots, a hundred and fifty feet water front and going back—"

"I'm familiar with the boundaries," Fullbright said coldly.

"It's nice land," Nick said. "I should get at least three thousand...." His voice fell off as he watched the other man.

"You paid seven hundred and fifty," Fullbright sat "Less than six years ago."

"That's right," Nick said. "But you yourself paid better."

Fullbright held up an almost transparent hand.

"Beside the point," he said. "Quite beside the point. However, if it would help you out at all, I'd be willing to consider a reasonable proposition. Say something in the neighborhood of fifteen hundred. That would be doubling your money."

"But, Mr. Fullbright," Nick said. "You know that land's worth a lot more today."

"All right," Fullbright said. "We won't haggle. I'll give you two thousand. Take it or leave it."

Nick stood up, his face red. The land was worth well over three thousand and he knew it. Fullbright knew it, too. But it would take time to move; it might take weeks or months. He started to turn away, to hide the fury in his face, before speaking.

Fullbright misunderstood the gesture.

"Twenty-five hundred," he said. "As a favor."

"How soon can I get the money?" Nick asked.

"As soon as we can have a deed drawn up," Fullbright said. "I'll call my attorney in Miami."

Nick nodded.

"I'll want it as soon as possible," he said. "We, me and Mrs. Cosmos, are anxious to close up and get out as soon as possible."

Fullbright stood up.

"I'll just draw up a binder and give you a check to keep everything in order. Say a hundred dollars?"

Nick nodded.

"Whatever you say, Mr. Fullbright," he said. "Anything you say."

"Do let me have Sam bring you something," Fullbright said, turning to ring for the Jamaican. "It will take me a few minutes to get an agreement typed out." He smiled. "I'm pretty rusty at that sort of thing," he said.

2

Tilden Flack sat in the firehouse, across the street from Nick's restaurant, slowly sipping from his pint bottle and watching the door of the restaurant until he saw Nick leave. It had been a long wait and it didn't improve Flack's temper. By the time he was ready to move, he was more than half drunk. He waited only until Nick was out of sight and then slowly got to his feet.

Walking over to the coke machine, he put a coin in and took out a bottle. It was lukewarm, but that didn't bother him. He used the drink for a chaser and downed the last of the whisky.

He shifted the holster around so that it rode his fat hip more comfortably, tipped his wide-brimmed black felt hat back on his head and left the firehouse. Crossing the street, he staggered just slightly.

When he entered the restaurant, his eyes quickly searched the place. He saw at once that the long room was vacant.

Instead of stopping at one of the booths or the counter, he continued on through to the double swinging doors in the rear. He pushed them open and entered.

Helen Cosmos was leaning over the sink, her slender, rounded arms half buried in soapy water. She looked up over her shoulder as she heard the creak of the doors. Seeing Flack standing there, a supercilious smile on his wide, ugly face, she frowned slightly and turned back to the sink.

"I'll be right out," she said.

Flack leaned back against the butcher's block. "Nick around?" he asked.

"He's out," Helen said.

Flack grunted. "Well, I can wait," he said.

Helen looked up from the sink, taking out her hands and wiping them on her apron. She took the apron off and threw it into a wire basket. Tossing back her blonde hair, she said, "Is there something you wanted in particular? Maybe I ..."

"Oh, I just wanted to see Nick," Flack said. He looked at her and smiled but it was more of a leer than a smile. "I don't mind waiting. Got all the time in the world."

Helen tried to keep the annoyance out of her voice when she spoke. "He may not be back for quite a while," she said. "Maybe I can have him call you."

Flack shook his head, still smiling. Standing less than a half dozen feet away from her, he slowly let his eyes travel from her face, down across her breasts to her slender waist and then on down past the shorts she was wearing to her rounded thighs. She was wearing one of her husband's shirts and it was open at the neck. He knew that there was nothing underneath it.

Helen felt her face flush under his glance.

"If you'd like to go out and sit down," she said hurriedly, "I can bring you a drink."

He shook his head.

"Maybe you can help me out at that," he said. "You see, I was up in Miami not too long ago and I ran across a funny bit of information. Seems there was this girl named Helen ..." He hesitated, looking into her face.

"Yes?"

"That's your name, isn't it?" Flack asked.

"There are a lot of Helens."

He nodded. "This Helen I heard about was a blonde, rather tall, slender, blue eyes, and a real nice figure."

She crossed the kitchen and flipped the switch which cut in the exhaust fan.

"Just what is it you're getting at, Mr. Flack?" she asked

"Oh, nothing much. It's just that this Helen I heard about used to work up in Miami. Miami and Palm Beach and sometimes in Jax. A hard-working kid, they tell me. That is, for a call girl, she was hard-working."

Helen swung around suddenly and confronted him, her eyes dark with fury.

"I don't think I'm interested, Mister Flack," she said "As a matter of fact, this kitchen is off bounds. If you want something, go on out into the restaurant and I'll serve you. Otherwise—get out!"

He moved quickly, crossing the room and standing so close to her so that she had to take a step back.

"Don't get snotty," he said, his voice suddenly hard. "Don't get one bit snotty. You think I don't know who you are? Don't know what you were? You think I can't spot a whore when I see one?"

His arm reached out and circled her waist and he pulled her body close.

"Who the hell do you think you are anyway, sister?"

For a moment she struggled and then as suddenly relaxed. She leaned back to look up into his face and her own was cold and bland when she spoke.

"All right," she said. "You know who I am; what I was. But right now I'm Mrs. Nick Cosmos. And I'm clean. There's no 'wanted' out for me; no one is looking for me. You may be a cop, but that doesn't mean one thing. So just take your filthy hands off of me and get out of here."

He hesitated for a moment, half raising his hand. She instinctively ducked, feeling the slap coming. But then he suddenly smiled and released her and stepped back.

"Now Helen," he said, "now Helen, don't act like that. Of course I got nothing on you. And I don't care what you were. It don't make no difference to me, not at all. But of course," he added slyly, "it might make a little difference to Nick. To your husband."

For a second she started to protest, to tell him that Nick knew all about her. And then it occurred to her that he would talk to Nick, would start something with him. Helen knew what Nick would do. It wouldn't matter to Nick that he was a deputy sheriff. Nick wouldn't take anything from him. Nick would hear just one word against her and he'd blow up. Helen knew what his temper was.

God, she thought, hasn't the poor guy got enough trouble already? Haven't I given him enough headaches? Why make any more difficulty for him? In another few days they'd be getting out, getting away from here and getting away from Flack and all the rest of it. It would be better not to have anything else happen. Better just to play along with this oaf. She'd handled a lot tougher dishes than this jerk, plenty of times in the past.

She took a step toward him and smiled.

"It might indeed," she said. "Yeah, it really might. But you don't look like the kind of fella who likes to go around making trouble. I can't see a big handsome guy like you picking on someone Nick's size."

For a moment he looked at her closely and then he too smiled. He shrugged his thick shoulders.

"Nick's O.K.," he said. "For a greaseball. What did you ever see in him, kid, anyway?"

"Well, you know," Helen said, cocking her head and pouting slightly. "It's nice to have a steady guy around."

"What you need," he said, "is a real man. A girl like you—" he was unable to keep his eyes from her breasts as he spoke and he was suddenly breathing heavily— "a girl like you needs someone who can give her the—"

"I need someone who can mix a good drink, right now," she quickly interrupted, as once more his hand went out toward her. Neatly she sidestepped him, smiling, however, over her shoulder.

"Let me just get a bottle and we'll mix up a couple."

She figured if she could stall around until Nick would return, he'd leave, planning to come back later, some other time when Nick was out. She'd make a date, a date that she wouldn't be there to keep. But in the meantime, she had to keep him quiet, keep him under control.

"Drink's fine," he said, "but meantime, how about—"

"I'm all hot and sweaty," she said quickly. "I want a drink first. We got plenty of time, all the time in the world. Let me put a couple of drinks down and then just run upstairs for a minute or two and freshen up. O.K.?"

He looked at her closely for a second and then nodded.

"Sure, kid, sure," he said. "A drink and you go on and 'freshen up'. I can stand the wait, I guess. And I can certainly stand the drink."

Helen went to the icebox and took out the chilled bottle of rum. She poured two water glasses half full, dropped an ice cube in each, and then filled up the rest with coke.

They sat across from each other at the kitchen table as they lifted their glasses.

"To us, honey," Flack said. He downed his drink at a single gulp and when he replaced the empty glass on the table, he didn't bother to wipe the spilled liquor from the stubble of his chin.

Helen lifted her drink slowly. "Yeah, to us," she said.

She heard the sound of a plane's engines, circling somewhere overhead, as she sipped the drink. Flack watched her like a hungry child staring through the window of a restaurant on Christmas Eve.

"What you say we take the bottle and take a little ride?" he said. "We could go out the Overseas Highway."

"No rush, Sweetie," Helen said. "I wanna get into something fresh. Why don't you take another shot and I'll just go up and—" She hesitated again, suddenly looking up at the ceiling. "That plane's coming in for a landing," she said. "You hear it?"

For the first time Flack became aware of the sound of the plane's engines. He too looked up, inquiringly.

"Damned if it isn't," he said. "Now I wonder what the hell a plane is doing coming down here? Sounds like he's going to try and make it on the beach. This time of year, no one comes here."

"Maybe you should go out and see."

"The hell with 'em," Flack said. "I'm a cop, not a God-damned welcoming committee. Anyway, anyone crazy enough to come to this godforsaken spot, don't deserve to be welcomed."

He stood up then, lurching a little and pushing the table so that the glasses jangled against each other.

"Come here," he said. "By God, come here. You can give me a little bit of—"

Helen quickly reached for his glass and the bottle and spilled another drink into the glass as he came toward her.

"We got time," she said. "Let's get a couple of belts down first."

He hesitated a moment.

"You didn't finish your last God-damned drink," he said.

"I'm finishing it now," she said. "Right now and then I'm having another to catch up."

She picked up her glass and drained it and Flack downed his second shot straight. As he turned to her again, she ran toward the back of the kitchen.

"Have another quick one," she called, "and I'll bet you I'll be back before you can finish it."

"You bet what," he called, belligerently.

"You know what," she said, coyly, disappearing.

Flack smiled with satisfaction and reached for the bottle. He splashed the glass three quarters full and lifted it. Before he had taken more than a swallow, he suddenly shook and began coughing, spitting the raw liquor on the floor.

He was still standing there, choking and coughing, his beefy face apoplectic, when Helen returned some ten minutes later. She stood in the doorway and stared at him.

"Go' dam' stuff wen' down wrong tube," he said, holding his hand on his stomach and retching. "Water."

Quickly she walked to the sink and drew a coffee cup full of water and then went over and handed it to him. He lifted it to his mouth and drank it, coughing once or twice when he finished.

"Come on," he said, tossing the cup to the floor. "Let's get outta this dump. Grab that jug and we'll get moving."

For a moment she started to say something and it was while she was hesitating that she heard the sound of the jeep as it approached. She recognized it at once and knew that it was Phil Hardin's beach buggy. She had heard the plane land while she had been upstairs and she guessed at once that Hardin had gone down to meet it and was returning with the passengers.

They'd stop at the restaurant. Everyone always stopped at the restaurant. It was the only place in town to stop at.

Flack had moved while she hesitated and now he was again in front of her. This time when he grabbed her, he backed her against the wall and his arm was like a steel band around her waist. His thick, flabby lips moved toward her and one hand held her head firm, fingers clutched in her blonde straw hair.

"Stop the God-damned stalling," he mumbled. "Stop horsing around. When I wanna woman, I wanna—"

He suddenly stopped speaking as both of them heard the slam of the outside screen door of the restaurant.

For a brief moment they held the tableau and then Helen squirmed and broke away. She put one finger to her lips and shook her head, nodding toward the front room.

He stared at her angrily a moment, his mouth pouting.

And then the two of them started slowly toward the front of the place, walking on tiptoe.

Chapter Six

1

For several moments the three of them stood there, frozen into complete immobility. It was Sally who made the first move. Slowly, almost like a figure in a slow-motion picture, she took her arms from around Tony Mason and reaching behind her, took his wrists and moved them so that he was forced to release her. She took a step backwards and the blood rushed to her face. Her mouth half opened as though she were about to speak, but no words came.

Tony himself didn't move. His expression was one of surprise and gradually it turned to indignation.

"Don't you ever knock?" he said at last. He took a step or two across the room and reached down to where Sally had laid her embossed cigarette case and he opened it and took out a cigarette and lighted it.

Socks Schroeder followed Tony with eyes filled with hatred. He still

Sally coughed and then spoke.

"Tony," she said, "this is Socks. Socks Schroeder. Have you two met ..." Her voice dwindled out in embarrassment.

"Oh, we've met," Tony said, his voice indifferent.

Schroeder took a sudden step forward, his fist doubled.

"Just what do you think you're doing with my girl?" he said. The fury in his voice matched his expression. "What kind of damned—"

Quickly Sally moved to stand in front of him.

"Oh Socks," she said, "for goodness sake, act your age." Her voice was embarrassed and she avoided looking into his face as she spoke.

Socks brushed her aside and took another step forward.

"I asked you what the hell you're doing with my girl?" he said, this time raising his voice and almost yelling the words.

"Your girl?" Tony shrugged as he asked the question. He looked bored.

"That's right, my girl. What the hell are you doing with my girl?"

Tony exhaled a cloud of cigarette smoke and turned to Sally. "Are you his girl?"

Sally, instead of answering him, looked at Socks and this time the blush was caused by fury rather than embarrassment.

"I'm not anyone's girl," she said. "Socks, I think you had better get out of here. I think—"

He didn't let her finish.

"I think I'd better stay," he said. "I think maybe I got here at just the right time. What do you mean, Sally, you are not anyone's girl? You know very well you and me—"

"Socks, please be quiet and leave," Sally said, a slight note of desperation in her voice. She moved and, reaching out, attempted to push him toward the door, but he failed to budge.

"I asked you a question, mister," Socks said. "Just what hell is going on here, anyway?"

"Socks, please go now," Sally said. "You are making a scene."

"*I'm* making a scene," Socks said, his voice neatly blending fury and indignation. "So I'm making a scene, eh? And just what do you think you and this damned degenerate Commie were making when I got here? You know very well, Sally, how it is between you and me. You know that your father wouldn't for one minute—"

"How is it between you and Sally?" Tony asked. "Tell me, just how is it?"

"Tony," Sally implored, "please. Please just let him go."

"I'm not going anywhere," Socks yelled. "And I'll tell you how it is," he said. "I'll tell you just how it is. Sally and me are going to get married."

"Socks, for God's sake," she said. "Are you crazy? Please get out of here. You know there's nothing between us."

He swung to her and there was no questioning the hurt surprise on his face as he spoke.

"What do you mean, Sally?" he asked. "What do you mean, there's nothing between us? My God, how about the other night, down there on the beach, huh? How about us going together now for more than a year? When a girl gives herself to a man it can only mean—"

Sally took her eyes from Socks and for a stricken second looked at Tony and then dropped her glance to the floor and the tears of anger suddenly came and she opened her mouth to speak but she had no words.

"Maybe you had better go at that," Tony said. "Maybe the lady would just as soon not hear any more."

"Listen, you," Socks said, "nobody tells me what to do."

"Socks," Sally said, "I'm telling you. I'm telling you right now. Get out of here. Get out of here and don't you ever dare come near me again."

"What has this sonofabitch been doing to you, Sally?" Socks asked. "What's the matter with you anyway? Is this any way for you to act with me? Any way for a girl who's going to be my—"

"I'm not going to be your anything," Sally said.

"Listen, Sally," Socks said, looking at her with pleading in his heavy, unintelligent face. "Listen, Sally. I don't know what this guy's been doing to you, what kind of line he's been handing you. But you just don't know what you're saying. You don't know what you're doing."

He turned again to Tony and the muscles in his arms tightened. "What the hell have you been telling her?" he asked. "What kind of a line have you been giving her anyway? And what have you got her hanging around here for?"

He looked at Sally's cigarette case, which Tony still held in his hand. "What do you want from her?" he asked. "Does she just come here to bring you cigarettes? Is that it? Or is it something else?"

He moved suddenly then and as he did his big body brushed against the easel. Unconsciously he hesitated, reaching out to keep it from falling. It was then that he saw the painting.

For a moment or two as his glance swept the figure, nothing registered and he was beginning to look away once more when his whole body suddenly froze. Slowly he turned back and an expression of utter shock and bewilderment came over his face as he recognized Sally's face. Slowly he lowered his eyes, taking in the full nude figure.

His mouth fell open and the blood rushed into his cheeks and he just stood there almost as though he were in a state of shock.

Tony stood watching him, his expression indifferent, almost amused. Sally also watched him, an embarrassed expression on her pretty face.

Slowly he took his eyes away and looked at Sally in hurt disbelief. "Sally," he said. "Sally! Oh my God, how could you?" He looked back at the picture again and then returned his eyes to the girl.

"You whore," he said in an almost inaudible voice. For a moment he looked as though he were about to break into tears.

"I've had just about all of this I want," Tony said. "I think—"

Before he could finish speaking Socks moved. He moved like a coiled spring and his arm shot out and his doubled-up fist caught Tony under the right eye.

Tony went over backwards, taking the card table with him.

"I'll kill the bastard," Socks screamed. "I'll break every God-damned bone—"

He was reaching down, grabbing Tony by the hair and beginning to pull the unconscious figure to its feet when Sally shot across the room and pushed herself between them.

"Socks," she screamed. "Socks! Stop it! Stop it this minute. Have you lost your mind? Are you crazy?"

He hesitated a second, looking at her blankly.

"Leave him alone," she said. "Leave him alone."

Slowly he dropped Tony back to the floor. Like a man in a daze he just stood there for a moment and then he walked back and stood in front of the painting.

Sally leaned down and took Tony's head and held it in her lap, brushing the hair back from his face. She was moaning and half crying.

For several seconds Socks stood staring at the painting. Suddenly he took in a great lungful of air and slowly expelled it. His eyes dropped and he saw the palette knife lying at the edge of the easel. His hand moved like a snake and then he grabbed the knife and slashed viciously, time and time again, at the painting until the canvas was slashed to ribbons.

When he had finished, he looked back to where Sally knelt beside Tony, who was starting to struggle to get up.

"Get up," he said, speaking to the girl. "Come on, get up. We're leaving."

Sally's eyes went from him to Tony, who was now standing, weaving slightly on his feet. She looked at him almost questioningly.

"Maybe you had better go," Tony said, speaking very slowly. "Yes, maybe you had better go now. Both of you!"

Slowly she stood up, still watching Tony. Her expression was bewildered and hurt.

"Are you coming now, Sally?" Socks asked. His voice was soft, almost gentle. There was no threat in it. His fury was utterly spent. "Are you coming, Sally?"

For another long moment she looked at Tony, but he had turned his head away and his shoulders were slumped dejectedly. He was looking at the floor.

She started to move toward him and then she hesitated. Her eyes went back to Socks.

Without uttering a word she moved over by him and he in turn moved off toward the doorway. He held the screen door open and she passed through it in front of him, without a word. Tony didn't look at them as they left.

Sally walked a step or so ahead of him as they wordlessly made their way back across the island to the town. Neither of them noticed the plane circling overhead, preparing for a landing on the sandy beach on the ocean side of the island.

2

It took Duke Flager only five minutes from the time his two passengers had left in the jeep to go into town to determine what was wrong with the engine of the plane. He was an excellent mechanic and he found the trouble almost at once. His hunch had been right and it wasn't serious. But it could well have been if he hadn't come in for landing.

Well, it was a simple matter. It would take not more than a half to three quarters of an hour to fix it up and fortunately he had the necessary tools and the replacement parts. There would be plenty of time.

Duke didn't like the way the weather looked. There had been those hurricane warnings, coming through for the last couple of days now. Of course the thing was supposed to hit well to the west, but Duke knew how those things went. All too often the winds, as they picked up, would shift suddenly and before you knew it, you'd find yourself in the middle of things. You could never really tell.

Of course, it was still pretty early in the season for trouble around these parts. Duke didn't have too much trust in the weather people. They were good, but they still made mistakes.

Anyway, he didn't want to be hanging around a minute longer than necessary. He wasn't too keen about this charter in any case and the sooner it was over and done with, the better all the way around. He'd be glad to complete the trip, collect his money and have it over and done with.

He was getting ready to work when he decided to turn on the radio and see if he could get a weather broadcast. It wouldn't hurt to check up.

Duke was the first person on Key Arroyos to learn that the hurricane had indeed taken a sudden turn in its course and was heading directly for them. The initial forecast was vague and the announcer wasn't able to say anything for sure, but there was no question but what the hurricane was heading in the general direction of the Keys. The velocity of the wind had picked up considerably and the storm was moving in fast.

When Duke heard the news, he cursed and quickly cut the set off. He jumped down to the ground and at once started working on the engine. It was probably because of his being in a hurry, combined with his anger at the weather bureau for not having given him advance warning, that he did what he did, made the mistake which was to cause him all the trouble. He had almost finished fixing the motor and was tightening one of the engine bolts when he exerted just a trifle too much pressure and the head of the bolt snapped.

For a moment he just stood there leaning over the engine and looking at it in disbelief. And then he cursed. "Of all the stupid, God-damned ..."

He knew the second the bolt snapped that he was in trouble. Not serious trouble and under most circumstances, it wouldn't amount to anything. He'd have to get an Easy-Out and extract the broken end of the bolt and put another one in. The trouble was he didn't have an Easy-Out or any other tool which could do the job. In Miami, or any regular airport, it would be the simplest thing in the world. Nothing. But here?

Well, he might manage something, but it would take time. He was still standing there at the side of the cowling and cursing under his breath, when he became aware of the man at his side and that the man was talking to him.

"Yep, a tough break," Phil Hardin said. "It happens, though, happens to me every now and then."

Duke looked over in annoyance and saw that it was the man who'd met him with the jeep and taken his passengers into town.

"I don't suppose there's a garage within miles," he said. "Jesus, of all the dumb tricks."

"I run a sort of a garage here," Hardin drawled. "Can't say as I ever fixed up no planes before but—"

"Have you got an Easy-Out?" Duke asked. "I'll have to get that bolt."

"Don't believe I have," Hardin said. "'Course I don't know exactly what an Easy-Out is exactly. Don't go in much for these fancy tools," he said. "But if you wanna get that bolt out, I can make up a little gimmick to do the job. Had lots of trouble with that sort of thing and I know how."

"Well how long will it take you?" Duke hurriedly asked.

"Can't rightly say," Hardin said. "Maybe twenty minutes, maybe an hour. Have to hook up the lathe and the belt's busted and—"

"Well, let's get started," Duke spoke rapidly. He looked up at the sky to the southeast and noticed that it had turned a peculiar yellowish purple. "I don't like the way this weather's building up. Got a report a few minutes ago and they say the hurricane is heading in this direction."

Hardin looked at the sky and shrugged.

"Never pays to rush things," he said.

"I want to be getting back."

"You can't trust those weather people," Hardin interrupted. "They never seem to know which way's up."

Duke looked at him for a moment in annoyance.

"Suppose you go and see if you can get that lathe going," he said. "How far a walk is it to your garage?"

"Six, seven minutes," Hardin said.

"Well, I want to get another weather report. You go on in and get started. I'll walk into town and meet you in a few minutes. Where did you take my passengers?"

"Dropped 'em off at the Greek's—the restaurant."

"You might stop by and tell them I'll be leaving as soon as I can get this thing off the ground. I'm not going to take any chances—want to get in the air as soon as possible."

Hardin nodded and walked toward the jeep.

Duke climbed into the cockpit of the plane and cut the radio in again. It took several minutes for it to warm up. This time he had no difficulty in getting a weather broadcast. And this time there was no doubt about it. Hurricane Bettina was definitely heading toward the Keys. Gusts up to fifty or sixty miles an hour could be expected before dark.

3

Tilden Flack's eyes narrowed slightly as, looking over Helen's shoulder, he watched the two men take seats in the booth opposite each other. Helen herself sensed his tension and she turned her head to look up at him. He nodded in the direction of the room and shoved her slightly toward the door. He himself turned, and walking quietly, returned through the kitchen and let himself out the back.

Helen entered the restaurant proper.

Stepping in back of the long counter, she picked up a dog-eared typed menu. She walked to the front of the room, stopping for a second to lift a fly swatter and strike out at random. There was static coming out of the radio and she turned it off as she passed by.

Then she went and stood next to the booth, holding out the menu. Neither man reached for it and neither one looked at her.

The bigger man, the one in the dark suit and sweat-drenched shirt, spoke.

"You run this place, Miss?" he asked.

Helen nodded. "Me and my husband," she said.

He looked up then, blankly. "How's the grub?" he asked.

Helen shrugged, holding out the menu.

"Who's your husband?" the big man asked.

Helen's hand, holding the menu, dropped and she took a step back, an expression of curiosity in her eyes.

"My husband?"

The slender one, the one who looked like a boy and wore the Stetson and the cowboy boots, turned his face and looked at her, smiling.

"My friend just wants to be sure he's a good cook," he said. He made it sound like a joke.

"My husband is Nick Cosmos," Helen said, a little too hurriedly, "and I don't know whether he's a good cook or not. I do most of the cooking. Anyway, it has to be good enough; we have the only restaurant in town."

"Cosmos," the big man said. He turned to his companion. "Now that's a nice name, isn't it, Gerald," he said. "Cosmos. Yes a nice name. I tell you what, Mrs. Cosmos, why don't you tell Mr. Cosmos to come on in from in back there and we can all sit down and discuss what he thinks we should eat. It's a hot day and Mr. Cosmos should have a pretty good idea."

"My husband isn't here just now," Helen said.

"Not here?" the big man said. "Then who is out there in the kitchen with you, Mrs. Cosmos?"

"Whoever it is, he's gone now," the one called Gerald said. "I heard the door close when he went out."

He looked at Helen and he was no longer smiling. "Anyway, I'm not hungry just yet. There's no hurry and we wouldn't want you to have to start cooking in this hot weather." He stared at Helen, "Would we, George?"

George shook his head.

"Certainly not," he said. He moved over on the seat and stood up, half bowing.

"I'll sit next to Gerald here," he said. "You sit down opposite us, Mrs. Cosmos. We want to talk to you for a minute or so. That's all right, if we talk to you, isn't it?"

Helen could feel the color leave her face. She was suddenly very frightened. She could sense the sinister undertones behind the voices. Slowly, hesitantly, she moved in and sat down.

"What do you want?" she asked in a thin, tight voice.

"Now, Mrs. Cosmos," Gerald said. "Don't you be upset. We just want to talk to you. There's nothing wrong in that now, is there? Just talking?"

Helen stared at him dumbly.

"This town is dead," George said. "I never saw such a dead town. Where is everyone?"

"It's a small place," Helen said weakly. "And the boats are out. This is a fishing town and almost everyone fishes and when the boats are out, why then ..."

"But some people are still around," George said. "For instance, the guy who just left by the back door. Who is he? No fisherman, that one, I guess."

"That was Tilden Flack," Helen said. "He's the deputy sheriff here." Her voice was weak and the man leaned forward to hear her.

"Tilden Flack," Gerald said. "The deputy sheriff. Well, well, who would have thought a deputy sheriff would be around a town this size. Would you ever have thought that, George?" he asked.

George shook his head, looking solemn.

"Who else is around town, Mrs. Cosmos?" Gerald asked. "Don't be bashful; just tell us. And why are you looking at the door? Are you expecting someone maybe?"

Quickly Helen looked at him and shook her head. They could be the men; they could be the ones Paul had sent down. She couldn't be sure, but she knew there was something wrong with them. There had to be some reason they had come to Key Arroyos. Strangers don't come to Key Arroyos, not this kind of strangers. These men weren't tourists, weren't sport fishermen. There had to be a reason for their being there. A reason for the questions and the way they acted.

There was only one thought in Helen's mind. She had to get out of the place and get to Nick. Keep Nick from returning to the restaurant.

"I have an appointment with the doctor," she said suddenly. "I'm late already and I have to go."

"Who was going to take care of the store," Gerald asked, "if you had to go to the doctor?"

"We could walk over to the doctor with Mrs. Cosmos," George said. "As a matter of fact, I been wanting to see a doctor and this might be just the time." He hesitated a moment and then stared at Helen. "What's the doctor's name?" he asked.

"Why—why Dr. Martins, Dr. Carter Martins."

"Dr. Martins," George said. "A deputy sheriff and now a doctor. Isn't that something, Gerald, for a town this size? A deputy and a doctor. Who else is in town, Mrs. Cosmos?"

She looked away, not answering. She wanted to get up and run, but she felt powerless to move.

"I'm serious," George said. "Who else is in town?" His hand shot across the table and the pudgy, childlike fingers gripped her wrist. Except that it wasn't the grip of a child. It was the cruel hard grip of a powerful man.

Helen's eyes opened wide in fear and shocked surprise at the sudden pain.

"Who else?" she asked dumbly.

"Answer George," Gerald said. "Who else is in town?"

"Why—why about everybody. There are fishermen's wives and children, the—"

"Skip the women and kids," George said. "What men are in town?"

She was sure then. Sure that these were the men. The men who Paul would have sent.

"Men?" she said. "The men?"

"A good-looking woman like you. I suppose that Mr. Cosmos, Nick, I think you said his name was, I suppose he—"

"Nick is away," she said, too quickly. "I think he drove into Key West."

COFFIN FOR A HOOD

"We'll skip Nick," Gerald said. "We know about Nick and the doctor and the deputy, but who else is around? Certainly someone else must be around. For instance, that guy who drove us here in the jeep."

"That would be Phil Hardin," Helen said. "He has a little repair business, sort of a part-time garage. He isn't very bright."

"Nobody very bright would hang around this kind of place," George said. "But keep on, who else is around?"

"Well, there's Mr. Fullbright. Richard Fullbright. He's a man from the north, but he lives here all year round."

Gerald looked at his partner.

"Fullbright," he said. "He doesn't sound fully bright, does he, George, living here all the year around?"

"I don't think he's very bright," George said. "Who else?"

"There's Mason, Tony Mason, an artist. And Socks and—"

"Socks?" George said. "Socks who?"

"Why Socks Schroeder. He's a young college fella. Used to be a basketball player. He was very well known."

Gerald slowly shook his head.

"Can't seem to remember anyone named Socks," Gerald said. "But then of course I can't remember every God-damned football hero who came down the pike."

"Basketball hero," George corrected. "The lady said basketball. What is this Socks doing down here, Mrs. Cosmos?"

"He works for the fish company, runs the warehouse."

In spite of herself she looked over at the old-fashioned clock hanging on the wall above the cash register. She saw that the hands pointed to five minutes after five.

"The doctor will wait," George said, seeing her quick look. "The whole town will wait. Even Gerald and I will wait. Now who else?"

He stopped speaking suddenly as the door opened. Phil Hardin walked in, whistling.

"Wait on the man," George said, letting go of her arm.

As Helen started to get up, Hardin approached the table.

"Say," he said. "I was hopin' you'd still be here." He stopped and pushed his straw hat to the back of his head. "That pilot fella of yours is havin' a little trouble with his machine. I gotta make him a thing-a-ma-jig, over at my shop, and he's in a hurry. Says to tell you—"

"What's wrong with his plane?" George said, suddenly tense and alert.

"Oh, nothin' serious. Just busted a bolt and I gotta make—"

"Well, go make it then," George said. "Why tell us your troubles?"

Phil scratched his head and laughed a little nervously.

"Well, he told me to stop by and tell you that he got a bad weather report over his radio and that he wants to take off as soon as we get his engine fixed up. Says he wants to get going before the hurricane hits."

"What hurricane?" Gerald asked.

Phil shrugged. "He says the hurricane's comin' this way."

Gerald suddenly stood up and stepped out from the booth.

"Listen, fellow," he said. "Get in that jeep of yours and go back and get that pilot and bring him here. Understand, get him and bring him here."

"He wants me to start fixing—"

Gerald leaned forward and put both hands on Hardin's shoulders, looking into the other man's upturned face and smiling.

"I want you to go get him," he said.

For a moment Hardin stared at him, his bulging eyes wide and his mouth slightly open. He gulped and quickly nodded.

"Yes sir," he said. "Right away, sir."

Gerald sat down again. He looked at Helen, still half smiling.

"Just what do they do when they have a hurricane here, Mrs. Cosmos?" he asked, his voice languid.

"There's the fish house. It's concrete block and people—"

"Hurricane, nuts," George interrupted. "I'm still trying to find out what all lives in this burg. There's a hundred houses around here."

"The fishermen live in most of them," Helen said hurriedly. "The others, the new ones over by the beach, they belong to the northerners and are empty this time of year. Outside of some of the old natives—"

"We ain't interested in natives," George said. "But I tell you what. You might just bring us a couple of bottles of beer and turn on that radio for a few minutes while we rest up and wait for that flyer. Then maybe we'll all take a short little sightseeing trip around the town. Eh, Gerald? A little sightseeing trip. That would be nice, wouldn't it?"

Gerald didn't answer him but turned to Helen.

"One beer," he said. "Make mine a milk. Chocolate milk. But take your time, ma'am. We got plenty of time. All the time in the world."

He took a sack of Bull Durham out of the breast pocket of his silk shirt and began to dexterously roll a cigarette as Helen started for the counter, her legs like rubber and her face white under its summer tan.

Chapter Seven

1

Phil Hardin wasn't actually simple-minded; the trouble was his inability to concentrate, to hold a thought for more than a moment or so at a time. His intentions, like his promises, were always good. He'd tell you that he'd pick you up in say Marathon or perhaps Key West on the following Tuesday and he really intended to keep his appointment. But then he'd get talking to someone, or maybe thinking about something, and he'd forget all about it and there you would be, waiting, and no Phil.

When he left the Greek's he had every intention of going right down to the beach and getting Duke Flager. He didn't like those men in the restaurant at all. There had been something about them which had frightened him and when he was frightened of anyone, he was particularly careful to do what they told him. And so he went out and got into the jeep and started it up and turned toward the beach. He was passing Doc Martins' house when he saw Socks walking down the steps.

He pulled over to the curb. Phil liked Socks. When he liked somebody, he wanted to talk to them.

"Hi," Phil said. "Hi ya, Socks. Where you goin'?"

Socks looked at him and glared and then, seeing who it was, he made an effort and smiled weakly.

"Back to the warehouse," he said.

"You want a lift down?" Phil asked. "I'm headin' that way."

Socks nodded and walked over to the jeep and climbed in.

"Been seeing the doc?" Phil asked, shoving the car into gear. "Never thought you'd need to see no doctor, Socks."

"Dr. Martins wasn't home," Socks said shortly.

"Not home?" Phil slowed down and shrugged. "Why a' course he ain't home," he said. "I took him over to the Cantios'. Mrs. Cantios is having ..." He suddenly jammed on his brakes. "Oh my gosh," he said, putting his hand to his mouth. "I was supposed to go back a half hour ago an' pick him up. By golly I plumb forgot all about it. Doc'll be mad as all hell."

He swung the jeep in a wide arc and started for the other end of town. "You don't mind goin' a little out of the way, do you, Socks?" he asked.

Socks grunted and hung on to the side of the wildly careening jeep.

"Take it a little easy," he said. "You want to wreck us? No, as a matter of fact," he continued, "I want to see Doc Martins myself. I want to see him very much."

"I thought you just left his house," Phil said, looking a little baffled.

Socks looked at the other man for a moment, perplexed, and started to explain all over that the Doc hadn't been home. But then he shrugged his shoulders and let it go. He'd gotten into these things before with Phil and he knew what would happen. Phil could drive you crazy with his talk.

"See the plane come in?" Phil said.

"I heard it," Socks said. "Is it still down on the beach?"

Phil nodded. "Sure is. Fellow broke down. I'm helping him get it started again."

"You are?" Socks said. "I thought you were picking up—"

"Yep," Phil said. "And tell you something. By the time we get that thing repaired, he ain't goin' take off from that beach at all. Not by a damn sight, the way this wind is building up. I guess you know we are going to have the hurricane."

"Where'd you hear that?" Socks asked.

"Fellow who runs the plane had his radio on and he got a weather report. Yes, sir, she's headin' this way and comin' in fast."

He slammed on the brakes and the jeep came to a dusty halt in front of a small, unpainted clapboard cottage.

"I'll go in an' see what's keeping the Doc," Phil said.

2

Duke didn't have any trouble finding Phil Hardin's garage. It was across the street from the closed movie house, a long, low, narrow building, and there was a freshly painted sign on the front. It read: Arroyos Garage—Cars Fixed, Boats Fixed and Machine Shop.

The place was wide open and Duke walked in. An ancient Rolls Royce, half stripped down, occupied the front part of the structure. Behind it was a work bench which supported a lathe and a drill press. Tools were scattered everywhere and the place was a mass of old spare parts, rusty machinery and junk. No one was around.

Duke yelled two or three times and waited and when he failed to get an answer, he cursed.

He walked out front and looked up and down the street. He didn't see the jeep, but he did see the restaurant. He turned and started for it. The sign above the restaurant was swinging wildly in the wind and Duke was barely able to read the legend, CAFE. He looked off to the southwest and he saw that the sky was completely black.

Entering the café, Duke was relieved to find his two passengers standing at the counter talking to Helen.

Duke spoke as the three of them turned at his entrance.

"Say," he said, "what happened to that yokel I sent in here to see you? The guy with the jeep. He's supposed—"

"Didn't he go down and get you?" George asked, putting his beer on the counter.

"Hell, I sent him up here to get to work on a lathe he has," Duke said, ignoring the question. "He isn't in his damned garage. If we don't get that engine fixed up before it all hits, I'm not going to get that plane off the beach at all."

His eyes went to the window and then quickly back and he saw the sudden surprised anger in the big man's face.

"Engine needed fixing," he said. "He was supposed to be helping me."

"How long will it take?" George asked. "We don't want to spend the night in this dump."

Duke shook his head, worried.

"The way she's beginning to blow," he said, "if I don't get her off the beach in another few minutes, I won't get her off at all."

"All right," Gerald said. "So you don't get her off tonight. It's as simple as that. You have to make repairs and we aren't ready to leave for a while anyway. So we just sit it out overnight, George—" he turned to his partner. "Sit it out overnight and this thing will blow over and then we can leave in the morning."

"I think we should leave tonight," George said.

"Listen," Duke interrupted. "Do you hear that wind? It will take another forty minutes to an hour before I can turn the engine up, assuming this idiot gets back here and gets to work. By that time it's going to be too late. Way too late. And if I don't find some sheltered place to get the plane in out of this wind, there isn't going to be any plane to take off."

"You mean ..." Gerald began.

"I mean," Duke said, "that the hurricane is coming this way. Right now. Just look outside. I got a weather report a few minutes ago and she's headed right for us. I don't know how serious it's going to be but it won't matter. I won't be able to put her in the air and the plane will be wrecked if she's left there on the beach."

"Then by God get down there and do something about it," George said, his voice ugly. He looked over at Helen. "What can he do about it?" he asked. "Is there some place around, some garage or something?"

"There's the fish house."

The voice spoke up from the door and the three men and Helen suddenly turned and looked around. They'd been so intent on their conversation that they had failed to hear Tony Mason enter the room over the wail of the wind.

"If you want a place for the plane," Tony said, "why, you can probably put it in the fish house there on the beach. There are large double doors that the trucks use and I think, if it isn't too large, you can get it in. The place is concrete and I should think it would be safe."

"I saw it," Duke said. "It'll be a job getting the plane to it, what with this wind the way she's blowing. We'll need a car of some kind to tow it. I'll have to have help."

"I'll give you a hand," Tony said. "And I saw Phil Hardin's jeep heading for the beach as I came in. He should be around there someplace."

Gerald, who had been staring at Tony's black eye, moved toward the door then. "Come on," he said, "let's get going. We don't want nothing to happen to that plane."

Duke turned to the door followed by Tony, but Gerald hesitated.

"You stay here, George," he said.

"Look," Duke said, "I'll need all the help I can—"

"Stay here, George," Gerald repeated. He looked at Duke again with that odd half smile on his boyish face.

Duke stared at him for a moment and then silently passed out of the door, followed by Tony and Gerald himself.

Turning toward the street, Tony shielded his face from the wind-driven sand. He looked through his fingers and recognized the short, round figure of the man waddling toward them against the wind.

"Hi ya, Nick," he said.

3

Sally Martins lay across the bed and buried her face in her arms. Her mind was in a turmoil as she thought back over the scene at the shanty, and she couldn't forget the expression on Tony Mason's face, the sardonic tone of his voice.

She remembered the way he had looked at her when Socks had told

COFFIN FOR A HOOD

him about them. She remembered his words, as he had stood there with the bruise darkening under his eye, telling them to go. Both of them.

Sally thought of Socks Schroeder and her relationship with him. She was remembering the time when she had returned to the Keys from school and had first met him. In the beginning he had repelled her; there was something about his too perfect physique, his fantastic athlete's body and vitality, which had antagonized her.

She hadn't taken him seriously. She found his constant talk of his career as a basketball player, his braggadocio and his utter self-confidence, more boring than offensive. He was neither bright nor witty; he had a surface education, but a minimum intelligence. On the other hand, there was no question about his dogged devotion to her, his worship of her.

If his manners were crude and forthright, at least his behavior had been circumspect. He hadn't made passes at her, but had been content to follow her around like a devoted slave. He took her to the movies in Key West and Marathon, bought her inexpensive dinners at roadside taverns and danced with her to hotel orchestras on the few occasions when he had enough money to take her to the better places. They went swimming together and had beach parties.

He was just about the only available male in the neighborhood and she was thrown in with him more because of the lack of anything else around than because of choice.

He treated her as though she were a minor goddess and it wasn't until their sixth or seventh date that he told her that he loved her.

She tried to laugh him off, and he'd been hurt. She'd let him kiss her and had been amazed to find that the sensation was not unpleasant.

Her father had accepted him with amused tolerance, not taking him seriously and never dreaming that she would. "An amiable ape," he had called him. And that was the way she too had thought of him until a month or so ago when things had suddenly reached a point where it was no longer possible to merely accept his physical company and ignore the man himself.

It wasn't until he had begun talking about marriage that she'd realized how serious he was. She'd scoffed at the idea and he had misunderstood her.

"Don't think I'm going to be in that fish house forever," he'd said. "Another year, that's all, just one more year. You may not know it, but I've been saving my money. And I had some money too, when I came down here. One more year and I'll have ten thousand dollars. And then I'm

going to open my own place. I've got it all lined up. A boy's camp, up
in Vermont. Ten thousand will swing it, will be plenty to start. I know
the exact place. They want ten down and there's a mortgage for
forty. But I can swing it. And I'll make money."

She could see how serious he was and the funny thing was she could
understand his confidence. He would swing it; he'd make a success of
it.

His next remark was unfortunate.

"Yeah, we can get married. And you'll fit right in," he said. "You'll be
the housemother."

That was when she laughed. She bit off the laugh quick when she
saw the sudden hurt look on his face. So she had done the same thing
she did before when she'd hurt him. She kissed him.

They were lying on the beach, at dusk, he in his short, tight trunks
and she in a Bikini. There was no one for miles around.

She'd leaned over and pulled him to her and kissed him and for a
moment he had held her. And then he had mumbled brokenly, telling
her how much he loved her. He'd rolled over, his strong muscular body
pinning her down on the sand.

She never did know what came over her and each time she thought
about it, afterward, she blushed with hidden shame. She'd thought of
nothing while it was happening, nothing but the pure animal pleasure. She tried to explain it to herself, telling herself that they were
young and alive and overflowing with vitality and that it had been the
natural thing to do. That essentially they were like all people their
age, healthy animals satisfying the appetites of healthy animals.

Certainly she had experienced no shame, no regrets at the time. It
was Socks who'd had the regrets, the moment it was over. He'd cursed
himself, crying his apologies to her, conscience-stricken and convinced that he had taken her against her wishes.

She was shocked to realize that she herself had felt nothing, neither
regret nor any particular sense of elation. With her it had been
purely a physical thing, a temporary sensation, pleasant enough
while it lasted, but meaningless the moment it was over and done
with.

For a while after that she had avoided him and he had misunderstood her and assumed that she hated him for what had happened.
But then they had started seeing each other again and he had re-
sumed his courtship, talking more and more about plans for an early
marriage.

She knew that she must bring things to a head; that she should let him know once and for all how she really felt. But she had been weak and she'd procrastinated, half not wanting to hurt him and half because it was the easy way out.

And then, a few weeks, ago, she'd met Tony Mason and started posing for him. It had taken up a good deal of her time and she'd seen less and less of Socks. The fantastic part of it was that until today, she'd never even dreamed that Tony could have any real meaning for her.

It was the telephone, ringing down in the living room, which finally brought Sally to. She waited for someone to answer, believing that her father was home, but when the ringing persisted, she finally got up and went downstairs. She was surprised to see that it was almost dark outside. Going through the kitchen to the living room, she saw by the kitchen clock that it was seven forty-five. She thought that the clock must be wrong; it would still be full daylight.

The call was for her father and it was from his friend, the druggist, up in Marathon. When Sally said that her father was still out, the man asked her to give him a message.

"We've just had word that the state police plan to close off the Overseas Highway," the man said. "Tried to reach someone in town but nobody answered at the firehouse. I thought you people down there should know in case any of you want to get out before this thing gets worse."

"Close off the Highway?" Sally asked. "What for?"

"The hurricane. It's coming directly this way and is expected to hit sometime late this evening. May not be much, but then again you can never tell. Anyway, the police are going to stop all traffic going west."

It was the first that Sally was aware of the impending hurricane, having until then been too busy with her own private storm.

"Better find your Dad and let him know," he said, and hung up.

For a moment or two she stood there, dazed. Then she went out on the porch and looked off to where the storm was building up in the southwest. The wind had increased and without thinking about it, she began taking in the porch furniture, wondering as she did it, what had happened to her father. Certainly the Cantios' baby must have been born by this time.

She closed the windows in the house and locked them, regretting that they had never ordered the storm blinds which they had discussed so often in the past. And then she decided to go over to the Cantios' and find her father. He would have to know; in a sense he was responsible for the town.

She decided that she would stop by the firehouse on the way. It was quite possible he would be there. She knew that frequently, toward evening, he'd go over for a quiet drink or two. He thought that she didn't know why he went there, but she'd known for a long time now. She knew about his public drinking and she knew about his private drinking.

4

The minute Nick walked into the café and saw Helen standing back of the counter, he knew something was wrong. He couldn't say just what it was that told him, but he knew. She was standing where she usually stood, behind the counter in the shadow next to the cash register and there was no one else in the place but the stocky, bareheaded man, sitting on the stool with the bottle of beer in front of him and staring at the wall. Nothing was unusual, nothing out of the way.

Nick started to open his mouth, to say something, when he saw the expression on her face. She was staring at him and there was no color in her cheeks. Even her lips were white. Her eyes were wide and frightened.

Quickly Nick looked again at the man with the beer, but he was merely sitting there, a middle-aged, heavy-set man with a bald head and a sweaty, commonplace face.

Nick took a couple of steps into the room and spoke.

"Say, wazza matter with you, kid?" he asked. "You look like you ..."

Helen lifted her hand halfway to her mouth and shook her head violently.

"My husband isn't in yet," she said. "He's not expected back for some time."

Nick stopped in his tracks, his eyes widening.

"What did you say?" he asked, completely startled.

"I said," Helen spoke again, her voice a dead monotone, "I said that Mr. Cosmos isn't here just now. You will have to come back a little later."

Nick ran a hand through his hair and cocked his head, looking at her with an odd, half-smile.

"Say, have you blown your top, kid?" he said. "Don't tell me you been hitting the bottle. Who do you think 1 am?" He looked at her as though she were telling a joke that wasn't quite funny.

Helen took her eyes from him and quickly looked over to where

George was sitting at the bar. George was looking directly at her. She started to open her mouth, to say something, but George interrupted her.

"You Cosmos?"

Nick looked at him and frowned.

"That's right," he said shortly. "Nick Cosmos. Say, what's going on here anyway? What the hell."

"Nick, Nick," Helen said, "These men ..."

"What men?" Nick, asked, looking utterly confused.

George slowly got up off the stool. He turned to Nick, his face bland and without expression.

"Your missus seems to be a little upset," he said.

Nick stared at him for a moment and then turned back to Helen. He gestured with his head.

"Come on in back," he began, and then, seeing the stricken look on her face, he moved quickly toward the counter.

Helen started for the back room and Nick followed her. He gave George a hard look as he passed him. They went through the door into the kitchen and the moment they were in the room, Helen turned to him.

"He's one of them," she said, her voice hysterical. "He's one of them, one of the men Paul sent. The other went away but he'll be back. Nick, get your gun, for God's sake, and get out of here. Hurry."

"That's right, Mr. Cosmos, get your gun."

Nick swung around. The big, heavy-set man was standing there, filling the opening between the restaurant and the kitchen. His left hand was in his pocket and his right hand was held up high, near his chest. There was a small, snub-nosed revolver in his hand.

"Yes," he said, "get your gun. Your wife's advice is very good. I don't know what is upsetting her; I don't know what's wrong with her. But take her advice. Get your gun. I'd like to have it. The way you people are acting around here, I don't think there should be any loose guns."

For a second or two Nick stood stock-still, staring at him. He looked then at Helen and spoke.

"I don't have a gun," he said. "I don't have any."

"You had better have a gun," George said. "Yes, you had better have a gun. Because unless you give one to me, I'm likely to believe you are holding out and I wouldn't want to take a chance on that. I'd rather shoot you now, just to be sure."

Nick nodded his head slowly.

"Oh God," Helen said. "Oh God, Nick, he's going to—"

"Tell her to shut up." George said. "Just tell her to shut up. And tell me where the gun is. I want the gun and then maybe no one will get hurt."

Nick hesitated a moment longer and then he hunched his shoulders in a gesture of futility.

"The drawer under the cupboard," he said.

George crossed the room, sidling along like a great crab and never taking his eyes off them. He backed up to the drawer and reaching behind himself, pulled the drawer open. He fumbled around for a moment and then he had the gun in his hand. He slipped it into his coat pocket without looking at it.

"All right," he said. "Now let's everyone calm down." He put his own gun into his other coat pocket.

"I'm getting hungry," he said. "Mr. Cosmos, you are probably hungry, too. Why don't you ask your wife to make us something to eat? We can go outside and sit down and she can bring us something to eat."

Nick looked at Helen and she nodded, dumbly.

"What you want?" Nick asked.

"Oh, anything," George said. "Anything at all. Except seafood. Seafood gives me indigestion."

5

Tilden Flack never did know quite what it was that had made him sneak out of the back of the restaurant when he saw the two of them sitting there in the booth. He didn't recognize them, either the man in the cowboy getup or the other fat, greasy-looking one. He didn't know who they were or what they wanted but for some reason, he sensed that they were bad news.

Flack was a man who worked largely by instinct and he never went looking for trouble. And so, looking over Helen's shoulder and seeing them, he turned and walked quietly to the back of the building and let himself out, closing the door as gently as possible after himself.

He was annoyed; sore because they had come in just when they had and interrupted him. By God, another few minutes and he would have had it the way he wanted it. She was willing; more than willing. It was turning out even easier than he had thought it would.

But then the two men had come into the restaurant, and for some reason seeing them had upset him and now he would have to wait. The thing to do was walk around a couple of blocks and enter the firehouse from the rear. From there he would be able to watch the restaurant door and see when they left.

It was a good idea anyway. He could use another drink and he had a quart of corn liquor hidden away in the firehouse. He'd just go over and get a couple of belts and pretty soon the men would go away and then he and Helen would get together.

He staggered as he walked, but he made it all right. The back door was open and he entered the firehouse. He wasted a little time, believing that he had put the bottle away in the locker which held the spare hose, but it wasn't there. He cursed under his breath and tried to remember. The trouble was he couldn't get his mind off Helen long enough to think clearly. By God, that was one girl. He sat down in a broken-backed chair and took out a cigarette and lighted it. He suddenly decided that he'd skip the bottle. He didn't want to get too drunk and already he had been sick once from drinking. That was the trouble with drinking; you get too drunk and the very thing you want to do, you can't. If he was going to see Helen, to take her, then he wanted to be half sober.

Ten minutes later he remembered that he had put the bottle on the shelf in the toilet and he went in and got it. He pulled the cork and took a quick slug and returned to the chair, which was propped against the wall next to the old fashioned pumper. He completely forgot to watch the door of the restaurant as he took the next couple of drinks over a space of a little more than half an hour.

The bottle dropped from his lap to the floor and the loosely inserted cork fell out and the liquor spilled into a spreading puddle at his feet. He didn't notice it, sitting there half falling out of the chair, his arms hanging almost to the floor and his legs spread out. His mouth was wide open and he snored gently.

He didn't wake up until some time after eight o'clock. He didn't wake up until he heard the door of the room open and he slowly opened his eyes and saw the outlines of the woman's figure as she stood in front of him.

Flack lurched to his feet.

"Com'ere, Helen," he said, slurring the words.

"I'm not Helen," Sally Martins said. "And I asked you, Mr. Flack, if you have seen my father."

It took him a moment to focus his eyes, a moment while he squinted at her and cocked his head to one side. And then he hiccoughed and belched, straightening up.

"Thought you were someone else," he said. "Who did you say you wanted?"

"My father, Dr. Martins."

Flack nodded his head slowly up and down, knowingly.

"Oh, Dr. Martins," he said. "The very good Dr. Martins. And you are Sally Martins and you're looking for your father, Dr. Martins. Well, I'll tell you ..."

"Please just tell me if you have seen my father," Sally said coldly. "I have to find him."

"Take it easy. Just take it easy, kid," Flack said. "How about a little drink and we can discuss it."

Sally shook her head in annoyance.

"Never mind," she said. "Never mind." She turned to leave.

Flack moved quickly, circling to stand in front of her.

"What's the matter, kid?" He asked. "You too good to have a drink with me or somethin'? You think you're too dam' good ..."

She knew that he was drunk and she'd heard stories about him when he was this way. She knew that he could be mean and nasty and she didn't want trouble.

"Not too good, Mr. Flack," she said. "I just have to find Dad. There's been a hurricane warning and I have to find—"

"Listen," Flack said. "You listen to me. Don't get the idea you're so hot. You or your old man either. I've had better than you a dozen times. An' as far as your old man is concerned, why he's nothing but a broken-down old quack who got drunk and—"

He reached out and took her arm, swinging her around so that she was facing him, close. "Yeah," he said. "A drunken bum, that's all he is. An' you ..."

She clenched her teeth in sudden fury and jerked away from him.

"Don't you dare say anything about him," she said.

"Oh come off it," Flack said. "Don't try to act so God-damned innocent. Everybody knows about your old man. Everyone knows how he got drunk and let a man die on the operating table. Why the hell you think he's hiding out down here? Anyway, the hell with your old man. An' the hell with you."

He reached out again, then suddenly and before she had a chance to move, he pulled her to him.

"So come on off it," he mumbled. "It's about time you got yourself smartened up. You ain't no better than anyone else around this place. No better at all. Just prettier."

As she stood there, more dazed by his words than his actions, he put his arm around her and leaned forward fumbling to find her mouth with his own.

For a second she was paralyzed with the suddenness of it and then she instinctively pulled back. But by now he held her firm and he was pressing his body against her, tipping her backward on her heels.

She cried out as they fell together to the floor.

He was like an animal, crawling over her and pawing and tearing at her clothes and she fought him viciously, trying to free her knee as she pushed against him.

It was the sound of the door opening that momentarily stopped him. He was half covering her with his body and she was smothering under his opened mouth as the sound froze him.

The voice was a casual drawl, indifferent and bored. "I don't like to interrupt anything, but are you the deputy sheriff around here?"

He moved like a slug, rolling off her and getting up on one knee. The figure stood in the doorway, silhouetted against the lowering sky and Flack at once recognized the outline of the cowboy hat. He pulled himself slowly to his feet.

"What the hell do you want?" he snarled.

"You the deputy?"

"I'm him," Flack said.

Sally slowly got to her feet, rubbing violently at her mouth. She stood, poised for flight, watching the man in the doorway.

"Well, they told me you might be here," the man said, still speaking in an indifferent, bored voice. "You got a phone call over in the café. Think it's your boss and he wants to tell you about the hurricane or something. Anyway, you better go over and take the call."

Flack grunted and shook his head to clear it.

"They're callin' me?"

"They're calling you."

Flack started toward the door.

"Just a minute, buddy," the man said, stepping into the room. "Just a minute. I'll take the gun."

Flack stopped dead. "You'll what?"

"I'll take the gun," Gerald said. He held his hand out. "I'll get it one way or the other," he said. He moved swiftly then and as Flack instinctively ducked, he hit him hard on the side of the face, knocking him to his knees.

"You don't hear good, do you fella?" he said. "The gun!"

Before Flack could move he reached down and jerked it out of the holster and, flipping it, caught it neatly and held it, muzzle pointed at the semi-prone figure.

"Now go over and take your call like a good boy," he said. "And talk real polite. I'll be standing next to you."

It was then that Sally spoke up.

"My dad will kill you," she said to Flack, her voice hysterical. "When I tell my father—"

Gerald slowly turned and looked at her.

"You must be the doctor's daughter," he said. "He was looking for you. He's across the street in the café. But I don't think he's going to be killing anyone. At least not for a while yet. Right now he's loaded to the gills and reciting poetry."

He stepped aside as Flack got to his feet.

"And now let's all go over and join the rest of the folks," he said. "They'll be worrying."

Chapter Eight

1

Hurricane Bettina not only left death and destruction and tragedy in its wake, it also left bitter controversy and recrimination. The United States Weather Bureau came in for a great deal of unfair criticism and abuse. In turn, natives of those regions most violently affected were accused of ignoring the warnings which were put out.

The real villain, however, was neither the scientists in the weather bureau, nor the indifference of the people. It was a matter of semantics. That and the fact that no matter how accurate and careful the weather people may be, a great storm is never entirely predictable and Hurricane Bettina proved to be no exception to this rule.

For at least three days before the hurricane hit, U.S. Navy fliers had been charting it, releasing periodic bulletins. For three days the people of the southern states had been warned.

The difficulty was a combination of the language used in the warnings, which was too technical to mean much to the average layman, and the fact that at the last minute the hurricane itself radically changed its course, picked up tremendous speed and struck where it was least expected.

Even at that, had people taken the warnings more seriously, much damage could have been avoided. Hurricanes are an old story in the Gulf area and it is true that a good many of them pass by causing only a modicum of inconvenience. It is also true that Hurricane Bettina was pre-season, coming at a time when most residents of the affected areas assumed they were free of danger.

Those who were cautious, the people who stood by their radios and checked the progress of the storm and took the proper precautions, were for the most part safe. But a great many refused to become alarmed and as a result were ill prepared to sit it out. In certain sectors, it would have made little difference in any case.

For instance, on Key Arroyos, it wouldn't greatly have mattered, irrespective of what preparations were made by the natives. By the time they learned that the hurricane had altered its course and was coming their way, it was already upon them. There was very little they could do. Already it was too late to leave the key itself. Being caught out somewhere on the Overseas Highway would have been infinitely more dangerous than seeking shelter and sanctuary on the island.

All in all, Arroyos may consider itself fortunate. Physical damage was comparatively heavy, but there was no loss of life—at least as a direct result of the hurricane itself. None was drowned; none killed by the great tidal wave which hit the island or by the flying debris.

The speed with which the wind picked up was fantastic. By eight o'clock it was blowing, at better than sixty miles an hour and increasing in velocity by the minute. By eight-fifteen the rain came and it came in a cloud-bursting blast, driving in horizontally from the southwest.

Arroyos was fortunate in several respects. The town had the physical facilities for sitting out the storm, represented by the steel and concrete-block fish house. The people of the town had had plenty of experience with high winds and hurricanes; they'd used the warehouse several times in the past under similar circumstances: The fact that almost all the men were away at the time was of little matter. The wives of the fishermen and their children knew exactly what to do. Within minutes after the rains struck, they were on their way. A self sufficient and experienced group of hardy natives, they didn't wait around for help or directions. They knew.

In all there were some twenty women and thirty-two children. The youngest was Mrs. Cantios' newborn baby. But even he proved to be no problem. Mrs. Cantios' oldest son, a boy of fourteen, alone and unaided got his mother and his newest brother into his cut-down hotrod and he had the family safely installed in the fish house even before the rain came. Mrs. Cantios herself had wanted to wait for the doctor, feeling that he was bound to return after checking his own home, but young Jimmy knew the doctor and knew his habits. He took no chances and it is just as well he didn't.

Dr. Martins was in no condition to help anyone, including himself, by that time. He'd delivered the infant late in the afternoon and even then he was half drunk. Later, sitting around the Cantios kitchen, he consumed the better part of a quart of corn liquor and by the time Phil Hardin and Socks picked him up and brought him back to the café in an effort to get some black coffee down his throat, he was barely able to walk. But he could still talk; in fact, he couldn't stop talking, speaking in his slow, beautifully modulated voice, pronouncing his words with studied caution and going on and on.

The warehouse was a mutually owned enterprise, built by the fishermen themselves who ran it as a cooperative. The building was at the end of the long beach, in a protected cove. On the south side was a landing wharf to which the boats could tie while they were being loaded. It was a low, one-story structure, some one hundred and ten feet long by forty feet wide. At the east end were great wide double doors, through which the trucks entered.

Rectangular, it was divided into three sections. The rear part, a room twenty by forty, was used for an office as well as a place to house the freezing equipment and machinery. At the moment the storage tanks were empty although Socks had started the icing machines in preparation for the catch which he had been expecting. This room also contained a Delco lighting plant, a precautionary measure in case the regular current was cut off.

Next to this was a somewhat larger storage room. The east end itself was one vast area in which trucks were sometimes garaged. It was in this section that Duke Flager had dragged his Cessna to protect it from the storm.

Immediately after the fish house had been constructed, a small hurricane had hit the Keys. As a result, the fishermen had fixed up the middle section as an emergency storm cellar, stocking it with camp cots, cooking facilities and canned supplies as well as water and other equipment which might come in handy.

Heavy tidal waves would sometimes swirl around the building, leaving inches of water on the floor, but the construction was solid and the walls and floors were bolted to steel and concrete piers, buried deep in the sand. There was little danger that the building would be damaged or washed away.

As a place of refuge, the fish house was ideal; it had only one slight drawback. This was the smell. A smell of fish which was typical of every fish warehouse in the world and a smell which was so strong that only those who were thoroughly used to it were able to stand it for any length of time without becoming nauseous.

This, however, presented no problem to the wives or the children of the Arroyos fishermen. They were thoroughly used to the smell of fish. Fish was the source of their income, it made up the principal part of their daily diet, it was a part of their lives.

The twenty women and their progeny moved into the warehouse without undue hysteria and almost as a matter of routine. Few bothered to take with them more than their most personal and valuable possessions. They left their homes and their furniture to fend for themselves as best they could. After all, they had little to leave and they had gone through this sort of thing several times before.

But with the other residents of the island it was a somewhat different matter.

2

The three of them were dripping wet by the time they reached the restaurant and Sally herself would have found it almost impossible to fight her way against the wind if it hadn't been for the tall slender man in the cowboy hat who half supported her as they fought their way through the wind and the rain. She was the first to enter, virtually pushed through the door by the two men.

By this time it was completely dark and it took her a moment to adjust her eyes to the light. Almost at once she saw her father, slumped on a stool at the counter and leaning down with his head on his folded arms. Socks stood next to him, supporting him on one side. As her eyes slowly took in the others in the room, and as she hesitated a moment, shaking the water from her hair and wiping at her eyes, she was suddenly struck by the absolute silence in the place; by the silence and the fact that the eyes of everyone in the room were on her. She started to move toward her father, started to open her mouth to speak.

But the voice behind her cut in and the words froze her into silence.

"Don't anyone move; don't anyone say anything!"

She turned quickly to see the man who had come into the firehouse take Flack by the arm and roughly push him forward.

"Get on that phone," he said.

Flack staggered a step or two and recovered himself. He moved slowly then to the telephone sitting on the counter next to the cash register. The receiver was off the hook and resting on the glass top of the case.

The eyes in the room went from Sally to Flack as he slowly put the instrument to his ear.

Sally quickly looked around the restaurant.

Nick and his wife Helen were standing close to each other behind the counter. Phil Hardin sat on the other side of her father, a dull, perplexed look on his plain, unhandsome face. His mouth was hanging open and he looked for all the world like a mentally retarded child, which, in a way, he was. Seated next to him and staring vacantly at the floor was a man who Sally at once guessed must be the pilot of the plane she had heard landing earlier. He was middle-aged, tall and leathery and he wore canvas trousers, a faded military shirt with shoulder taps and dark sun-glasses. There was a streak of grease on his lean, square chin.

At the side of the room, sitting in one of the booths, was Tony. He carefully avoided Sally's eyes when she looked at him.

The other man was also a stranger. A thickset, heavily fleshed man wearing an incongruously dark business suit which looked as though he'd been using it to sleep in, he stood straddle-legged, in the center of the room between the booths and the counter. His short arms were at his sides and one of his hands was in the pocket of his coat. The other held the stump of a cigar. His bald head was glistening with perspiration and he watched Flack as the deputy picked up the telephone.

Flack coughed and turned and spit on the floor. He leaned down and spoke in a hoarse voice.

"Hello," he said. "Hello."

They could hear the static coming over the telephone wires, above the wail of the wind. Twice more he spoke into the phone, yelling hello and then he hesitated and listened.

He shook his head, dazed, and turned away, putting the receiver back.

"Nothing," Flack said. "Line went dead."

"We'll all be dead if we don't get out of here and over to the warehouse," Socks said in a furious voice. "What is all this business anyway? What—"

"Shut up!" The fat man turned and stared at Socks, his eyes cold. "We'll go when I say we go."

Sally had crossed the room and she sat down across from Tony.

"What's it all about?" she asked, keeping her voice low. "Who are these men? What do they want? Don't they realize ..."

Tony gestured for her to be quiet, shaking his head. He leaned across the table so that his voice could reach her, but not be heard above the crashing noise of the storm outside.

"I don't know," he said. "I helped the one in the sunglasses get his plane into the warehouse. When we got back, the man who brought you here—his name's Gerald—was with me. He and the fat one flew in on the plane. The fat one told Gerald that Nick had pulled a gun on him. From then on they just sort of took over. They seem to be some kind of gangsters."

Gerald had gone to the radio and was fooling around with the knobs, but was unable to get anything except static. He banged the box and cursed and turned to face the others. As he did Dr. Martins groaned and suddenly lifted his head and looked around the room. His bloodshot eyes focused on Sally and he shook his head to clear it and spoke.

"It's getting late," he said, very distinctly. "Getting very late. No time for you, my dear, to be ..."

The lights suddenly flickered and went out and he stopped speaking. A moment later they came back on, but very weakly.

The fat man moved toward the door.

"All right, everyone," he said, "let's get going." He took the gun out of his pocket and waved it around to include those in the room.

"You, football hero," he said, looking at Socks. "Help the old man there. Get one of his arms and one of you other guys get his other arm. I want you all to stay together and I don't want anyone getting fancy ideas. We're going over to this warehouse."

"Now see here." Flack spoke up suddenly and he sounded completely sober. "See here. I don't know what this is all about, but I represent the law."

"You represent nothing," Gerald said. "Do what he says."

"We should check and see that the people in the town—" Socks began, but again the fat man cut off.

"The hell with the people in the town," he said. "You already told us the fishermen's wives and children are at the warehouse. We got no time now to be fooling around. Anyone who hasn't made it is just plain out of luck. So come on, let's get going."

"There's Mr. Fullbright," Nick said. "Someone should see that he's reached."

George shot a quick look at Gerald and the younger man shook his head.

"We're staying together and we're going now," George said. "Get that drunk off the stool."

"Don't you dare speak of my father that way," Sally spoke up suddenly, getting to her feet.

"Shut up, lady," Gerald said. "Just do what he tells you to do. You're damned lucky we're taking the old man at all. If he wasn't a doctor, and we didn't think we might have to use him, we wouldn't even bother with him. So get moving, all of you, let's get going."

Gerald reached down and picked up the doctor's small black bag. "I'll just carry this along myself," he said. "You sure, Doc, it has what I want in it?"

Dr. Martins looked up at him blankly for a moment, and then nodded.

"Yes—yes," he said. "It has what you want."

"O.K. Let's move then."

He shoved the door open and a blast of wind and rain swept into the room. As he did, the static coming over the radio faded out and a voice came over the instrument, clear and sharp above the sound of the roar of the storm.

"... and latest reports are that the road below Marathon is impassable. It is expected ..."

The voice stopped as suddenly as it had started, once more drowned out by a series of shrieks and squeals.

Slowly they trooped out of the room. Socks and Phil Hardin held Dr. Martins up between them and he seemed to have some idea of what was happening as he staggered to the door. They were followed by Nick and Helen. Tony and Sally were directly behind them. The others trailed along.

Already there were several inches of water racing through the streets and stray bits of debris were blown about at random by the high-shrieking, rain-filled winds.

As the group passed down the street, Sally looked across at her home and saw that the wind had broken in one of the front windows and that the porch roof was gone. The lights had been left on in the downstairs part of the house but as she watched, they flickered and went out.

Someone behind her had picked up a powerful flashlight and had it trained on the ground. Up front, Socks and Phil leaned into the wind, one on each side of Dr. Martins. They didn't need a light to find their way, but they had to be careful to avoid large areas of water and flooded spots, as well as fallen trees and parts of buildings blown about by the gale.

The warehouse was less than a half mile away, but it took the group more than half an hour to reach it.

From a distance they saw the dim lights shining through the narrow windows of the big building and Socks knew that someone had cut the generator in. He knew that by now all main electric wires leading onto the island were down.

3

Richard Fullbright first became aware of the possibilities of Hurricane Bettina when he got the telephone call from his attorney in Miami. He had contacted the lawyer as soon as Nick Cosmos left in order to facilitate the transfer of Nick's two lots, which he realized he was getting at a complete steal. They discussed the matter at some length and Fullbright was about to hang up when the attorney mentioned the hurricane.

"Looks like you're in for a blow," the lawyer said.

Fullbright asked what he meant and the lawyer relayed the most recent weather report.

"Think it might be a good idea for you to drive up to Miami," he said. "The way your place is situated, you could have trouble, serious trouble if you get high water."

"This house is built to take anything," Fullbright answered, slightly indignant.

"With those big windows?" the lawyer said. "And right at water level? You don't know what these storms can be. You should close up the place and get off the Keys if you want to play it safe."

"It's not too bad here now," Fullbright answered. "No, I'd much prefer to be here in case of trouble."

"Well, it's up to you."

Fullbright hung up and called Sam.

"We're in for a little bit of weather," he said. "Maybe you better get out the storm shutters."

Sam nodded.

"I've been getting the reports over the radio," he said. "I've already started putting them up. But, Mr. Fullbright, if this hurricane hits, you don't want to be in this house."

"We'll stay here," Fullbright said. "Just see that the porch furniture is taken care of and things are shipshape."

"I seen these things in the islands," Sam persisted. "It could be mighty dangerous."

Fullbright shook his head in irritation.

"Don't be a fool, man," he said. "Just do as I tell you. Check around and see that there's nothing loose to fly about. Get the shutters up. Get started now."

When Sam left he went over and poured himself a Scotch and soda. Purposely he turned off the radio. He didn't even want to hear about the storm. With the money he'd put in the place, no storm was going to bother him.

By eight-thirty, however, even Richard Fullbright was forced to admit that he had made a mistake. He was standing in the big living room, looking through a crack between the shutters, when the line of palm trees, which he'd brought down from Miami and had planted less than a month previously, heeled over in the wind and then slowly lifted their roots. He yelled for Sam.

"Get down to the village and get some help," he ordered. "Get some men up here and see what you can do about the bushes. At this rate we're going to lose—"

"I don't think there is anyone around," Sam said. "The fishing fleet hasn't come in and all the men are off."

"There has to be somebody," Fullbright said angrily. "You get on down there and dig up someone. We're going to need help around here."

Sam shrugged.

"Yes, Mr. Fullbright," he said.

It was while he was gone that the rain really started coming down, and before he was back, the floor of the house was covered by almost an inch of water. The winds drove it under the doors and around the windows and Fullbright stood paralyzed as he watched it, unable to do more than stand there and curse.

And then the lights went out.

Sam was back within a few minutes. He had difficulty pulling the door open and when he came in, he was accompanied by gallons of driving water. He was swinging a gasoline lantern.

"There's no one," he said breathlessly. "They are all gone down to the warehouse. No one left in town at all."

His eyes were wide and he was breathing heavily.

"We better get out," he said. "Things are blowing all over and several of the shanties have already gone."

Fullbright looked grim. "Get the car out," he said. "Get the car while I start packing up."

Sam shook his head.

"Car won't do no good now," he said. "It's bad here, but if we go out on that highway and hit those bridges, it would be a lot worse."

"We could make Key West," Fullbright said.

"Mr. Fullbright," Sam said, "I don't think so. That last radio report—the state police warned against trying to drive. Said the safest thing to do was stay where you are."

"Well, we can't stay here. You can see ..."

"We should go down to the warehouse," Sam said. "That's where everyone else is. That's where we should be. It's the safest place."

For a minute or so Fullbright hesitated. "All right," he said, "let me have the light for a couple of minutes. You pack what you think we'll need. Hurry. I'll be back in a minute or so and we'll leave."

Sam was back in the living room when Fullbright returned. He'd packed two suitcases, one with clothes and the other with whisky and a few cans of food. Fullbright himself had a large attaché case in his hand. Going toward the door, Sam attempted to take it from him.

Fullbright hung on to it possessively.

"No," he said. "No. I'll handle this. You just take the bags. Bring the car around to the back. We should be able to make the warehouse all right."

"Car's no use now," Sam said. "The whole road down to the garage is washed out."

They had to walk it, fighting every inch of the way through the rain and the wind and if it hadn't been for Sam, Fullbright would never have made the distance. As it was, they were the last to arrive at the fish house.

Chapter Nine

1

Duke Flager twisted his head and took off the earphones, then reached out and clicked the switch on the radio. He pushed back the canopy top and climbed out of the cockpit of the plane and onto the soaked concrete floor of the warehouse. He saw that they were watching him, waiting expectantly for what he would have to say. But he took his time, reaching for a cigarette and lighting it, before speaking.

"Well," he said at last, "that's it. Bridge is washed out somewhere west of here and Key West is cut off. Road's out to the east. We're completely cut off. All lines are down."

He stopped and looked at his wrist watch. It showed ten minutes after three.

"That was the station in Miami," he said. "Hard to get it clear with all the static, but from what I understand, we're just about in the eye of the hurricane. It's expected to reach its peak in another hour."

For a moment no one spoke and then Gerald, sitting at the card table in the rear center of the room and under the flickering light hanging from the ceiling, moved his chair back and stretched.

"Another hour," he said. "So what does that mean? When will it die down? When will we be able to get out of here?"

Duke looked at him and shrugged.

"Hard to say," he said. "As far as the wind is concerned, I'd say it will keep up for another six or eight hours. But as far as leaving ..."

"We'll be here until they can get someone in by either helicopter or by boat," Socks interrupted. "No one is going to get off this island."

"We're getting off." The fat one, the one they called George, quickly spoke up. "We're getting off. Just as soon as you can get this plane out of here and put it in the air. How soon would you say that will be?"

Once more Duke shrugged.

"No way of telling," he said. "Certainly not until the wind drops down to somewhere around ten or fifteen miles an hour. Even then—"

"Even then what?"

"Well, it will depend how the beach is; whether I can get a clear space for a runway."

"We'll clear a space all right," George said. "You sure you got that engine fixed okay now? Sure we won't have no trouble?"

"Not with the plane," Duke said. "Not if the weather is right and I can get a clear space."

He walked over to the table and pulled up a chair, sitting down a foot or two away from where George was standing.

"There's nothing to do but wait," he said.

Socks moved out of the shadow where he'd been leaning against the wall.

"I should go and check those generators," he said.

Gerald turned and stared at him coldly.

"You ain't going anywhere," he said. "Nobody's going anywhere. We're all staying right here; right here until this thing lets up."

"That's right," George said. "We're staying right here. What's the matter, football, you nervous or something? Why don't you come on over and sit down and just take it easy. You got no place to go. You can tell us about when you were a college hero. Come on, tell us some more about those ball games you played in. Basketball you said, didn't you, kid? You must have been real great. Come on, tell us about it."

Socks spread his feet and glared at the fat man.

"I was great," he said. "They all said so. The biggest sports writers in the country. Let me tell you ..."

Sally stepped away from the cot on which her father was lying and moved under the wing of the plane until she came to the jeep. Tony was stretched out on the seat and he moved over as she stepped into the car and sat down next to him. The jeep itself had been pulled around so that it stood between the plane and the great double doors of the building. It was at the opposite end of the room where most of the others sat under the single naked bulb hanging by a long cord from the ceiling. The jeep was in almost complete darkness and Sally knew that if they kept their voices low, they couldn't be heard above the sound of the wind and the rain.

She reached out and found Tony's hand and took it between her own slender palms. Her fingers were like ice.

"Tony," she said, "Tony, what is it? What's wrong? What's happened to everyone? Why is everybody so strange?"

"It's the hurricane," he said.

"No it isn't," she said. "It's something else. Something about those men."

"Don't think about them," he said. "Just try and stay clear of them and don't think about them."

"But I have to think about them," she said. "Why did they ask Dad all of those questions? What were they trying to find out?"

"They asked all of us questions," Tony said. "I don't know why. I don't know anything, except that they're some kind of gangsters and they just happen to be here."

"But they just don't happen to be here," Sally said in a low voice. "Don't you see, they came here. They came here on purpose. And since they've been here something's happened. Something's happened to all of us. It's as though everyone is scared to death. Don't you see? Can't you tell? Take Nick and Helen. Or Mr. Fullbright. Why, he acts as though he's in some sort of—"

"Socks seems to be doing all right," Tony said. "At least if he's frightened it isn't interfering with his autobiography."

"Socks hasn't the brains to be frightened," Sally said. "But why are they keeping us all together like this? They don't seem interested in the others, the women and children in the other part of the building. Why is it only us?"

"You're beginning to imagine things," Tony said. "Don't. Don't let it get the best of you. How's your father feeling?"

"He was getting better, almost sober. But I left him for a minute or so a few minutes back and somehow he got hold of another bottle. He had a pint flask when I got back to him. I think Flack gave it to him. Flack was with him, talking to him and trying to pump him. I think those others put him up to it."

"Flack's more afraid of them than anyone else," Tony said. "Did you see his face while they were questioning him, asking him about who he knew up around Miami? He was green."

"I wouldn't care what they did to him," Sally said. "It's the others I'm thinking of. I was talking with Helen and Nick. Helen told me that they are killers, professional murderers. She says they came down here to get Nick."

"Why would anyone want to get Nick?"

"I don't know. All I know is that Helen's almost paralyzed with fear. I started to question her, but Nick made her keep quiet."

"I don't think it's Nick," Tony said. "What could Nick have done? No, if they came here looking for anyone, I'd say it was Flack. Flack, or possibly Fullbright."

"Fullbright?" Helen turned and looked at him curiously. "Why Fullbright? Of all people."

"I don't know why," Tony said. "I only know how he's been acting. Ever since he and Sam got here. The moment they began questioning him, asking about the north and what he did up there, something happened to him. He's lost his arrogance, his assurance. For the last hour or so, he's been sitting back in the corner there, looking like a ghost."

"He's afraid of the hurricane," Sally said, "He's not used to it."

"It isn't the hurricane," Tony said. "He wasn't frightened when he got here and the man's no fool. He knew as soon as he and Sam made the warehouse that they were safe. No, it isn't the hurricane. It's something else. It's something that was here when he arrived."

Sally was silent for several minutes. She pressed his hand again and then slowly removed her own.

"I'm going back to Dad," she said. "I can hear him beginning to mumble again. And Tony ..." She looked up at him, pleadingly, "Tony, stay away from Socks. Don't answer him when he tries to talk to you. He's been trying to get you into a fight all night. Stay away from him."

"Go back to your Dad," Tony said. "Don't worry about me. I can take care of myself."

She started to get out of the jeep and then hesitated for a moment. "I can't understand what's come over Dad," Sally said. "He's never acted like this before. Oh, I'm not kidding myself. I know about his drinking: I guess everybody does. But there's something very strange about him this time. Always before, no matter how much he drank, he'd snap out of it if anything came up. But somehow now it's different. He isn't making any effort. None at all. All he does is lie on that cot and mumble. Keeps talking about the old days. Long, disjointed sentences that don't make any sense at all. And half the time he looks at me as though he doesn't remember who I am."

"He'll be all right," Tony said. "Just stay with him. Try to make him sleep."

Sally nodded and stepped to the ground.

"You try and sleep too," she said.

2

Flack had it figured out. There was no longer any question in his mind. From the very second that tall slender one in the cowboy hat had slugged him and taken his gun, he'd suspected, and now he knew. He didn't recognize them, of course, but he knew the type. Knew just what they were. They were killers; professionals. And if they were killers, they had to be working for the syndicate. There was only one syndicate.

He could tell by the way they acted, the questions they asked. And he'd had a chance to question Duke Flager while the pilot and Phil Hardin had been working on the plane during the early hours of the night. What Flager had told him, made it sure.

They were killers and they were here on business.

He didn't want to think about what that business was.

It was funny how fast he'd been able to sober up. An hour after they had arrived at the warehouse, it was just as though he'd never taken a drink. That first hour hadn't been too bad. They'd all been busy then, busy in spite of the exhaustion and the weariness of fighting the hurricane while they struggled against the wind and the rain to get to the place.

The two of them had taken over at once. It was their party and they'd run the show. Flack had thought that they would go in with the others, the women and the children. But Gerald and George had their own ideas about that.

George had herded them together in the main room of the warehouse, the room where the plane was being temporarily stored, and George had stood guard over them while Gerald, accompanied by Socks, had inspected the rest of the building. The two had returned, after several minutes, lugging a half dozen canvas cots, a few provisions and the primus stove. There'd been very little talking.

When Fullbright and his colored boy Sam had shown up, dragged in half-drowned and exhausted, they had sent Sam in with the women and children but ordered the older man to stay with the rest of them.

It wasn't what they said or did. It was what they didn't say. They had ordered Duke and Phil to get to work on the plane and it was obvious that they would wait only long enough for the weather to clear and then they would be off.

But Tilden Flack knew that something was going to happen before they left. That's when he started to think again about those other years, began to think about Cicero and Cicero's brother, whom he'd murdered.

It was while they were baiting Socks that Flack went over to the cot on which Doc Martins lay, half conscious. Flack waited until the girl left him and he sidled over under cover of the semi-darkness. He had the bottle which Phil Hardin had given him.

The drink acted on Doc Martins the way he hoped it would. The old man took a shot and coughed and then quickly reached for a second one. Flack held back. He'd started talking then, started asking questions. Maybe there was something in the Doc's bag, some drug or something the doc could give the younger one, who'd been interested.

But it was useless. The old man rambled on and on. He didn't even remember the two men; didn't remember them coming into the restaurant. And then he'd started to sing and someone yelled for him to shut up and Flack left him.

It was when Duke got the report that they were completely cut off that Flack got his idea. If the roads were out it meant that they were isolated. It meant that the only way out, until rescuers showed up, would be by the plane.

Someone was bound to come to them as soon as the hurricane was over. But before help could arrive, those two, that fat, sinister man in the crumpled suit and that other one who looked like a boy, would have plenty of time to do whatever it was that they had come to Arroyos to accomplish; have time to do it and get away on the plane.

There was only one way to see that they were powerless, one way
to spike their guns. The plane would have to be disabled. If they knew
that the plane couldn't get off, that they too would be trapped on the
island until help arrived, they'd do nothing.

Tilden Flack was far from being a hero. On the other hand, he was
not a fool. He wasn't at all sure that he himself was marked as the
victim. It could very well be one of the others.

It could be Dr. Martins, who Flack knew had got drunk years before
and botched up a plastic surgery job up in Chicago, losing his patient.
It could be Socks Schroeder, who'd sung in front of a grand jury. Flack
wasn't sure; couldn't be sure. Or it could be Flack himself.

Had he been positive that it was one of the others, he'd have done
nothing. He'd have let events take their course. But there was that one
possible chance that it was himself they had come down to kill. In that
case he had to do something.

There was no running away, no place to hide. The only thing left for
Flack to do was to use his brains. And that was how he reached the
decision about the plane.

The plane must be disabled.

The trouble wasn't in getting Phil Hardin off alone in a darkened
corner of the room and talking with him in privacy. The raging storm
outside more than insured privacy; even a yell within the great room
could barely be heard a few feet away. And the room itself was all dark
shadows, the single light bulb hanging from the cord over the card
table at which George and Gerald sat while they passed the time baiting Socks Schroeder casting only a dim light which penetrated but a
few feet in a circle around the group of huddled figures.

No, the trouble wasn't a matter of opportunity or of privacy. The trouble was in penetrating the dull-witted mind of Hardin himself. At no
time had Hardin had any fear of the storm itself; nor had he any particular fear of the two strangers amongst them. For the hurricane he
entertained merely annoyance, knowing that it was wrecking his
garage and workshop. For the strangers he felt an alien sense of dis-
like. He neither understood them nor liked them.

Flack he did understand. Flack was a deputy sheriff and Flack represented the law. He neither liked nor disliked Flack, but Flack was
a known quantity and it was because of this that he listened to him
and tried to follow his reasoning.

They stood together, in a far corner of the room, with the silhouette
of the plane between them and the others and Flack leaned his
heavy, dirt-streaked face close to the other man's ear as he spoke.

"I'm swearing you in as a sort of deputy," Flack said, "and it's up to you to follow orders. These men are criminals, killers. They're down here to murder someone. And when this blow is over, that's what they are going to do. They're going to kill someone, maybe kill us all. And they'll get away with it, too."

Hardin's eyes bugged and he stared witlessly at the other man.

"Kill someone?" he said. "Kill us? Why? Why would they want to kill us?"

Flack took him by the arm in a tight hard grip and half shook him.

"It doesn't matter why," he said. "They'll do it. I'm telling you they'll do it. You saw how they been acting. You saw their guns. You saw how they took over. As soon as this thing's ended, there's goin' be trouble."

Hardin nodded at him dumbly, looking more witless than ever.

"What we goin' do ..." he began.

Flack's grip tightened on his arm.

"Keep your voice down," he said. "Just listen. So long as they got that plane to get away in, they can do it. They can shoot us all and then take off before help can get here. I know it and they know it. The plane's the answer."

"The plane?"

"Right, the plane. Don't you understand? It's the plane which will make it possible. But if the plane wasn't here, if they couldn't get away after the storm is over, then we'd be safe. They won't do anything if they know that help will come sooner or later. That people will come and find them here. Can't you understand?"

"But the plane is here," Hardin said. "Hell, they know the plane is here. They know that flyer fellow and me fixed it up."

"That's just the point," Flack said. "They know you fixed it up. They know they can get away. That's why we have to do something to un-fix it. That's what I'm talking to you about. That's why I'm swearin' you in as a deputy to help me. We've got to get to that plane somehow or other and fix it so it can't take off."

"But we just got through fixin' it so it can," Hardin said.

Flack cursed him under his breath.

"You idiot," he said. "Try and listen to me. Try and understand. You've got to get back into that plane. Got to do something to it. Jerk out the wires in back of the instrument panel; do whatever is necessary to put it out of commission."

Hardin shook his head dumbly and shrugged.

"Why me?" he said. "Why me? How can I do anything? That flying fellow is in the plane and he'd see me. He'd never let me come near it."

"You fool," Flack said. "Don't you understand? They know I'm the law around here. They'd never let me get near the inside of the plane. But you they wouldn't suspect. You've already been working on it. All you have to do is listen and follow my orders. Go to the plane and tell the pilot I'm over here and I've got a bottle. Tell him I want him to come on over and have a drink. Tell him I want to talk to him a second or two. Then, when he leaves, you get in the plane and do what you have to do."

"They'll see me getting in," Hardin said.

"What if they do? You were in it before. They'll also see you talking to the pilot and they won't suspect anything. Now just do as I say. Go on over and get him and do what I tell you."

Hardin hesitated for a long moment and then slowly nodded his head.

"How about a slug outta that jug first," he said at last.

Flack pulled the pint flask out of his pocket. His voice was heavy with impatience as he handed it to the other man.

"Take it easy," he said. "I want a shot left for the pilot."

Hardin put the flask to his lips and took a long pull. He handed it back after a moment or so and shook his head, wiping his lips with the back of his hand. A moment later he turned and started for the side of the plane.

Twenty feet off, at the opposite side of the room, Helen Cosmos looked up and watched him with only faint curiosity. She sat on the side of the cot, next to her husband, holding one of his hands in both of her own. She continued speaking in the same low, intense voice which she had been using for the past fifteen minutes, keeping her lips close to his ear so that he could hear and understand her words.

"You've got to try it, Nick," she said. "You've got to try it. I think the wind is down a little now and the worst of the storm is over. But in any case, if you can make the door and get outside, you'll have a chance. It's dark enough that they won't notice if you stay close to the walls."

Nick felt the pressure of her hands and sensed the shiver that went through her slender body.

"I don't want to leave you here alone," he said.

"It isn't me that they care about," she said. "Don't you see, it isn't me. No one is going to hurt me. It's you they came to get. Stay here, wait until daylight, and it will be too late. Then you won't have a chance. God knows, I don't want you out in that hurricane, but at least that way you got a chance. Stay here and you have no chance."

"But, kid," Nick said, "they haven't done anything yet."

"It's only because they have time. They wouldn't do anything before, earlier, because they had no way of getting away. They had to wait until the plane was repaired. And then, once it was, the winds and the rain kept them here. But sooner or later the storm will be over and then they'll be free to go. Don't you understand? Can't you see that they are just waiting, just marking time? No, Nick, you have to do it— have to do it now. If you wait much longer, there'll be no chance at all. Nick, for God's sake, if you've ever loved me, you got to do what I ask. You got to try and make a break for it. If you can get back to the village you'll be O.K. You can find something still standing, some place to hide out."

He hesitated a long time and at last nodded.

"O.K., kid," he said. "O.K., if that's what you want. You're the boss. Tell you what, I'll stroll over and pick up a couple of mugs of coffee. See where everyone is, what everyone is doing. I wanna get the lay of the land before I start out."

He reached into his pocket and found the cigarettes and held the pack out and she took one. He struck a light for her and held it as she drew in the smoke and then he lighted his own. Before he blew out the match, he looked at his watch. It showed four-fifteen.

3

Richard Fullbright slowly opened his eyes, staring straight ahead and not blinking for several seconds. The realization that he must have fallen asleep suddenly came to him and his first reaction was one of amazement. Asleep? My God, how could it have been possible?

It must have been his complete physical exhaustion, the battle to reach the warehouse and his near drowning as Sam had helped him through the torrential downpour and the terrible winds which would have carried him off his feet, had it not been for the colored man.

As though that hadn't been enough! That and the realization that by this time his beautiful house was wrecked, probably completely washed away and ruined. But then, when at last they had arrived, found their sanctuary, this other thing had had to happen to him. This thing which he had known in the back of his mind was bound to happen sooner or later and to which he had blinded himself.

No wonder that for those first minutes and hours he had been paralyzed with fear. No wonder he'd been unable to think clearly, unable to do anything but cower there in a state of complete collapse. No wonder, even, that at last he had actually slept, fallen unconscious from total exhaustion.

He was an old man and there was only so much he could take. For a while there—it must have been just before that merciful sleep had overtaken him—for a while, he'd been ready to give up. Ready to toss in the sponge. Everything had seemed to crash about his head at once.

But slowly now he was beginning to regain his shattered senses. Slowly he was coming to. The sleep is what he had needed to recoup his strength.

He was slumped against the side of the wall, almost in the corner and just outside of the perimeter of light cast by that single naked bulb, but there was just sufficient reflection for him to see the face of his watch. It was a little after four, but because of the shadows, he couldn't quite make out the slender minute hand of the timepiece. He was surprised to realize that instead of sleeping for hours, he'd been unconscious barely sixty minutes.

He moved slightly and groaned in pain as the nerves of his stiffened and cramped body reacted. He knew that he would be a sick man by morning, but the aches and pains of his body were an old story and they didn't worry him unduly. The thing was that his mind was once more back to normal. His mind was as keen as ever and it was sharp and alert as it always was when he felt it necessary to call upon it. There was that and the fact that the fear, that terrible, paralyzing fear, was no longer with him.

Not, of course, that he was kidding himself. He was still afraid. He still knew the danger he was facing. He still knew the position he was in and he wasn't discounting it. The difference was that he was able to think clearly. And when he thought clearly, he always found an answer.

He began to relive the earlier hours of the evening. Those first hours after he had arrived at the warehouse and found the two of them there.

It hadn't taken him long to realize what it was all about. He'd met men like these two before; knew them at once for what they were. Cheap hoodlums; paid killers. In the early days, when Knocky and Sol and Manny had first come to him and he'd agreed to go in with them, to front for them in that Casino deal, there had been plenty of boys of that type hanging around. Of course, later on, after he'd assumed control and taught the others a few things about how to really handle a business, those types hadn't been necessary. Cheap, paid thugs. Willing to do anything for a price.

He knew now, now that he was thinking clearly again, just where he'd made his mistake. It was the mistake he'd always warned the others about. He'd underestimated his opponents. Underestimated them because they were essentially stupid men. It was a mistake so many people made and it was a mistake which was always fatal.

He'd been a fool to think that those three, those men who'd been his partners, had been fooled by him. They'd found out. Probably brought accountants in and gone over the records. They hadn't been satisfied in thinking that they were merely stealing the business from him. They must have guessed that it was just a little too easy.

They were pigs; greedy, selfish men, not satisfied with getting their hands on the place and having it all. They wanted what he'd taken in the past. He'd been living in a fool's paradise thinking that he could get away with it. But that was all water under the dam; all beside the point. The only thing important now was the moment. And at this precise moment, as he sat there in his soggy clothes and looked across the room at the group around the table, he knew that he must do something.

Knocky and Sol and Manny hadn't forgotten him. They'd sent their goons down, and had put a price on his head.

It was exactly what he could have expected them to do if they found out. His mistake had been in thinking they wouldn't find out.

Instinctively his small, immaculate hands closed tighter on the attaché case he held on his lap.

He couldn't be sure, of course, but he could guess. The price? Well, judging from what he knew about things, you can get a man murdered for anywhere from five hundred dollars to twenty-five thousand. It all depended on who the man was and where the thing was to take place.

This would be one of the more expensive kills. Not because he was important or anything like that. Of course it would be different if he hadn't retired; hadn't moved south. Up north, back home while he was still active, it would have cost a lot to get him killed. Down here it would be cheaper. But not too cheap.

Still and all, he guessed that it was not more than ten grand. That would be just about right.

Once more he clutched the attaché case, almost fondling it. That attaché case was his insurance. The case and the hundred thousand dollars which it contained.

If they'd kill him for ten thousand, certainly he had a little bargaining power with a hundred grand. The thing to do was to buy out as cheaply as possible and to convince them that there would always be more coming.

He was refreshed now, felt almost elated. It was a game and he was always good at games. He decided that the best time to make his pitch would be at once. They would be tired and sleepy and relaxed. Now was the time.

He looked over again at the group around the table and started painfully to pull himself to his feet. It was then that the sudden, high-pitched scream cut through the sound of the wind and the storm and froze him as he was halfway to his feet.

Chapter Ten

1

For the second time Socks saw Sally leave the cot on which her father lay and cross the room toward the jeep. He knew that Tony Mason was in the jeep and the thought infuriated him. Lunging to his feet, he started away from the table.

"I'm still talking to you, college," George said. "Come back here."

Socks hesitated for only a second and then once more moved. Before he had taken more than a step, Gerald was on his feet, the gun in his hand as though by magic.

"George still wants to talk," he said.

"Listen," he said, "why don't you guys leave me alone? I'm going over there. I want to be with my girl."

"Your girl's being taken care of fine," Gerald said. "Come back and talk with George."

Socks' face reddened and for a moment he hesitated. Gerald reached out and took him by the arm.

"Back and sit down," he said. "We want to hear more about you being a basketball hero. Want to hear more about how honest you were. How you weren't afraid to tell that grand jury all about those bad, nasty boys who threw the games."

"Now listen," Socks said. "Listen here. That damned artist is over there with my girl and I don't like—"

"An artist?" Gerald said. "Don't you worry about no artist. Why hell, fellow, those guys are all pansies. Your girl couldn't be in safer hands. So come on back here now like a good little hero and talk to George."

For a moment more Socks hesitated and Gerald casually lifted the gun and scraped his cheek with the barrel. A tiny spot of blood showed in an instant on Socks' face, and his hands clenched and his jaw tightened.

"If you didn't have that gun," he said. "I'd—"

"But I do have the gun," Gerald said. "Anyway, I don't like you very much. I don't think I like you at all. Maybe I'll do the artist a favor and just ..."

He stepped back, lifting the barrel of the weapon and Socks stood there staring at him. George spoke up quickly.

"Take it easy, Gerald," he said. "Take it easy. Don't let him be any more of a hero than he has to. I know these athletes aren't very smart, but I think he's smart enough to do what we tell him."

Socks slowly relaxed and stepped back and pulled the chair out and sat down.

"We got a lot of time to kill," George said. "You aren't the brightest boy in the world, but you do keep me awake and I just don't feel like I should go to sleep for a while. So come on. Tell us some more."

2

"And if he hadn't walked in when he did," Sally said, "Flack would have—"

Tony interrupted her, squeezing her arm and pointing over to the table.

"He just slapped your boy friend with his gun," he said. "It looks like Socks is trying to get himself killed."

"He isn't my boy friend," Sally said, irritation coloring her tone. "And you aren't listening to me. I'm telling you what happened in the firehouse with Flack. You don't seem to care."

He took her by the shoulders and turned her so that she faced him, shaking her.

"Of course I care," he said. "I care a great deal. But right now there are other things. Right now I'm worrying about what's going to happen, not what has happened. Those two are up to something and I can't figure out what it is. And several things are going on. First Flack and Hardin were off together in the corner and talking. Then Hardin went back to the plane and now Duke is with Flack. They're up to something and I want to know what's going on. I want to know."

"Tony," Sally said. "Tony, stay out of it. There's nothing you can do.

Nothing at all. At least they aren't interested in you. So stay out of it."

"I've been staying out of things too long," Tony said. "That's been my trouble—staying out of things. I've thought that I could just turn my back, walk away...."

"Oh, Tony."

Suddenly she was in his arms and her own were around him and she was searching for his mouth. "Tony—Tony."

Quickly he kissed her, holding the kiss for barely a moment and then he gently pushed her away.

"I've got to find out what's going on and why," he said, "I've got to know."

3

"What the hell does he want to see me for?" Duke said. "I don't want to see anybody, don't want to talk with anybody. All I want to do is get some sleep and sit this out."

"Well, I don't exactly know," Hardin said. "All he told me was that it was important. Said it would only take a minute or two and he wanted you to come and talk to him for a second. Yeah, just a second. And also, by the way, he said maybe you'd like a shot. He's got a pint of booze."

Duke looked annoyed.

"He would have," he said. He shrugged and moved in the seat of the cockpit. "Well, what the hell. I got plenty of time and I guess it won't hurt. We won't be going anywhere anyway for a while."

He opened the door of the plane and got out. "Don't go falling asleep in that plane," he said. "I'll be back in a minute or two and I don't want to have to haul you out."

He stepped to the wet cement floor and started over to where Flack crouched in the shadows.

Across the room, Gerald watched, but made no move.

There was a dim red light on the dashboard and for moment or two, after Duke left, Phil Hardin looked at the instrument panel with interest.

By God, one of these days he was going to pick up an old plane and start fooling around with it. These machines weren't half as complicated as he'd thought them to be. Hell, after helping Duke on the machine, he could see it would be duck soup. He'd love to get his hands on one.

He started to fool with the dials, idly twisting them, and it was then he pulled a knob and the door of the small compartment fell open. He reached in and his hand felt a paper bag. Pulling it out, he opened it and held the contents under the glow cast by the dimmed red light. He was holding a sliced chicken sandwich in his hands.

Slowly he began to munch it. For the moment he completely forgot why he had come to the plane. Forgot all about what Deputy Sheriff Flack had ordered him to do.

In the corner of the room, Flack was having his own problems. He knew that he must hold Duke Flager for exactly a certain length of time. Should Duke return to the cockpit of the plane too soon and before Hardin had an opportunity to disable the engine or the controls of the plane, the whole plan would be wasted.

On the other hand, Duke must return while Hardin was still at work sabotaging the machine. This was essential to his plot. The sabotage itself would be wasted unless the two gunmen learned of it long before the takeoff. Otherwise they might well go into action at any moment. They must know that the plane was unable to take off and as a result they would be accountable for anything they did when rescuers finally showed up.

Flack had no compunctions so far as Hardin himself was concerned. He knew what would happen if George and Gerald found that he was damaging the plane.

"All right," Duke said. "All right, now I've had the drink, what is it you wanted?"

His voice was surly. From what he'd seen of the deputy, he didn't like him and he wanted to get back and sleep.

"Well, it's like this," Flack said. "You flew them two here. I was wondering why they came, what they wanted?"

"Why don't you ask them?"

"Well, they don't seem like the kind of boys to ask questions of," Flack said. "I thought maybe you—"

"I mind my own business," Duke said. "They chartered the plane, told me where they wanted to go and that's it. I don't get nosey about my passengers."

"Look, mister," Flack said, "maybe you should of got nosey. You got a license to protect, you know. Another thing, I'm an officer down here and when I ask questions, I expect answers."

Duke got up from where he was squatting on his haunches. He started to turn away. He was taking no guff from a crumb like this. He'd heard George and Gerald questioning the deputy and he knew that Flack was both without guts and without authority. The only authority Duke recognized was force, and right at this moment the two mobsters had the force. He didn't know what Flack wanted and he didn't care. He wasn't going to get into the middle of things.

Realizing that Hardin still would need time, Flack quickly got to his own feet and reached out and grabbed the other man by the arm.

"Listen," he said quickly. "No reason to get huffy, pal. What the hell, we're just having a friendly drink and I was just asking a question or two. No harm in that, is there? Now let's have another slug and let's not get into a hassle. I wasn't meaning any harm, fellow."

Duke either had to physically pull away from the other man or stand still and so he hesitated a moment and then turned back.

"I just don't like questions," he said. "O.K., I can use another shot." He reached for the bottle.

It was while he was lifting it to his mouth that Sally happened to look up from where she was sitting with Tony and saw Gerald's silhouette as he stood beside the cowling of the Cessna. Saw him raise his hand and point the gun. Some instinct must have told her what was about to happen. She screamed a split second before the crash of the shot.

Gerald only fired once. Even before the crack of the pistol had stopped reverberating throughout the confines of the room, he jammed the gun between his belt and his trousers and reached in through the opened door of the plane. A moment later he jerked back and Phil Hardin followed, falling headlong to the concrete floor.

Gerald drew back his boot and kicked him viciously twice.

"The son of a bitch," he said. "He was monkeying around with the wires in back of the dashboard. I'll kill the bastard." He fired two more quick shots.

George was at his side and he held his own gun in one pudgy hand. The other held the flashlight and its beam was trained on Hardin.

"Get 'em all over there under the light," he said in a tight, hard, voice. "All of them. What the hell is this? What's going on here, anyway?"

Sally followed Tony out of the jeep and she was unable to keep her eyes from the crumpled figure of Hardin as she passed. Tony held his arm around her and he looked straight ahead.

Duke was back by the plane by this time and Gerald jerked at the sleeve of his jacket.

"Get in and check that plane," he said. "If this bastard has done anything to it, I'll cut his heart out—if he isn't dead already. And from now on don't leave the seat of that plane. Anything else happens to it and you're elected. Right off, you're elected."

George was back under the light and he slowly swung the spot around the room. When it rested on Fullbright, huddled in the corner, he yelled across at him.

"Come on," he said, "come on, over here with the rest of them. We've been too nice to you people and you don't want it that way. So we'll change it. All of you now, over here."

"He shot that man down in cold blood," Socks suddenly spoke up, his voice unbelieving. "Shot him right down in cold blood."

"Shut up," George said. "Shut up or you'll get it next. You're overdue anyway."

Socks stared at him for a moment, his face bare of expression. Then he slowly moved to the table and slumped into a seat.

Gerald had returned to the group and now he came up to Tony and jabbed him in the ribs.

"Go over and get the old man," he said. "That drunken doctor. Get him off that couch and on his feet. I want him to look at that bum, want to find out if he can talk. He's got some explaining to do."

He turned to face the others.

"The rest of you pull up around this table. All of you. Find seats and sit down. Nobody's going to wander around from now on. You're all staying right here."

Gerald walked back to the plane and for several minutes spoke with Duke. He didn't look down at Hardin, who still lay on the ground under the opened door of the cockpit.

"Plane's O.K., George," he said when he returned. "I don't know what he was up to, but if the doc gets him on his feet, I'm damned sure going to find out."

4

It was well past six now and there were faint traces of daylight coming through the narrow windows of the building. The sounds of the storm had abated somewhat but the wind still whistled and roared outside and they could hear the rumble as driftwood and rubbish was tossed against the concrete sides of the building.

The great tidal wave had struck somewhere around five o'clock, raising the water level on the floor several inches, but it had drained off and now there was nothing but the thin coating of sand and mud awash on the concrete,

Phil Hardin lay on a cot next to the table under the light. There was a makeshift bandage around his head, soaked red with blood. His eyes were closed. Dr. Martins sat on a chair beside the cot and held his wrist. After a moment or so he looked up.

"No pulse," he said. "He's gone."

The old man's voice was firm, but his hands were shaking badly, and his face was pale and drawn.

"I must lie down," he said. "I'm not feeling ..."

Gerald stood next to the doctor and his foot suddenly kicked the half opened black bag. It turned over and several small bottles and vials rolled on the concrete floor.

"You're going to feel a lot worse before we're through here," he said. "You told me you had something in that bag for me; told me a God-damned lie."

"I thought you meant sleeping pills," Dr. Martins said. "I thought ..."

"You thought! You're a damned liar. You knew what I wanted." He raised his hand in a threatening gesture, but the doctor didn't move, merely stared at him coldly.

Gerald hesitated and then shrugged and turned and moved off. "We're not through here yet," he mumbled.

Dr. Martins moved away from Hardin and dropped to a second cot a few feet further from the table. He stretched out flat and closed his eyes. Next to him, Helen and Sally sat on a third camp cot. Helen's eyes were closed and she looked as though she were asleep, but she was sitting absolutely erect, supported by her hands which were tightly grasping the edges of the cot at her sides.

Sally started to get up as her father lay down but Gerald, sitting at the table, quickly spoke.

"Sit down, sister," he said. "He don't need you. All he needs is time to get over his hangover."

George looked up from the table, his eyes red and angry.

"Everyone stay sat," he said. "This thing is dying down now and you won't have too much longer to wait. Go over and see what that damned pilot is able to pick up on the radio, Gerald."

Nick and Flack both looked up as Gerald left the circle. Neither Socks nor Tony, however; raised their eyes. Socks sat with his head on his arms at the table and appeared to have fallen asleep. Tony merely sat, staring into space.

Gerald had to pass in front of Fullbright, where the old man sat on the fourth cot, in order to get to the plane. He was brushing by him when he felt the man's hand pull gently at the edge of his jacket.

Richard Fullbright had finally made up his mind—finally reached the decision after hours of thinking about it. He knew that time was running out, knew that he would have to make his move. And so he reached up and as Gerald passed by, he pulled gently at the youth's coat.

Gerald turned, but was unable to hear the words which must be coming from the narrow, white-lipped mouth. He hesitated and then, with a look of irritation, leaned down.

"I want to talk to you," Fullbright said. "I must talk to you."

"Talk," Gerald said. "Go on, spit it out."

"Alone," Fullbright said. "Away from the others."

Gerald had difficulty making out the words, and leaned closer.

"Come on," he said. "Come on, spit it out. What the hell's on your mind?"

Fullbright looked around worriedly and then raised his voice.

"I must talk to you alone," he said. "It's important. Very important."

"What's important about it?"

"A matter of money," Fullbright said. "A matter of twenty-five thousand dollars."

For a moment more Gerald hesitated and then he turned to face George.

"This one wants to talk to me alone," he said.

George looked back blandly and called out his answer.

"Well, go ahead and let him talk. But see what's coming over that radio."

"Come on," Gerald said. "Come on."

Fullbright got up, still clutching the attaché case.

"You need that to talk?" Gerald said.

"Yes."

Duke told Gerald what he knew.

"The reception is bad," he said. "Inside the building like this, the reception—"

"Just give it to me," Gerald said. "Never mind the lecture on electronics."

"Well, she's going out as fast as it came in. The peak of the storm was around four this morning. Hit all the way from Key West up to Tameralda. Terrific damage as near as they know."

"The hell with the damage," Gerald said. "Just give me the facts. When is it going to be over? When can we leave?"

"I can't tell for sure. The worst is over already. But there's still plenty of wind. It should die down within another three or four hours. The coast guard hopes to get helicopters in by this afternoon."

"That means—"

"That means that if we can get the plane out of here, and that if we can clear a spot on the beach and it hasn't been wiped out, we might be able to get away sometime after twelve o'clock, if the wind does die down."

"O.K." Gerald said. "Stay with it. Keep the set turned on and stay with it." He turned to Fullbright. "Stay here," he said, "I want to give George the news. I'll be back."

5

Helen slipped off the cot and edged over until she was next to Nick. She spoke to him in a quick desperate voice as Gerald and George leaned close to each other and talked.

"Now," she said. "Now, Nick. Make a run for it. If they see you, I'll do something to distract them. This is your chance, honey. You've got to take it."

"No," he said. "No, I'm staying."

She looked at him and her eyes pleaded desperately. "Please," she begged, "Please ..."

He again shook his head, his eyes tired but determined. "I'm staying," he said. "Whatever happens, I'm staying. I saw what they did to Hardin. For nothing. No, these men are crazy. They're killers and they're crazy. I don't know what they are going to do, but I'm not running. I'm staying right here with you."

Once more she started to plead with him but looking into his face, she saw the determination and realized there was nothing she could say. Nothing she could do. Nick Cosmos would stay there, at her side, no matter what.

She lowered her eyes then and only lifted them a moment later to watch as Gerald once more left the group and walked over toward the plane.

"Come on," Gerald said, taking Fullbright by the arm. "Over in the jeep. We can talk there. And you can tell me what you got to tell me. Tell me about the twenty-five thousand dollars."

Richard Fullbright waited until they were seated beside each other in the jeep. It was no longer necessary to yell to make himself heard and for this he was glad. The storm was dying down fast and he knew that he would have little time. He didn't want to waste it; wanted to make every minute count. Every word count.

"I know why you came," he said. "You and your friend."

Gerald turned quickly and stared at him, the muscles of his mouth tightening.

"I know," he said and he tried to make it sound casual, to keep the fear and the worry out of his voice. "Yes, I know that Knocky sent you. Knocky and Manny and Sol."

"You know who sent us?"

Fullbright almost smiled. There was no question about it; none at all. The man was interested; probably amazed at his, Fullbright's, calmness, at his seeming indifference.

"Knocky and Manny and Sol," he repeated. "Who was it made the arrangements, by the way? Was it Knocky? It must have been."

"You're telling me," Gerald said in a neutral, flat voice. "Don't ask, just tell."

"What were they going to pay you—five thousand? Or were they going to be real big and give you ten for the job?"

"I said don't ask, tell." Gerald's voice was suddenly ugly and Fullbright knew at once that he was beginning to overplay it. He spoke up quickly.

"Whatever it is they offered," he said, "it's peanuts. But then the boys always were a bit cheap. You should do business with a man who doesn't believe in being cheap."

"We should?" Gerald said.

"Right. A man like me, for instance," Fullbright said. "That's why I have a proposition for you."

Once more, Gerald looked at him curiously.

"You have a proposition? What is it?"

"Simply this," Fullbright said. "Instead of making five grand, or maybe ten, and having to do a job, I'm offering you twenty-five thousand, twenty-five thousand dollars in hard cash, not to do the job."

"You are offering us twenty-five thousand?"

Fullbright could see the way the man's mind was working. He knew the type, knew the mentality of a paid killer. It was simply a matter of price, the right price.

"I'm not talking blue sky," he said. "Look—see this." He reached down and shot the latch on the attaché case, opened it so that his companion could see the neat stacks of green bills.

"This is money—hard cash. Not promises. Cash. You boys will be leaving here in a short while. You have a plane and a pilot. There's no reason you have to go back to Miami, have to go back north. You can take twenty-five thousand dollars of this money and go just about any place you like."

"We can?"

"Yes. Don't you see, if you do what you came down here to do, it will be impossible for you ever to go back anyway. Too many people know you have been here. Too many people have seen you. You'll have to run anyway."

Gerald nodded slowly.

"And this thing we came to do," he said slowly. "If we do it we will have to run. So, suppose we do it and take your money anyway and run?"

Fullbright almost smiled.

"Just the point," he said. "Why not just don't do it? And instead of stealing the money and running, I'm giving it to you. I'm giving it to you of my own free will so that you won't have to do what you were told to do. You won't have to do anything. Just accept the money which I am offering you as a free gift. And then have the pilot fly you into Cuba or Puerto Rico or even back to Miami if you like."

"And this Knocky and Manny and Sol," Gerald said after a long minute. "Wouldn't they be just a little annoyed about that? Wouldn't they be just a little upset?"

"Not if you give them back the money they paid you," Fullbright said quickly. "See, make it an extra ten. Twenty-five for you boys to cut up between yourselves and the ten to give back to them so they won't be upset. You can tell them about the hurricane—say it was impossible to reach Arroyos."

Gerald nodded slowly, his face thoughtful.

"Sit here," he said. "I want to talk to George."

He climbed out of the jeep and left and Fullbright breathed a long sigh of relief. It was in the bag. He'd been lucky. The man had understood and he'd make his partner understand. And he'd been satisfied with thirty-five thousand.

Quickly, while he was still alone, he reopened the briefcase and took out four of the neatly banded packets. He knew by the feel what they were. Three of them contained ten thousand dollars each and the other held five thousand.

He was holding them on his lap when George walked to the jeep. George didn't get in and sit down but merely stood next to it.

"Gerald says you want to give us some money," he said.

Without speaking, Fullbright held out the cash.

George took it and shoved it into his pocket without as much as looking at it. And then, carefully and slowly he reached for the snub-nosed gun.

Fullbright felt the blood leave his face and for a moment he was unable to find his voice. His eyes opened wide and he struggled.

"Hand me the bag you got there," George said.

"Listen. Please, for God's sake listen," Fullbright said. "You can't—"

"I said hand me that briefcase."

Fullbright slowly lifted the attaché case and held it out. His voice suddenly went all to pieces as he stuttered out the quick words.

"There's more," he said. "More—lots more. As soon as this is over, as soon as I can get into Miami and get to my bank ..."

He stopped, and seeing the other man's cold, unblinking eyes staring at him, froze suddenly in his fear.

"You're giving this to us because you like us, aren't you?" George said in a soft slurring voice.

"I'm ... I'm ..."

"You talk too much," George said. "Even for a guy as generous as you are, you talk too much. Now get out of that jeep and get back over there with the rest of them. Get over and shut up."

Chapter Eleven

1

No hurricane is completely and totally predictable but it was a singular characteristic of Hurricane Bettina that it changed its course so unexpectedly and so radically. It was a second characteristic of that particular storm that even while it was being carefully charted, it behaved in an erratic and peculiar fashion. Once having reached its peak in velocity and speed of travel, it swept across its chosen path with fantastic rapidity and having created its havoc and destruction, passed on and died out in the areas over which it created tragedy and disaster with an almost phenomenal suddenness.

By noon of Wednesday morning, had one been able to blind oneself to the aftermath of the hurricane, it would have been impossible to believe that so great a disaster had ever occurred. The great winds had died down to ten or twelve miles an hour and there was a bright sun in the clean, cloudless sky. It was a beautiful tropical day, a trifle chilly for the time of year, but aside from this, as lovely as one could wish. The only thing which marred it, so far as the middle keys were concerned, was the devastating wreckage in the small towns and settlements where houses and trees had been either swept away or piled up in great heaps of rubble.

2

It wasn't until the fat man told Socks to see that the wives of the fishermen and their children were locked in the back room where they had been sitting out the storm that they realized the time had come. That was at ten o'clock.

At ten-fifteen the small door at the side of the temporary hangar was opened a slit and Gerald slipped out. The sun was just beginning to show and the wind was still high, but he was able to fight his way through the tangled debris and circle the warehouse.

To the west the tidal wave which had accompanied the storm had cut a deep gulley through the beach, which was still filled with water. But the rain itself had stopped and the tide was rapidly receding.

He fought his way to the end of the building and saw that the wharves had been carried away but that the beach off to the east, where the plane had originally landed, was still intact. It was, however, cluttered with driftwood.

In front of the great doors through which they had dragged the plane was more driftwood and part of the remains of the wharves themselves. He returned to the interior of the building and spoke for several minutes with George.

"All right," he said, following their whispered consultation, "All right. I want everyone up. Except the women. You two—" he looked over at Helen and Sally—"you two get some coffee going on that stove. And make up some kind of breakfast. Then we're all going outside."

Dr. Martins stood up, looking very old and feeble.

"Something should be done," he said, pointing to the cot on which Phil Hardin's body lay, "something should be done about him."

"The hell with him," Gerald said. "He's dead. But you others, you and you and you—" he pointed to one of them after the other, to Socks and Tony and Flack and Nick—"you are all coming outside with me. We got a job to do. We're going to clear the junk away from in front of the doors and then we are all going down to the beach and start clearing that. We're going to make a runway so we can get this plane off."

Duke Flager strolled over from the plane.

"Ought to have a long rope and a block and tackle," he said. "Then we can use the jeep here. It will make it easier."

"Right," Gerald said. He turned to Socks. "You got it?" he asked.

"There's a rope in the back room," he said.

"Go with George and get it," Gerald said. "Get whatever we're going to need."

Within a half an hour they had eaten and started the work. Dr. Martins, Richard Fullbright and the two women stayed inside and George was with them, sitting at the table with his eyes half closed. But he didn't sleep. Each time one of them moved, his heavy lids lifted like automatic shutters and his cold, expressionless eyes would stare out at them. He smoked incessantly, coughing and spitting, but he didn't move.

It wasn't until they heard the engines of an airplane somewhere off in the distance that he went to the door and looked out. He called something and a few minutes later again went to the door.

The wind had been blowing a gale when they'd opened one of the doors in order to get the jeep out, but by noon, when once more the door was opened and the jeep returned, accompanied by the men, it had died down to merely a brisk blow.

Socks, Nick, Flack and Tony trooped in first and the jeep followed. Duke was driving it and next to him sat Gerald. He held the gun loosely in his lap. All of them looked exhausted.

George closed the door after them.

Instinctively they went to the group who had been left in the building and Helen reached for the coffee pot steaming on the stove.

Duke and his two passengers huddled a few feet off.

"What was that plane I heard?" George asked. He looked at Gerald and the other man shrugged.

"Weather plane out of Miami, probably," Duke said. "Making a spot check."

George nodded. "That runway all set?"

"The runway's set," Duke said. "But we ought to wait a little longer. There's still plenty of wind and I'll have to take off against a cross current."

"Wait how long?"

"Half an hour, maybe an hour."

George looked over at his partner, who nodded.

"Make it half an hour," George said. He looked down at the watch on his chubby hairless wrist. "Exactly one half hour. Twelve-thirty on the button. Then we take the plane out."

3

He could hear the faint echo of a child's crying somewhere in the back of the building and somehow or another the thin, high whine almost drove him crazy. God damn him, he thought, why can't he stop? What has he got to cry about?

Tilden Flack had never cared for children and it infuriated him now that the mere sound of a child's cry should bother him, should distract him when there was so much he had to think about. And there was almost no time in which to think.

He wished he knew exactly what the clock read, wished he knew how much of that vital half hour had passed. If he could only think of a plan, think of something he could do. But there was nothing, nothing at all but to sit there and wait.

He tried to force his mind to think of those others with him, of Socks and Nick and Doc Martins and Fullbright. Tried to reason out that it must be one of them. That it couldn't be he, Flack, who'd be elected.

The terrible part was in knowing why they had waited this long. If it were Doc or Fullbright, there was no reason to wait. Neither was of any use in getting the plane out, or clearing the runway.

Just sitting here in the chair and looking at George and Gerald as they stood a few yards away, each holding a gun in his hand and just standing there, was enough to drive a man crazy.

It had taken a physical effort to stay still, not to try and run. But running would be the very worst thing he could do. He must wait for exactly the right moment. He knew that if he moved, made any effort to escape, they'd shoot him down like a dog. And there was always that one possible chance that he wasn't the intended victim. Always a possible chance.

A couple of feet away, Helen sat once more on the edge of a camp cot and her husband sat beside her, holding one of her cold hands. They didn't speak. No one spoke. Helen was just as glad. She didn't want to talk. Didn't want Nick to hear her voice for fear he would know what she was planning to do.

She'd made up her mind.

Any minute now the two killers would make their move. They'd suddenly tell everyone to stand up and they would probably line them up against the wall and then the guns would spurt leaden death and Nick would crumple and fall and Paul, the man who had owned her up in Miami, would have had his revenge. Nick would die and it would be because he had loved her and been good to her.

She knew now that there was nothing she could do to save him and nothing he could do to save himself. But there was one thing she could do. She could die with him.

The minute those guns were lifted, she knew exactly what she was going to do. She was going to throw herself in front of him and at least they would take it together. They'd go out together. She and Nick.

It was funny; she wanted to cry, wanted to break down and let the tears come. But she had no tears and so she just sat there, holding Nick's hand, and waited. She knew how much time there was left. There was no time.

Richard Fullbright was no longer frightened, no longer felt any sensation except complete exhaustion and complete defeat.

He'd realized from the very moment that George, the fat one, had rudely jerked the attaché case out of his hand. George and that other one were just cheap killers as he'd known all along. Paid assassins. But once more he'd overestimated. He'd assumed that they'd listen to reason; that they'd be practical about it. He should have known better.

They would behave the way all of their kind behaved. Without imagination and without sense. They didn't have the brains to understand that killing him would benefit them nothing. They only knew that they'd been ordered to do a job and they were going to do it. And because they were cheap crooks and murderers, they had no compunction about taking his money and going right ahead with their plans.

Fullbright didn't even want to think about them. They were nothing, less than nothing. Merely the mechanical means to an end. He didn't want to think about Knocky and Manny and Sol, either. The real villain was fate. The real villain was his own essential stupidity. He should have known all along that there was no way of beating the system. No one ever really beat the system.

Well, at least it would soon be over. He was an old, tired and beaten man and he'd made his pitch and it hadn't worked. He almost looked forward to this last act. He only hoped that there would be no pain. He didn't believe he could stand much more pain. But even that wouldn't matter, of course. The thing was now in the hands of God.

It was the first time that Richard Fullbright had thought of God in a good many years.

Doctor Martins was glad about one thing. He was sober, cold, stone sober. He wanted to be sober when it happened. He wasn't sure, wasn't at all sure. But he'd had this peculiar sense of impending tragedy for hours now and he knew something terrible was about to happen.

He could guess, but guessing was really no good at all. Guessing would get him nowhere. The thing to do was to concentrate on what he knew, not on guesswork.

He was glad he'd spoken to Sarah.

"Stay with Tony," he'd said. "If anything happens, stay close to him. Nothing will happen to him, nothing ever happens to men like him. God protects the Tonys. And if something should happen to me ..."

"Nothing will happen to you, Dad." She'd quickly interrupted him. "Nothing."

"Listen to me, Sarah," he said. "Listen to me. Do what I tell you to do. Just for now. Just until this is over and done with. And then, later on, I want you to do whatever you like. Don't take my advice ever again, don't take anyone's advice. Do the things you want to do and live your life the way you want to live it. But now ..."

She'd reached up and put her arms around him and held him and he'd had to stop talking because they were watching and he didn't want to irritate them.

But he'd had the sense of disaster and he knew. He thought back to the past, to the things he had done, and he knew. It would be him or it could be one of the others, but the main thing was that Sarah would be all right. No one would harm her.

Alone of all the people in that vast room, only Socks Schroeder had no fear, no sense of expectancy. The sole emotion which crowded his mind was one of fury. It was a double-barreled emotion.

First there were those two gangsters. They'd been ordering him around, goading him, all night. He hated them, hated everything they represented. And he hated himself for letting the guns in their hands cow and bulldoze him. Without those guns he could have taken them in his hands and broken them in two. Torn them limb from limb. They were vicious animals, thieves and killers.

He remembered the way they had shot Phil Hardin down in cold blood and his lips whitened and the muscles in his great arms and body tightened and strained. They were men like those others up north who had tried to bribe and corrupt him. And he had to stand here, powerless.

It wasn't that he was afraid. It wasn't that he wouldn't be willing to risk being shot. But he had enough sense to know that he'd have no chance. They kept well away from him and never gave him the opportunity to get his hands on them. One of them was always at a distance and he knew that before he could do anything, the leaden bullets would find his body and stop him.

That alone was enough to drive him crazy. But there had to be this other thing.

Socks knew now at last that Sally was lost. He couldn't tell just how he knew, but he did. She'd been his and now she was lost to him. In spite of what they'd had together, she was gone. The strange part of it was that he no longer blamed that artist fellow. Somehow or other he had come to realize the truth. It wasn't the artist, much as Socks despised and hated him. It was Sally herself. Sally actually preferred the other man, who was really no man at all.

It was an unsolvable situation and thinking about it led him nowhere. It was better to think of those other two, the two who were just about to get into the plane and take off.

He wasn't finished yet; no, it wasn't over yet. There still might be some slip, some opportunity to get his hands on them. He knew them for what they were and he hated them and if the chance developed, they'd see what was what.

He wasn't afraid and couldn't understand the fear he detected in the others. No one had to be afraid of criminals. You only had to be honest and decent and wait your chance.

4

Unconsciously Duke Flager's eye went to the clock on the dashboard, as it invariably and automatically always did when he was checking the broadcast over the radio set. The hands of the clock pointed to exactly twelve-thirty, but the fact failed to register in his mind. He leaned back on the seat of the Cessna and for a moment merely sat there, a look of utter and complete surprise on his normally bland, expressionless face. And then slowly his mouth opened in a circle and he released a low whistle.

He said, "Well, I'll be God-damned!"

He removed the ear phones and slowly moved to the edge of the seat. He was reaching for the door of the plane and had his hand on the latch when the door swung open.

"O.K., pilot," Gerald said, "It's time to move."

For a moment Duke looked at him with unseeing eyes.

"We're ready," Gerald said. "What the hell's the matter with you?"

Duke shook his head as though to clear it. "Why—"

"Listen, get on the ball, brother," Gerald said. "It's time we got going. I want you to stay in the plane. I'm going to have the jeep pull up in front of you and we'll tie a rope on and pull you out. Pull you down to the beach and then George and I are climbing in and we're taking off. You got everything set?"

Duke nodded. "Everything's set," he said.

"Be sure it is. I don't want any trouble from you. And don't warm up the motor until we get the plane on the beach."

Duke nodded again and he pulled the door closed as Gerald stepped back. Once more he opened his mouth, the words coming out just under his breath. And once more he said the same thing.

"Well, I'll be God-damned!"

5

They stood there, that odd-looking pair, the tall one in his wide gray Stetson, white Dacron suit (no longer neat) and his high-heeled cowboy boots. The sheer silk shirt was sweated now and the string black tie even stringier. His boyish face lean and angular, dark expressionless eyes and fine jawline; stomach flat beneath the ornate buckle.

The other one was actually the taller but looked squat because of his great girth. A man somewhere between thirty and fifty. Heavy-rimmed glasses unable to hide the deep black circles under his eyes. The Semitic face and the blue chin needing a shave more than ever. Brown shoes no longer polished, but the nails on the short fingers of the babyish hands still retaining their beautiful manicure.

They stood there and each held a gun in his hand and they were silhouetted by the sun streaming in through the wide open doors of the warehouse.

In front of them, close together in an even line were the others. All but Phil Hardin who still lay dead on the cot behind the plane.

First Tony Mason and next to him Sally. Doc Martins, half supporting Richard Fullbright. Nick and Helen Cosmos and then Flack. At the end of the line Socks Schroeder.

Not more than ten yards separated the pair from the others.

Just in back of them Duke, seated in the cockpit of the plane, was watching through the plexiglass, fascinated. It was George who spoke.

"Slowly," he said, "in exactly the order you are now. Over against the wall."

He raised the point of his gun a fraction of an inch, indicating the high cement wall at the south of the room.

"Just as you are and slowly," he repeated. He stepped forward as they began to move, holding out an arm and putting it in front of Tony. "Except you," he said.

Sally stopped and her face paled.

"Keep moving, sister," George said. "You." He took Tony by the arm. "You get in the jeep. Swing it around and back it up in front of the plane. Stop about fifteen feet in front of it, by the end of the tow rope. I'll tie it on."

Out of the corner of his eye Tony saw Gerald move slightly to the left as he climbed into the jeep. He saw the others, standing there against the concrete wall.

He turned the key and started the engine and it roared to life and he quickly throttled it down and then rolled forward, cutting the wheel slightly so as to pull up on a line with the plane and well in front of it.

Pushing in the clutch, he waited for the jeep to come to a full stop. He looked into the rear vision mirror and saw that George had stepped directly behind him, between the jeep and the plane. He put the jeep into reverse.

George had shoved the gun into his side jacket pocket and was stooping to pick up the end of the rope.

Once more, just before releasing the clutch to move the jeep back to the plane, he looked off to the side.

Gerald, looking for all the world like some figure in a grade B Western, was standing there straddle-legged, the gun held almost casually, facing the people who stood against the wall. His head was half turned as he also tried to keep one eye on the jeep.

Tony shoved down with his right foot.

The jeep leaped like something alive, hurtling backward.

George's heavy, misshappen body was crushed into the front of the Cessna before he had a chance to let out more than one single, high-pitched scream.

He was conscious of the gunfire, conscious of the shattering glass of the windshield. He knew that the other one, the tall thin boy in the cowboy suit was standing there almost dead in front of him and firing. He knew that the lead was smashing into the jeep and into his own body.

With a deliberate, agonizing slowness, so as not to stall the engine, he again shifted. And then once more the jeep was driving forward, away from the wrecked plane.

He caught up with the flying figure in the wide gray Stetson and the white Dacron suit on the hard concrete pan, just beyond the doors of the warehouse. He could feel the shock as the wide steel front bumper of the car hit the man's back and shattered his spine.

And then he knew nothing.

Chapter Twelve

1

Duke Flager finished inspecting the damage to the front of the Cessna and sadly shook his head. He turned and walked back into the warehouse and over to the silent group which stood around the figure lying on the cot.

Dr. Martins looked up as the pilot approached.

"How is he, doc?"

For a moment the doctor's tired eyes looked down at his patient and then he spoke in his slow, modulated voice.

"Considering everything, fine," he said. "For a man with a bullet in his right shoulder, a man who's been all cut up by flying glass and a man who was shot at from close range at least six or seven times, he's fine. He has concussion, probably from banging his head on the windshield and he is still unconscious. But that's to be expected. He'll live."

Once more he looked down at the figure on the couch.

"Don't paw him, Sarah," he said to his daughter as she knelt holding tight to Tony Mason's hand. "He's still a pretty sick boy, even if he is going to be all right."

"And the others?" Duke asked. "Those two out there."

Dr. Martins shrugged. "Both dead," he said.

Socks Schroeder elbowed his way through the others.

"And a damned good thing," he said. "A damned good thing. If they weren't, by now one of us would be dead."

"Yes," Flack said, "one of us. But which one? That's the question. Which one?"

Duke shook his head.

"No one," he said. "No one, or, that is to say, no one unless you did something foolish, like Hardin did, and tried to stop them."

They stared at him for a moment, unbelievingly, and Socks again spoke up, his voice indignant.

"You're crazy," he said. "Crazy. They were killers and they came here to kill."

"Right," Flack said. "They came to kill. To kill one of us. Otherwise, why Arroyos? Why did they come to—"

Once more Duke interrupted.

"Why Arroyos?" he repeated. "Why Arroyos? Well, I guess in a sense, they came to Arroyos for the same reason most of you came here. Because they were running away. Of course I don't know what you people are running away from and to tell you the truth, when the engine trouble and the storm brought me down here, I didn't know what they were running away from. I didn't know much of anything about them. But just before we were getting ready to take off, as I was getting the plane ready shortly after noontime, I got a broadcast out of Miami. A news broadcast."

He had their attention now, their full attention, and he hesitated a moment, as though to savor the drama of the situation. Then he continued.

"Yes," he said, "I got the broadcast. And I learned who they were and what they were. Until then they were merely two men who'd chartered my plane to take them to Cuba, get them out of the country. But the broadcast cleared up several things. The police put it on the air. The young one was named Gerald Claudio and the other was George Banner. And they were killers all right, killers on the run. Two days ago they shot down a man named Paul something or other. He was some sort of racketeer, or gambler and he was mixed up in drugs and white slavery. They killed him and they were running away. Arroyos was just an accidental stopover in their flight. Like, I guess, it's a temporary stopover for all of us."

For a moment there was complete silence, and then suddenly a woman sobbed.

Nick Cosmos put his arm around his wife and slowly led her away from the others.

Duke slowly shook a cigarette out of a crumpled pack.

"In a way," he said, "they're lucky. They can stop running now. They're dead. They've found their sanctuary in Arroyos."

THE END

OPERATION–MURDER
- - - - - - -
Lionel White

Chapter One

They reached the summit some time just before daybreak, and a thin, powdery snow had fallen, covering the macadam surface of the highway and making it treacherous and almost impassable.

The driver hesitated momentarily, then shrugged and downshifted until the gears clashed into low. Again the great blue and silver bus was moving on the downgrade, following the tortuous curves and hairpin bends of the road as it dropped into the valley where the town nestled—nestled warm and alive and vulnerable under the shadows of the crystalline crags of the surrounding ranges that stretched westward to the Continental Divide.

She knew that it was bitter cold outside and she shivered slightly and edged away from the mist-fogged window at her right-hand side. She had the entire seat to herself, for which she was glad. In fact, with the exception of the driver and the two others, she had the entire bus to herself. Only those with urgent business braved the treacherous weather and high altitudes of this section of the Rockies so deep in winter.

The narrow, twisting road reached on endlessly as they wound their way down between canyons of tall spruce and fir; down past the snow line. She knew they were losing altitude with each turn of the great, winter-ribbed tires. There was an odd sensation somewhere deep in the air passages behind her ears as the pressure within her sought release and after a while the sound of the engine changed and she barely heard it.

The driver exercised extreme caution and once or twice she could feel the wheels slip and lose traction momentarily as the great machine lurched off the crown of the road. But he was an excellent driver and he always swiftly regained control so that at last, just as the first streaks of daylight came, she was able to see the town far ahead and below. It didn't look at all like those small villages and hamlets in the Adirondacks which she had known. It had none of the picture postcard qualities which had always endeared them to her.

Four or five scattered street lights could be seen and even as she watched, a window in first one house and then another would open a yellow eye as early risers began a new day.

It was a place of human habitation, all right, a sanctuary in these grim, forbidding and endless ranges. But somehow it had the quality of rawness; the sterility of a cardboard movie set, as though it were not designed to be lived in but only to be observed and then discarded. In a sense that was what the town did represent for her.

Half a mile from the town she again lost sight of it as the bus picked up speed and dipped into a hollow. And then, before she knew it, they had arrived and the bus was pulling up in front of the all-night gas station and luncheonette on the main street of the hamlet.

The driver set his emergency brake, but didn't cut his ignition. He stood up slowly and with one gloved hand tipped the peaked cap back on his head and stretched widely and yawned. He turned to where she sat, two seats back and to the right of the aisle. "This is it, miss," he said.

He smiled, exposing a double row of very even, very white teeth. "You're in luck, restaurant's just opening. Rest of the town's still asleep. Not that it matters much," he went on. "It's asleep in midday, too."

He reached for the lever which jackknifed the front door open.

The sailor who lay stretched across the wide back seat stirred in his sleep and muttered something and then coughed. The other one, the old man in the sheep-lined jacket and wide-brimmed Stetson, sitting opposite, suddenly opened his eyes and stared without turning his head. He cleared his throat and took out an old-fashioned silver watch and looked at it under the turned-up lights.

She reached up for the cloth coat hanging from the hook by the window and, edging into the aisle, put her arms into its sleeves and knotted the belt around her slender waist. She found her overnight bag and started for the door. The driver was standing outside, waiting, his breath making a vapor pattern in the cold air. He held out a hand to help her down the steep double step.

She smiled her thanks, the smile magically erasing the tired lines of sleeplessness from her face, nodded and then turned and walked across the ice-covered concrete apron and entered the luncheonette. The driver reclosed the door, all but a crack, and followed her into the cheerful neon brightness of the room. He went at once to the counter and the stout, dark-haired woman pouring a pitcher of steaming water into the coffee urn looked over her shoulder at him and smiled.

"Some night."

"Some night is right," he said. "Make it black, and a couple of sugar doughnuts with it."

The waitress nodded. She replaced the top of the urn and reached for a thick white cup and filled it and put it in front of him. She put two doughnuts on a saucer and placed it beside the coffee. Then she walked over to where the girl had taken a seat halfway down the counter and looked at her inquiringly....

It wasn't five minutes later, while the girl was still waiting for her own coffee to cool enough to swallow, that she heard the sound of the bus as the driver gunned the motor. In another moment there was a subdued roar and he threw the machine into gear and pulled out into the road.

There was a brass-rimmed clock on the wall over the cash register and she glanced at it from time to time. At seven o'clock, while she was still waiting for the bacon and eggs which she had ordered, she suddenly smiled. In exactly one more hour, she thought. One more hour and he'll be here. Here at last. And we'll be together from now on.

She tossed a strand of straw-colored hair out of her eye and then, almost surreptitiously, looked down to where the fingers of her left hand were spread on the green linoleum counter. It was still there, that thin, plain gold band, where he had placed it on her third finger just ten days ago. It was still there, a symbol of love and hope and faithfulness. Just as his last words were still in her mind.

"Darling, I love you. Just trust me and believe in me. It won't be long. Ten days, that's all, just ten days. And then I'll meet you there, in Twin Valley, and we'll go on up to the cabin and we'll have our honeymoon and the honeymoon will last forever."

Thinking of the words, she thought of Frank Scudder, the man she had married for better or for worse. Time hung suspended as, motionless and with her wide gray-blue eyes blindly staring at the fly-specked mirror behind the counter, she sat there and sought to recapture from her memory her picture of him.

Frank—tall, slender, as dark as she was fair. Frank with his wide shoulders and narrow, athlete's hips, his strong square hands. The angular face almost too thin and the large, heavily lashed eyes. The high cheekbones with their twin spots of color; the spots of color which were the only indication of the thing that was wrong with Frank.

Some time later she again looked up at the clock and was amazed to see that half an hour had passed and the best part of her breakfast was still on the plate in front of her.

She felt the sudden draft as the outer door was opened and in spite of herself, she turned quickly on the stool so that she could see who entered. At once a disappointed look clouded her eyes. She realized, of course, that she still had half an hour to go.

She felt nervous, and somewhere, in the very back of her mind, was this odd little thread of worry, the feeling that something wasn't quite right—that eight o'clock would come and she'd still be here waiting.

The voice cut into her thoughts. "Ma'am," he said, "ma'am, I hate to have to tell you, but you're sitting here with your elbow in your eggs."

For a full ten seconds she stared up into the friendly, amused gray eyes, shaded by the wide-brimmed hat of a state trooper, and then quickly she looked down. She had been sitting at the counter, daydreaming, her left elbow neatly resting in the yellow yolk of the partly eaten egg on her plate. She blushed, stood up and reached for a paper napkin.

The dark-haired waitress came over, smiling, and held out a damp rag. She began to wipe her sleeve furiously. The trooper turned away and shed a fleece-lined leather jacket, hanging it on a clothes tree, and then removed a heavy sweater and his hat, putting them on the chair between himself and the girl. He loosened the extra belt which held his gun, but didn't remove it.

"Just getting off, Clarke?" the waitress asked, bringing hot coffee without waiting for an order.

"Getting off," he said, "and going right back on."

"You look like you already had enough for one stretch," the woman said. "Something going on?"

He lifted the steaming coffee and, blowing across the top of the cup but carefully keeping it away from his lips, he said, "Plenty's been going on. Surprised you didn't get it on the radio."

"Radio's busted. What's—"

"Hell broke loose over at Ogdenville," the trooper said. He frowned. "Bank robbery sometime last night. A town deputy spotted them while they were finishing the job. They shot him."

"What—"

"That's about all we know just yet," the trooper said. "Except the deputy isn't likely to live and the gang made a clean getaway. May be headed this way."

He finally took a chance that the coffee wouldn't scald his lips as the waitress poured pancake batter on the iron grill.

The Indian came at ten minutes after nine.

Tina Scudder would never have taken him for an Indian if it hadn't been Millie, the waitress, with whom she had by this time reached a certain degree of intimacy as a result of an incident that had occurred shortly after eight-thirty.

It had been too silly for words: Tina Bennet Scudder, trained nurse, experienced mountain climber and skier, suddenly slumped to the red-checkered linoleum floor of the luncheonette in a faint.

The trooper had long ago left, hurrying out to relieve one of his fellow officers who had been setting up a roadblock by the pass; a half dozen or so breakfast patrons had come and gone, and she and the waitress were again alone in the place when it happened. One moment and she'd been there, slender hands nervously tearing at a pack of matches and the next thing she knew the dizziness had overcome her and she'd slipped off the edge of the round stool and fallen to the floor. She couldn't have been out for more than a minute or two at the most and fortunately, she hadn't hurt herself when she'd fallen.

"The altitude," Millie said. "You aren't used to it up here. We're over eight thousand feet up, you know." While she'd talked, she had helped Tina to one of the booths and, miraculously, had conjured up a water glass half-filled with brandy which burned her throat as she choked it down.

"This room's too hot, anyway," the woman continued, patting Tina's hand and leaning over and looking into her face with worried, motherly eyes. "Are you waiting for someone, honey? Is there anyone I can send for?"

But the brandy had already reached her stomach and the warm glow it made brought her back to normal and she was quick to speak. "I'm all right," she said. "Just that I guess that long bus ride and all and—"

"Well you just sit here and take it easy. I'm going to get you another cup of good hot coffee and maybe you'd better loosen that jacket. This altitude, you know."

Tina nodded. "Yes," she said. "Yes, I guess I'm not quite used to it."

Millie had already turned and started for the counter and Tina's eyes followed her heaving, bulging figure for a second, then once more went to the clock. He was already three quarters of an hour late. She knew that something must have happened. He had been so very definite about it. He'd left no possible room for error, no free time at all for waiting.

"Eight o'clock," he'd said. "You can count on it, darling. Your bus arrives just before seven and you'll have time for a good warm breakfast and by the time you're on your second cup of coffee I'll be there."

But he wasn't there. He wasn't there at eight; he wasn't there at nine. And at ten minutes after nine, the Indian arrived.

The door opened and he came in, shaking snow from his bare head and brushing the flakes from his shoulders with lean, ungloved hands. His complexion was as dark as a Negro's and the cheekbones were high and sharp under the jet eyes. He wore a leather windbreaker, a pair of corduroy riding britches and high, fur-trimmed boots. He was extremely tall for an Indian, standing about six foot three, and his shoulders almost filled the doorway as he passed into the room. He had the waist of a young girl. The most surprising thing about him was his hair. It made no difference at all that he shook the loose snow from his head; his hair was short, crew cut and dead white.

Naturally she had looked up quickly when the door opened, half rising from her seat and hoping against hope that it would be Frank. Sinking back then, disappointment heavy in her, her worried eyes had turned to Millie who sat across the table.

Millie saw the disappointment and turned and looked over her shoulder. "Cramden's Indian," she said, her voice low and throaty. "But don't worry, dear. Your man will be along any minute, I'm sure. Probably just held up by this foul weather. Now you just sit here and take it easy. I'll be right back."

Yes, just take it easy. But how could she take it easy? God only knows what could have happened. She tried to control her thoughts; tried not to think about it, but she couldn't help herself. Oh God, she never should have listened to him, never should have come on alone. It was her own fault. She should have stayed with him, no matter what he said. He was in no condition to be driving through snow-clogged roads. She silently prayed that it hadn't started again, that the red blood hadn't burst from the tortured lungs ...

Millie was back again and she was leaning over her and there was a square white envelope in her hand. "It's for you," she said. "That is, if you're Mrs. Scudder, Mrs. Frank Scudder, this is for you. The Indian brought it."

She couldn't control the shaking of her hands as she tore open the envelope. It had to be from Frank. There was no one else in the whole world who knew where Tina Bennet Scudder was on that particular Monday morning in the first week of March. She read:

Tina dear—
    I am sending this by Joe from the lodge. Got in earlier than I planned so came right out. He'll drive you out and I'll be here waiting. Everything is fine.
                                                    Frank

She stood up and crossed the room to where the Indian stood motionless, staring out over the snow-packed street to where the jagged silhouette of the mountain range rose in thin blue air beyond the town.

Chapter Two

The whine of the car's motor as the driver raced the engine and the back wheels spun on the snow-covered pavement reached Cy Butler's ears as he started to reach for the cash register and ring up the sale. He changed his mind and then took a step over so that he faced the window. Using the sleeve of his jacket, he rubbed a circular spot of frost from the pane and looked out across the street toward the bus depot. A moment later he turned back and looked at Charlie.

"The Indian," he said.

Charlie Hanson nodded. "Yeah. I saw him. He stopped by the gas station and filled up a few minutes ago."

"He was by here, too," Butler said. "Loaded up with provisions enough for an army. Guess those people who rented Cramden lodge for the winter are here. Guess whoever took it over took the Indian along with it."

Charlie Hanson's thin, bitter face turned toward the window and his voice was petulant.

"If they did," he said, "I feel sorry for 'em." He didn't look sorry, though, he merely looked vindictive. "But I guess anyone crazy enough to rent that place in the middle of winter is crazy enough to do anything. Can't understand, when I got a perfectly good hotel here in town, why some damned fool would want to—"

"You got a good hotel, Charlie," Cy said, "but did you ever try to eat one of those meals you serve?"

Hanson looked at the other man with distaste. "Nothing wrong with my food," he said. "And that's no way for you to be talking either, Cy. You wanta remember I buy groceries from you and if you don't like the way I serve—"

"You buy your groceries from me, Charlie, because I'm the only grocery store in town. Same as I buy my gas from you because you got the only pump in town."

Cy Butler laughed as he said it. He liked to get a rise out of Charlie and they'd gone through the same routine a thousand times before and it never failed. He changed the subject. "You hear who took the lodge?"

"Asked that damned Indian," Charlie said, "but you know him. He just grunted—put on that goddam 'ugh, me no speak 'Merican' act. Hell, he speaks good as I do. Went to college down to Boulder didn't he? Damned bastard—"

"Maybe he didn't like the way you asked," Cy said.

"I ask the way I please. Anyway, the hell with 'em. The Indian, the Cramdens and whoever was crazy enough to take the place. Ring up that damned bill—I gotta be gettin' back to the place."

Butler again reached toward the register. Punching out the sums, he spoke over his shoulder. "This weather must be raising hell with the roads," he said. "Newspapers haven't come in from Denver yet. Sort of anxious to take a look at 'em."

"Can't believe anything you see in the papers," Charlie said, sourly.

Cy nodded in good-natured agreement. "Sure," he said. "But I heard over the radio about that bank robbery over in Ogdenville last night. Understand they shot a deputy."

"Banks are a bunch of damned robbers themselves," Charlie said. "Serves 'em right. Turn about's fair play." He picked up the bag of groceries and walked toward the door. A blast of icy air blew into the store as he stepped out and closed the door.

Lowering his copy of the late edition of the *Rocky Mountain News*, Harry Bamberg, the brakeman, took the stub of cigar from his mouth and spit halfway across the car, aiming with unerring accuracy at the discolored brass cuspidor on the floor at the end of the tier of bunks. His other hand reached for the heavy porcelain mug of steaming black coffee. He took a sip of the scalding liquid and then belched. The cigar went back into his mouth and he spoke around it, not looking up.

"Eight thousand bucks," he said. "God damn it, imagine that. Eight thousand bucks, and for that they go and shoot a deputy sheriff." He raised his face and blue-veined, thyroid eyes stared across the oak table at his companion.

Horace Bello stood leaning over slightly, his two large calloused hands grasping the back of the armchair. His thick body slowly weaved back and forth, almost as though he were keeping time with the rhythm of the train.

"Kinda funny," he said.

"Funny?"

"Well, you know what I mean. Here we are, carrying about five or six million dollars and safe as a bug in a rug, and some fool sheriff gets himself shot up for a lousy eight grand."

The brakeman nodded. His eyes went to the forty-five in the holster strapped to the other man's waist. Then he looked up to the rack on the side of the caboose which held the two submachine guns, the double-barreled shotgun and the rifles. His expression was lugubrious. "Ain't nobody goin' touch this train," he said. "Money's as safe as though it was still in the mint down in Denver."

Bello nodded. "Yep," he agreed. "It's safe enough, all right. First place, I don't guess nobody, outside of the mint people, of course, and some of the bank folks up north, even know we make this run. And even if they did, what could anyone do about it?" He shook his head sagely and then went on to answer his own question.

"Hell, we only got the engine, the car and this caboose. And armor plate on all of 'em. Butch up there with the engineer, Cal in the car and you and me back here. They wouldn't have a chance."

Harry agreed. "Not a chance in hell," he said. "No, I don't worry about no stick-ups. Nobody's crazy enough to fool around with government money anyway. Only thing bothers me is this damned weather. She's getting cold as hell out and that snow's really beginning to come down. Just hope we don't have no trouble in the pass."

Bello pulled the chair back and sat down, stretching out his long legs. He reached for the tin coffee pot and poured himself a cup. "Expect trouble?" he asked.

Harry grunted.

"Never can tell," he said. "You're new on this run, but I been on it for twenty-two years now. We've had plenty of trouble in the past. Remember back in 'forty-nine. One hell of a snow and there was a slide up beyond Twin Valley. Came down in Yellow Horse Canyon about twenty minutes after we went through. Then, after we crossed the trestle, we hit a second one in front of us. Couldn't go back and couldn't go ahead. Stuck there for four solid days before the plows got in from the Wyoming division point."

"You have any trouble?"

"Nothing. Nothing at all," Harry said. "We just plain sat it out. Had plenty of grub, like we always have, enough coal to keep the potbellies going and keep up a head of steam in the boiler. Plenty of blankets and we was really snug. Only thing is we were four days late and those banks just had to sit on it and wait for their dough." Bello nodded. "Well, that shouldn't have bothered 'em," he said. "After all, we just change this money for the worn-out stuff they turn back to the mint. But they might have worried about several million dollars trapped in the mountains."

"Nothing to worry about," Harry said. "You gotta remember one thing. If we couldn't get the money through, it was a damned sure thing no one could get to us. No, this is a money train, but it's just about the safest damned money transportation that there is. They may be able to knock off these small-town banks—" and one hand vaguely pointed at the headlines in the newspaper on the table in front of him "—but you can bet your ass they can never bother us."

The wind suddenly veered and a thick cloud of smoke from the engine up ahead wallowed down and blew past the windows of the caboose. They could hear the hissing of the gigantic steam pistons as they labored up the long grade.

Bello walked over and looked out of the side of the car and a moment later, as the wind once more shifted and smoke cleared away, he saw the long thin line of snow-covered highway running through the gorge paralleling the tracks.

For a fleeting moment he saw the dark silhouette of the stalled car, like a small black bug in the center of the road. The figures of two men were beside it and they seemed to be struggling with shovels. He couldn't really be sure as a moment later it was out of sight. Bello shivered and went back to the table.

"Hell of a time to be stuck," he said.

Ahead, in the engineer's cab, young Butch Hanrohan looked out through the inch-thick bulletproof glass at his elbow and spotted the stalled car on the road. Quickly he nudged the engineer, turning at the same time with a complacent smile on his face.

"Okay," he yelled above the roar of noise in the small compartment. "Okay—give." He held out his hand.

For a second the engineer turned his head and then he faced back again and watched the instrument panel. He shook his head.

"Come on," Butch yelled, "give. Half a buck. That car was going up the grade."

"It was stalled," old Peterson said. "God damn it, the car was stalled."

"Stop your quibbling," Butch said. "The bet was I get a half for every car going up the grade, you get a half for every one going down. They were headed up."

"Car was stalled," Peterson said. "Wasn't going anywhere. Just standing still."

He'd been waiting for this to happen for the last hour. Not, of course that he wasn't planning to pay off. But he liked to ride the kid; liked to get his goat. And he knew that Butch was just a little burned up already. He'd collected a buck and a half from the guard on the three cars they had already passed during the several miles that the tracks ran alongside the road and he felt good about it. It wasn't that he gave a damn about the money; the main reason was that Butch, this new kid they'd put on as a guard a short time back, hated so to lose. And now he really had him going.

It was hard for them to hear each other over the noise made by the powerful steam engine, but Peterson had formed the habit of reading lips. He knew what Butch was saying all right, but he pretended he couldn't hear. The madder the other man got, the happier he felt about it. He'd just let him stew for a while, and then he'd pay off. Take some of the starch out of him.

But it didn't happen quite that way because a mile or so further on, they passed another car and this one was definitely moving and it was coming down the grade.

Without thinking about it, Peterson took a crumpled dollar bill out of his pocket and handed it to the younger man.

"Change," he yelled.

Butch looked at him and leered. "We're square," he said. "This just takes care of that other one—the stalled one." He laughed.

A moment later and they hit the tunnel and when they came out after a couple of minutes, the road was no longer in sight.

Far up the tracks they could see a black smudge. That would be the first stop and they'd be there for only about five minutes. Just long enough to drop the canvas bag and then go on. It was the first of the dozen stops they'd make on the six-hundred-mile haul before they came to the end of the run, where they would wait over for two days and then start back.

Peterson pulled the cord over his head and the sound of the whistle, thin and high on the cold air, carried back into the cab....

Back in the armored car, just behind the engine, Cal Treacher barely heard the sound of the engine's whistle. Cal sat slumped in a canvas deck chair, his heavily booted feet resting on the rim of the guard rail going around the potbellied iron stove. His eyes were closed and his hat pulled forward so that it covered part of his face and shielded him from the bright bulb hanging from the ceiling of the car. But he wasn't sleeping.

Cal was wishing that this trip was over and done with. It was his last one and it put a period to thirty-five years of service with the company. Thirty-five years was a long time. Not that much had happened during those years. Of course there had been Betty and the two boys and little Betty. Gone now, all of them: the older boy buried somewhere on a South Sea atoll, Jim back East and making money hand over fist as a veterinarian and little Betty planning to marry that Indian fellow up in Twin Valley. Big Betty had been dead for fifteen years. He was all alone and on his last trip. And then it was going to be Florida and the sun and fishing and just lazing around.

He opened his eyes, pushed the hat back on his head and looked across the car to where the sacks of money lay. Six, maybe eight, million dollars. And it didn't mean one goddam thing to him. Not a thing. He had it made already. The pension and Florida and the sun and just lazing around.

Cal yawned and then smiled secretly to himself. He shifted a little in the chair and reached down and moved the bulk of the gun he wore on his hip. He'd sure as hell throw that iron away when this trip was over. Yeah, throw the gun away along with the rest of the encumbrances of those thirty and more years. He had it made.

Another few days.

He had it made.

Shifting his position with that odd, catlike grace which so frequently characterizes the movements of very fat men, Dave Liebman stretched out and found the dial of the small portable radio and with a click muted the instrument. He stared blindly out of the window of the tourist cabin—not seeing the endless blanket of white snow of the Colorado Plains at all, but seeing the sands of Miami Beach instead, and spoke without turning his head or moving anything but his thick red lips.

"I don't like it, Stanley," he said, "I don't like it at all."

Stanley Kubet, thin to the point of emaciation as he stood in his long underwear in front of the small round sink, leaned forward slightly so that he could get a better view of his lathered face in the cracked mirror. His lean jaw jutted and he pulled the skin taut on the left side of his face with one hand as the other wielded the straight razor. He made no answer and continued shaving.

"He didn't have to do it," Liebman said. He stretched out a pudgy hand for the box of chocolates on the table next to him. "It was stupid; no goddam reason for it at all. We already had him tied up and cuffed and he was just laying there on the floor and for no reason he plugs him."

Stanley nicked the point of his chin and swore. He turned then and stared for a moment at the other man.

"For God's sake," he said, "shut up until I get through. You want I should cut my goddam throat?"

Liebman reached for another candy. "You're crazy to shave in this weather," he said. "Catch your death of cold when you go outside."

"I'm not going outside. We sit right here for at least another twenty-four hours. But you're right, he shouldn't have done it."

Dave nodded. "Another thing," he said. "I'm not sure I like it, his taking the money."

"Oh hell," Stanley said. "That part's okay. At least that way, if we get hooked up in a roadblock and they go through us, we're clean."

"And suppose he gets hooked up?"

"That's his problem. But don't worry about that baby. Don't worry at all. If they stop him, you can worry about the guys who set up the block. He can take care of himself."

"He's tough, all right."

"Plenty tough."

"The funny thing is," Liebman said, "you'd never take him for a hood. My God, he talks like a college professor. Even looks like one. And with that bum lung and all—why my God, he don't look as though he could take on a ten-year-old girl in a fair fight."

"I'd match him with a pen full of tigers," Stanley said. "You don't know that boy. I was with him in Korea. I saw how he operated. He uses a machine gun as though it were an extension of his right arm. And he don't know what fear is."

"That was before he was in the hospital," Dave said.

"The hospital's what makes the difference." Stanley washed the soap from his face and reached for the dirty towel hanging at the side of the sink. "He was always tough, always had plenty of guts. But the hospital is the difference. It's something else with him now. He's not only tough, he's a goddam desperado. Don't care for nothing at all. Except money."

"That's just it," Dave said, plopping another candy into his mouth. "That's what worries me about him. He don't care; maybe he feels he's got nothin' to lose. Maybe he just—"

Stanley turned around and faced the fat man. His voice was sharp and annoyed when he interrupted. "Listen, Dave," he said. "Get something straight. He's okay. He's the kind of guy we have to have for this thing. Sure he's tough; maybe he's a little crazy too. But he's got the moxie. He's got brains. Who the hell else would ever figure on knocking over a bank just to get the running money to take care of the really big job? Another thing—you wanna remember I know him; know him well. We kicked around long before the army days. Frank was smart enough to keep out of jail although he pulled plenty. But he never hung out with hoods or bums; he played around with decent people. It was the war taught him to be a killer. He used to finger jobs and plan them, but he never went for the rough stuff himself. He's different now."

He shrugged then and walked over to the table and found his pipe in the ash tray. He sat down and started to clean the bowl.

"Well, the bank thing was all right," Liebman said. "All right, except he shouldn't have killed that guy. But you know—" a thick finger went to his mouth and he twisted his face as he inserted a dirty fingernail between two front teeth to dislodge a fragment of food "—you know, Stanley, you gotta admit it sounds screwy. Christ—a train robbery! A month ago anyone told me I'd be in on a deal like this I'd have told 'em to blow the snow away. Why nobody's pulled a train robbery since Jesse James left the script for Jesse Lasky."

"But it makes sense," Stanley said. "It makes damned good sense. You agreed with that yourself, didn't you?"

"I agreed," Liebman said. "Yeah, I agreed all right. But I didn't figure we'd be in for a killing before we even got started."

"Had to get the run-around dough," Stanley said, shortly.

"I'm not worrying," Liebman said. "Just wonder if he made the lodge all right."

"He made it, you can bet on that. That kid knows what he's doing."

Liebman stretched and then slumped down on the bed. He pulled two pillows under his head and lay for a minute or so staring at the ceiling.

"Well, I'm going to get some shut-eye," he said. "I hope this damned weather don't get no worse—it's going to be tough enough tomorrow." He sighed and closed his eyes. "I still wish to Christ I was in Miami."

For several long moments Stanley just sat, staring at the other man. Finally he breathed a long sigh and lifted long legs so that his feet rested on the seat of the other chair. "Wish I had a paper," he said.

Dave Liebman opened one eye. "Wish I had a broad," he said. "This kind of goddam weather, I wish I had me a nice, warm, well-fed little—"

"Don't knock yourself out, kid. Where we're goin' there ain't goin' to be no broads—thin, fat or otherwise. Ain't goin' be nothing but snow and wind and ice and money. Yeah boy, money! Money enough to buy all the floss between here and the end of the world."

"I could use one now," Liebman whispered between half-closed lips.

A moment later he was gently snoring.

Stanley watched him for several minutes and then he spoke in a soft voice. "For a guy who's always talking dames," he said, "you sure as hell don't get much action. No, not much action, kid."

Chapter Three

He didn't want to talk.

She'd tried, made several feeble, ineffectual attempts to open a conversation, but he had merely sat there beside her, his face blank and uncommunicative, and grunted. There were, of course, a lot of unanswered questions in her mind. But in a sense she was really just as glad to have a chance to think. There were so many things to think about.

And so the two of them drove on through the snow-covered winding mountain roads in silence, she busy with a thousand and one private thoughts of her own, and the Indian, tall and stiff and silent behind the wheel as with almost fantastic dexterity he avoided skidding and losing control of the car on the treacherous, icy surface of the wind-blown roadway.

She knew that she'd have plenty of time to think. The Cramden lodge, Frank had told her, was some thirty-five miles out from the town, up there somewhere above the snow line among the crags which seemed to rise sheer into the chilled blue, cloudless skies. The trip would take time. Even with the snow tires and chains, the old car found the going difficult. It was an ancient Packard sedan and the heater was barely adequate. The Indian kept the windows hermetically sealed so that their mingled breaths clouded the glass and made visibility poor, but in spite of the lack of draft and the heater, the interior was freezing cold.

It was so strange, Frank not meeting her as he had planned to do. She guessed that he must have arrived a day or so early and gone directly up to the lodge to wait. But then why hadn't he left word at the bus depot? And why hadn't he come in town himself instead of sending the Indian?

For a moment a worried frown creased her forehead. She hoped that he hadn't become ill, hoped that the old trouble hadn't started all over again. She turned in the seat so that she faced the driver. "Mr. Scudder—he's all right, isn't he?"

The Indian looked straight ahead and nodded briefly. "He's all right."

"I sort of expected him to meet me—to come and ..." her voice died out. The Indian gave no sign he had heard her. A moment later the car skidded violently as the tires hit a patch of ice and he was busy then controlling the wheel and getting the heavy machine back on the road. His face was stolid but she sensed the annoyance in him and so she faced forward once more and decided to let him concentrate on his driving. It was obvious that he didn't want to talk to her.

She concentrated on thinking about Frank.

For ten days now, she had spent most of her waking hours thinking of him, remembering the hundred and one things about him; all of those particularly individual characteristics which distinguished him from a thousand other human beings and added up to make Frank, the man whom she loved and who loved her. Most of the things that had happened during the time they were together had blended into a sort of total picture, except of course that afternoon out on the ski slope, the afternoon when she had first realized that she loved him.

She would never forget that afternoon.

It had been such a relief getting away from the hospital. Even for the few hours. Not that she didn't like the hospital and her work there, but it had all been very new to her and on that particular day she had grown tired of seeing the sick and the dying and had felt the need for fresh air and change, the sight of raw, healthy nature unencumbered by human beings. Particularly sick human beings.

It had been her day off and she had left the hospital early and gone into town where she had rented the skis and gotten directions to the slope. The man in the sports shop had driven her out himself, after she'd picked up sandwiches and a container of coffee at the local drugstore.

"You want to be a little careful, miss," he'd warned her. "That's a pretty rugged bit of country and you'll probably not find anyone else around in case you get into trouble. We don't get anyone much up here except on weekends, this early in the season."

She'd thanked him, but also had reassured him that he wouldn't have to worry about her. She was an old hand when it came to winter sports.

And so, around one in the afternoon, after she'd made a couple of long, graceful runs down the two-mile incline and wearily trudged her way back up each time, she'd taken off the skis and found a protected spot under a large blue spruce and sat down to have her lunch. Her cheeks had been bright red and her eyes were sparkling. She'd felt beautifully alive and the flesh of her body tingled.

The spot she had chosen for her break was about two thirds of the way up the slope, but off to one side in a sort of hidden valley, dotted with ancient blackened tree stumps left over from a forgotten forest fire.

She was halfway through with her second sandwich, feeling warm and pleasant and just the slightest bit sleepy, when she had looked up at the horizon and that's when she had first seen the tiny figure flashing in the high sun and zigzagging down the slope. For a moment she had watched, fascinated as she observed the neat long slaloms the skier made as he wove in and out of the trees.

Suddenly she had leaned forward and her mouth opened as though she were about to scream a warning. The skier had swerved far to the left and was heading at an incredible speed directly toward the broken field of stumps where she had found her temporary refuge.

She realized that at the tremendous speed he was traveling it would take a miracle to keep him from being crushed against one of those jagged stumps. She did scream then, trying to warn him but knowing all the time that her voice would never carry that far.

For a moment he disappeared behind a hillock and then, almost at once, he was again silhouetted against the snow-white backdrop, twice as large this time, and coming directly at her. She got to her feet and waved her arms desperately, in an effort to make him change his course.

It was too late now, however, and he was entering the valley. She watched, frozen in a sort of hypnotic horror, as she saw him twist and turn, weaving between those deadly, fire-black trees. She was waiting now for it to happen. It had to happen. She tried to turn her face, to take her eyes away.

And then, even as she stood there, faint with expectancy of the horror which she was sure she would witness, he had miraculously twisted, turned, and side-stepped, executing techniques which took him in and out of danger in breath-taking fractions of seconds, until finally he had come to where she stood and had neatly executed a sliding stop.

And there he stood, a little half-apologetic, half-proud grin on his dark face, directly facing her and breathing heavily as he leaned forward on his two poles.

"And fancy meeting you here, among these dark forest ghosts!" he said. "This must be my lucky day."

For a moment, as she let the sigh of relief escape, she was so mad that she didn't recognize him. "Oh—you fool!" she said. "You idiot—you could have been killed."

"I certainly could have been," he said. He laughed, leaned down and started to loosen the skis from his heavy boots.

It was then that she realized the man was a patient from the hospital back in the town. But at the moment, her mind was still preoccupied with the terrible risk he had taken and the fright he had given her and she didn't at once think about the fact that he was a patient and that he should not have been there in the first place.

"You are going to tell me that you are Miss Bennet, one of the nurses from the hospital," he said, "but I'm not going to believe you. You are really a Saint Bernard dog and that thermos bottle you have there contains a warm nectar to sustain the weary mountain traveler. Of course I mean a nice lady Saint Bernard, and you are actually a good fairy who only changes into a Saint Bernard when it is necessary."

"I am neither a Saint Bernard, nor am I a good fairy. But this container does contain a nectar, after a fashion, and I think you may have some although you don't deserve it after the fright you gave me."

"I frighten myself at times," he said.

Her anger hadn't lasted. That was one of the things which she quickly discovered about Frank; it was impossible to stay mad at him for any length of time.

He'd shared the container of coffee and they had sat there and talked, comfortable in little twin hollows of snow. First they'd talked about the skiing, and then, after she told him that she knew he was a patient at the hospital, they'd talked about that for a few minutes.

But he hadn't wanted to talk about the hospital. "They sent me up there to die," he'd told her and there had been the stain of bitterness in his voice. "To die, along with the rest of the forgotten ones. I hate it. If I have to die, then—"

She had cut him off quickly. "They sent you there to get well," she'd said sharply. "To cure you."

He laughed, but she saw that his eyes were very sober. "No," he said, "you're a nurse and you should know better. They don't really care; they just want to get us out of sight. They don't want to be reminded. Sick dogs go off and hide themselves, but sick human beings have to be sent off into hiding, either by friends and relatives or by a government which no longer has any use for them."

She knew better than to argue with him. "Anyway," she said, "you shouldn't be here. You—"

This time he interrupted her. "Fantastic," he said.

She looked at him, startled. "What is fantastic?"

"My good fairy, who is really a lovely lady Saint Bernard, has become a schoolmarm. I am about to hear a lecture on the care and treatment of government wards." She knew that he was laughing at her.

"You shouldn't be here at all," she continued, and then she said, "but I am rather glad you are. It's lonely, skiing by oneself."

"I wanted to be alone, until I saw you," he said.

"No one should want to be alone." They had let it go at that.

Then, after they had rested, they'd finally got up and strapped on their skis and they'd made two more runs, only this time he had stayed on the proper slope and he had taken no wild chances but had been content to follow her down the long curve of the mountainside.

Later they had gone back to town, returned the rented skis and then gone to the taproom in the hotel. He had nodded at a table in the corner where four other patients sat drinking beer, and she had spoken to a nurse she knew. They found a secluded spot over by a window looking out on the street of the town and he had ordered buttered rum punch for each of them.

And they had talked.

They say you can know a person all of your life and really not actually know him at all; never penetrate the heart of that person or understand his innermost feelings and thoughts. But by the same token, it seemed to her that within the almost pathetically short time they had spent together, they'd found out everything of real importance there was to know about each other.

It wasn't just that he was attractive in a physical way, or that he had an odd, whimsical manner of speaking and made small jokes about the hospital and people they both knew there. It was something more subtle than that. Perhaps, basically, it was that each of them reacted to the loneliness and to some subtle sense of insecurity they found in the other....

Walking back to the hospital, later, she found that her ungloved right hand was in his left hand. That was when the incident occurred.

The driver of the car had been going much too fast, considering the icy condition of the road. He had turned into the street from the left-hand side, some thirty yards in front of them, heading the car in their direction. When he had first sensed that he was going into a skid, he'd done the worst possible thing and jammed his right foot on the brake pedal. The car had gone immediately into a side skid.

Frank had been watching ahead and he saw at once what was happening. He hadn't bothered to yell a warning. Instantly he'd freed his hand and pushed her so violently that she'd been forced to take two or three quick, stumbling steps before she fell into the snowbank at the edge of the road. He fell across her prone body a split second later and then the car had come to a stop, its fender crunched against a tree, not two feet from them.

She was pale and shaking as the driver of the car climbed out and came toward them. But Frank was already on his feet. He made no attempt to help her. She herself was looking up at the frightened face of the car owner when it happened.

Without a word, Frank drew back his arm and a moment later his doubled-up fist struck the other man full in the mouth. As the man went down, he hit him a second time. Then he raised his heavy ski boot.

"Don't—oh don't!" she cried. She was on her feet now and she had moved quickly so that she was beside him. She reached up and held onto him.

He hesitated, and then he turned and looked down into her frightened face.

"God!" he said. "My God, he could have killed you."

His own face was dead white and he was trembling. And then, before she knew what had happened, she was in his arms and his mouth had found hers.

Even as she had clung to him, the thought passed through her mind. It was me, she thought, me that he worried about. He didn't even think of himself. He, too, could have been killed, but it was the thought of my danger which brought on that sudden insane outburst of fury.

Frank was still shaking with anger, his face white and his mouth thin and straight over gritted teeth as they continued on their way a few minutes later. She had understood then that he felt no sense of fear at their near escape; that he had only been consumed with an overpowering and uncontrollable anger at the man who had put her in jeopardy.

The hemorrhages had started just as they turned into the hospital grounds. It was then, as she was helping him the rest of the way to the hospital that she was sure that she loved him.

She knew that she was in love with this tall, thin, wide-shouldered man who had a tiny spreading infection buried deep in his lungs.

For a second then, as she thought about it, she was frightened. But quickly she shook her head to clear the thought away. She could cure him. She knew she could cure him. Even the doctors were willing to admit that much. It was just a case of time. Time and rest and the loving care which she could give him....

In a sense she was sorry that he'd been so impetuous about their marriage. She believed it would have been much better if they had waited, if she'd stayed on nursing a while longer and he'd stayed on as a patient. But she loved him and she understood him and she could see his point.

"Sure," he'd said. "Sure, I got the bug in the army. But I'm damned if I'm going to spend the rest of my life in a veterans' hospital. No, not me. I've seen enough of them—the others who've come for the cure and then come back again and again."

And because she'd loved him, and been willing to marry him and spend her life with him, she'd listened to him and then agreed with him.

She remembered his words now, the words he had spoken just before they had left, he to fly out to San Francisco and she to take the train to Denver and then the bus up to that strange little cardboard village.

"A friend of mine," he'd said, "up in Ogdenville. Runs a sort of bank up there. He owes me money. And now he's written and is willing to pay it." He was going to San Francisco first, however, to pick up his car.

She'd asked, of course, why his friend couldn't just mail or wire the money. But he'd explained that he had to go personally for it. She'd wanted to go with him. That was when he became vague and explained that it was something he had to do alone.

She was to go to Denver and then on to Twin Valley by bus and to get there on the morning of March first. On Monday morning. The cabin was up in the mountains, north of the village, and he'd already made the arrangements. He'd meet her at the bus depot at Twin Valley at eight o'clock sharp.

It was all very strange, but then again, it was Frank. It was a part of Frank, this mysteriousness and this strange way of doing things. Possibly it was one of the things about him which had attracted her in the first place.

Frank was like no one else; no one she had ever known. Of course, at twenty-two, with time out to learn nursing and time out to bury first a mother and then a father, a girl had not had too much time to know a great many people.

They'd had so little time to really tell each other about themselves, less than two months from the day they first met until the day they were married. But it really hadn't mattered. It was like Frank said. "Hell, honey, the past isn't worth talking about. It's the future that counts."

Well, the future was about to start.

Chapter Four

He had waited until the Indian left the lodge and the throb of the Packard's engine had died out in the distance before he moved from in front of the great fireplace where the logs crackled and flamed and threw a comforting blast of warm air into the room.

Frank didn't think of him as the Indian; he thought of him as Joe Moon, the name under which he had known him during those years they'd spent together in the army. They had been companions, not friends. He didn't have friends. But the two years together had established a sort of mutual respect and understanding between them. In a great many ways they were—alike; both quiet men who wished only to be left alone. Each, in his own reserved way, had gradually accepted the companionship of the other as a natural thing.

Moon hadn't been expecting him to arrive when he did; hadn't been expecting him until late in the day. But he'd asked no questions, not even after hearing the radio broadcast on the portable battery set and learning about the bank robbery in Ogdenville and the shooting of the deputy sheriff. There was no doubt that Moon was aware of the thing that had happened and no doubt that he realized that Frank was involved. But he'd asked no questions and Frank had offered no comment. He'd merely waited until well after sunup and then written out the note and told Joe to take it in and give it to the girl and bring her out to the place. He waited until the car had left before doing what he had to do.

It was a shame, naturally, that he'd had to change his plans and come directly to the lodge. But after what had happened, and particularly after the close shave when he'd been stopped at the roadblock, he'd not dared to go into Twin Valley. He couldn't risk a second search. As soon as the other man had left, he got up, and putting on his heavy mackinaw and hunting cap with the ear flaps, he left the lodge and went out to where he'd parked the coupe in the four-car garage at the back of the building.

The snow, which had been falling since long before daybreak, had already obliterated the tracks he'd made some six hours earlier.

The light was bad, once he'd pulled the overhead doors closed, but he needed little light for his task. It didn't take him long. He had the spare tire off in a matter of minutes and although he felt the same deep thrill of excitement he always did when he saw money—lots of money—he was unhurried as he pulled the stacks of bills from the inside of the rubber casing.

He left the money on the cement floor as he carefully replaced the tire on the rim. Then he turned and, picking up the bundle of bills, all neatly wrapped in paper bands indicating their denominations, he went back into the lodge and removed his outer garments. Going into the larger of the three bedrooms, he lifted the mattress of the huge double bed and carefully placed the money between the cardboard which covered the springs and the mattress itself. He didn't bother to count the bills.

Returning to the main room, he began coughing and he took out a handkerchief and spit into it. The linen was stained red when he returned it to his pocket, but if he noticed, it didn't seem to worry him. Once more he slumped in the great leather chair in front of the fireplace and his eyes went to the watch on his wrist. Staring into the fireplace, he spoke aloud.

"I'll be glad to see her," he said. "Damned glad."

His body was still as the minutes went by and he continued to stare into the fire. He was tired and he had had no sleep in more than thirty hours. The lack of sleep, however, was of no consequence. He was a man who needed little sleep, irrespective of what the doctors said. He begrudged every unconscious hour and long ago he'd made it a habit to get along with as little as three or four hours of sleep each night and to find additional rest in long periods of complete physical immobility, his body utterly relaxed, but his mind keen and awake as he would lie back in a chair in an almost trancelike state.

Quietly sitting there, he tried to think of her. Of Tina, his wife, the girl he loved and who would soon be with him. He wanted to remember everything about her, wanted to recapture, even now, each fragment of their time with each other and each inconsequential moment they had spent.

In spite of himself, however, his mind kept wandering, kept going back to the robbery. Finally, with an annoyed shrug, he shifted his position and at the same time, mentally capitulated to the dictates of his thoughts. He discarded Tina and began to recall the events of the previous night.

The business of the deputy had been unfortunate. Coming in like that, right in the middle of things—it had damned near screwed up the whole deal. Thank God, Liebman and Stanley hadn't panicked. Not that he expected Stanley would. But the other one, Liebman, that gross, obese man whom Stanley had brought in on the job—he wasn't at all sure about him. Tough maybe, but stupid.

He'd squawked about killing the guy. And even Stanley'd seemed a little upset about it. But God damn it, didn't they understand? Didn't they realize that he'd had no option? Just suppose they'd merely gone off with the money and left him tied up there in the darkened lobby of the bank. Why hell, their descriptions would have been broadcast within hours. Sure, they might have made a getaway all right. But it would have wrecked the big plan. And Frank wasn't going to let anything wreck that plan.

For a moment he wished that he hadn't had to bring those two in on it. Wished that he and Joe could do it alone. But quickly he corrected his thinking; he knew that they'd need help. Stanley and the other guy might not be perfect, but then who was? He had to take a chance on someone. And at least those two were experienced.

Once more, however, he began to worry. Not about Stanley; Stanley could be counted on. But Liebman was not only a glutton, he liked to drink. Drinking didn't mix with the sort of thing they had to do.

He shifted again in the chair and shrugged. Well, the hell with it; he'd just have to take Stanley's word for it, have to believe that the guy would work out. It wouldn't matter anyway, once the thing was over and done with. None of them would matter. Then it would be just the two of them—he and Tina.

A small frown puckered his forehead for a moment. He was going to have to tell her; sooner or later, she'd have to know.

Half an hour later, as he was putting another log on the fire, he heard the labored throb of a car's engine somewhere far off to the south. He immediately took down a pair of 7x50 field glasses from the mantelpiece over the fireplace. A moment later and he'd once more pulled on the plaid coat and the cap and was out of the house and standing on the wide veranda. Lifting the glasses, he directed them along the road leading up to the lodge. It took him a minute or so before he centered them on the small black dot down past the valley and up the other side of the mountain.

It was a jeep, with the canvas top up, and it was coming fast. He couldn't tell for sure, but it looked as though there was only one man in the car. There was no doubt about its destination. The road ended at the lodge.

Returning to the house, he stripped off the coat and went at once to the bedroom. Opening a tan cowhide bag, he searched under the stack of shirts and found the .25 automatic. Putting his right foot on the bed, he pulled up the cuff of his trousers and slipped the gun into the holster strapped a few inches above his ankle. Then he returned to the living room.

The sound of the car's engine was clearer now and he moved hurriedly. He took the double-barreled shotgun from the pegs where it hung on the wall and laid it carelessly on the long oak trestle table. As he did so, he snapped off the safety.

Five minutes later and he was standing at the partly opened door as the jeep pulled to a stop in front of the lodge. When the door of the vehicle opened, he saw that the driver was alone in the car. Alone and wearing the uniform of a state trooper.

Clarke Upton walked across the foot-high patch of snow separating the driveway from the front porch and climbed the steps. He stopped then and stamped the loose snow from his feet, at the same time looking over to where Frank stood in the doorway. He smiled.

"These jeeps are sure cold," he said. "Great little snow buggies, what with the four-wheel drive and the low gears but cold." He took off his wide-brimmed hat and leaned down and dusted the white flakes from his putteed legs.

"I guess," Frank said. He too smiled. "You better come in and warm up." He opened the door wide.

Upton followed him into the living room and at once walked over and turned with his back to the fireplace. For a moment the two of them stood facing each other, after Frank had closed the door and turned back into the room, each with a quizzical smile on his face, each surreptitiously studying the other.

Upton broke the silence. "Saw your smoke from the highway," he said. "Thought I'd just stop by and make a check. Where's the Indian?"

Frank crossed the room and went to the leather chair. He sat down carefully and crossed his legs.

"Gone into town," he said. "My name's Scudder, Frank Scudder. I've taken the place for a couple of months. Wife and I are spending our honeymoon up here."

The trooper looked up, slightly surprised. "Your wife?"

"Yes. She's in Twin Valley and Joe—the Indian—has gone in to pick her up. I got in earlier than I expected and came right on out. We've rented the lodge from Mrs. Cramden and Joe is staying on and cooking for us and taking care of things."

Upton nodded. His hand went to his shirt pocket and he took out a crumpled pack of cigarettes, extending them to the other man.

Frank hesitated a moment and then reached for one.

"Shouldn't," he said. "Got a touch of trouble"—he gestured vaguely toward his chest—"and I guess my wife would raise hell about my smoking. But one won't hurt I don't think. You see," he hesitated for a minute and then went on, looking into the fire and avoiding the other's gaze, "we're really up here for a sort of double purpose. This high, dry climate is supposed to be good for me. I've been sick. We're combining a honeymoon with a sort of rest cure."

Upton nodded, sudden sympathy in his face. He understood. Hell, he'd seen plenty of them. The Rockies, especially around Denver and the highlands of Colorado, were filled with lungers.

For a moment he said nothing as he held a lighter out and then, after Frank had leaned forward and drawn on the cigarette, immediately coughing badly, he lighted his own. Backing off a foot or so from the fire, he said, speaking slowly, "You say your wife is in Twin Valley? Were you planning on meeting her there, by any chance?"

"Why yes," Frank said. "The fact is I was. But—"

"Guess I must have met her then, this morning," the trooper said. "Pretty girl, just under medium height with blonde hair and blue eyes? Waiting in the bus depot?"

Frank looked up quickly. "Yes," he said. "Yes, that sounds like Tina."

Upton smiled. "Hell," he said. "She was waiting there when I stopped by for coffee. Seemed kinda worried. How come you missed—"

"I was supposed to meet her at eight, but I got into town around four and I didn't want to wait around. So I came on out and sent Joe in. Guess he must have picked her up already. Surprised you didn't pass his car on the road," he added.

"Fact is," Upton said, "I didn't come out the usual way. Took a detour as I wanted to make a stop-off over at the Simkins' place. Probably missed him then." He stopped and took several puffs and then looked directly at Frank.

"You must have been driving all night," he said.

"No. I stayed over in Denver. Hit a tourist camp on the edge of town. You see, I came in from Salt Lake City—'Frisco before that—and around eight o'clock last night I was pretty tired from driving and so I hit this tourist camp."

He stopped talking then and felt in the inside of his jacket pocket and took out a small rectangular card. Looking down, he read from it.

"Small's Motor Court," he said, and held out the card so that the other man could see it. Upton didn't look at it and Frank dropped it carelessly on the table at his side.

"Yeah, I got in fairly early. Don't sleep well and woke up around midnight. Place was pretty cold so I finally pulled up and left. Decided to come directly on to the lodge."

Upton nodded. "Know how it is," he said. "Nothing worse than not being able to sleep."

"By the way," Frank said, "would you like a cup of coffee? There's a fresh pot on the stove in the kitchen. Or perhaps a shot? They tell me whisky's good for this kind of weather."

"Well, I might try the coffee," Upton said. He didn't, however, make a move to get it but stood still with his back to the fire. "Can't take a drink, unfortunately, not while I'm on duty."

"Duty?"

"Yes, worse luck. You see, there was a bank job over in Ogdenville. That's west of Denver, county seat. Someone broke into the bank there and cleaned it out. Deputy sheriff happened by and apparently started in after them. He was shot."

"Heard something about that on the radio," Frank said.

Upton nodded. "Yeah. We got a dragnet out all over the state. It's out of my territory, of course, but we've had orders to check around. That's how I happened to stop by."

"Looking for anyone in particular?" Frank asked.

"Can't rightly say. We figure it must have been either three or four of 'em. They had to go somewhere. They got away in a car. Course, we don't know much yet, but we are checking on strangers."

"Say," Frank suddenly exclaimed. "I guess that's what it was all about!" He looked up quickly. "I was stopped early this morning by a roadblock somewhere north of Denver. They sure went through me and even searched the car," he added.

"Yes?"

"Yeah. Didn't tell me what it was all about, but they held me while they checked back on the tourist camp."

Upton nodded and flicked his butt into the fireplace. "You and the missus from San Francisco?" he asked.

"New York," Frank said. "I was a patient up in a Vet's hospital in Saranac. Mrs. Scudder was a nurse there."

"Oh, I thought you said—"

"We were married a couple of weeks ago," Frank went on quickly.

"Unfortunately, we didn't get to start our honeymoon right off. I had to go out to the coast, business I had to get straightened out there. Tina, that's Mrs. Scudder, cleaned up things back East and we arranged to meet here—that is in Twin Valley."

"Well, I'm glad you're getting together," Upton said and smiled. "Sure wish you all the luck in the world. And I guess I'll just take you up on that coffee now if you don't mind."

Frank stood up. "Would you mind putting the light on under the pot?" he said. "I don't understand these kerosene stoves yet very well. It's still warm but I think ..."

"I'll get it. You just take it easy."

As Upton went toward the kitchen, Frank turned and went into the bedroom.

"Be right with you," he called. He closed the door and then quickly took the .25 from his leg holster and slipped it under the pillow on the wide bed. A moment later and he returned to the living room.

Frank was back in the leather chair when the trooper came into the room some five minutes later carrying two thick mugs of steaming black coffee. Setting them down on the oak table, his eyes went to the shotgun and he quickly looked over at Frank.

"Yours?"

"Belongs to the place," Frank said.

Upton reached for it. He lifted the weapon and quickly broke it, exposing the shells in the twin barrels. There was a startled expression on his face.

"Hell," he said, "this thing's loaded. And the safety catch is released. That's mighty careless of the Indian. Mighty damned careless. Not like him at all."

Frank quickly spoke up.

"He was showing it to me just before he left," he said. "Afraid it was my fault. I was fooling around with it. I'm not used to sporting guns," he added.

Upton nodded. "The Indian's all right," he said. "A little odd and people around here don't understand him very well. But he's all right. A good boy."

"Yes, I know."

Upton glanced at him with a curious expression. "You know?"

"Well, yes. You see, it was through him I heard about the place here." He went on to explain. "Joe and I were in the army together for a while. This last one, in Korea. Spent two years in the same outfit. We've kept in touch since."

"Oh. I see. Well, then you know him better than I do."

"Guess I do."

"You'll be in good hands," Upton said. "He knows this country like a mountain goat. Born and raised here. One of the best skiers and hunters in these parts. You know, I'd have been a little worried about you people up here alone," he added. "We get some mighty rough weather and don't be at all surprised if you get snowed in for several weeks at a time. In fact," he looked out the window for a moment and then turned back, "in fact, the way this weather is making up, I wouldn't wonder but what you're in for one right soon. Hope you got plenty of provisions and everything."

"Joe's taking care of that," Frank said.

"Good," said Upton. He stood up and reached for his coat. "Have to be pushing off, I guess."

He hesitated for a moment at the door. "I don't want to worry you," he said, "but we have a hunch the guys who pulled that bank job may have headed up this way. Tell Joe to keep an eye out when he gets back. And if any strangers should drop around, well ..."

"I'll let Joe handle it," Frank said.

"He's the boy can handle it," Upton said. He smiled and opened the door. "Take it easy," he called. "And good luck."

"You too," Frank said.

Chapter Five

There was a signpost where the road forked off to the left and the legend next to the arrow showed that they had come twenty-nine miles. By now they were high in the mountains and the air was thin and dry. It was very cold. The Indian had kept the car in second for the latter half of the drive and they'd climbed steadily. Only two cars had passed them since they'd left the town.

The surface of the highway out of town had been covered with snow and ice, but Tina sensed at once that they had left concrete pavement behind and were now on a little used dirt or gravel road. Waiting only until he had gone a sufficient distance to be out of sight of the main road, the Indian slowed down and then stopped. Tina looked over at him in sudden alarm.

He reached for the door latch, at the same time speaking out of the side of his mouth. "Be just a minute," he said.

She started to blush as he climbed out of the car. She was surprised to see that he walked in front of the Packard and stood staring down at the road. For the first time then she noticed the twin pair of tire tracks. It was still snowing, but the flakes were thin now and coming down much lighter. Even from where she sat she was able to see that a car must have turned in not more than an hour or so before they themselves had made the turn. Either the same car, or another, had passed the spot, making fresh tracks, a few minutes before.

For a long moment the Indian studied the tracks and then he shrugged and returned to the front seat behind the wheel.

"Must have had a visitor," he said. For the first time he turned and looked at her. It was an impersonal, neutral sort of look. Neither friendly nor unfriendly.

"It's awfully lonely up here," Tina said rather aimlessly.

"It's lonely."

The conversation ended there and the Indian was now devoting his full attention to driving the car. He kept his wheels in the tracks of the other car and after half an hour of slow and careful maneuvering they came to a tall, weather-worn wooden arch. At some time in the past there had been a legend across the top of it, but the words had faded and been eaten away by the winds and rains until they were no longer legible.

The moment the car rolled over the crest and the lodge itself came into view, nestling on the side of a steep hill between two great snow-capped humps, she fell in love with it. The main building was long and low and with a great sweeping roof which went on past the walls to protect wide verandas. A wide, rectangular stone chimney reared into the sky at one end of the structure and there were two other shorter brick chimneys at the opposite end. Although it was mid-morning, the small paned windows were uniformly covered by heavy drapes and the great copper-studded door which led into the lodge seemed almost forbidding.

Beyond the building was a second structure which could only be a barn or garage. It looked large enough to hold a dozen cars. There were two or three other small outbuildings and next to one of them were stacked several cords of firewood.

As the Indian pulled to a stop in front of the great door, it opened and Frank stood there, a faint smile on his face.

Tina, in spite of the excitement of her arrival, noticed at once that he looked very tired. She was out of the car almost before it came to a stop. And then, in no time at all, she'd crossed the porch and was in his arms.

The Indian drove on to the building behind the lodge.

An hour later Tina sat alone in the living room. She was huddled in the big leather chair, Frank's dressing gown corded around her waist, and the flickering shadows from the fire played across her face in the subdued light as she stared into the yellow flames. Frank had gone out to the back of the house and she could hear the sound of his voice as he and the Indian talked.

It was a beautiful room; a room that would have made any girl—any bride—happy and contented and secure. The sort of room designed to give a feeling of warmth and sanctuary. A forty-foot-long, beamed ceilinged, pine paneled room, the north wall completely filled by the massive rough stone fireplace. Heavy monk's cloth drapes were drawn across the windows and she guessed that they were there chiefly to act as an insulation against the cold.

Aside from the great blazing logs in the fireplace, the room was lighted by kerosene lamps, which even this early in the afternoon had been lighted. There were several shelves of books, simple but well-worn and well-made pieces of furniture and sundry brass and copper cooking vessels hanging from hooks on the walls. The kerosene lamps, combining as they did with the reflections from the log fire, gave out a warm, soft light, a light which might be difficult to read by, but which was designed for dreaming and for peace and contentment.

It was all so strange. Here she'd been in the place for an hour or more, alone in the lodge with Frank, and although they had talked almost incessantly, she realized that they'd said almost nothing. There were so many things she had wanted to know, so many unanswered questions. But it seemed that each time she had started to ask Frank about the last ten days—where he'd been and what he'd been doing and how he felt—he'd changed the subject and it had been she who had answered questions.

The man who had driven her out, the Indian, apparently had put the car away and then stayed out in the barn behind the garage unloading the supplies and keeping himself busy. He had not appeared until a few minutes ago. It was rather odd that he'd chosen just the moment he did to come into the room. She had just finished asking Frank about him.

"The strangest man," she said. "It wasn't that he was unpleasant, or even surly. But he just seemed completely occupied with his own thoughts. Hardly even spoke to me all the way out from town. It was almost as though I wasn't even in the car at all."

"He'll be all right," Frank said. "A good man and, from what I've heard, a pretty good cook. Rough cooking, that is. We have to have someone here," he went on. "This place is heated by the fireplace and there are Franklin stoves in the bedrooms. Need to have someone for bringing in the wood and keeping things going. And he sort of comes with the place. He was caretaker for the owner. Name's Joe Moon."

"Well, I guess he's all—"

She had stopped suddenly then as her eye caught the movement at the door leading into the room from the kitchen. The Indian stood silent and tall in the passageway. She had heard no sound; there was no telling how long he'd been there.

Frank quickly followed her eyes. It was the Indian who spoke first, however.

"Things are all set, kid," he said. "I'm ready to take off." He twisted his head and then turned and went into the kitchen. It was obvious that he wanted to talk to Frank alone.

It had been his words that had so surprised her, not that he'd wanted to talk to Frank. If he was leaving to go somewhere, she guessed that that would be only natural. But the words and the way he had delivered them. It was almost as though he and Frank were old friends. As though they were equals; there had even been a trace of warmth and affection in the way he'd said it.

She was still thinking about it when she reached over to the table at her side and blindly fumbled for the pack of cigarettes she'd laid on it when she sat in the chair. Instead of the cigarettes, however, her hand brushed against a small rectangular card and without thought she turned and looked at it. She picked it up and held it so that the light from the fireplace made the words legible. She read: "Small's Motor Court—Denver's Best—At the Edge of the City."

She was still looking at the card when Frank once more returned to the room. At the same time she heard the outside kitchen door slam shut.

Frank walked over to her, smiling. Almost carelessly he leaned over her shoulder and his lips brushed against the back of her neck. He saw the card in her hand and gently reached over and took it from her.

"Stayed there for a few hours' rest last night," he said, at the same time putting the card in his pocket.

She looked up at him then, startled. "But Frank," she said, "I thought—"

"Joe's gone," Frank interrupted. "Had to drive into Phillips for the rest of the supplies."

"Phillips?"

"Yeah. A town up over the Divide. It's a pretty rough haul and he won't be back until morning. At least we'll have our first night here alone."

He pulled a chair up and sat beside her, as she turned in her seat so that she could see him.

"Frank," she said, "there's something I don't quite understand. The way he spoke to you—it was as though you were old friends. Why, he called you 'kid.'" She sounded almost indignant.

He answered without looking at her. "I know," he said "Guess I forgot to mention it to you, but I used to know him a long time ago. Fact is, he was in the army with me."

Her eyes were wide as she stared at him. "But Frank," she said, "why in the world didn't you tell me? I had the idea ..."

He shrugged and turned and his smile flashed. "Hell, honey," he said, "that's how I happened to hear about this place. We've kept in touch with each other and he wrote that the lodge would be available this winter. Guess I just forgot to mention him."

She nodded, but the perplexed expression remained in her eyes. "He acted so strange," she said, rather weakly. "You'd think, knowing you and all, well, that when he met me he'd sort of ..."

"He's a strange guy," Frank said. "But he's okay. We were buddies. Anyway, the hell with old Joe. He's gone now and he won't be back until morning. It's just you and I now, darling."

The next few hours passed swiftly. They were busy getting unpacked, starting fires in the auxiliary stoves in the kitchen and bedroom, finding dishes and linens and various things they would need to get settled for the night. There was little opportunity for idle talk.

Once, soon after dark, they stopped for a few moments and Tina fried hamburgers which they ate on split rolls and washed down with mugs of steaming coffee.

By then they were too tired to do anything but turn in for the night. Even conversation would have been an effort.

Finally, exhausted, they turned down the lights in the great living room long after darkness had dropped down from the towering peaks and the snow-clad valleys had lost all identity in the blackness.

They chose the largest of the bedrooms. It was as it had been that night ten days ago; the one night they had spent together during their short marriage. They exchanged few words.

Willingly, gladly, she gave herself to him. There was the pain again, the sharp, unusual physical pain. But she felt love and an odd, vicarious feeling of passion which offset the pain and made it all right with her. Although she had come to him without experience, she knew what to expect from her nursing training.

When he hurt her, she bit her lips and pressed even larder against him. His hands on her fine breasts were caressing and gentle and he kept his lips pressed to the soft hollow of her neck. She wanted him to kiss her lips, even though she knew the danger of his doing so. But he wouldn't.

Because she loved him and wanted him to have all of her, she blotted from her mind her own purely physical feelings, discarding her lack of sexual reaction as merely an indication of her lack of experience. He was a man of strength and of strong desires, that she knew. But she was amazed at his sexual drive and the insatiable passion which brought him to her again and again.

Once, late at night, she thought of the stories she had heard in the sanitarium of the fantastic sexual desires of men who suffered from lung trouble. At once she was ashamed of the thoughts, and although she wanted to turn over and sleep forever, her arms went out and around him and she pulled him to her again.

That was Monday, the first real day of their marriage. Very late, she at last fell asleep, her body tired but a soft smile of happiness on her lips.

That was Monday.

They heard the first of the radio broadcasts while they were seated across the table from each other in the large combination kitchen and dining room the following morning.

They had got up very late. She had been the first to awaken and she had looked over at his head, lying dark and handsome on the white pillowcase next to her own. There were deep shadows beneath his closed eyelids and she saw that the dark stubble of his rough beard had grown.

She had a fleeting desire to lean over and gently kiss his cheek but instead she turned and crawled quietly out of her own side of the bed. She wanted to hurry and get the breakfast started; to have water hot and waiting when he was ready to get up. She could have sworn that he was dead to the world and that nothing would have aroused him, but no sooner had her feet touched the ice-cold floor than he spoke, without opening his eyes.

"Toss a log in the fireplace," he said, "if the fire is still going, that is.

By the time you're back I'll be up and getting things going."

It was a characteristic of his that later on never ceased to amaze her, this capacity to awaken at the very slightest sound and to awaken fully and completely with none of that normal transition period from sleep to wakefulness which all other people seemed to have.

The embers were still smoldering and when she returned to the bedroom, after throwing a couple of logs in the great fireplace, he had already disappeared into the small side room which held the chemical toilet.

She went out to the shed to draw water from the well, and although she was still tired and half asleep, the clear, sharp air brought the blood to her cheeks and gave her a sense of fresh life. It was a glorious morning. Turning back to the house with the bucket of water, she stopped for a moment and breathed deeply.

From far across the valley came the shrill, forlorn cry of a railroad train's whistle as the engine rounded a curve. Somehow or other it was a friendly sound, in spite of its qualities of loneliness and sadness.

Later, he cooked the sausages and eggs while she made coffee and toast. He was all ready long before she had the toast buttered, and he went to the bedroom and brought in the small battery-powered radio set. He put it on the table and at once turned the switch. They got the end of a news program. The announcer had just finished the national news and was getting into local events.

She wasn't really listening until she realized that he was talking about the bank robbery at Ogdenville, on Sunday night. She first became conscious of the words when she heard:

"... and early this morning, after lying in a coma for more than twenty-eight hours without regaining consciousness, Deputy Sheriff Boyd Carson died in Denver General Hospital. Sheriff Carson was shot down Sunday night by unknown gunmen whom he intercepted while they were robbing the safe of the Ogdenville National Bank of more than eight thousand dollars. Police officials working on the case have established a state-wide dragnet in an effort to find some trace of the Ford ranch wagon which was reported last seen leaving Ogdenville shortly after the crime took place. Programs on this station will be periodically interrupted to bring you any late developments in what is turning out to be one of the biggest manhunts in this part of the country. And now we will bring you the opening market prices as quoted by—"

Frank reached across the table and whirled the dial, finally stopping when he found a station broadcasting hillbilly music.

"Frank," she said. "Frank, what with the excitement of seeing you and getting settled and everything, I haven't asked you a single question yet about what you've been doing for the last ten days. Where you've been and so forth. Wasn't Ogdenville where you went to meet that man who was to pay you the money?"

Chapter Six

Dave Liebman stared at Stanley as the words of the announcer came from the set. His face paled, but he said nothing until it was over. Then he quickly snapped off the switch. His hand was shaking as he took the cigar stub from his mouth.

"Christ," he said. "We gotta get out of here. We gotta get out of here fast."

"Easy, boy," Stan said. "Easy. You heard it. You heard him say Ford ranch wagon. We ain't going anywhere in that car now."

"But we can't stay here. My God, the guy runs this place saw the car when we drove up and checked in. Sooner or later he's going to put two and two together. Even if he didn't hear the broadcast, he'll be getting a paper and he'll read the story there. And then he's going to remember."

"Yeah. But Frank's boy is due any minute now." Stanley looked at his watch. "He should be here already. We can't do a damned thing until he comes. If we try to take off now, we'd be picked up within a dozen miles. Another thing, the car's in the shack connected to this room. No one can see it. And we came in while it was still dark. We don't know for sure if he even seen the Ford. All he knows is we drove up and I went to the door. The lights from the car were on the door and he was facing them when he answered the night bell. He couldn't have seen what kind of car it was then. Another thing, he was in his nightshirt. After I signed in, he started back for bed the same time as I left the office to pull into the shed. He might not have seen the car at all."

Dave didn't look relieved. "Maybe he didn't and then again maybe he did. But I don't like it. I don't like it one goddam bit. Where the hell is that friend of Frank's anyway? He should be here by now."

"Take it easy," Stan said once more. "He'll be along. Anyway, there's plenty of Fords and plenty of Ford ranch wagons."

"Sure, sure," Dave said. "Plenty of 'em. And you can bet your ass everyone's going to be stopped and the cops are going to question—"

"Let them question," Stanley said. "It still don't mean that they can tie us in."

Dave threw the dead cigar into a wastebasket and sat back on the stiff chair. "That damned fool, shooting the cop. Hell, it was insane. This whole damned caper is gettin' fouled and—"

"Good God," Stanley said, "take it easy. There's nothing we can do. We just gotta wait. He should be here any minute now."

"And then what?"

"Then we leave with him."

"And the ranch wagon?"

Stanley hesitated and he frowned. "Well," he said, "I don't know just ..."

He stopped suddenly and both men were still and alert. Dave started to say something and Stanley quickly put his finger to his lips. A moment later and the sound of the car pulling into the yard came to them clearly. Stanley was the first to reach the window.

"It's the Packard," he said. "It's him."

Stanley went to the door and inched it open, but Dave stood well away from it. His right hand rested lightly on the butt of the gun which he had pushed down between his belt and his stomach.

Joe Moon had to stoop to enter the room.

He nodded at Stanley, but his eyes went to Dave. He noticed the other man's hand on the gun and he smiled thinly. "Sorry I'm late," he said. "Got held up by a roadblock about twenty miles back. The law is sure out in force."

"We just heard the broadcast," Stanley said. "Some guy spotted the ranch wagon when we were leaving. Don't think they got the license number, but they spotted the car."

"And where's the car now?"

"In the shed, next door. We leave it here and it'll be picked up for sure. It's hot, and the guy who runs this place will be able to give a description of us."

"He see the car?"

"Not sure," Stanley said. "Don't think so, but we can't be sure."

"Okay," Joe said. "We'll do it this way. You," he indicated Stanley with a nod of his head, "get your coat on and get over to the office. Get him in some kind of conversation and see that he don't look out of the window. He's alone in the place—runs this dump in winter without any help and there don't seem to be no one else checked in. Keep him busy for a few minutes. While you're doing it, your partner can get in the wagon and start out." He turned to Dave.

"Turn left when you pull into the road. Go about three quarters of a mile and make a right. It's a sharp turn hard to see. Looks like a cow path. But take it. Go in couple of hundred feet. I'll wait for your partner and we'll pick you up within fifteen or twenty minutes."

"And then what?" Dave asked.

"There's an abandoned quarry up that road. We dump the car. Chances aren't even one in a hundred that it'll be found before spring. Just be sure no one sees you pull off the main drag. Better get started."

Five minutes later Stanley left the house and went to the tourist camp office. He had to knock several times until the door was opened. They gave him two or three minutes and then Dave, bundled in a long coat and with a scarf around his neck, went out to the shed and started the engine in the Ford. He let it warm up for a minute or two before backing it out of the shed. Stanley was back in the cabin before the sound of the car's motor had died away in the distance. Wordlessly he collected their luggage and Joe helped him out of the place with it. He didn't speak until they turned into the main road.

"I think everything is okay," Stanley said. "I asked the guy who checked us in where I could find a Buick garage. Told him we were having clutch trouble. He was half in the bag and looked like he'd been drinking for a week. Said he thought we had an Olds. I don't think he even knew that you'd driven into the place. Don't think we got anything to worry about with him."

"I hope not," Joe said. "You careful about any prints you might have left?"

Stanley looked at him and smiled. "We're pros," he said.

They found Dave standing beside the station wagon on the narrow dirt road which was lined by twin rows of tall pines. The trees had helped to keep the snow from drifting and there were only two or three inches covering the surface of the road.

Joe pulled the Packard up behind the other car and got out. "You guys stay here," he said. "I'll take care of the Ford. It'll take me about fifteen or twenty minutes."

Dave was lighting a fresh cigar when he heard the distant sound of a splash a few moments later.

When he got back to the car, Joe opened the door but made no move to get in. Stanley was sitting in the front seat and Dave was stretched across the back.

"How're you boys on identification?" Joe asked.

"Okay," Stanley said. "Driver's licenses, gas credit cards, social security numbers—the usual. Dave there is George Fox, from Hoboken, New Jersey, and I'm Morton Frieheit from Bayonne. I'm a beer salesman and Dave is supposed to be a bartender."

"Good," Joe said. "And are you carrying any iron? I saw your part-ner had a gun in his belt."

Stanley nodded. "Of course," he said.

"Well, let me have it."

Dave Liebman leaned forward in his seat. "What did you say?"

"Let me have it. Everything you've got. You can't afford to have any kind of a weapon on you. There's every chance we'll be stopped and questioned before we get up to the lodge. There's the possibility that you'll be searched. You can't have no artillery found on you!"

"But suppose," Stanley started, but Joe cut him short.

"Listen," he said, "this is my end of it. I'm supposed to get you there, and get you there without trouble. Frank gave me my orders and I'm doing what he says. So give me your guns. You wouldn't have a chance in hell," he added, "in any case. The troopers out this way shoot first and ask questions afterward when they see guns."

Reluctantly Dave pulled the revolver from his waistband, handed it over. Stanley took a .45 automatic from his shoulder holster and laid it on the seat. Then he unstrapped the holster itself and put it beside the gun.

"How about the luggage?" Joe said.

Without a word, Dave opened a pigskin bag and took out two more guns, one a Luger and one a twenty-two target pistol.

"Any of these hot?" Joe asked. No one answered him.

Without another word, he picked up the guns and walked off into the trees at the side of the road. He was back within minutes.

"Okay," he said, climbing behind the wheel. "One of you guys get out and walk back to the road. I'm going to have to back this car out. I want to be sure no one's passing when I do."

Once on the highway and heading north, he spoke to Stanley, who sat beside him.

"Be sure you got the story right, now," he said. "Any one stops us, you two guys are just in from the East; I picked you up this morning in Denver and you're coming up to the lodge for a two weeks' vacation. You're going to do a little skiing and just sort of resting up. I know most of the troopers in these parts and they won't question the story, just as long as you say the right thing."

"We'll say the right thing," Stanley said.

"I'd feel a hell of a lot better if I still had that gun," Dave rumbled from the back seat.

"We got all the guns you can ever use at the lodge," Joe said. "Just take it easy. We'll be there in a couple of hours."

They didn't pass more than a dozen cars during the entire trip. There was no roadblock. Only twice was there any further conversation.

An hour after they had left the tourist cabin, Dave again opened the pigskin bag and took out a pint flask. Removing the cork, he took a long pull from the bottle and then tapped Stanley on the shoulder. Stanley turned, shook his head, but accepted the flask. He held it out to the driver. Joe spoke without taking his eyes from the road.

"Never take the stuff when I'm driving," he said. Stanley shrugged and handed the flask back to Dave, who took a second drink and coughed violently afterward.

"A man can freeze in this goddam car," he said.

Later, after they had taken the fork in the highway leading to the cabin, Dave once more spoke. "Christ," he said, "I'm damn near frozen. And I'm half starved. Didn't get a goddam thing to eat yet this morning."

Joe spoke without turning his head. "We'll be there in a few minutes now. The girl will probably have some coffee on and there's plenty of food."

Stanley turned and looked at Dave with a startled expression. Dave leaned far forward on the seat.

"The girl? What girl?"

"Frank's girl," Joe said.

Dave and Stanley stared at each other wordlessly. Dave's mouth was open and there was a peculiar look on his face. "Frank's girl? Well, I'll be God-damned."

The minute that he handed her the plain envelope, with nothing on it but her name, neatly printed out in block letters, Betty Treacher knew what would happen. They'd wait, the two of them, until she'd left the gas station, and then they'd start. Start wagging their dirty vicious tongues.

Monty, the attendant, the one who'd handed her the letter, wasn't so bad himself. He was just a simpleminded, middle-aged man who was too stupid to think for himself. He just played up to that other one. No one else but Charlie Hanson would have given Monty a job of any kind and so it was only natural that he'd be Charlie's stooge.

But Charlie himself was something else. Charlie had a mean, dirty mind. He was a filthy, tight-fisted bitter old man and she hated him.

Of course Joe had left the letter with Monty to give to her, but she knew very well that Monty had told Charlie about it. It wasn't just that Charlie didn't like Joe; Charlie didn't like anyone. Naturally, he especially hated Joe: had hated him ever since he'd found out that she and Joe were going together.

Crossing the street to the combination luncheonette and bus depot, where she went each noon for a sandwich and a milk shake, Betty remembered when she herself had worked for Charlie. Her dad, who'd known Charlie since they were boys together, had got the job for her. That had been almost five years ago.

Tall, wide-shouldered and with a fine, full bosomed figure, Betty wasn't a particularly pretty girl, but she had a healthy clear complexion, rather routine features and really beautiful, long auburn hair.

Charlie Hanson, in spite of the difference in their years, had fallen in love with her almost from the very beginning. At least he'd said it was love, and he'd shown no hesitancy in pressing his feelings on her. It had been difficult, particularly as he repelled her in a physical way which made even his presence offensive, but she'd managed. She'd managed fine until the time when Joe Moon had come back and settled down.

She and Joe had taken to each other right off. And that was when Charlie stopped asking her to marry him and instead, tried to get what he wanted without bothering about any formalities. She'd had to quit her job, of course.

It was just as well. The job with the phone company paid almost as much and she didn't have to look at Charlie Hanson all day long.

Yes, she and Joe and gone for each other right from the first. But somehow or other, they'd never got around to making it final. Joe had drifted from one thing to another. He'd opened a small garage and repair shop, but that hadn't worked out. Joe liked his fishing and hunting too much and anyway, most of the men in the town and the ranchers around the countryside did their own repair work.

He'd drifted off then for a year or so and when he'd returned, less than eighteen months ago, he'd taken the job out at the Cramden place, as a sort of caretaker. They'd started seeing each other again.

The fact that Joe was a full-blooded Indian hadn't made anything easier. The people in the town didn't think much of Indians, and her dad hadn't liked the idea. Betty didn't really care too much what the town people thought; she cared even less what her father thought. Her father was pretty much like old Charlie Hanson—a bitter, selfish old man. All he wanted was enough money to be able to quit his job and take his pension and go down to Florida and die in the sun. He didn't give a damn about his children or anyone. Just another selfish old man.

Betty never had been able to forgive him for taking her out of high school in her second year and putting her to work. It was right after her mother died. No, she didn't care about her father, one way or the other. The only person she really cared about was Joe.

Sitting in the restaurant, she ordered the usual sandwich and milk shake and while Millie was getting the food for her, she tore open the envelope. The note was very brief.

> Kid: Passed through late and left this with Monty for you. Going to be tied up for several days as we got people staying at the lodge. Will try and get in early next week. And that deal I was telling you about is going to come through I'm pretty sure. Get ready to tell the phone company to shove it. I think this is really it and if everything works out, we'll shake this damned town for once and all and soon.
>
> Joe

Betty smiled secretly to herself as she refolded the sheet of paper and put it back in the envelope. Men were really such fools. Even Joe, sweet and smart as he was. Did he think he was fooling her for a minute? As well as she knew him? Good Lord, after all of those questions about her father and his job as a guard on that money train? After getting the time schedules from her? After that business about the dynamite? That in itself had been the first tipoff, when he'd found out from her about the dynamite stored away in the shack up in the hills by the construction gang working for the telephone company. In the beginning, of course, she hadn't even suspected. But later, he'd disappeared for several days and during that time the shanty had been broken into and the dynamite stolen.

She'd known then that it must have been him.

Sure, Joe wasn't like most men; he didn't talk much. But little things here and there had tipped her off. She could guess what he was up to.

And she didn't care. She didn't care one damned bit. Let him do what he wanted to do, what he had to do. Let him get the money any way he could. She'd share it with him and with pleasure. Neither of them owed society one damned thing. Not one thing.

She was just as glad he didn't take her into his confidence. She was smart enough to not want to know the actual details. But she'd help him out any way she could. Any way at all.

Millie put the sandwich and milk shake down in front of her and smiled. "Some weather," she said. "Looks like we're really going to get some winter at last."

"We've had plenty already," Betty answered, "so I guess a little more won't hurt anything."

Millie drew a cup of coffee and came back and leaned on the counter and the two talked as Betty ate her lunch. Millie was one of her few friends in the town. Millie didn't disapprove of her affair with Joe. She didn't refer to Joe as "the Indian." At least not in front of Betty, she didn't.

At the exact moment that Betty Treacher was finishing her lunch in the bus depot in Twin Valley, her father, Cal Treacher, was inserting his false teeth and preparing to eat his lunch in the caboose of the money train as it crossed the Wyoming border and entered Idaho. His words were mumbled and half lost as he spoke with his hand still in his mouth.

"Of course I know I shouldn't be back here," he said, his tone petulant. "God damn it boy, I been guarding this train for better 'n thirty years. But by hell I been coming back to this here caboose every noon for the last twenty of 'em and I'll still come when I want to. I don't like eating alone."

"Nothing to worry about," Bamberg said. "Take it easy, Horace. Cal knows what he's doing."

Horace Bello blushed and sat down across the table from the other two men. "Well, I just asked if you wanted me to stay in the car while you're back here," he said. "I just thought—"

"Car door's bolted and the train's movin'," Cal said. "Just simmer down and let's have some grub. Our next stop ain't for another four hours and we can get a game of hearts in if you want."

Chapter Seven

Tina, hesitant and embarrassed, nevertheless reached out and took the roll of bills from his outstretched hand. "But, Frank," she said, "you don't understand. It wasn't a loan, darling. It was our money. What's mine is yours." Frank shook his head and at the same time closed her hand over the money. "I'm an old-fashioned husband, Tina," he said. "I don't live on my wife's money. It took you a couple of years to save up that thousand dollars, you told me so yourself. It was bad enough

I had to borrow it, but now I'm giving it back. And don't worry, I've got more. Plenty more."

Tina nodded, the baffled expression still in her eyes. They were again sitting before the great open fireplace, a low table in front of them on which were the coffee cups and sandwiches. It was just after noon and they were having lunch.

"But I don't understand," Tina said. "Where did you suddenly get all of this money? You told me, back at the hospital—"

Frank put up his hand as though to stop her words. "I get my pension checks," he said. "And I got the money from that fellow in Ogdenville. We won't have anything to worry about. We'll be all set for a long time to come. Just don't worry, and don't ask questions. As I told you, I'm an old-fashioned guy. It's my job to worry about the money."

He reached for his coffee cup and turned so as to face the fireplace squarely. "We'll talk about something else," he said. "How about a little skiing this afternoon?"

For a moment she didn't answer and then she stood up. "I'll put this away," she said, indicating the roll of bills which she still held in her hand. She went into the bedroom and after a few moments returned.

"Frank," she said, "if you were in Ogdenville, why—"

He looked up at her sharply, annoyance on his normally calm face. "Listen, honey," he said, "the hell with Ogdenville. And the hell with all these questions. I don't like to be questioned. I'm a big boy and I don't like—"

Her eyes widened. There was a shocked expression on her face. "But Frank, I'm not—"

"Damn it, let it lay!" His tone was suddenly sharp and he almost yelled the words. "Let it lay, leave it alone. Don't be one of those goddam curious, nagging wives."

He stopped as suddenly as he had started and he stood up and came and leaned over her chair, putting his arms around her. One hand went under her chin and he lifted her face so that she looked into his eyes.

"Baby," he said, "what the hell? Are we fighting? Let's not. We don't have anything to fight about. It's just that I don't like questions and all that sort of thing. Guess I've lived alone too long. You just have to get used to me. All I want you to do is be happy. Take things the way they come and be happy. I'll take care of you; I'll do all the worrying, if there's any to be done. And now, how about the skiing?"

"Do you think you should be going out, Frank?" Tina asked. "After all, you've had a pretty rough trip and you still look awfully tired.

Maybe it would be better to just sit around."

"I feel fine," Frank said. "The air won't hurt me; in fact, even the doctors said a little exercise is good. So let's get out while there's still a high sun. We can take it easy and just sort of look the place over."

"Well." Tina hesitated. "Well, if you say so. I'd like it. There are skis?"

"Everything," Frank said. "Joe has everything here we'll need. I'll get some clothes on and go out in the barn and select a couple of pair. You start getting ready."

"When is he coming back?" Tina asked, getting up from the chair. "The Indian—is he going to be—"

"He doesn't like being called the Indian," Frank said. "And he'll be back sometime this afternoon." He patted her affectionately on the shoulder as she turned toward the bedroom.

"By the way, he'll have a couple of guys with him. They're going to be staying on for a week or so."

She stopped and turned toward him, surprise and chagrin in her face. "A couple of guys?" she said. "You mean he's bringing—"

"Yeah." He said it casually. "Joe's bringing in two men who are going to be staying here. They'll be doing a little skiing and so forth. On a vacation from New Jersey."

"But Frank. You didn't tell me anything about anyone else being here." She couldn't keep the disappointment out of her voice. "Isn't it going to be just a little crowded?"

He put his arm around her shoulder and looked down at her. "Don't worry about it, baby," he said. "You know, this is a sort of expensive proposition and by whacking it up, it makes it a little easier on us. They won't bother us at all. They'll have the bedroom at the other end of the lodge and won't be in our way at all. You'll never know they're here. Anyway, it'll only be for a week or two."

As he finished speaking he went into the kitchen to get his heavy coat.

Tina slowly turned and walked into the bedroom. For the moment she was too stunned to say anything more.

It didn't make sense; didn't make any sense at all. Not only the Indian, but now two complete strangers to share their honeymoon. And as far as cutting the expenses, well, that made even less sense. Dividing the rent for a mere two weeks out of the several months they planned to spend at the lodge was a drop in the bucket. And anyway, Frank had just said he had plenty of money now.

She heard the door slam as he left to get the skis and for a few moments she stood in the center of the bedroom, motionless and just thinking.

Everything was so strange. Frank's evasiveness she was getting used to. She understood that he never liked questions. But these other things. First, his failure to mention having known the Indian. And then his staying in the tourist court outside of Denver on Sunday night, the very night she had arrived by train and had to wait to take the bus out to Twin Valley. She still couldn't understand why he hadn't met her there in Denver and driven her out as long as he had been in or near the city at the time.

He had never explained his failure to meet her in Twin Valley and she was left to draw her own conclusions.

He'd been in Ogdenville; he'd been in Denver; he hadn't met her. He'd avoided Twin Valley and he suddenly showed up with money, a lot of money. He didn't want questions. He and Joe Moon were old army buddies and two strangers were coming to share their honeymoon.

Tina sat down on the edge of the bed. It didn't add up. It didn't add up at all. Did it?

Her face was suddenly very pale and her lips were trembling. Her eyes opened wide and she stared at the wall across the room. Or did it? Did it add up? Did it make sense?

Good God, what was she thinking! What in the name of all that was holy was getting into her? Was she crazy or something? Was she beginning to have hallucinations?

Quickly she stood up and crossed the room to look at her white face in the mirror over the dresser. She'd have to get hold of herself. She'd have to—

The back door slammed and Frank's voice came to her from the kitchen. "All set, Tina," he called. "Get yourself ready. It's beautiful out. Cold and clear and beautiful. Snow's stopped coming down and is just right. Not too sticky."

Tina reached for the heavy woolen ski pants hanging on a hook on the wall where Frank had put them when he'd unpacked her trunk, the trunk which had been sent on ahead by express before she'd left the East. Before answering, she shook her head, as though to clear it of the thoughts which had begun to poison her mind.

"A couple of minutes, honey," she called back. "Give a girl time to get dressed. And you might put the rest of that coffee in the thermos bottle," she added. "That is if you can find one."

Ten minutes later, going toward the mountain with her hand in Frank's, she thought: It's beautiful. Beautiful and I'm happy. Really happy for the first time in my life. But I must learn to curb this silly imagination of mine. I've got to stop having these weird fantasies.

The sound of the train whistle interrupted her thoughts. Frank turned to her, his breath making a cloud of vapor in the cold air. "Let's try it over that way," he said, pointing toward the hill off to the north. "Maybe we can find the railroad tracks."

In many ways, that afternoon was the happiest that Tina had spent in the twenty-two years of her life. Thinking about it, later on, she couldn't have told exactly why. They didn't talk a great deal. They didn't do much of anything, except slowly climb the snow-covered hills and then make the long sweeping runs into the valleys. They rested and took sips from the thermos of coffee which Frank carried and again started plodding up the slopes. They laughed often at nothing in particular, except that they were carefree and happy.

The exercise and fresh air seemed to agree with Frank and he coughed very little. His cheeks were flushed and looking at his lean, handsome face above the wide shoulders, Tina found it hard to believe that there could be anything wrong with him, that he could be fighting the germ of tuberculosis.

But she didn't let her mind rest on that thought; she reacted to his gaiety and laughter and the happiness in him and she too was gay and happy.

They found the railroad tracks, some four miles from the lodge and followed them until they came to the place where the trestle carried the single pair of iron rails over the deep gorge. They turned off to the right then and took a long bare slope down into a valley covered with hemlock and spruce, and rested a while.

She smoked a cigarette and Frank wanted one but she shook her head and told him it wouldn't be good for him.

"None of the things I love are good for me," he said, "except you."

She laughed and kissed his cheek and he rolled her over on her back in the snow and wanted to make love to her then and there, but she squealed and escaped and, blushing, told him that he was crazy. He admitted it and stood up and reached for her again. They held each other wordlessly for a long time.

Late in the afternoon, as the sun dropped to the rocky hills off to the southwest, they started back. It was some two miles from the lodge that they came to the edge of the precipice. It was at the ridge of a high, naked mountain, far above the timber line, and they came upon it without warning. They had been climbing, puffing hard from the exertion, when suddenly they reached the summit. Tina was in the lead and Frank quickly caught up with her.

"Watch it," he said sharply, reaching for her arm.

She had expected the land to slope off on the other side, the same as it had on their approach to the top. They slowly approached the edge and she peered down. There was a straight drop-off. A drop of more than two thousand feet. She shuddered, stepping back a pace. Far below she could see the jagged, ice covered rocks in the valley.

The rim of the cliff extended for a little over three hundred feet, and then the drop became gradual until it formed a long gorge. "You can tell by the old stump over there," Frank said, pointing to a lightning-blackened pine to his left. "You have to watch out for it. If you ever went over that edge, you wouldn't have a hope."

Once more Tina shuddered. No, you wouldn't have a hope. She thought how easy it would be for a skier, who didn't know about it, to plunge into that treacherous gorge. And then, a second later, she thought of something else. She stopped and turned toward him.

"Frank," she said, "Frank, how did you happen to know about it? How—"

He drew her on, not looking at her. "Oh," he said, "I was here some years ago. Before the army. I just happened to remember it."

The happiness suddenly went out of her. She remembered also, re-membered only too well.

He had told her, back there in the hospital in Saranac, while they were making their plans. She even remembered his words. "Always wanted to see Colorado," he'd said. "Been one of the ambitions of my life to get out in those mountains."

As the heavy Packard made its way through the snow and ap-proached the lodge, Joe Moon was busy with his own thoughts. For the first time he was beginning to have doubts. There was nothing wrong with the scheme; it was the people who were in on it. Of course Frank was all right. He knew Frank and he could count on him. He had to admit, however, that the girl was a surprise, the blonde nurse whom he introduced as his wife. The more Joe thought about it, the less he liked it. God knows, they'd have enough problems without some dumb kid to take care of.

Joe wondered how Frank was going to get around it; he obviously hadn't told her anything and from what Joe'd been able to figure, the girl thought Frank was on the up and up.

And then there was the business about the bank over in Ogdenville. The only thing Joe knew was that Frank had indicated he and those other two were going to pull a job and pick up some running money, on their way up to the lodge. Joe had thought he meant a small stickup of some sort. He'd never dreamed that Frank would consider a bank robbery as a small job for running money. And killing that deputy sheriff—Joe didn't like that at all.

He didn't like one of his passengers, either. The tall thin one, the one named Stanley, seemed all right. Looked like he could handle himself even if he was a little old for what they had to do. But this other one, this gross, fat man with his chewed cigar and his flask of whisky. Where did he fit in? How could he help? He hadn't said much, but what he had said, Joe didn't like. The guy looked and acted and talked like a cheap racketeer, or a muscleman for a protection mob. Joe wondered how Frank had even happened to select him.

For a moment he felt a sense of guilt. Why should he question Frank's integrity, particularly at this stage of the game? Hell, if he lacked confidence in Frank, he should certainly never have gone this far with the thing. After all, it was he who had known about the train and the money it carried. It was he who had wormed the details from Betty and started planning the crime. It was he who had looked up Frank and invited him in on the deal. And he'd been glad enough to leave the business of recruiting the others to Frank. Frank had the contacts and the experience.

Well, it was too late now to start worrying. There was only one comforting thought about the whole deal. It would all be over soon. Then he would have the money, the money which meant so much to him. The money that was going to buy him the freedom for which he had waited all these years.

He'd have to stay around for a while, until things cooled off, but at least those other two would be gone. That was the plan—once the job was over, he and Frank were to stay on and the other two would blow.

Pulling into the yard in front of the lodge, Joe was quick to see the twin channels that the two sets of skis had made. He didn't stop in front of the place, but drove around to the barn in back. Getting out, he raised the garage door and then took the Packard inside. Stanley and Dave tumbled out of the car, shivering in the cold, and followed him to the back door of the house. Dave carried his pigskin bag and Stanley, moving slowly, carried a large suitcase.

They took their outer clothes off in the kitchen.

"Where's Frank?" Stanley asked, walking over and holding his hands over the stove. "Thought you said—"

"Must have gone out," Joe said.

Dave grunted. He took the flask from his pocket and drank from it.

Taking it from his lips, he tipped it upside down and a couple of drops trickled to the floor.

"That's that," he said. "Hope to God you got some whisky in this dump."

"Take it a little easy on the booze," Stanley said. "We got plenty of time."

"I'm hungry," Dave said. "How about something to eat?"

"I'll get something started," Joe said. "Why don't you two go on inside by the fireplace."

He walked into the other room himself and put logs on the fire, which had died down. "Be warmed up in a few minutes," he said.

Dave waited until he'd left the room before he turned to Stanley. He spoke in a low voice. "You hear what he said?" he asked. "You hear him? Said Frank had a goddam woman up here with him."

Stanley nodded. "Yeah," he said. "I heard him. But I can't figure it. I can't figure it at all. Christ, we only split out Sunday night. Where the hell would he have had a chance to pick up a girl? And what in the name of God did he want to bring her up here for?"

Dave leered. "Easy enough to figure what he brought her for," he said. "The same thing you bring a girl any place for. But how did he manage to find one so soon? My God, those things don't just hang around the roads waiting to be picked up. Well, it doesn't matter. Might be a good idea, especially if we gotta hang around here for any time. After all, we're all in this together and what's for one is for—"

Stanley looked at him sharply. "Don't get any cute ideas," he said. "If Frank's got a girl here—and I have to see that to believe it—it's his girl and I wouldn't advise you trying to cut in. You know how Frank is."

"Yeah, I know how he is," Dave said. "A son of a bitch! Anyway, maybe she's got a sister."

"Dammit," Stanley said, "can't you keep broads off your mind for ten minutes? We're up here to do a job—a big job. Wait till we do it; wait till we get the dough. Then you can get all the women you want. You can feed your fat gut, get drunk and get laid, but let's stick to business until we're through with what we have to do."

"Better tell that to Frank," Dave said. "He's the one's got the dame."

Joe came to the kitchen door. "You guys want to wait for Frank, or you want to eat now?" he asked.

"Now," Dave said.

"Come into the kitchen then," Joe said.

Stanley took the chair next to the stove and Dave sat down so that he faced the kitchen door. Joe took the pot of beans from the oven and put it in the center of the table. He put the loaf of sliced bread next to it and then went back to the stove and ladled a dozen hot dogs from a pan of boiling water into a large bowl. He carried them to the table.

"Coffee'll be ready in a few minutes," he said.

Dave looked at the food and then his eyes went to the paper plates in front of him. He looked up at Joe.

"Christ' sake, fellow," he said, "you call this garbage food? This may be good enough for you black—"

The other man's words cut him off in mid-sentence. They came in a soft, almost friendly voice. "You fat son of a bitch," Joe said. "Just say it. Go ahead and say it. Black what?"

Dave raised his eyes and saw the bread knife in the other man's hand. He saw him standing there, straight and motionless, halfway across the room.

Slowly Dave got to his feet. He was a good foot shorter than Joe but he outweighed him by at least sixty pounds. His bloated, chapped cheeks were fire red and he spoke through clenched teeth.

"Put that knife down. You hear me, put that God-damned knife down. If you think I'm afraid—"

Stanley quickly jumped up from his chair. "Oh for God's sake," he said. "What the hell's the matter with you two?" He turned to Joe. "Hell, he didn't mean anything," he said. "That's just Dave's way. There's no sense in fighting."

The kitchen door opened suddenly and all three quickly turned to face it. Frank Scudder stepped into the room. Behind him, they could see the girl, her face drained of color.

"Is somebody fighting?" Frank asked. He stared at them for a full half minute in dead silence, his eyes ice cold. "Is somebody fighting?"

He took another step into the room. He spoke to Tina over his shoulder. "Go into the bedroom," he said, "and take off your things. I'll be in in a few minutes."

He stood to one side as she passed him, looking straight ahead. The eyes of the other three men followed her as she walked past them.

When the door closed behind her he spoke again.

"My wife," he said. "Let's sit down."

Chapter Eight

Now she knew. Unequivocally and beyond the faintest shadow of doubt—the terrible truth was inescapable.

Tina Bennet Scudder, sitting in the deep old-fashioned chair in front of the log fire and staring at the cold figures of the calendar thumb-tacked to the wall above the mantel, knew at last. The calendar told her that it was Tuesday, March the second. Whatever lingering doubts she may have entertained had been dissipated half an hour ago when she had crossed the room on tiptoe and held her ear close to the kitchen door. It was probably the fat man's voice that she had heard.

"Yeah," he said, "we ditched the ranch wagon. Got rid of the guns, too. I don't think there's a chance they can trace us."

Even now, as she sat huddled there with Frank's bathrobe wrapped around her and with the flickering shadows playing across her pale face, she could hear them. The heavy door was not thick enough to completely shut out the low mumbling of their voices as they sat around the table and talked.

She wasn't terrified; in no sense was she even frightened. It was something different. Frank was still Frank. He was still the man she had married and whom she loved. Nothing had changed that. Nothing, she thought, ever would. But she had uncovered a facet of his character which she had never dreamed existed, a part of him that she found impossible to reconcile with the part that she knew and loved.

In a way it was almost parallel to the physical thing, the tuberculosis. The façade was healthy and strong and good, but behind that façade was a deadly killing germ which, if not arrested and erased, would slowly grow and eat its way into the very heart and soul of him.

She had known about the tuberculosis when she fell in love with him and when she married him. She had known it was there and she had been determined to devote her life, if necessary, to purging it and cleaning it out so that Frank would be in fact what he so eloquently appeared to be on the surface.

Wasn't it true that if a man needed help to cure the ills of his body, he might also need help to cure the sickness of his soul? And because this illness, which she had now discovered, was an illness of the mind, would she be justified in deserting him? In running away? She didn't think so.

Her eyes were moist and it was not the smoke, backing down the chimney periodically as the wind changed direction, which caused it. It wasn't self-pity. She was remembering back, remembering back those few short hours. How happy, how foolishly, blindly happy she had been!

She looked down at the table, at the tray of food which Frank had carried in from the kitchen more than an hour ago and which still lay there, the food untouched.

"Going to be tied up for a while," he'd said. "You go on and eat. Sit in here in front of the fire. I'll be with you later."

Nothing else, no explanations.

Now, she was afraid of explanations. She was afraid of what he would have to tell her, and he'd have to tell her something. It had gone much too far. Even Frank must realize that. She didn't know which would be worse—lies, or the truth.

Half an hour later, when Frank opened the door and came into the room, she had already left. He went to the bedroom and entering, saw that she had climbed into the high double bed. A turned-down kerosene light on the table beside the bed cast a faint glow in the room. For a moment he stood in the doorway, watching her. She could feel his eyes on her face as she lay there under the heavy quilts. She breathed, evenly and slowly, her mouth partly opened. Her body had the stillness of deep sleep.

But she wasn't asleep. She wondered if she'd ever sleep again.

He closed the door softly and went back to the kitchen.

That was Tuesday.

There was a high, cold front coming down from the bleak upper reaches of Canada and the wind out of the northwest was raw and bitter, driving the snowstorm before it. By the time the money train reached Idaho, it was obvious they were going to be in for some very rugged weather.

Cal Treacher was upset about it. Not that he was really worried, it was more annoyance. This was his last trip and he didn't want anything to happen; didn't want any delay. He'd made the trip often enough, God knows. And it had happened often enough—those long layovers while they waited for the great rotating plow to open up the roadway. If they were in luck, the layovers would take place in one of the small towns or cities along the route, but more often than not the storms or the great snow slides had caught them between stations and they'd had to come to a halt in some lonely pass and just sit it out until help came.

It could happen again; it could happen on this, his last run.

Well, if worst came to worst, he'd probably know before they reached the end of the line. He'd be able to telephone Betty, down in Twin Valley. In case they were going to be delayed, she would have to see to things in Denver. Of course she'd have to take a day off to go down to the city, but he'd be willing to make it up to her for her lost time. His rent at the boardinghouse was paid until Monday night and he didn't want to get stuck for an extra month. She'd have to see that his bags were taken out and checked, take care of the other things he'd planned to do himself, just in case they didn't make it back on time.

God knows, it wouldn't hurt her to give him a hand. He'd helped her out often enough.

Betty was the only one of his children who'd really proved a disappointment to him. The older boy's death had hit him pretty hard, but in his secret heart, the pride which he had felt in having a son who was a hero went a long way to compensate for the tragedy. And the younger one had turned out fine. Sent his dad expensive Christmas and birthday presents and had never given him any trouble at all. He'd started in earning money before he was twelve years old, what with his paper routes and working after school and all. He'd managed to put himself through high school and college on his own earnings. He'd been no trouble at all.

But Betty was something else again. The Lord only knows where she got her character from—certainly it wasn't from him and it wasn't from her mother, either. She'd always been a spoiled brat. And she'd turned into a bitter, discontented woman.

No, he couldn't say much for his daughter. And now this last business, this going around with that God-damned Indian, even talking about marrying him. Well, he hated it. That's all, he hated it. He sighed and took his pipe from his thin, sardonic lips. It'd serve her right though. Serve her damn well right. Probably all she deserved, an Indian.

Up ahead in the cab of the locomotive, old Peterson squinted his eyes and stared at the track bed as the great wheels under him ate up the miles. He too figured that they'd have a little trouble with weather before getting back to Denver. Figured they might be a day or two late, but he didn't care. He wasn't going anywhere, and he still had another five years before he'd be retiring. He'd just as soon spend the time one place as another.

Peterson had known Treacher for a good many years and he knew how anxious the other man was to make this last trip of his on schedule. He wasn't mean or vicious in any sense, but he couldn't help wishing that they would be late. The mean, miserly old bastard, it would serve him right. Peterson had never known Treacher to go out of his way in his life for anyone else; never known him to do a kind or generous thing. There was no reason providence should look out for him. The final decision, in case they hit really heavy snowdrifts on the return trip, would be up to him, the engineer. He wouldn't let Treacher's anxiety to get back on time interfere with his decision. If he thought they should lay over, or wait it out, that's what they'd do. Let the old man stew in his juice.

"If this keeps up, those passes are going to be bad," he yelled, above the sound of the locomotive.

Butch Hanrohan, standing next to him, stared out the window at the swirling snow and grunted.

Harry Bamberg felt the same way Cal did about being late. But for a completely different reason. He had a wife and three young kids back in Denver and he hated every minute he had to spend away from home. After twelve years of marriage, he still couldn't get used to staying away overnight, in spite of the fact that more than two-thirds of the nights of his married life had been spent in the celibacy of a bunk in the caboose of an onrushing train.

"We're going to be late," he said to Bello. "Sure as hell, we're going to be late. Just look at that damned barometer."

Horace Bello looked at it but it didn't mean much to him. And he didn't care in any case. Horace was thirty-two years old and he was engaged to a girl in Reno. She was working as a hostess in a gambling joint and they were saving every cent they could. As soon as they had enough money to handle the down payment on the tourist court, they were going to quit their jobs and get married.

In a way, the later they were, the better it would be. He wouldn't be hanging around town spending his dough. Every night he spent on this train meant that he saved a whole day's pay. The food and the bed were free, as long as he was on the train. Hell, they could be six months late as far as he cared.

"Let it snow," he said. "Hell, let's have a blizzard."

"Wait till you get married," Bamberg told him. "Just wait, boy. You'll feel different."

"I been waiting two years now," Horace said. "A little longer ain't goin' make much difference."

Trooper Clarke Upton spent Tuesday in bed. He kept a room at Charlie Hanson's Twin Valley Hotel, but he took most of his meals over at the bus depot luncheonette, even if it did make Charlie mad. He'd had the room now for more than two years and nobody could understand why he stayed on there. For the same money, he could have rented a small house and certainly almost any place would have been more comfortable.

The fact is that Trooper Upton liked the room, bare and miserable as it was. He liked it because just as long as he stayed there at the hotel, he felt that the assignment was only a temporary one. He had to feel this way, otherwise he'd have quit the service altogether.

Upton hated Twin Valley. He was from Colorado Springs, and he liked a big town. But for two years he'd been up here in Twin Valley and although he'd put in for a transfer each three months with monotonous regularity, he was still here. But as long as he kept the hotel room, he didn't feel trapped.

Twin Valley was a sort of out-of-the-way place and one of the few advantages of being stationed there was that he could do things pretty much as he wanted. It wasn't a matter of regular hours or anything like that. He had so much territory to cover, so many check points to make. The responsibility was his, although of course he had to report in to division headquarters regularly. But at least there was no one breathing down the back of his neck all the time.

Upton didn't take advantage of the situation; he was a very good trooper and very conscientious about his work. He took it seriously. If he hadn't, he'd have quit long ago. It was unusual for him to spend the daytime around the hotel or even in the town. Certainly it was unusual for him to spend it in bed.

But he'd been on duty for more than thirty-six hours by the time he turned in on Tuesday morning. The worst kind of duty, too. All on account of that damned bank job over in Ogdenville. Upton didn't mind action, didn't mind hard work. But just hanging around, sitting out in the snow and ice and cold at a roadblock—that was something else again. He would have welcomed trouble.

But nothing had happened and he guessed that his superiors had finally decided the guys who'd pulled the job had made a clean getaway. In any case, he'd been told early Tuesday morning to turn in and so he'd gone back to his room in Twin Valley and hit the bed. He had been so tired that he hadn't even bothered to eat or wash but just stripped down to his heavy underwear and climbed in between the blankets. He woke up late in the afternoon, pretty well rested and hungry.

As usual, there was no hot water and yelling down to Charlie failed to improve the situation. So he took a lukewarm shower, shaved and changed into fresh clothes. He strapped his gun to hip and went over to the tiny office he shared in the same building that held the telephone company's switchboard and the town clerk's office.

He called into headquarters and learned that nothing had happened on the Ogdenville robbery.

It was just six o'clock and he knew that Betty Treacher would be getting off. He and Betty often ate together. Betty was one of the few people in the town with whom he was friendly. Clarke Upton was only twenty-eight and one of these days he was going to find the right girl and settle down and have about six fine kids. He knew just what kind of girl he was looking for. Betty Treacher was just about as different from her as he could imagine. But nevertheless, he liked her. The fact that he sort of felt drawn to her, and that she liked him, was probably the result of both of them being pretty lonely and feeling like outsiders in the town.

Betty was a year or two older than he was, but she wasn't a bad-looking girl at all and she had a really fine figure. There wasn't anything wrong with her in that department. She was bright enough, in fact, just a little too bright, a little too sharp. She was always getting in trouble because of her sarcastic, cutting remarks. And she was hard. Clarke hadn't been around a great deal, hadn't messed around with many girls. But he knew that she was hard all the way through. She gave the impression of a girl who'd had plenty of experience.

Leaving the tiny office which was barely big enough for his desk, Upton crossed the hall toward the room, an exact duplicate of his, where Betty worked the switchboard. He was remembering the first time he'd dated her.

It had been a couple of years ago, a few weeks after he'd been assigned to the territory. Just about the same time in March. He'd rented a sleigh and taken her to a barn dance seven miles away in the next village.

They'd had a pretty good time and before the night was over, they'd killed the bottle of bourbon he'd brought along. On the way home, he'd turned off at a side road and parked. She'd let him kiss her but the minute he tried to go further, she'd stopped him. He still remembered her words and his own sense of shock when she'd spoken them.

"You probably want to sleep with me," she'd said. "Most men do. Well, let me get you straightened out. I've slept with a lot of men, at one time or another. But that's all over now. I've got a guy; some day maybe we're going to be married. He isn't around now and I'm not even sure when he's coming back. But I'm waiting for him. I'm just telling you so that you'll have it straight. I like you. I'd probably go to bed with you, if it wasn't for him. But that's the way it is and that's the way it's got to be."

She kissed him again and held him close for a minute or so. Then she'd taken out a cigarette and lighted it and said they might just as well get back.

A week later her guy came back to Twin Valley. The guy was Joe Moon, the Indian.

Since that time, there'd been no more dates. They saw a lot of each other, of course, having offices in the same building, and because each of them lived alone, they met often in the restaurant where they had their meals. They usually sat at the same table and talked while they had dinner. She never told him much about herself, and he didn't talk about himself. They talked mostly about the people in the town, whom neither of them liked much, or about the weather or the news events of the day.

Once or twice a week Joe Moon would show up and usually Betty and he'd drive out somewhere and spend the evening together. If Joe ate with her in the restaurant Clarke would sit at a separate table. The two men had a nodding acquaintance and that was all.

Clarke often wondered about him, wondered when if ever he and Betty were going to get married. But he never asked questions; it was none of his business.

Once Joe had got drunk in the town and Upton had found him passed out on the street. He'd driven him out to the lodge and put him to bed. It was the nearest thing to trouble he'd ever had with him. Betty, meeting him a few days later, had thanked him.

"He can't drink," she said. "Can't hold it. One drink and he's gone. Thanks for taking care of him." Clarke hadn't been surprised. He'd never known an Indian who could hold whisky.

Betty was coming out of the door of her office as he approached. Wordlessly, the two turned and left the building. They crossed the street and entered the luncheonette, taking their usual table well to the back. Looking at the typewritten menu, which never changed and which he knew by heart, Upton said, "Goulash again. Report says we can expect some cold weather before the week's over, and plenty of snow."

"Maybe I'll be lucky and the telephone lines will come down," Betty said. "Nothing like an enforced vacation."

"In this town?"

Betty laughed. "You got a point there," she said.

"Well, one thing," Upton said, "the snow won't be bothering Joe. That snowmobile he rigged up will get him in town no matter how tough the going gets."

Betty looked up at him and shook her head. "Not this weekend I don't guess," she said. "He's getting some people settled at the lodge. They're up for the winter."

Chapter Nine

When he returned to the kitchen after looking in and seeing Tina apparently sleeping in the bed, Frank carefully closed the door and went over and sat down in the chair facing the other three men across the round table.

"She's sleeping," he said. "You can go ahead and talk—not that there's anything to worry about. I've told you already you don't have to worry about her."

Joe was the only one who looked at him. He nodded his head slightly and then spoke, almost reluctantly. "Of course it's none of my business," he said, "but I don't quite get it. Why did you want to bring her up here?"

Dave Liebman spoke quickly, without looking up. "It's everybody's business," he said. "We're all in this together, ain't we? We're all taking the same chances. Nobody tole me anything about a broad being in on it."

Frank paled as he stared at the fat man. The tiny muscles around his jaw tightened and he leaned forward in his chair.

"You got anything to say, Stanley?" he asked in a hard, tight voice.

"I agree with the others," Stanley said. "I don't get it."

"All right!" Frank got to his feet and leaned over with his hands spread out on the table. "All right, I'll tell you. We agreed that once we get the dough, we'll bring it back here and bury it. That right?"

The others nodded.

"So we also agreed that I'm to stay on, along with Joe, in case everything goes the way we plan. That I'm the one—and Joe—who'll be taking the grief when the rumble comes. And you can bet that it's going to come. You can bet that we'll be questioned. Everyone within fifty miles of this place is going to be questioned. Everything being equal, I can take it. So can Joe. Neither of us has a record. Joe's supposed to be here—he works here. And I've got to have a good reason for being here, too. Well, what the hell better reason can I have than that I'm spending my honeymoon? They can check that and it'll check out."

"Sure," Stanley said, "you gotta have a reason. But I thought the reason was going to be on account of your health."

Frank turned to him and he spoke as though he were talking to a child.

"Listen," he said, "you still don't get it. The health part's fine, except for one thing. I was already up in the mountains, back in New York State. In a hospital, to be exact. There wasn't much reason for me leaving to come somewhere else in the mountains. Except for one thing. I married my nurse. And they don't keep married patients and their wives in Vet hospitals. So, when I got married, I established a good reason for getting out and finding another place. A good reason for coming here.

"They can check back on it; they can check on Tina. They won't find a mark against her. Everything I tell them can be cleared. All they are going to have to do is take one look at my wife and they'll know she couldn't be mixed up in anything.

"Once we've pulled this job, and if things go the way they should—and they have to because we're going to wait for just exactly the right time—then you two guys blow. It's all arranged. They're going to know that it took more than two guys to do it. But they don't know you've been here and you won't be here when they get here to check up. There's just going to be me and my wife and Joe. And not one damned reason in the world to suspect us."

Dave looked up slowly. He spoke softly, not looking at Frank. "Yeah, me and Stan are going to be on the lam and you'll be here with the dough."

Frank swung quickly to face him. "So what," he said. "Isn't that the way we arranged it? Isn't that what we agreed on? God damn it, isn't that why we knocked over that bank, so that you bastards would have running money? And another thing; you won't be on the lam. You'll be gone and you'll have dough to hold you over in Mexico until things cool off. But you won't be on the lam. The law won't even know you exist. They won't know who they're looking for. You'll be safe."

He stopped and slowly sat down. He still stared at Dave and there was a cold, calculating look on his dark, lean face.

Stanley spoke. "Dave didn't mean anything, Frank," he said. "We know that the dough is going to be all right. We're not worrying about that, not at all. It's just—well, it's this business about the girl—your wife. You know, it was kinda unexpected."

"She don't know anything about all this, does she?" Joe asked.

"No."

"Well then, how do you know—"

"I know," Frank said. "She's my wife, see. She's in love with me. What the hell's the matter with you guys, anyway? Do you think I'd marry someone I couldn't trust? Don't you think I know what I'm doing?"

"You going to tell her about it?" Stanley asked.

For a moment Frank hesitated. He'd like to say no, like to tell them that she wouldn't know. But he knew that she'd have to know. She'd have to know if she was going to be trusted. Otherwise, something would be bound to come out.

"She'll know," he said. "Yes, she'll know all right. And you won't have to worry about it, either. Not one little bit."

"Then I think you better start telling her pretty soon," Joe said, dryly. "You never know when someone may stop by here, and we don't want her tipping anything off. She knows these guys are here now, you know."

"I'll tell her," Frank said. "Just take it easy. I'll tell her."

Dave's fat fingers were drumming on the top of the table and he stopped suddenly and reached for the thick porcelain mug which sat in a puddle of spilled coffee. He picked it up and then, seeing that it was empty, quickly put it down.

"More coffee?" Joe asked.

"Naw. But I could use a drink. This goddam cold goes right through me. What I need is a shot."

Frank nodded at Joe who stood up and went over to a cupboard over the sink. He opened it and took out a bottle of rye. He took the tin cap off with his thumbnail and then pulled the cork. Putting the bottle down on the table, he went back and got three shot glasses, putting one in front of each of the other men.

Dave reached for the bottle.

"Make mine light," Stanley said. Frank said nothing and waited until the liquor was poured and then reached for the glass. Dave looked at Joe Moon.

"How about you, chum?"

Joe shook his head. "Don't take the stuff," he said.

Dave downed his drink quickly and then poured a second shot. He finished it while the others were still on their first drink and poured a third.

"Better take it easy, fellow," Joe said. "That stuff really hits you hard if you're not used to this altitude."

"How would you know?" Dave said, his voice nasty. "I thought you didn't drink."

"Oh, for God's sake, Dave," Stanley said. "What's the matter with you anyway? What are you so touchy about? The guy's right. I know. You gotta watch it this high up."

"I never have to watch it," Dave said. "I just hope we got a good supply. By the way, how long you figure before we're set to go?"

Frank looked at Joe, who hesitated a moment and then spoke.

"We can't tell," he said. "Everything has to be just right. We have to wait for the return trip in order to get the money in used bills. They make the run about twice a month and the next time she's due will be this weekend. Saturday afternoon. But that's the least of it. The weather has to be exactly right. It's got to be snowing and snowing good. Otherwise we'd leave tracks. On the other hand, too much snow can ruin things. Too much snow, or an avalanche along the line, and the train gets stuck miles away from here, we're out of luck. So it has to be just right."

"Well, how does it look now?" Stanley asked.

"This could be it," Joe said. "Right now it looks fine. But tonight's only Tuesday. There's no telling what it will be doing on Saturday."

"And if we miss this weekend, we gotta wait another two weeks?"

Joe nodded. "Yes. And maybe we miss then and it'll be another two."

"Christ," Dave said, "we could miss all the way along the line. We could miss until summer."

Frank interrupted as Joe started to answer. "Sure," he said. "Sure we could. But that's the way it's going to be. Remember, we're shooting for big money, about the biggest hunk of money that anyone's ever gone for. So what if we have to wait for a month, or even a year, or two years? You think you can make a million bucks in that amount of time any other way?"

"There's no way we could cover our tracks in case there isn't any snow, is there?" Stanley asked.

"Not a hope," Joe said. "Not one in a million. Another thing, it has to be a good wet snow and coming down hard. We won't know how much time we'll have. Can probably count on three or four hours at the very least and with luck, it may be two or three days."

"Two or three days?" Dave looked up sceptically. "How you figure that? Hell, once that train is late ..."

"Two or three days if we're lucky enough to have a blizzard, at just the right time," Joe said. "If we have really tough weather, the train could get stuck somewhere along the line and they wouldn't worry too much down in Denver about it. It's been stuck plenty of times before."

"Then let's hope for a blizzard," Stanley said.

Joe shook his head. "No," he said. "No, that's not good either, unless the blizzard starts just about the time we pull the job. Otherwise the train might be tied up long before it gets this far."

Dave pouted, shaking his head again. "Christ," he said, "we can be here forever. I just hope you got plenty of food and plenty of booze. Looks like it might be a long winter."

"We got plenty," Joe said.

"Good." Dave stood up and reached for the neck of the bottle. "In that case, I'll just take this along to bed with me. That is if you show me the bed."

Joe stood up and walked to the door leading into the living room. "I'll take the boys to their room," he said. "Hang around, Frank, and I'll come back and have another cup of coffee with you before hitting the deck."

"Do that," Frank said.

When Joe returned to the kitchen five minutes later, he carefully closed the door behind him. Frank was over at the stove, reheating the coffee. The Indian sat down and took a pack of cigarettes from the breast pocket of his plaid shirt. He rubbed a hand through his strange white hair and stared down at his feet until Frank returned with two cups. Looking up, he spoke in a tired voice.

"I don't like that fat one," he said. "He can be trouble."

Frank nodded. "Yeah, Joe," he said, "I know."

"Trouble," Joe continued. "He drinks like a lush; a disagreeable drunk, too. How'd you happen to cut him in?"

"I had to have someone," Frank said. "I don't know much about him, but Stanley says he's okay. Stanley's worked with him before. Stanley I can trust. He's quiet, but he's a good boy in a pinch. He says the fat one's good with dynamite. Knows his business. And we had to have someone who can rig the job."

Joe grunted, but didn't look less worried. "The man's a pig," he said. "I'd like to have him do his work and then go."

"We'll need him all the way through," Frank said. "I know he doesn't look like much, but it's going to take four of us to handle this. Four is the least—we could use a dozen."

"Not if he knows what he's doing," Joe said. "Once that train goes off the rails, and at the right place on the trestle, we shouldn't have much trouble."

"You never can tell. There can always be trouble."

"The trouble can start here," Joe said.

Frank looked up at him. "Here?"

"Yeah. That guy gets drunk and you never know what can happen. The kind of thing we're doing, it's risky having a drunk around. I only hope this weekend works out. I don't want to be stuck here with him, not for any length of time."

"It could be this weekend, all right," Frank said. "Weather reports so far are perfect. You're sure about your dope on the train?"

"I'm sure," Joe said. "I've already explained it to you. I get my information through the girl. Her old man is the guard in the money car. She's keeping in touch with him."

"Isn't that going to look suspicious?"

"It could," Joe said. "Except for one thing. This'll be the old man's last trip. She's helping him get packed up and ready to take off when he retires. So she's got a reason for keeping in touch with him. He's going to give her a call when they reach the turn-around point. By then we'll have a pretty good idea if the weather is going to be all right."

Frank nodded. "But how about the girl herself?" he asked. "You sure she's okay?"

"She's okay. I haven't talked with her about the job, but she knows there's something in the wind. And she'll be safe as a church once it's over."

"How's she going to feel if something happens to her old man?"

"It won't bother her one bit. He's a mean, stingy old bastard and she's always hated him. She won't care."

For a long time Frank sat silent, thinking. He finished his coffee and took a cigarette out, but then put it back without lighting it.

"Maybe we should take care of her after it's over," he said.

Joe looked up at him sharply. He wasn't quite sure what the other man meant by "take care of."

"It won't be necessary, Frank," he said. "I'm marrying her, once this is over and done with."

Frank stood up and stretched. "Good idea," he said. "I guess I better get to bed now. If we're all going out tomorrow to look the spot over, we should get some rest."

"We're all going?"

"You and me and Stanley," Frank said. "Dave should stay here and start working on the explosives."

Joe stood up and crossed again to the stove. "I'm going to have another cup of coffee," he said. "You go ahead and turn in." He hesitated a moment, and then added, "You'll have to warn that fat boy to be careful, just in case anyone should stop by. He'll have to keep out of sight. And Frank—" again he hesitated for a moment, but at last went on, not looking at the other man—"your girl, she's going to be all right if someone should come around?"

"She'll be all right. I'll explain a few things tonight," he said.

He went out of the kitchen and passed through the living room and softly opened the door of the room in which Tina was sleeping.

Frank undressed quietly in the shadows cast by the kerosene lamp. As he was about to lift the bedcovers and crawl in beside her, Tina opened her eyes and looked at him, her face blank and expressionless. Frank reached over to turn off the light.

"Leave it on, Frank," Tina said. "Leave it on for a few minutes. We have to talk!"

"We can talk in the morning, honey," Frank said.

"No. No, Frank," Tina said. "We must talk now."

There was a sudden sharp crashing sound, from somewhere in the lodge. It sounded like a bottle dropping and smashing on the floor. A moment later there were mumbled curses and then once more the lodge was quiet.

"Now, Frank," Tina said.

Stanley Kubet waited until Joe Moon's footsteps receded and he heard him enter the kitchen and close the door, before walking over and sitting on the edge of the bunk bed. It wasn't a large room and it held only the two bunks, a small round table and a couple of straight-backed, uncomfortable chairs. In the very center of the room was a small potbellied stove whose chimney went up straight into a hole in the ceiling which was protected by a round iron guard. There was a good fire in the stove and the bottom half of it was cherry red. A stack of cut wood lay in one corner.

Against the wall opposite the door was a small window and under it was an old-fashioned washstand on which was an empty basin. Faded but clean towels hung on hooks next to the window, which was curtained in a heavy red material. There was a hooked rug on the floor and the waxed pine walls were bare except for a two-year-old calendar. A kerosene lamp hung from the ceiling. The room was very warm.

Dave Liebman was already sprawled on the other bunk, his head resting against the wall. He had opened his shirt at the neck, taken off his tie and kicked off his boots. He held the whisky bottle in his right hand, which hung almost to the floor, one large thumb covering the unopened neck.

"No glasses," he said. "This is a hell of a dump."

Stanley looked up at him, frowning. "Jesus, Dave," he said, "you oughta lay off that juice."

"Nuts," Dave said. "It's going to be uncomfortable enough here. A man's gotta have something."

"It'll be all right," Stanley said. "We won't be here forever. But you don't want to get drunk. Not now you don't."

Dave hitched himself up until he was sitting on the edge of the bed. His bulging eyes stared at the other man and then he deliberately lifted the bottle and took a series of long swallows.

"For God's sake," he said. "Go to bed. What's it to you what I do? You don't have to worry about me. And nobody tells me what to do. If I wanta get drunk, I'll get drunk. Just don't let it worry you. Don't let it worry you one little bit. I been drunk plenty of times before and I'll be drunk plenty of times again. What I gotta do, I can do drunk or sober."

Stanley said nothing, but turned and began undressing.

Yeah, it was true all right. Dave had been drunk plenty of times before. And it had never interfered. The man had a fantastic capacity for booze. His great belly seemed to hold gallons of the stuff and it was true that it never interfered with what he had to do. Dave was an expert with explosives and he knew his business through and through. Stanley had worked with him enough to know that.

It was also true that the big man got in trouble. Often and always when he was drinking. But it wasn't because of the drinking. It was because of the women. He'd get drunk and then he'd get ideas and he'd start things. That's how it always happened. Usually in a bar or a nightclub. Stanley reflected that at least there was no danger of that here. Here, Dave would just get drunk.

Stanley climbed into bed and turned and faced the wall.

"Okay, pal," he said. "Get as goddam slopped as you want. But remember; you got work to do tomorrow."

Dave ignored him. He drank another slug from the bottle and then carefully sat it on the floor. He took off one sock and scratched his foot between the toes. Then he leaned back on the bed and again reached down for the bottle. For a long time he just lay there, silent and inert, holding the bottle and staring at a spot on the ceiling....

During the course of the next hour and a half, Dave finished the bottle of whisky. As he lay on the bed and drank, Dave Liebman was thinking of women. Each time he remembered a different girl, and for brief moments recaptured the sordid details of his encounter with her; he'd then lift the bottle and take another slug.

He'd started out in Brooklyn some twenty years ago as a laborer with a construction gang, right after he'd gotten out of the trade school. He'd been strong, and big for his age, even then. And he'd been smart. Within a couple of years he wangled a union card, although they were pretty hard for an apprentice to get, and started specializing in explosives. He went into that end of the work for two reasons: contractors found it hard to get men interested in what was the most dangerous field in the business, and the jobs with explosives paid the highest wages. Even then, in his late teens, Dave needed money. He was already getting fat and he never was much to look at. And already he had an obsession for girls. It was unfortunate that girls failed to find him attractive, but Dave soon realized that money made the difference. Money was the equalizer.

In two more years, Dave put on an additional fifty pounds and became an organizer for the union. It gave him a little more money and a lot more freedom. But by this time Dave needed a lot more money. He started shaking down contractors as well as running a loan-shark racket on the side.

He did his first stretch when he was twenty-four on an assault and battery charge after he'd beaten up a laborer who welched on a loan. He did his time in Sing Sing and it was there that he made the contacts which paid off so well when he got out.

The union didn't want any part of him once he'd served his time but it no longer mattered to Dave. He'd made the right connections and he knew a lot of people who had use for his particular talents. For the next few years Dave wandered around a lot. He had a number of jobs but none of them took much time. And they paid amazingly well. Working for a mining company in Pennsylvania, he blew up the home of a union leader conducting a strike—and three weeks later planted a bomb in the car of the vice-president of the mining company. Both sides, he found out, paid equally well.

The next time he was arrested it had nothing to do with his work. He was arrested on a rape charge after he'd half killed a seventeen-year-old waitress whom he'd picked up in a tavern and taken to a cheap hotel. He jumped bail and returned East where he tied in with a bank mob.

He made money but he spent it as fast as he made it. He spent it on liquor and on women. The women were, almost without exception, professional prostitutes and he had an insatiable appetite for them. Because of his reputation for brutality, however, he found even these women difficult to obtain.

It was indirectly because of this that he lost his mob contact; he attacked the thirteen-year-old daughter of a friend one day while the friend wasn't home. Neighbors heard the child's cries and called the police. They didn't get Dave, who'd heard the sirens as the police car screamed up to the house, but the girl's father heard the story from his daughter and he let it be known that he'd take care of the matter in his own fashion.

Dave met Stanley not long afterward while both of them were hiding out in Miami Beach. He'd been with Stanley ever since and Stanley had always managed to keep him out of serious trouble. Stanley saw to it that he got the kind of women who wouldn't make trouble, and took care of him when he got drunk.

They'd pulled half a dozen jobs together, but none of them amounted to a great deal. Not until Frank had contacted Stanley. This was going to be the big one—the real job. The jackpot.

Thinking about the job, Dave began to think of the men who were in it with him. Stanley was all right. He could get along with Stanley. Frank he didn't know much about. Frank wasn't like any hoodlum he'd ever known before. The guy seemed to know his business, except that maybe he was a little crazy. Kill crazy.

The Indian didn't count. He was just the local fixture. Dave went back to thinking about Frank. "Goddam lunger," he said in a husky whisper. "Wonder what that broad wants with him?" He began to think about Tina. Now there, by God, was a real woman. He reached for the bottle and lifted it to his lips and drained the last few drops. Jesus, what he could do with a broad like that.

His head fell back on the pillow and the bottle slipped with a crash to the floor. He cursed, not realizing that the bottle was empty, but didn't get up. His eyes closed and a moment later deep, strangled snores escaped from his open, too-red lips.

Chapter Ten

There was no use in even trying to sleep. Looking at the tiny face of her wrist watch where it lay on the table at the side of the bed, Tina saw that it was well after four o'clock. There was still a faint glow from the stove, but the air in the room was freezing cold. She'd insisted on having the window wide open, knowing that the fresh air was the best possible thing for him.

Now she was cold and she hadn't yet found sleep. Not since they'd stopped talking more than an hour ago and Frank had turned over on his back and left her lying there, wide awake and her mind in a hopeless turmoil.

Moving as quietly as possible, she slipped out of the side of the bed and found her bathrobe and slippers. She crossed the room and opened the door into the large paneled living room. The logs in the fireplace were still glowing and she went over and poked them to bring a flame to life. Pulling the heavy leather chair around so that it was only a few feet from the hearth, she sat down.

She wanted to cry, but her eyes remained tearless as she stared into the blaze. The one, single thought kept coming back again and again. Yes, he's sick. Sicker than I ever dreamed.

She remembered back to that first time she had met him and the incident of the hemorrhage, when she had helped him to the hospital. As a nurse, and as a woman, the sight of that flow of blood had merely served to increase the depth and drama of her love and to make her determined to stay with him and by him and to make him well and whole.

Why couldn't she feel the same way about this? She was more than a woman in love, or a nurse, now. She was his wife. Was a disease of the soul actually any different than a disease of the body? If she were loyal and faithful during the siege of one, shouldn't she remain so, when she discovered the other?

The words he had spoken, the things he had told her and the answers that he had given her questions, proved that he was desperately sick in mind as well as in body.

The strange part was that she had felt no fear, hadn't even felt as though he was a stranger. It was almost as though she had known all along. She had accepted it as fact, the same way she had accepted the hemorrhaging as fact. The thing which shocked her now was his own attitude, his own inability to understand, even though one knew this was part of the disease itself. He simply had no realization that he was wrong.

"Wrong—right?" he had asked. "Who can say what is wrong or right? Was it wrong that I should have been in an army, killing men for seventy-five dollars a month instead of being in college? Was it wrong that I should have come out with t.b.? Was it wrong that the government should have taught me the trade of killing and is it wrong for them now to object if I practice that trade?"

"Oh God, Frank," she'd said. "Can't you see, can't you see the difference? Don't you believe in anything? Don't you know that it is wrong to steal and to kill?"

"It's wrong to be poor," he'd said, his voice hard and uncompromising. "It's the great sin—the greatest of all. It's wrong not to have money. It's wrong to have a pair of lungs which are slowly being eaten away. I've only got one life. I'm doing what I have to do. Without money, you don't live. The strong men get it and the weak ones don't. There's no justice, and even you should know that. It really doesn't matter what weapons a man uses. Some use superior intelligence, some use an abnormal capacity for work, or an abnormal cupidity. Some stay legally within the law. But they are the same, all men. They use what they have, whatever tools are at hand, to survive and to get the things they want and need. And that's what I'm doing. I'm using the trade the government taught me and I'm using what strength I have."

She'd tried to reason with him but it was like talking to a deaf man. He had an answer for everything. "If a man has nothing it is either because it wasn't given to him, or because he was afraid to take it, one way or the other. It's easy enough to talk of moral values, when you've already got yours. Easy to discuss principles on a full stomach and from the upholstered seat of a Cadillac. The only freedom you'll ever find is the kind you can buy. And it takes money to buy it. I'm getting money the only way I know how to get it."

"But Frank," she pleaded. "Can't you understand; don't you know that there's such a thing as crime, and wrong as—"

"The world's filled with criminals," he'd interrupted, "all kinds of criminals. In my opinion the only real criminal is the man who refuses to fight to live; to get the best that there is. Do you think I'd be any less a criminal if I sat back and let you work for the rest of your life to support me and to take care of me? If I let you go without things, the things other women have? If I let you slave and grow old and tired and sick to make enough money to keep me in medicine and food and lodging? Would I be an honorable man if I did that?"

"My God, Frank, I'd be happy—happy to work and to slave for you. To help you and get you well again. To ..."

"What I've done, I've done," he said. "There's nothing more to say."

"You don't want to tell me anything about it, do you?" she'd asked then. "About these men ..."

"Only this," he said. "They were with me. We took some money. They're here now for a few days and then they'll leave. It's all over and done with and there's nothing more to say about it. You must forget they are here or that they ever were here once they have left. It's all over and there's nothing more to be said."

He'd gone to sleep then and she'd lain in the bed with wide-open eyes and stared through the darkness blindly....

Not for one moment did she consider leaving him. Tina Bennet Scudder was not only a nurse, she was a woman in love. And Frank was the first man whom she had ever loved. She would cure him of this illness just as she would cure him of that other illness. To cure him she must understand him. She must go on loving him and help him to eventually become the man she had believed he was when she married him.

It was only then, as she reached this decision, that the tears came. She was glad now that she hadn't insisted on knowing the details of what had happened in Ogdenville. That he had helped in the robbery of the bank, she knew. But in her heart she was convinced that he'd had nothing to do with the shooting of the deputy sheriff. He was terribly mixed up and confused and bitter and he'd done a terrible thing. But he wasn't bad. No, he was sick, but he wasn't bad.

Tina crept back to bed just before daylight. He stirred restlessly in his sleep as her arms went around him and her body conformed to the curves of his.

Joe Moon was setting the fire in the kitchen stove when he heard the thump. He looked up quickly and then silently glided out of the room and crossed to the bedroom in which he'd left Stanley and Dave. As he reached the door he heard the mumbled curses. It was just after daybreak.

Dave Liebman lay on the floor for a full two minutes after he fell out of the bunk. His eyes were open and bulging and it took him that length of time to realize where he was and what had happened to him. He slowly pushed himself up to a sitting position and then cursed loudly as he felt the sliver of broken glass on which one great buttock rested. Quickly, almost agilely, he leaped to his feet. His hand reached around and rubbed his backside. Then he coughed and spit into the corner of the room. He went to the window and pulled back the curtain, shivering.

Joe opened the door and looked into the room.

For a second Dave stared at him, then moved over and took his coat from a hook on the wall and put it on.

"Fell out of bed," he mumbled.

Joe nodded.

"No liquor," Dave said. "My God, I feel awful. I gotta have a drink."

Joe turned and started back for the kitchen. Dave followed and when they reached the other room Joe opened the cabinet and took out a half-filled bottle.

"Rye?" he asked.

"Anything," Dave said. "I gotta have a drink."

Joe handed him the bottle and Dave went back to his bedroom. He sat on the edge of the bed and his hands trembled as he twisted the cork from the bottle. He had it to his lips as Stanley spoke. "For Christ' sake—already?"

Dave finished the drink and carefully sat the bottle on the floor.

"Go back to sleep," he said. He himself climbed into the bed without removing his coat. He took the bottle into bed with him, and placed it under the covers.

Joe put the coffeepot on and then went over to the sink and drew a second basin of water which he put on to heat for washing. He returned to the small alcove off the kitchen where he slept and got his soap and razor and other toilet articles. Stripped to his waist, he stood in front of the small mirror over the sink and carefully shaved. When he was through he washed thoroughly, rinsing in ice cold water, and then ran a comb through his white hair. After he'd put on his shirt, he sliced several strips from a side of bacon and put them in a cast-iron pan to fry. He set a single place at the kitchen table, as he didn't figure the others would be up for at least an hour or so. As far as the fat bastard went, he'd probably drink himself into a stupor and then be out for the rest of the day. In a way, Joe hoped he would. At least then he might get it out of his system and be all right for later in the week when they'd really need him.

There was just one thing; he'd better keep the hell out of Joe's way. Joe Moon didn't like drunks. He didn't trust them and he was afraid of them. He knew what whisky did to him and he privately thought it did the same thing to other men. It made him crazy.

Joe ate his breakfast and when he finished he left the dirty dishes on the table and got into his heavy lumber jacket and pulled a peaked cap over his head, the type that had ear muffs attached. He drew on a pair of thick-mittens and then left the lodge.

Going to the large barn in the rear, he entered by the side door. Frank's car and the Packard were side by side in the barn, and in the stall next to them stood the snowmobile. Walking over to the machine, Joe looked at it lovingly. He'd designed and built it himself and he was proud of it.

The machine was a sort of large sled built on a pair of sixteen-foot runners which resembled long, extra wide skis. On a framework between them was the superstructure. This supported a small, powerful Lycoming gas engine and the airplane propeller, which faced the rear of the machine. Behind the propeller was a large square rudder, which, along with the engine, was controlled from a high seat in the front of the machine. This seat was wide enough to hold three men. Just in back of the seat there was a large, box-like contraption which could be used for hauling material, or, in an emergency, two or three more persons.

Joe had built in a gas tank and several other essential accessories. It was an odd looking contrivance, but it was amazingly efficient. The engine itself was air-cooled so that there were no problems with freezing. Regardless of how bad the weather was, the machine could get him where he wanted to go, just as long as there was snow on the ground.

Checking to see that the runners were tied down to rings in the cement floor, Joe then set the controls and stood at one side of the propeller. Slowly, against the compression of the engine, he turned it over several times. The extreme cold had made the oil thick and sludgy and he had difficulty in turning the blade.

He returned to the controls and turned the ignition key. The engine took hold on the third try and at once the narrow confines of the structure were filled with the roar of its exhaust. After idling the machine a minute or two, Joe walked over and opened the door to let the monoxide fumes escape.

He allowed the motor to warm up for about fifteen minutes and then cut the ignition switch with a smile of satisfaction.

On leaving the barn, he instinctively checked the lock on the heavy steel door leading into the cement-block tool room. Inside were the dynamite and the guns.

When he finally returned to the kitchen, he found Stanley and Frank standing next to the door and looking out the window toward the barn.

"What in the hell was that racket?" Stanley asked. He was pulling suspenders over the shirt of his long flannel underwear.

"I warm her up once a day," Joe said.

"How does she look?" Frank asked.

"Fine. We'll have no trouble with her, none at all." Joe went to the stove and shook the coffeepot. "You guys ready for something to eat?"

"I could eat a horse," Stanley said.

"I'll just have coffee." Frank sat at the table and pulled a cigarette from a pack, coughing as he did. "I wonder if you would mind fixing up a little juice and an egg for Tina," he said. "She isn't feeling very good this morning. Still pretty tired from the trip and the altitude is bothering her a little. I'll do it myself, if you want to show me where the stuff is."

"I'll be glad to do it," Joe said. "Just take it easy." He looked over at Stanley. "How about your partner?"

"He's in bed—passed out. Funny thing, I never knew him to go out like this before. I tried to get him up when I heard the sound of that engine, but I couldn't make him budge. He's lying there like a dead man."

Frank looked up quickly. "You sure he's all right?"

"He's all right," Joe interrupted. "Just drunk. Came in here a while ago and got another bottle. I warned him about this altitude, but he wouldn't believe me." He looked over at Stanley. "How much of that one did he put away?"

"Most of it."

Joe shrugged.

"He'll be through then for the day," he said. "With what he had last night, that's enough to do it. We can forget about him for a while."

Joe gave them hot cakes and bacon and coffee and the three of them sat and talked while they ate.

"It'll be best to take the snowmobile this morning," Joe said. "There's always the chance that we might come across someone; not a very big chance, but it's possible. If we're on skis, we'll be sure to be spotted and it will be hard to account for the three of us. In the machine, at least we'll see whoever's coming and one of you can keep down out of sight. We'll have a chance to get away before anyone can get close."

"There any more machines like that around?" Stanley asked.

"A couple over the other side of the Divide," Joe said. "None right around here. I can get away from anything except a helicopter or an airplane—and there's not much chance of one of them snooping around."

"How about Dave?" Stanley asked. "Suppose someone comes to the lodge?"

"Not much chance of that either," Joe said. "Anyway, the girl will be here. She can stall them off and we can arrange for her to put out a signal for us that I can pick up with the glasses if anyone's around when we return. There's a clothesline outside and she can hang something on it to dry. I'll be able to see it. The only thing worries me is about that fat guy inside there. He's gotta keep out of sight."

"How long will we be gone?" Stanley asked.

"Two hours. Maybe three."

"He'll be okay for that long," Stanley said. "He's out like a light and once he gets to sleep he's a heavy sleeper. He'll be sober when he wakes up. He always is, no matter how much he drinks. And he knows that he doesn't dare show his face. He'll be all right."

"I'd take the booze from him in any case," Frank said.

Stanley stood up. "You take care of what's around here," he said. "I'll go in and case our room and be sure there's none there. But I'm sure he'll be all right. He won't let liquor interfere with this. He gets drunk, but he won't let it interfere. He knows he has to keep hidden."

Stanley left and was gone for several minutes. He returned with a partly filled bottle of rye in his hand.

"Out cold," he said. "I left him a note in case he should wake up before we get back. There's no chance of that, though. Anyway, I left the note and told him to sit tight. Just to be sure, I turned the key in the door from the outside."

"Yeah? And suppose he wakes up and finds himself locked in?"

"I told him that I locked the door because someone might come while we're gone. But don't worry, he's out cold."

"Okay then," Frank said. "I guess we'd better get going. I'll take the stuff in to Tina if you have it ready, Joe. And I'll tell her about the signal and what to do if someone should show up."

He picked up the tray and left the room.

Tina was sitting up in the bed when Frank came in. Her long hair hung down and caressed her shoulders and her eyes were dark smudges. She looked tired and sick.

"Frank," she said, "I thought I just heard an airplane."

"You heard an airplane motor," Frank said. "Joe was warming up the snowmobile. We're going to take a short ride."

"We?"

"Yes. Stanley and Joe and myself. Be gone a couple of hours or so. Now try and eat some of this." He put the tray down at the side of the bed. Tina made no move toward the food.

"And the other one? The fat one?"

"He's in his room, locked in. He got drunk and passed out. You won't have to worry about him. He won't move for hours. We'll be back long before he comes to."

"Where are you going, Frank?"

He sat down at the side of the bed. "Listen kid," he said. "Either you're with me or you're against me. Either—"

"Darling," she said. "Darling, I'm with you. You know that, Frank. But I'm worried. I want to know what's happening. I want to know."

"Nothing's happening. We're going out for a short ride. As a matter of fact, we're checking on a way of getting Liebman and Kubet out of here. Just sort of reconnoitering. If you want to help, if you want them to leave, then just do as I say. Be a good girl and do as I say."

"I want them to go," Tina said.

"They'll be going. But you must help. The main thing is that no one knows they have been here or are here now. It isn't only them, it's me, too. If they are found here, then I'm in for it too."

Tina nodded, looking at him with dumb, frightened eyes.

"So the main thing you have to remember is that should someone show up, don't let them know that there's anyone in the place but yourself. You can say that Joe and I have gone out and will be back soon. Don't open the door, not for anyone."

"Are you expecting someone to come around?"

"No. No one at all. But there's always the remote possibility. That state trooper stopped by the other day. He could just possibly come back."

Quick fear came to her face and she gave a slight gasp.

"Oh, don't worry," Frank said. "He isn't looking for anything. It's just that now and then he stops by to see if everything is okay. But there isn't much chance he will. He was here only a couple of days ago. Now go ahead and eat some breakfast. You'll feel better if you eat."

Tina automatically reached for the glass of canned orange juice. But she merely held it for a moment and then put it back.

"Frank," she said. "Frank, you're not planning something else? You're not going to get into more trouble? Do something—"

He leaned down and kissed her, stopping the words.

"Stop worrying," he said. "I told you it was all over. Everything will be the way you want it now. We just have to get rid of Dave and Stanley. It'll take a few days and then they'll be gone and everything will be all right."

"I wish you wouldn't go out," Tina said. "I wish you'd just stay here now. Let them go, but you stay here."

Frank shook his head. He fought to keep the irritation out of his voice. "That's why I'm going out, baby," he said. "We've got to make plans for their leaving. Just do what I say. Take it easy and trust me." He turned to leave the room and then came back. "There's just one other thing."

He explained then about the warning signal; explained what she had to do in case anyone came to the lodge. Reluctantly she agreed to follow his orders. She agreed, not to protect the others, but to protect Frank. She couldn't let anything happen to him, not until she'd had the chance to nurse him back to health; to nurse his mind back as well as his body.

She was getting out of bed and starting to dress when he finally left the room. Ten minutes later she once more heard the roar of the airplane engine as Joe started up the snowmobile out in the garage. She stood at the window and watched as the machine gathered speed and took off over the snow toward the north. There were two figures huddled on the front seat. The third man, and she guessed it was Stanley, seemed to be crouched in the luggage box in the rear. As she watched, his head and shoulders ducked out of sight.

Tina went back to the bedroom and made an effort to eat the food which Frank had brought in on a tray. She finished the juice but ignored the rest of it.

He'd said not to worry. That it was all over and done with. It was like telling a man in the shadow of the electric chair not to worry. She began to wonder where they had gone and what they were doing. Could it be they were planning something else—some new and even more terrible thing?

It was then that she remembered what Frank had said about leaving the fat man behind.

A peculiar expression crossed her face.

At that moment she heard the sound of curses coming from the other end of the lodge. Frank had been wrong about one thing. The fat man was not "out for the day." The fat man was awake and stirring.

Her face assumed a hard, determined look. She stood up and started for the living room. She had no fear of being alone in the house with that gross and vulgar man. She was glad that she was alone with him.

If Frank were planning anything, the fat man would know. He'd know all about it. And she also must know. If she was going to help Frank, going to protect him, she had to know.

Slowly and steadily she passed through the living room and walked to the door of the bedroom in which Dave Liebman had spent the night.

Chapter Eleven

He was awakened by the high-pitched whine of the engine as the snowmobile left the yard. For a long time he just lay there, an obese, insensitive mass of flesh, motionless and obscene under the tent of blankets which covered him. The dark hair which grew on his cheeks stood out against his pale skin like clumps of brush on a dirty field of snow. Bloodshot black eyes buried in the fat rolls at each side of his nose and the two thick, over-red lips made the only color to relieve his yellow face. His mouth was half open as he breathed heavily.

Minutes after the sound of the engine had died in the distance, he slowly crawled from the bed. The note had been lying on his chest, and it fell to the floor as he started to get to his feet. He saw it at once and reached down to pick it up. Reading it, he cursed under his breath.

So, he'd probably still be sleeping when they got back! That's all they knew about it. Damn them, they shouldn't have left without waking him up. They shouldn't have gone off and left him like this. Be gone for only an hour or so, eh? That was just great.

He looked around for the bottle he'd remembered getting earlier and saw that it was gone. Once more he looked at the note. Stanley had written that he wanted him to sober up so that he'd get to work. That was just great, too. What the hell was the matter with them, anyway? Drinking never interfered with his work. And how long did they think it would take him to set the caps and rig up and test the detonator? An hour, at most an hour and a half. And hadn't they told him nothing could happen for several days at the earliest? He had all the time in the world.

He pushed his feet into his boots and stood up and stretched.

God, he felt awful. He hadn't slept much, but then he never did sleep a great deal. He shouldn't feel this bad, not on the amount of liquor he'd drunk. But then, of course, he hadn't eaten—not that garbage the Indian put out—and maybe there was something to this business about altitude after all. He felt a lot worse than he should have felt, everything else being equal.

What he needed was a drink. A drink would fix him up—and then he'd see what there was to eat.

He went to the door; the knob turned but the door didn't open—it was locked from the outside. He swore.

He was still standing there, swearing in rage and frustration, when he became aware of knocking on the door.

For a moment alarm came into his face and his hand instinctively went to his belt. His eyes darted toward the window and he was about to move when he heard her voice.

"Are you awake? Can you hear me? Are you awake in there?"

Relief quickly replaced the fear in him. "Yeah," he said. "Yeah, I'm awake. Open the door, will you?"

The key turned and the door opened.

"They must have locked it by mistake," she said, and smiled at him.

The smile surprised him even more than her words. He just stared at her.

"Yes, they must have locked it before they left, forgetting you were in here. Would you like some breakfast?"

She smiled again, turned and started for the kitchen.

As he followed her across the living room, his bloodshot eyes on her slender body and on her long blonde hair hanging loose to her shoulders, he thought for the first time in years of that other girl. The thirteen-year-old girl whom he'd raped so long ago, and who had caused him so much trouble....

She went at once to the stove and opened the cupboard next to it. "I can make some coffee," she said, "and we'll see what else is around."

His mouth opened and he started to tell her not to bother—that what he wanted was a drink. Instead, to his surprise, he said something else altogether. His words were a little blurred but his voice was oddly soft.

"I'll wash up. Be right back." He returned to the bedroom and Tina began searching through the food stores. Behind the cans of milk she found the whisky. She took a bottle from the half-filled case and carried it over and set it on the table with a glass.

She only had a couple of hours, three at the most. But she was going to learn what she had to know. If there was any hope of saving Frank, she had to know everything about the past and the future. It would be unpleasant, but treating the sick was usually unpleasant....

Almost without exception, no man ever really believes he is ugly or repulsive. This is particularly true, oddly enough, of the men who are least attractive. Dave Liebman was no exception to this rule. Of course he knew he was overweight, that he was not exactly a matinee idol. But he felt that he had other virtues which made up for the lack of physical attractiveness. When the women he had known had failed to react to his overtures, even though they were being paid to do so, he labeled them frigid or queer and dismissed them from his mind.

Back in the bedroom he found the pitcher of cold water and splashed some of it into the large crockery bowl on the dressing table. He stripped to his waist and shuddered as he dipped pudgy hands into the bowl and began to wash. For a moment he thought of shaving, but then discarded the idea. He had very tender skin and shaving was always an agony; with cold water it would be sheer torture.

From his pigskin bag he took a clean white shirt and put it on over a fresh undershirt. Before buttoning up the shirt and putting on the bow tie, he ran a broken-toothed comb through his scraggly, reddish hair. Looking at himself in the cracked mirror, he felt a lot better.

It was always like this when he was coming out of a drunk; he had an overwhelming sex desire. He felt the old excitement coming over him, making him tense and nervous.

That was the trouble, of course. Even under normal circumstances, he was almost impotent. When he'd been drinking heavily, he always had the urge, but the greater the desire, the less he could satisfy it. It was a horrible contradiction and one which infuriated him.

He had been thinking about her when he went to sleep, and here she was, looking for him. The second Frank had taken off, she'd come sniffing around. Well, he guessed she knew a real man when she saw one. And he guessed she could use a real man, after hanging around with that thin, half-dead lunger for a while.

Frank had said she was a nurse. Dave Liebman knew all about nurses. They were all whores at heart, every damned one of them. They had all the answers; he knew why the doctors and interns kept them around. They didn't fool him a bit, not one damned bit.

He hitched up his trousers and tightened his belt and returned to the kitchen.

Tina looked up as he came into the room. "Coffee's ready," she said, smiling and indicating the place she had set at the big round table. "And I've got the breakfast coming up."

He saw that she'd poured a mug full of steaming black coffee and that there was a second cup in front of her where she sat across from the place she had prepared for him. He moved over and fell into the chair. When he noticed the whisky he reached for the bottle and poured a couple of ounces into the coffee. He held the bottle out.

"Try it," he said. "Best thing in the world to start the day. Lot better than cream and sugar."

She started to shake her head and then changed her mind. She wanted to do everything she could to make him friendly. She smiled and took the bottle and poured a small amount into her own coffee.

"Sounds like a good idea," she said.

He grinned, showing his bad teeth, and nodded. Already he was beginning to feel a little better. He lifted the cup and although the hot liquid burned his mouth and throat, he didn't put it down until he'd drained it. The headache had started to recede even before she got up to get the coffeepot again....

Sitting across the table and watching as he stuffed the spoonfuls of food into his mouth, Tina remembered back when she'd first started out as a probationary nurse. It had been the hardest thing she'd ever done in her life, and many aspects of it had been utterly repulsive.

This fat, gross man wasn't sick, of course, but if she was going to find out what she had to know, she'd have to look at him in the same light as she looked at her patients. She'd have to smile when she felt like throwing up, she'd have to say pleasant, encouraging words when in her heart she wanted to say, Oh God, why don't you just go off somewhere and get out of the sight of decent people.

"It's going to be a nice day," Tina said. "Looks as if the sun is really going to shine. It's a shame they didn't wait for you."

Dave looked over at her and spoke, his mouth filled with food. "The hell with 'em," he said. "It's a lot nicer right here. You didn't finish your coffee."

"Well, I guess it's cold now. Shall I heat up some more for you?"

He shook his head and reached for the whisky bottle.

"Had enough coffee," he said. "It's better straight." He poured his coffee cup half full.

Tina toyed with an unlighted cigarette and spoke casually, not looking directly at him.

"Have you and Frank known each other for very long?" she asked.

"Very long?"

"You know," she said, "I mean before Ogdenville."

For a moment or so he stared at her, his eyes suddenly small and sharp. He grunted then and wiped some food from his shirt front.

"What do you know about Ogdenville?" he asked gruffly.

She looked at him and forced a smile.

"Everything," she said. "A good job. I was worried, but I guess with you along, there wasn't anything to worry about."

The sharp look faded and he nodded his head rapidly, his expression smug. "A cinch," he said. "Lead-pipe cinch."

She looked at him admiringly. "I guess all the jobs that you and Frank have been on have been a cinch."

She saw by his reaction that she'd said the wrong thing. Saw at once the quick suspicion in his eyes.

"All the jobs?"

"Well—" She shrugged and tried to make up for the slip. "Well, I just assumed that you'd been working with Frank before. He's never mentioned you, but I thought you'd been in on the others."

"I don't know about any other ones," he said. He lifted the cup of whisky, and she knew that his suspicion of her was crystallizing and that he was withdrawing—he wouldn't say anything more.

Quickly she stood up and walked around the table. She reached across him so that her breast brushed his shoulder. She reached for the bottle and spoke.

"I'll have another myself," she said. "You'll get ahead of me if I don't protect myself." She laughed and went back to her chair.

God, he thought. God, she hasn't got a goddam thing on under that sweater. Probably just put on a skirt and sweater and those slippers and came right out of the bedroom. He felt the saliva glands moisten his mouth and he gulped. She'd deliberately done it; he knew she had. Deliberately leaned over him so that he could feel the curve of her body.

"How long you been married?" he asked suddenly. "How long you know Frank?"

"Oh," she said, her voice deliberately casual, "long enough. A couple of months, anyway. We got married a week or so ago."

"Yeah? How do you like it?"

She caught the double meaning behind the question, understood the leering insinuation in back of the words. She felt an almost irresistible desire to lean over and slap his vulgar, flabby face. Instead she looked up at him under her lashes and smiled.

"Don't you know?"

He laughed. "Frank's all right," he said. "I just met him myself a short time ago, but he's a right guy. Lucky, too," he added. He stared at her face and then his eyes went to her breasts and he let them stay there. "Real lucky."

"It's going to be fun having people around while we're up here," she said. "A lot better than being here alone. Two people alone can get awfully tired of each other after a while. You know, sort of get cabin fever or something."

He didn't look up, just nodded.

"Yes, I was glad when you and that other man showed up. Not that he looks like so much, but it's going to be nice to have someone to take a drink with now and then. Frank doesn't drink hardly at all and that Indian—well, I understand he never drinks."

Dave raised his eyes. "Trouble is," he said, "we won't be here very long. Not after this weekend, if the weather's right and we can do the job. So we won't have much time to get friendly. Not unless ..."

She had to be very careful; she knew how suspicious he was. He'd already caught her up once, and she could take no chances. What he had just said confirmed the suspicion she had already formed. They weren't here just hiding out; they were planning something else.

She couldn't ask him directly. There was only one way; he was proud and egotistical and vain and she'd have to appeal to that side of his character in order to get him to start boasting. Also, he wanted to impress her.

She well understood how dangerous it was to tease him. But if she wanted to help Frank, she had to know what he was involved in.

"They should have taken you along with them," she said. "I should think they'd need you. Not, of course, that I'm not glad you're here. I don't like to be alone. This is a real lonely place and I'd be afraid, here all by myself. But they shouldn't have left without you—locking you in your room and everything."

At once he frowned. Yeah, the bastards, they shouldn't have locked him in the room. Didn't they think he'd have enough sense to stay out of sight in case anyone showed up?

Suddenly a second idea came to him. Was it because Frank was afraid to leave him alone with the girl? Was it because he didn't trust him—or because he didn't trust the girl?

He pulled himself to his feet and staggered slightly. That whisky was stronger than he'd thought. "Come on," he said. "I'll help you with the dishes. And how about a little music, huh? That radio work?"

Tina reached over and turned the dial. She played with it for a moment or two and then found a station broadcasting music.

"You just take it easy," she said. "I can handle the dishes all right."

He lumbered around the table and stood next to her.

"Come on," he said, putting an arm around her slender waist. "Come on, baby, that's good stuff. Let's dance."

She was unable to control the shudder that went through her as he pulled her close to him and his arm tightened around her.

They were almost of the same height and his pale, thick-lipped face was no more than an inch from hers as he held her. His feet remained motionless and she felt a quick moment of panic. His foul breath almost suffocated her. She started to pull away and at once felt the strength in his arms as they tightened around her.

The sound of the auto horn came then, over the soft notes of a guitar coming from the radio.

"Quick," she cried. "Someone's coming!"

For a moment he just stood there and she made a supreme effort and pushed herself free from him. She ran into the living room and looked out the window. He was beside her in a moment, moving with amazing speed for a man as fat as he was.

They both saw the jeep at the same time. It was about five hundred yards away and coming directly toward the house.

He turned and ran for the bedroom. "The dishes," he yelled. "Clean 'em up quick. And don't let 'em in if you can help it."

She hurried back to the kitchen and put the bottle in the cupboard. She didn't bother with the dishes; they'd have to stay there. It wouldn't matter anyway, she reflected. She wasn't going to let anyone in. Turning quickly, she grabbed up the pile of clothes and in a moment had opened the back door and gone out into the snow. She found a couple of shirts and threw them over the line, using the clothespins already on it to hold them, and then hurried back into the house. Rushing into the bedroom, she kicked off her slippers and found a pair of shoes.

There were footsteps on the porch as she entered the living room.

It was the trooper whom she'd met in the bus depot in town on Sunday morning. For a moment, standing there in the half-opened door and looking up at him, she felt that she would faint. Her first thought was that he had come for Frank, but she quickly realized it couldn't be that, it couldn't be he'd discovered the hide-out and knew that Frank and the others were there. They wouldn't have sent one man alone. No, they'd have come in force if that was it.

But the relief was short-lived. It must be something else. It must be that Frank and those other two had been picked up somewhere.

"Hello there," Clarke Upton said. He smiled at her and took off his wide-brimmed hat and knocked it against his leg. "Hello. How've you been doing up here?"

He stood waiting for her to ask him in. Reluctantly, she stood to one side.

"My husband isn't here," she said. It was an inane remark, but she didn't know what to say.

He moved then and passed her and entered the living room. He turned and smiled again.

"Cozy," he said. "It's nice to get in out of the weather. Sun may be out, but I can tell you it gets cold. Especially in that jeep. Got a heater, but it isn't much good."

She nodded, watching him with wide eyes.

"Anyway," he said, "I didn't come to see your husband." He opened a couple of buttons on his jacket and took out a plain white envelope. "Joe around?"

"No—no, he and Frank went out for a while. I think Frank wanted to take a ride in that contraption and see something of the country. I don't know when they'll be back. Not for quite a while, I don't think."

Upton shook his head. "That snowmobile," he said. "Some machine. You're smart you didn't go along. Compared to it, my jeep's a Pullman. I must admit, though, that Joe can really make it move. Goes places no one else can get in these mountains. But it's sure cold. Freeze you to death if you aren't dressed for it."

Tina nodded, dumbly, still standing by the door which she hadn't completely closed.

Upton looked down at the letter in his hand.

"Oh, yes," he said. "I brought this up. It's for Joe, from his girl down in Twin Valley. She knew I was coming up this way and asked me to drop it off." He held out the envelope and Tina took it from him.

"Wanted to stop by anyway, just to warn you people."

Tina looked up at him with wide, questioning eyes. "To warn us?"

He laughed quickly. "Oh, nothing to worry about," he said. "Just that we're expecting a real tough storm this weekend. She's blowing in from the northwest and is due to hit here Friday or Saturday. Chances are if it's as bad as we expect, you people'll be snowed in here for a week or more. Wanted to let Joe know so he can be prepared for it."

Again she nodded, still not moving. "Is there any danger?"

"No, not so long as you have plenty of fuel and food. We get these blizzards several times a year. They're real bad, if you get caught unexpected or if you happen to be out in them. But as long as you stay inside and can keep warm, there's nothing to worry about."

He rubbed his hands and his eyes went around the room. For a moment he hesitated, as though waiting for an invitation to sit down. But Tina said nothing.

"Guess I'll be moseying along," he said. "You'll remember to tell Joe—and give him the letter from Betty?"

"Yes, yes," she said quickly. "I'll remember."

For a moment then, as he started toward the door, she had an almost irresistible desire to tell him everything about Frank and Ogdenville and that terrible fat man hiding in the bedroom. To tell him about the mysterious job which was planned for the weekend.

She felt like rushing to him and burying her head on his broad chest and crying.

He had the door open and he was buttoning up his jacket. "Well, take care ..."

"Oh," she said quickly. "Oh, you must excuse me. I wasn't really expecting anyone and your coming so suddenly surprised me. I don't know what I could have been thinking of. You must stay, at least long enough to have some warm coffee. Or perhaps, in this weather, a drink."

He smiled then and closed the door.

"Wondered if you weren't going to ask me," he said. "Sure, I'll take you up on that coffee. Need it in this kind of weather. No drink, though. A little too early in the day, and anyway, whisky and this altitude don't mix too well."

"Just take off your things and warm up in front of the fire," Tina said. "I'll bring you a cup right away. I just have to warm it up."

"Sounds fine."

"And maybe something with it? Eggs, or—"

"No, just the coffee will be fine, Mrs. Scudder. It is Mrs. Scudder, isn't it?"

Tina said yes, it was Mrs. Scudder.

In the kitchen, her eye went at once to the clock over the stove. Frank had been gone for two hours.

Chapter Twelve

She waited until the sound of the jeep had died in the distance before she threw the coat over her shoulders and went out and took down the garments from the clothesline. For a moment she stood there, looking off into the distance, to where a great stand of spruce stood far to the north. Beyond them rose a steep cliff, almost covered with fir, and she could see the wind blowing gusts of snow on its upper, bare reaches.

It will be beautiful in the spring, she thought. In another three or four months, it will be covered with columbine and gentian and paintbrush and it will be beautiful. She wondered if she'd be there to see it.

Quickly she turned and went back to the house.

He was standing in the center of the kitchen, the whisky bottle once more in his hand. He gulped, his head back, and then went to the sink, dipped up a cup of water and took a short drink, and then once more put the bottle to his mouth.

She closed the door and stood watching him.

His eyes were bleary as he finally put the bottle down and stared at her.

"Why the hell did you tell him to come in?" His voice was no longer soft. "Are you stupid, damn it? You want trouble? Why'd you let him in?"

She dropped the clothes and took a step forward and started to force a smile.

"Why—why—"

"You're a nosy bitch, too," he said. "You were pumping me before; and then you ask a cop in."

He dropped the bottle on the table and moved toward her.

She spoke quickly, striving to keep the fright out of her voice. She knew he was drunk and suspicious and dangerous. He was no longer just a simple, fat, lecherous fool.

She said, "Don't worry about him. He stayed just for a few minutes. I didn't want to—"

His hand reached out and he pulled her to him. "You just like men."

He jerked her close and his thick mouth suddenly pressed against her lips. She struggled, tried to escape from his bearlike embrace, but she was powerless in his grip.

He pushed her back so that her thighs were against the rim of the heavy table and he leaned over her, his thick knee crushing between her legs. One hand held her by the back of the neck and the other suddenly tore at the sweater and came up under it.

She cried out as the thick fingers found her naked breast and tightened. His lips fell from her mouth and down to her neck and then she felt his sharp teeth as he bit into the soft flesh.

The pain was so intense for a moment that she thought she wouldn't be able to stand it. He was doing something with his hand that was agonizing and she opened her mouth and screamed. He was tearing at her clothes then, his body imprisoning her against the table.

Once more she opened her mouth to scream, but the sound never passed her lips, for the heel of his hand struck across her slender throat. She knew a moment of agony, and felt consciousness leave her as he half dragged and half carried her into the bedroom....

Twenty minutes later Tina sat on the edge of her bed, her face buried in her arms and her whole body quivering as sobs shook her slender shoulders. Her clothes were in shreds and her tears mingled with a slender ribbon of blood that was dripping from the corner of her bruised mouth.

Dave Liebman stood across the room and stared at her, his breath coming in short, tortured gasps.

"You ain't hurt," he said. "You ain't hurt, so stop that goddam bawling. Stop it, or I'll—"

His voice suddenly stilled as he lifted his head and turned toward the window. He listened for a moment and then took a step toward the door.

"It's them," he said. "They're coming back. Get off that bed and get into some other clothes."

He took a quick step toward her and his bloodshot eyes stared into her face as she raised her head.

"You say one word about this," he said, "and I'll kill you. I'll kill you and I'll kill that guy of yours. Understand?" He moved closer to her.

Tina looked at him and nodded dumbly.

He turned then and left the room, still breathing heavily. Tina slowly got to her feet. She heard the roar of the engine outside.

Joe had stopped at the far side of the stand of fir and taken the skis which were tied to the side of the snowmobile. Strapping them to his heavy boots, he turned to the other two.

"I'll just take a look and be sure everything's all right," he said. "Be back soon. Better stay close by."

He started off through the trees, the binoculars hanging from the strap across his shoulders.

"Christ, he better not be long," Stanley said. "I'm damned near frozen."

Frank took off his dark glasses and wiped his eyes.

"It's cold, all right," he said. "He shouldn't be long."

But it was almost an hour before Joe returned. When he did he told the other two that he had spotted the jeep in front of the lodge. He'd recognized it as belonging to the trooper, so he'd waited until it had left and then waited an additional half-hour.

He started the engine again and they came slowly in, watching carefully. When they reached the lodge, Joe left the snowmobile parked at the rear and the three men climbed out and walked up onto the veranda.

Reaching the front door, Joe was surprised to find it unlocked. He pushed it open.

Dave Liebman stood a few feet inside the room.

"About time, God damn it," he said. "What's the idea?"

"Who was here?" Frank asked. He stopped suddenly. He'd noticed the smear of lipstick on the other man's mouth. Without a word he strode across the room and opened the bedroom door.

"The trooper, huh?" Joe said, walking into the kitchen.

Stanley quickly moved over to Dave.

"You fool," he said in a low voice. "You damn fool, you got her lipstick all over your face. Get in and get it off quick."

Tina had stripped off the sweater and was standing half naked at the side of the bed when Frank entered the room. Her face was tear-streaked and her hair a rumpled mess. The tweed skirt was badly torn.

For a second he just stood there and stared at her. He saw the great blue and purple bruise on her breast and then his eyes went to the tooth marks on the side of her neck. He saw the tiny drops of blood.

His own dark, saturnine face was bloodless and his hands began to tremble.

Without a word she rushed at him and his arms went around her. She was sobbing as she buried her head in the hollow of his shoulder.

"Frank, oh Frank," she said. "Thank God you're here."

He stepped away from her suddenly and went to the closet. She came to just in time to see him whirl around with the gun in his hand. In a second she once more had her arms around him.

"No! No, Frank! You can't. It wasn't his fault. He was drunk; he didn't know what he was doing. And I let him out. I didn't have to, but I let him out."

He struggled to break her hold, but she had an amazing amount of strength. "Wait," she pleaded. "Wait. Not now, Frank. Not that way."

They stood for a full minute in silent struggle and suddenly he started to cough. He stood back from her and bent over and the deep, terrible sounds came up from his chest. The gun dropped from his fingers.

The paroxysm lasted for several minutes. At last he looked at her and spoke in a choked whisper.

"All right," he said. "All right. Get some clothes on."

It was an hour before Frank left the room. He had put the gun away and each of them had calmed down. She'd wanted to make him lie down to rest, but he wouldn't.

She told him about the trooper's visit and handed him the letter which he'd brought for the Indian, and she told him about the storm warning.

"Don't worry," he said. "Don't worry, baby. I'm all right now."

"Just get rid of him, Frank," she said. "See that he leaves. He's evil. He's a dirty, vicious, evil man. Promise me you'll see that he goes. I can't stand to stay here in the same—"

"I'll see to it," he said. "Just stay here and rest, honey. I'll see to everything."

"And be careful, Frank. He's dangerous. Don't let him hurt you."

He laughed, without humor. "Hurt me? Don't worry. He won't hurt me. He won't hurt anyone."

He found Joe in the kitchen.

Joe tore the letter open and read it and then looked at Frank.

"From Betty," he said. "She heard from her old man. He telephoned her from up in Wyoming. Told her they're starting back but that the weather is very bad up that way and he's afraid they may get stuck somewhere coming over the Divide."

"The Divide?"

"Yeah—and that would be just about right—if they manage to get over. It would put them just where we want them."

"How'd she happen to write—and send it up by a cop?" Frank asked.

"She and the cop are friends," Joe said. "She often sends letters up by him. He makes the rounds up this way every so often. And she wrote because she says she'll have to go into Denver this weekend and do some things for the old man in case he gets stuck. I usually see her on weekends."

As he finished speaking, Joe looked at Frank closely for a moment, his eyes worried.

"Say, you feeling all right, boy?" he asked. "You're looking mighty pale. Hope the trip—"

"I'm okay," Frank said. "But Tina tells me the trooper said we can expect a blizzard this weekend. This will probably be it. And we got damned little time. I want to get that fat bastard out in the garage and have him rig up the explosives. See if you and Stan can get him sober enough to get him out there now." He hesitated just a moment. "Another thing," he said, speaking carefully, "be sure Stanley goes out with him. I want Stanley to watch everything he does. I want him to know how to do it—just in case."

"Just in case?"

"Just in case," Frank said. "You know, the guy's a drunk. Always a chance he could crack up at the last moment. So be sure Stanley's with him and sees everything he does and learns how to handle things if he has to in an emergency."

Joe nodded.

"You go on out too," Frank said, "and I'll be along in a while. I want to go over those guns with you."

"Sure," Joe said. "I'll go in and get the others."

Stanley sat on the bench at one side of the small square room and he waited until Joe and Frank had returned to the house before he spoke. It was freezing cold and he stayed as close as he could to the gas lantern, which threw out a brilliant light and a small amount of heat. Dave Liebman worked over the dynamite at the long bench on the opposite side of the cubicle.

"Christ," Stanley said, waiting until he was sure the others were out of hearing, "Christ, did you see how that boy handled the submachine gun? He took the thing down and had it back together in no time at all. The guy's a whiz. And he shoots it just as well as he handles it."

Dave grunted. "He's too damned quick to shoot," he said.

Stanley nodded slowly.

"You should remember that," he said quietly. "The next time you start fooling around his woman, you should try and remember that."

Dave looked up quickly. "Aw, what the hell," he said. "He don't frighten me. Anyway, what the hell's he want a woman for? Without a gun in his hand he's nothing. What good's he to a dame?"

"I wouldn't know," Stanley said. "But I wouldn't want to mess around with him, that's for sure."

"He don't frighten me at all," Dave said. "Anyway—" he looked over his shoulder and leered at the other man—"that's some piece he's got in there."

"You trying to tell me—"

Dave winked. "Can I help it if broads go for me?" he asked.

Stanley snorted. "What did you do," he said, "get her in a corner and try—"

"I didn't have to try."

Stanley stood up and yawned. "Well, whatever you did, or you plan to do," he said, "hold it until we get through with the job. We don't want no damn trouble now." He walked over and peered over Dave's shoulder. "Why you putting that wire there?" he asked.

"That's the induction coil," Dave said. "Steps up the juice. You have to be very careful and see this switch is cut out before you make your tie in with the sticks. Now—" He went on explaining. He was still talking when the door opened and Joe came in, carrying a plate of sandwiches and a thermos bottle of coffee.

"Go on back to the house," he said to Stanley. "Yours is inside. Anyway, Frank wants to talk to you for a second."

Dave looked up. "Listen," he said, "how about a drink?"

"I'll be back in a few minutes," Joe said. "I'll bring you one then. How's it coming? You almost through?"

"Another half-hour," Dave said.

Stanley and Joe went back to the house and when they walked into the kitchen, Frank was back sitting at the table. He looked pale.

"How's he coming?" he asked.

"Good," Stanley said. "Almost through. He wants a drink."

Frank nodded. "You watched what he was doing—understand it?" he asked. Stanley looked at him quickly. "Sure, I guess so," he said. "Why?"

"Well, he could always get boiled and screw things up," he said. "I just want to be sure that in case he does ..."

"Oh, I could handle it all right," Stanley said. "But Dave's a real expert. Anyway, don't worry about him gettin' drunk. He'll be all right when the time comes. Hell, he'll be all right. He'll have to. We're going to need him afterward, after the trestle goes."

"I know," Frank said. He stood up and reached for his coat and ski cap. "Where's the bottle?" he asked. "I'll take him a shot. Otherwise he's liable to quit working and come for it...."

Dave looked up when the door opened and Frank came into the room. He quickly dropped his eyes. He'd been expecting one of the others.

Frank went over and sat on the bench. He took the bottle out of his jacket and held it out.

"Here's the booze."

Dave grunted. He stopped working and reached for it. As he pulled off the cap, Frank stood up. He lifted the seat of the bench and then leaned down and did something to the floor underneath. A moment later and he lifted the trap door.

"You ever see this?" he asked.

Dave took the bottle from his mouth and walked over. "What?"

Frank pointed.

"Down there," he said. He took the flashlight from his pocket and aimed the beam down past the opened seat of the bench. There was a deep, dark hole. The beam died out on the steep walls before hitting the bottom.

"Goes down about eighty feet," Frank said. "Used to be a well. Been there for years, Joe tells me. That's where the money's going to be. That's where we hide it. Nobody but Joe knows about this hole. It was sealed up and Joe came on it accidentally while he was building this room. Probably no one has even thought about it in years, if anyone's still living who remembers."

Dave leaned over and looked again. Then he stepped back. "Looks like a good spot." He went back to the workbench.

Frank put the trap door back and then put the seat down. Then he sat down again himself and crossed his legs.

"You about through?"

Dave grunted. "Just about. Ran through the whole thing with Stanley, although it was a goddam waste of time. Just dismantling the stuff again. Can't haul it while it's connected up. Too dangerous."

"Take another drink," Frank said.

"What?"

"I said, take another drink."

Dave swung around and looked at him.

"Say, what's the—"

"I just want you to have another drink. Go ahead. Maybe I'll even join you."

Dave looked at him in surprise. His hand went to the bottle and he held it out.

"You first," Frank said.

Dave looked at him for a second and then lifted the bottle and put his head back.

Dave wanted to laugh. He almost choked as the liquor ran down his throat. Jesus, this was one for the books, he thought. It was some laugh. Here he'd just finished taking the guy's wife and Frank was passing out drinks to him. And Frank must have guessed. Must have known that something had happened. There'd been the lipstick on his mouth, and Dave knew that the girl had not time to repair the damage to her clothes before Frank had walked into the bedroom.

Yeah, he must know. And instead of getting mad and squawking, he was passing around whisky! He'd had Frank wrong all along. Yellow, that's what he was. Plain yellow. He didn't want trouble. Not even when a guy took his woman, he didn't want trouble. He swallowed the liquor already in his mouth and took a deep breath and then another long swallow. It was then he heard the words.

"Good-by, Dave. You dirty, fat slob."

The shot came as Dave started to take the bottle from his lips.

It was quickly followed by three more shots, the automatic leaping in Frank's hand where he held it on his lap. The first bullet caught Dave under the chin and, as his head fell, the next three made a perfect line up the front of his face with the last one crashing the bridge of his nose exactly between his eyes.

The bottle crashed to the floor, its neck neatly severed; the liquor began slowly to seep across the cold cement.

Frank had to kick one fat hand out of his way to open the door.

Passing through the kitchen, Frank didn't look at either of the men who stared at him.

"Better get rid of him—down the well," he said. "I'm going to bed. Dead tired. See you in the morning."

Tina stared at him, her eyes wide with fright, as he came into the room and carefully took off the heavy jacket and threw it over the back of the chair. She was still staring at him, her face bloodless, when he brought the glass of water and held out the two pills.

"You better take them," he said. "They put you to sleep, and you can use it. So can I. I'll take a couple myself."

Without being conscious of it she reached for the pills. She spoke when she had them halfway to her mouth. "Frank— Oh, God, Frank, you didn't ..."

"Take the pills," he said.

Chapter Thirteen

Betty Treacher talked to her father over the telephone on Wednesday morning, just before seven o'clock. By seven-thirty she'd made up her mind. She'd get a note off to Joe by Clarke Upton if he was going out that way and then she'd arrange to get the substitute in some time on Friday and she'd take the bus down to Denver.

It wasn't so much that she wanted to do the old man a favor; she didn't care enough for him for that. But from Joe's note it looked as if he wouldn't be getting in for their usual weekend date, and she didn't like the idea of being stuck in the town all alone. Not with the storm coming, she didn't. God knows, the place was dismal enough at best. But with no Joe, and snowed in—well she just couldn't face it.

So she'd go down to Denver and do what the old man had asked, in case he failed to show up himself. If he did show, well, then she'd have dinner with him and say good-by. It would probably be the last time she'd ever see him.

Not that she gave a damn, but he was her father, and this one last time wouldn't really matter. She hoped only one thing—that Joe had been serious when he wrote that note and that now something would happen; something to get both of them out of the place once and for all.

She called the central exchange later in the day, after getting the note off to Joe, and arranged for the substitute to show up.

Thursday was a nice day, clear and cold. Friday started out the same way, but along about noon the snow started—the snow and the wind. Listening to the weather reports, she was glad that she'd made the decision she did. It certainly looked as if they were in for it.

She caught the Denver bus at two o'clock Friday afternoon.

She'd have herself a ball in Denver. It was just too bad that Joe couldn't be with her.

Old Peterson knew they were in for it as early as Wednesday night. Up at the junction point, well to the north, the weather had already started closing in. He could tell, even though the snow hadn't really started coming down yet. He'd gone through it often before.

They had several stops to make, and two layovers, and he doubted very much if they'd get any further than the Divide. He knew what those passes were, once it really got rough.

Things went just the way he figured they would. They made the usual stops, picking up and dropping off the money sacks. Horace Bello and Cal Treacher took turns riding in the cab with him and Butch Hanrohan filled in now and then. Treacher, of course, was supposed to stay in the money car itself, but he liked to change around.

Harry Bamberg, the brakeman, came forward from the caboose now and then, and everything went pretty much as usual—except the weather kept getting worse, and the further south and east they got the worse it became.

Once, early Friday morning, they were held up for several hours in a deep canyon where the snow had drifted high over the twin rails. But the plow showed up finally and cleared a path and they got through. They spent that night at a small station a little north of the state line and started out very early Saturday morning. By this time there was no doubt about it—the blizzard was blowing full force.

Peterson, with whom the final decision lay, was tempted to stay holed up, but after arguing for a while with Cal, he finally decided to go ahead and try and make it. He figured if they could just get across the Continental Divide, they'd have a fair chance of pulling into Denver, if not quite on time, at least early enough to enjoy part of a weekend.

By noon, however, he knew that it was a lost cause. They'd never get through. Already the drifts were piling high, and several times they'd come to an almost complete halt as the engine had labored through the drifts.

Peterson looked at his watch. It was a little after three o'clock. They'd been making miserable time.

Even blinded by the snow, he knew exactly where they were, about a mile from the long trestle which crossed the deep gorge some thirty miles or so from Twin Valley. They wouldn't make Twin Valley that night.

At least, with the wind howling at better than sixty miles an hour, the tracks over the trestle would be clear. He'd take the train that far, and stop on the far side. It would be the best spot he could choose as long as they were going to be snowed in for a while.

Cal Treacher looked out of the small window as he sensed the slowing down of the train.

"God damn it," he said, under his breath. "He's goin' to stop." He, too, knew exactly where they were. He started down the aisle toward the rear of the car. He was unlocking the heavy steel door leading to the platform, ready to cross over into the caboose, as the wheels under him reached the first ties of the long trestle.

"I'll never make it now," he said. "Never."

Neither Joe Moon nor Stanley Kubet saw Tina Scudder until Saturday morning. They saw very little of Frank, either. It was all right with Stanley; he'd have been just as happy if he never saw Frank again. The business with the deputy sheriff in Ogdenville had been bad enough. Even then he'd begun to regret ever getting mixed up with the thing. Now this thing with Dave Liebman was just about the last straw.

It wasn't that he didn't think Frank was justified; it wasn't even that he gave much of a damn about Dave. But there was something about the way it had been done; something about that cold, precise manner of Frank's. Like an executioner. It wasn't something that had happened suddenly, when he'd merely lost his temper and blown his top or anything like that. No, it was calculated murder.

Stanley was pretty tough himself, but there was that strange, almost inhuman attitude in the other man which shocked and frightened him. In spite of his conviction that the train job was going to succeed, he wished he was well out of the whole thing.

Joe Moon hadn't liked it either. And in his case, too, it had nothing to do with the victim. As far as he was concerned, he was glad to see the fat man dead; he'd disliked him from the very first. Another thing, it would make it only a three-way split.

What bothered him was the timing—why the hell couldn't Frank have waited? But he had done what had to be done. He and Stanley had gone out to the barn in back of the lodge. They'd lifted the trap door over the abandoned well, and together they'd hauled the great inert bulk over and had lifted it to the edge. Joe had prayed that it wouldn't get stuck on the way down.

It hadn't—he could tell when he heard the thud at the bottom, long seconds after he'd pushed the body over the edge.

Stanley had helped him with the concrete, mixing cement and carrying the freezing water from the well, and at last they had got the job done. Joe was taking no chance on the smell which would come in the warm spring months if he didn't get it covered up.

Once, very late Wednesday night, Frank started to cough in his sleep and it woke him up. He felt very groggy, but he climbed out of bed and found the light and the matches. He put on his bathrobe and slippers and then turned and looked at Tina. She hadn't awakened. He noticed that her face was very flushed and he put his hand on her forehead gently. She was hot; she must have a fever.

He stayed up for a long time and then at last returned to bed. He didn't awaken again until well after sunup the next morning. Tina was still sleeping, lying flat on her back and taking long, deep breaths. Her face was still flushed and there was a fine film of perspiration on her forehead, although the room was cold.

Frank put more fuel in the stove and went into the kitchen. Joe was dressed and sitting at the table having breakfast.

"Breakfast?" he asked Frank.

"No. Just some juice if there is any."

Joe got up and opened some canned orange juice. "Got a weather report," he said. "Clear today with high winds—and very cold. Barometer's beginning to fall, though, and we can expect snow and a lot of it within forty-eight hours."

"Good," Frank said. He picked up the juice. "Wife isn't feeling well," he said. "Think she's beginning to run a fever. She'll probably stay in the room today."

Returning to the bedroom, he saw that Tina was still sleeping. When he poured the juice into a glass, he also put in two sleeping pills.

Going back to the bed, he gently shook Tina by the shoulder. It took several minutes to awaken her. When at last she stirred she stared up at him without expression.

"You're very hot," he said. "Perspiring. I think you have a little fever. Better take this juice."

For a full minute she looked into his face, unseeing. Then she turned away again.

"Tina," he said, "I want you to drink this."

She spoke in a whisper. "I don't want anything."

He reached down and put one arm under her and lifted her to a sitting position.

"Drink it," he said.

Tina took the glass and drank. Then she dropped back on the bed and closed her eyes. Watching her still face, he saw tears form and roll down her cheeks. He turned and left the room. He knew she'd go back to sleep; that she'd sleep the better part of the day.

Along toward eleven o'clock, he put on his clothes and went out to the barn. Stanley was still in his own room, but Joe was puttering with the snowmobile.

"Going to do a little skiing," he said as Joe looked up when he came in.

Joe nodded. "Be careful," he said. "Easy to get lost around here." He hesitated, looking inquiringly toward the house.

"She's sleeping," Frank said, interpreting the look. "Stanley's getting up." He nodded his head to the door leading into the square concrete room.

"We took care of him," Joe said. His voice was surly. For a moment Frank hesitated as he reached the door, the skis under his arm. Then he turned back.

"You and Stanley can split his share," he said. "I didn't do it because—"

"I understand," Joe said. "I understand. It's all right. And we'll split it three ways. I could have done the same thing easy enough."

"Okay, Joe," Frank said. He left the barn and once outside stooped to strap the skis to his boots.

The sun was very bright, and he put on the dark glasses. They gave him a little relief, but after he'd been out for a couple of hours, he turned back once more in the direction of the lodge. He had a headache and the sun reflecting off of the snow was making it difficult for him to see well. He took it easy coming back.

Tina and Frank had soup and crackers together in the bedroom around seven o'clock that night. Tina still felt the effects of the pills she'd taken and her mind was foggy and unclear. It was very hard for her to remember things.

One thought kept going through her mind: it's over. All over and done with. There's nothing left now but to get away as fast and as soon as possible, as soon as her strength returned.

Several times he looked up to find her eyes on him, and once or twice she opened her mouth as though to say something, but then looked down and was silent.

He was very gentle with her and insisted on sponging off her forehead with a damp cloth. After she'd eaten, he took the dishes back to the kitchen, and when he returned he asked her if she didn't want to have him bring in the radio.

She shook her head.

"I just want to sleep, Frank," she said. "Just sleep." She closed her eyes and lay on her back, breathing softly. He watched her for a long time and at last undressed and climbed into the bed beside her. For a long time he lay awake in the dim light cast by the turned-down kerosene lamp. Finally he fell asleep.

When Tina woke on Friday morning, the fever had disappeared. She felt very weak, but she knew that she was all right—as all right as she'd ever be.

Frank lay next to her, breathing heavily. She didn't look at him.

She knew it must still be early; the sun hadn't risen yet, but she could see a gray sky through the window and knew it was almost daybreak. Large driving flakes of snow drifted past the window as she watched. She could feel the house shake as blasts of wind struck from the north.

He killed the man, she thought. Of that there was no doubt. He'd gone out to the barn and he'd taken a gun and killed him deliberately, in cold blood. What had happened in Ogdenville was something else. He'd been in on that robbery, and a man had been shot. But she hadn't believed he could have had anything to do with that part of it. God knows, the other had been bad enough.

But taking a gun and shooting down a man in cold blood!

There was no point in fooling herself any longer. It didn't matter now whether she loved him or not. Nothing mattered as far as her own feelings were concerned. She couldn't fool herself any longer. It wasn't an illness; it wasn't like the thing which was wrong with his body. It wasn't like the disease which was eating away his lungs. It was murder.

She began then to cry softly, muffling the sounds so that he wouldn't awaken.

She had to face the truth. Frank was a criminal; he was a murderer. All his gentleness, all his love for her—and she didn't doubt his love—none of it altered the facts.

Then she remembered what the fat man had said about the job they were going to do over the weekend.

She lay there, sick with fear of the moment Frank would awaken.

Chapter Fourteen

Tina Scudder knew that this day, Saturday, would be the one.

Long before she opened her eyes, before Frank noiselessly slid from the bed at her side, she knew. Lying still and motionless, it was hard to tell where the dream had ended and the reality had begun. The dream itself had been terrible enough, but now that she was fully awake, nothing seemed changed.

It was not yet daylight, but she must have been conscious for at least half an hour. He was over at the dresser now, leaning down and writing the note with the aid of the shielded flashlight. He'd dressed in the darkened silence of the room.

Several times she was tempted to say something, but she didn't know what to say. And the feeling grew within her, the sure knowledge that today was to be the day. Whatever was to happen would happen now—some time during this Saturday in March. Every instinct in her wanted to make her cry out to him, "Frank! Frank, don't."

But she remained silent and frozen. In her heart she knew that there was no holding him, that nothing she could do or say would matter.

He had loved her, she knew; he still loved her. But it wasn't a love which would allow him to listen to her or be controlled by her.

He finished the note he would leave for her, then switched off the flashlight, and came toward the bed. He leaned down over her and she felt his lips softly brush her forehead. She wanted to cry.

The door opened then and closed behind him. For a moment she heard the sounds from the far end of the house as the others moved about, getting ready.

Joe was standing over the stove, putting short logs on top of the dying coals, when Frank entered. He looked up and nodded, saying nothing. Leaving the draft open at the bottom of the grate, he stuffed a crumpled newspaper under the old fire and lighted it with a kitchen match to hurry a blaze along. He straightened up and walked over to the window and stared out for several moments. Turning back once more, he spoke in a low, tired voice.

"Wind's shifted and coming in straight from the north," he said. "Snow's still coming down very heavy, and the temperature has dropped down to five above zero, and getting colder. I don't like the wind. Going to make some bad drifts."

Frank went to the window and looked out.

"It's what we want, isn't it?"

Joe waited until he'd put the coffeepot on before answering.

"Yes and no. Those drifts get too bad and the train will never make the trestle. And then there's Stanley. What about Stanley?"

The door opened as he asked the question and Stanley Kubet came into the kitchen, pulling on a heavy woolen sweater.

"What about me?" he asked.

"It's this weather," Joe said. "We want it snowing, but if it gets bad, the train may not even get through."

"But what about me? What did you mean by that?"

Joe shrugged. "Just this. Let's say the train does get through and everything goes as we planned. But then, if the drifts start really stacking up and everything gets closed in, we won't be able to get you out tonight. I wanted to get you down to Boulder and drop you off so you could pick up the bus before midnight. We've gone all through it several times. First back here to get rid of the money and leave Frank and then I take you to the outskirts of Boulder. That way I'll be able to get back long before anything is found out. But if this weather really closes in—"

Stanley looked from one man to the other, his eyes worried.

"There won't be any trouble about that," Frank said. "If things get so bad you can't get out, then no one is going to be able to get in. So Stan comes back here and stays until we can move. There'll be no danger just so long as he's gone before anyone can come around asking questions."

Joe nodded, his expression dubious.

Stanley still looked worried.

"Listen," Frank said, "what's got into you guys? Hell, things are coming along just the way we wanted them to. We knew all about the chances we'd have to take when we planned the thing. Are you getting cold feet now?"

"No. No, but you know how it is just before a job," Stanley said. "I always get a little jittery." He moved over and sat at the table.

Joe said nothing. He turned back to the stove and started getting the breakfast ready.

"Everything's set," Frank said. He took a fat wallet out of his pocket. "There's six hundred bucks here," he said. "Identification cards— everything you'll need. You know what to do, where to go."

"Six hundred?" Stanley looked at him in amazement. "What do you mean, six hundred?"

"That's right, six hundred," Frank said, his voice harsh. "What the hell's the matter with you, anyway? Suppose you should get picked up and questioned. Do you want more than that on you? Could you account for more than that? It'll be plenty to get you as far as San Diego. By that time we'll have sent some more along. When you get into Mexico City, we'll have the rest of the eight grand there waiting for you. It will keep you until we can make the break and meet you."

"But I thought I was to start out with twelve hundred," Stanley said. "I thought ..."

"That was when Dave was going with you," Frank said.

Joe made pancakes and fried up ham and eggs, but none of the men ate much. Sipping his coffee, Frank rubbed his eyes.

"Can't understand it," he said, "something's wrong with my eyes. Seem to have caught some sort of infection. Last couple of days I've had a lot of trouble seeing, especially when I get outside."

Joe looked over at him and nodded slowly. "Touch of snow blindness, probably," he said. "It hits a lot of people. Be sure you wear dark glasses. It should go away in a day or so."

It was still dark when they finished breakfast and prepared to leave. Joe saw to it that each of them wore as many clothes as possible.

"Can't tell how long we'll be," he said. "This thing is blowing up into a full-scale blizzard."

All three of them wore ski caps with ear protectors and were careful to put on dark glasses. The last thing Frank did before leaving the house was to put the flask of brandy in his jacket pocket.

The snowmobile had been packed and made ready the night before. Joe had been very careful in stowing the dynamite and caps. Three sets of skis were strapped to the side of the vehicle and in the bottom rested the guns, wrapped in heavy blankets.

The engine was cold and it took a long time to get it started. When they eventually pushed the machine out of the barn, the snow was coming down steadily and blowing across the yard in blinding gusts. It was still not quite light and Stanley wondered how he'd be able to tell where they were going.

The raw, snow-driven wind cut into their faces, and before going a mile, Stanley was almost frozen. Frank was cold, but he ignored his discomfort; he was tense and keyed up, thinking only of what they had to do. None of the men spoke, as the combination of the wind and the sound of the high-powered engine made communication impossible.

Joe Moon was beginning to regret the entire project, he was wondering if the whole crazy scheme wasn't impossible—or whether, after all, he wanted to do it.

Stanley Kubet's mental processes were working along an entirely different line. He had no advance regrets for what they were about to do; he had only, somewhere deep within himself, a fear that the train wouldn't arrive.

Frank was thinking of only one thing—the money which would buy him the freedom and the luxury and the life he longed for.

By eight o'clock they reached the site of the trestle. The snowmobile swooped down into the valley and came to a halt between the first of the series of great arches which supported the slender steel rails, far overhead. By the time they had taken the dynamite from the vehicle and carried it down the ravine to the foot of the second arch, the snow had already drifted and erased the tracks which they had made in reaching the place.

Joe and Stanley did most of the work, but Frank was with them as they tracked back and forth. His breath came in short, torturous gasps and he was beginning to cough. His arms and legs were like lead as he trudged behind the others.

More than an hour went by before they had the explosives planted and the wire laid. The snowmobile was then moved back away from the trestle some hundred yards and the detonator box connected. They rigged a small canvas tarp over the box to protect it.

Joe hung a second tarpaulin from the side of the vehicle and the three of them sat hunched in the lee of it in an effort to protect themselves from the wind.

Frank took the flask from his pocket and held it out. He spoke in a hacking, weak voice which barely carried to the others over the roar of the storm.

"Better have a shot," he said. "We'll rest a few minutes and then get the guns out."

Joe looked at the flask and shook his head, but Stanley reached for it.

"Plenty of time," Joe said. "She won't be through for an hour or so anyway, and it may be a lot longer. May not show up at all." He secretly hoped that the train wouldn't show; that somewhere north of them it had been held up by the drifts.

As the other two men drank from the flask, he hunched up his knees and settled down in the snow for the long wait. He was warm and snug in his heavy woolen clothes. If it hadn't been for the thoughts going through his mind, he would have fallen asleep.

By noon on Saturday, Tina had made her decision.

She had gotten up as soon as the sound of the snowmobile's engine had died. It was almost as though she had known what was in the note he'd left for her; known without having to stand, shivering, in front of the dresser in her pajamas, as she read the few brief words.

"I will be back some time late today. Nothing to worry about. Try and get a good rest. Frank."

Nothing to worry about.

The words were so typical, almost symptomatic of Frank and what was wrong with him. She smiled bitterly as she reread the note. *Try and get a good rest.* That too was typical. He had committed a robbery, he had killed a man—or perhaps two men—and even now he was out doing some new and terrible thing. And he told her not to worry and to try and get a good rest.

They might be the words of a man who loved her, but they were not the words of a sane human being. For a long time she sat in front of the fire in the living room, listening to the wind whistling outside, as she stared into the leaping yellow flames. Several times she thought about breakfast, but she had no desire for food.

Once during the morning she went into the kitchen and turned on the radio and listened to a weather report. The winds were increasing and heavier snow was expected. Blizzard warnings were out for the entire region. Motorists were warned to stay off of highways and several main roads were reported closed.

As the hours passed, she found herself waiting with increasing tension for the return of the men. Fear was beginning to come over her—not for herself, but fear of what they might have done.

Shortly before noon she went once more into the kitchen. She realized that she would have to have something to eat, no matter how little the idea of food appealed to her.

It was after lunch that she came to her decision to leave. No sooner had she reached this decision than she suddenly found the lodge and the surroundings alien and terrible. She must go at once, blizzard or no blizzard. She dared not wait until he returned. She knew that once he came back, she'd no longer have the strength to leave.

She found paper and the pen in her writing case and sat at the kitchen table as she composed the letter. It wasn't long, and it explained everything.

She addressed the note, and then she looked out the window, but could see only the heavy snow. Quickly she put on heavy clothes and her ski boots and opened the front door. She saw that the snow was ten or twelve inches deep, and that it had drifted to depths of several feet in many places. She knew then that using one of the cars to escape from the lodge would be impossible.

Once more she went back inside. Carefully she made her preparations. In one of the bookcases there was a detailed map of the region, which she remembered seeing when they'd first arrived. Pulling it out, she studied the location of the lodge. The nearest hamlet was some ten miles to the east, a tiny dot on the map which she knew could be no more than a store and a house or two.

She felt her heart sink as she looked at it, knowing that to find it in the storm would be almost impossible, even if she had the strength to fight the blizzard. It was then that she noticed the thin line indicating the railway track. The track coming from the northwest ran through the town. She remembered the ski trip she and Frank had made several days ago; they had found the tracks where they crossed the trestle. The place couldn't have been more than three or four miles from the lodge.

Carefully she traced the line of the rails on the map and saw that their closest approach to the house was due north, only a few miles.

She knew that if once she could find the tracks, all she would have to do would be to follow them into the town.

If she were to leave the lodge and travel in a northerly direction, sooner or later she would have to cross the rail line. The skis were in the barn where she had left them. By twelve-thirty she'd closed the door behind her for the last time. She carried nothing but the clothes on her back.

The last thing she did before leaving the lodge was to take the note and place it on the kitchen table, weighted down by the china sugar bowl, where it would be seen when the men returned.

By ten o'clock Saturday morning, State Trooper Clarke Upton knew that he was going to have trouble. He'd spent Friday night at a small town some seventy-five miles northwest of Twin Valley and had left early in the morning in his jeep for the return trip. Before going a mile he'd been forced to put the car into four-wheel drive. At the end of five miles he'd climbed out and put the heavy chains over the snow tires.

Once or twice he'd been forced off the road by drifts, and had made wide detours. But it wasn't really until he'd started climbing to pass over the Divide that he began to realize how bad things were—and by this time it was too late to turn back.

He got stuck for the last time at a little before eleven. The fact that he was unable to get the jeep out of the drift into which it had skidded didn't particularly worry him. He knew exactly where he was. He'd traveled the trip a hundred times.

Taking the snowshoes which he carried with him, he strapped them to his feet. And then he removed the small compass from the dashboard. Fourteen miles due south by southeast was the Cramden Lodge, the closest human habitation. He'd have to cross one bad range and make a long detour around the summit, but he had plenty of time. He wasn't in any hurry and he knew that his safety lay in avoiding panic and conserving his strength.

He wasted five minutes while he slowly ate a chocolate bar before starting.

Trooper Upton was four miles from the trestle when the sound of the explosion reached his ears. Tina Scudder, approaching from the opposite direction, was less than a mile and a half away.

Chapter Fifteen

"It won't come. Not now."

Stanley looked at the others, his teeth chattering as he spoke. He was numb with cold, and the biting wind had turned his narrow face a blue purple. But more than the wind and the cold, the tension of waiting told on him. His nerves were frayed and jagged and his ears ached from the cold and the strain of listening.

Joe nodded. He also felt that too much time had passed; that somewhere up north the train had finally come to a halt, held up by the heavy drifts.

Only Frank remained optimistic. The excitement which had been building up all day had a far different effect on him than on the others. It seemed to warm him through and through. He felt the cold hardly at all. There was a feverish light in his eyes and although the biting, snow-laden wind brought an incessant stream of tears, he repeatedly wiped the moisture away and stared off across the snow clad hills.

"We'll wait," he said, tersely. "We have to wait. They're bound to get through sooner or later."

Stanley looked over at the Indian, but Joe was noncommittal. In a sense Joe felt that both men were right; the train was probably already snowbound—but there was nothing to do but wait and make sure. Looking off toward the trestle he gradually began to visualize what would happen when Stanley pushed down on the plunger and the dynamite charge exploded. For the first time the very enormity of the scene which would take place was coming to him. But he knew it was too late to back out.

"I'm freezing," Stanley said. "I can't take much more of this."

Joe held out the flask which still contained a few ounces of liquor.

"Drink this," he said. "And move around a little. Get your blood circulating. It's dangerous to sit still in this kind of weather."

"If we could just start some sort of fire," Stanley began.

"We can't," Frank said. "We'll just have to wait."

Joe looked up and started to say something, and then closed his lips and stood tense and listening. Far off he heard the faint sound of a rumble. He shook his head and motioned for the others to be still. Neither Stanley nor Frank, however, heard the sound for another three or four minutes.

"She's coming," Joe said at last. "I can hear her over the ridge some-where. She's coming."

Stanley was shaking badly as he stood up and stared into the wind.

"Get to the box," Frank said in a cold voice. "Get on that plunger, Stan. Quick."

"We got time," Joe said. "Sound carries a long way in this air." His eyes went over to the spot where the plunger box had been placed on the white snow, and he shook his head slightly.

Frank turned to Stanley. "Be sure," he said. "Very sure. Don't let her go until the engine is well out on the trestle."

For a moment Stanley looked at him blankly, and then he nodded. He moved off and Frank quickly followed him. Joe watched the two of them for a moment and then he shrugged and walked over to where the snowmobile squatted. He leaned against it and watched the tres-tle. By this time, he could hear the approaching train very clearly. It would be in sight any moment.

Joe shook his head slowly. "I'm a fool," he said. "A damned fool."

Neither Frank nor Stanley heard him. The engine of the money train, heading back to Denver, from its northern run, was rounding the bend and bearing down on the trestle. Through the snow, Frank could see the silhouette of the engineer as he leaned forward and reached for the throttle. The engine slowly approached and started out across the trestle, followed by the money car and the caboose.

Frank shouted at Stanley.

"Now!"

Of the five men on the train, Cal Treacher was the only man who realized what must have happened. Even before the explosion, Cal had an inkling of what was taking place.

A moment after Peterson began to pull back on the throttle to bring the train to a slow stop on the opposite side of the trestle, Cal realized that their speed was slowing down. He knew that the engi-neer had made up his mind and that he was going to come to a stop and wait the storm out.

This knowledge infuriated him; he was anxious to get back to Den-ver and get this last trip of his career over and done with. Peterson was a fool, a stupid old fool with neither guts nor ability. All he had to do was keep on going and they could make it. Stopping was a de-cision which they should all share. Of course, technically, the re-sponsibility was with Peterson, but nevertheless he should consult the rest of them.

Cursing under his breath, Treacher quickly started forward. He was crossing the threshold of the doorway to get aboard the engine when he happened to look out. He saw the snowmobile clearly. A short distance from it he spotted Frank and Stanley, and saw Stanley suddenly lean down as he pushed the plunger in.

Of course he didn't know what was happening or what was about to happen. He acted instinctively, because for years he had trained himself to be prepared for the unexpected. He saw three men in a spot where he had never seen anyone before. He saw three men standing near the trestle in the middle of a blizzard, and he sensed that the train was going to come to a halt. He didn't hesitate, but reached for the high-powered rifle which rested on the rack next to where he stood.

His hand had closed firmly around the stock of the gun when the sound of the explosion crashed into his ears. A second later, as he stood dazed and shocked, the coupling between the engine and the money car snapped and the quick jolt threw him forward and onto the small open platform. He fell from the far side out into the open void above the canyon, even while the money car was following the engine out across the twisted rails, to plunge downward. Treacher landed a hundred feet below in a deep snow bank, still clutching the rifle. Although the sudden long drop knocked him senseless and he landed bruised and badly shaken up, he suffered neither broken bones nor serious injury.

Old Peterson himself went to his death convinced that a human error, an error of his own, was responsible for the disaster. The last conscious thought he had was one of regret for not having decided to stop the train long before it reached the trestle. Of course if he had stopped earlier in the day, the accident could have been avoided. He was wrong, however, in thinking the fault lay with himself. He never realized that the accident was caused by the blowing up of the trestle, but died thinking the bridge across the canyon had been taken out by the storm itself.

Peterson had already pulled back the throttle to slow the train and was reaching for the air brakes when, looking out the window at his side, he saw the road bed in front of him seem suddenly to rise in the air and disintegrate. By the time his hand had pulled back the brake lever the great locomotive was already plunging down into the canyon.

As the engine left the rails to ride out for a brief moment into empty space, its great driving wheels still racing madly, it turned with almost agonizing slowness on its side, and then like some fantastically graceful diver, nosed down so that when it finally struck it landed head-on. The boiler burst with the contact, and a cloud of live steam momentarily engulfed the steel monster as it exploded into fragments.

Somewhere deep in the inferno were old Peterson and Butch Hanrohan, both of whom rode the engine to their death, frozen to their positions in the cab by sudden shock and surprise. Neither man had time to develop a sense of actual fear.

The explosion would have been a highly dramatic spectacle, but for the three men who watched, the blowing up of the trestle was dwarfed by the drama of the death of the train itself. It was like watching the death of some weird, prehistoric monster, and although the whole thing was over and done with in a matter of seconds, to those who watched it seemed that time stood still and that it would never end.

The money car, which had broken loose from the engine at the moment of the explosion, followed after the locomotive almost like a dutiful wife, making the same graceful arc in the air. But instead of crashing nose first, it twisted at the last moment to fall on its side, missing the great pile of rocks on which the engine had crashed, to land in soft packed snow. But the weight of the car was enough so that it cracked open all along one side, and it lay there like some huge obscene worm which had been neatly split down its middle.

The wheels of the caboose jumped the rails when the explosion came, and rode the ties out onto the trestle. The strain broke the couplings and for a moment it looked as though this last car, with her two passengers, Harry Bamberg, the brakeman, and Horace Bello, the guard, might be saved.

Moving with the studied caution of a figure in a slow-motion picture, it slowly proceeded down the track and had almost come to a stop when it finally reached the yawning gap in the trestle which had been created by the blast. The front trucks went out into space and there was a grinding, splintering crash. Then the main body of the car followed the front wheels and hung on for a moment, until finally it too fell, turning slowly end over end to land in the canyon several hundred feet from the shattered money car.

The caboose was largely made of wood, and was crushed into kindling when it struck the rocks. Within minutes it was a mass of flames from the fire started by the potbellied stove. But by this time both of the car's riders were already dead, smashed into oblivion in the heart of the wreckage.

Frank was the first to speak. He didn't look at the others and he spoke in a low, husky voice, but it probably wouldn't have made much difference if he had yelled the words. They wouldn't have heard him.

"Jesus!" he said. "Jesus Christ!"

Stanley still leaned over, his hands glued to the handles of the plunger, frozen in a half-stooped position but with his head lifted and his wide, frightened eyes on the burning wreckage of the caboose. Joe Moon stood at his side, arms akimbo and feet widespread. Every drop of blood had left his dark face and his skin looked yellow and dead. His mouth was open, but he didn't seem to be breathing at all.

Frank had to jerk his arm several times to get his attention.

"The guns," he said. "Get the guns, quick." He pushed him toward the snowmobile.

It took both of them to free Stanley's hands from the plunger and they had to help him along to get him into the snowmobile and propped up on the seat. He seemed in a state of complete shock. Joe himself moved like an automaton as he took Frank's orders. He managed to get the engine started and he steered the machine almost blindly as they approached the spot where the money car lay on its side.

Frank sat between the other two, the submachine gun cradled in his arms. He was cursing steadily, in a slow, soft monotone.

Stanley found it impossible to look at the wreckage as they approached. His eyes were lifeless as he stared at the snow under the runners of the vehicle. Joe himself kept his eyes straight ahead. He drove automatically as he steered the snowmobile to a spot some fifty feet from the wreckage of the money car.

Frank's face was feverish with excitement and his thin lips twitched. He seemed utterly unaware of the other two men. He leaped to the ground as they stopped and turned toward the money car.

The shock of the long fall into the snow bank had knocked Cal Treacher unconscious, but he was out for less than a minute. He still had no clear idea of what had happened, and for several seconds after he came to, he just lay there. Then, groaning painfully, he began to struggle to get himself out of the snow bank. It took him several minutes, but at last he was on his feet. He still carried the repeating rifle.

The old man's faded eyes took in the wreckage of the train with shocked disbelief. He was off to one side of the engine, almost midway between the flaming caboose and the money car. At last, slowly and painfully, he started to struggle through the drifts, walking toward the spot where the money car lay on its side. The car itself was between him and the snowmobile, which had just come to a halt.

Cal Treacher rounded the end of the car, half crawling and half walking, as Frank leaped to the ground not twenty yards away.

By this time both Joe Moon and Stanley were watching Frank. They remained on the seat of the vehicle, motionless, apparently waiting to be told what to do. Neither of them noticed Treacher, but Frank saw the man at once. He could see his features clearly, and Treacher didn't seem to be looking at them at all, but was looking off over their heads.

Blood from a gash on Treacher's brow dripped down into his eyes, and his mind was dazed and confused. Things had happened fast, too fast. But one thing was very clear. The money train had been wrecked. Something must have caused that wreck. It had been his job to protect the cargo on that train, a cargo of millions of dollars. At the moment that cargo was, as far as he knew, still lying in the broken car a few yards off.

But coming toward him was a man carrying a machine gun.

Instincts which had been generated by some thirty-five years as an armed guard motivated Cal Treacher when he lifted the repeating rifle, and it came to life as he staggered toward the trio of men.

Frank had raised the submachine gun and his finger was pressing the trigger before Cal had sent more than a half dozen slugs in their direction. The soft-nosed bullets from the machine gun virtually cut Treacher in two, not ten feet from the car. But by that time the damage had been done.

Treacher's first slug had smashed into the magneto of the snowmobile's engine. A second one hit the gas tank, which at once flamed up. The third slug took Stanley Kubet neatly between the eyes, and he died as he fell from the seat of the machine.

Frank paid no attention to Joe Moon as the Indian leaped to the ground and began a futile attempt to put out the fire. He dropped the machine gun and was struggling through the snow toward the money car even as the other man yelled at him.

"Frank," Joe cried. "Frank, for God's sake, the gas tank's on fire!" He stopped then and stepped away from the snowmobile. The flames were shooting up high in the air and Joe leaned down and dragged Stanley's body several feet away. When he next looked up Frank had already struggled halfway to the money car.

"Frank," he cried once more. "Frank, come back."

He heard the other man call something over his shoulder and watched him continue toward the money car.

Joe turned back to the snowmobile. One quick look and he knew he'd never be able to put out the flames. He made no attempt to do so, but instead walked around to the windward side and unstrapped two sets of skis.

"The money is no good now," he said aloud. "No good at all." Tying the skis to his heavy boots, he again circled around until he stood over Stanley. He leaned down and felt for a heartbeat and then, after a moment, slowly stood up, shaking his head.

For several long minutes he stood there and stared over to where Frank had disappeared into the money car.

He turned slowly and watched the burning snowmobile. It was then that the old feeling crept back, the feeling of inertia and frustration which he had always had. It was like all of those other times when, at the last moment, just as success seemed to be within his reach, fate had stepped in to crush his hopes.

He knew only too well what the destruction of their means of escape meant. He understood the tragedy of that accidental shot which had fired the gas tank of the snowmobile. There would be no hope of removing it, no hope of hiding what would be left after the flames died down. Sooner or later, after the wreck was discovered, they would find it and they would know.

Stanley was dead, and there were only himself and Frank left, and Frank was obsessed with the desire to kill and destroy, dying of tuberculosis and gone mad with his desire for money.

The money was there, all right; all they had to do was take it. But how far could they get? Back to the lodge? Then what?

Joe Moon knew the country, and he knew the weather. He knew full well that there would be no chance of getting one of the cars out, no hope of successful flight. The very thought of flight, with the law forever getting closer, made him feel more and more depressed. The one thing which had attracted him to the plan in the first place was the fact that it had seemed fool-proof, that no one could tie him to it, that once they had the money they would be safe.

But it was all spoiled now. The destruction of their means of escape and the forced leaving of a trail which would lead directly to them had ruined everything. This time the failure was absolute and complete.

He finally turned and started off with long strides, heading directly west. He knew that he had no chance; he'd just go until they caught up with him.

The car lay on its side, twisted and distorted and split open like a cracked lobster. It lay almost buried in the deep snow, but still Frank had a hard time climbing up over the end and crawling in. Frank had to take off the dark glasses in order to see anything at all in the half light and it took him several minutes to adjust himself so that he was able to see into the murky interior. But shafts of light came down through the cracked side, and they helped a little.

In the frenzy of his activity, he wasted a good many minutes, but at last he found what he was looking for. It lay at the far end of the car, on its side, with its four short castored legs in the air. The tarnished round dial was on top and he climbed over the huge old safe to reach it. He was muttering and cursing as he tore at the great iron door. During those first few moments he seemed unable to realize that the safe was locked; that although it had been upset and banged around, it was still as invulnerable as it had been before the crash.

At last, crying and cursing, he fell back and began to cough, shaking and shuddering. He slid back off the safe into a pile of shattered glass. His eyes fell then and he saw the machine gun. Quickly he reached down and picked it up. With a laugh, he pointed it at the safe, pressed the trigger, and held it.

Only a miracle kept one of the ricocheting bullets from striking him. It wasn't until the magazine was finally empty that he dropped the gun. He stepped forward and almost gently felt the great iron door of the safe. And then slowly he shook his head.

He turned to find his way back out of the car. He must go back and get Joe and Stanley. They would help him open the safe. He remembered suddenly the dynamite caps and crow bars and chisels which they had packed in the snowmobile in expectation of this situation.

Yes, he'd get Joe and Stanley. He was weak, too weak to handle this by himself.

Chapter Sixteen

The sound of the explosion reached Tina's ears while she was still a mile and a half from the trestle. She halted momentarily and stared into the distance ahead, a puzzled expression on her face. She couldn't imagine what made the noise and after a minute or so, while she stood still and rested, she stopped trying to guess.

It was heavy going in the snow, but she was not tired. She'd had enough experience in the mountains to take it slowly, and she knew that if the blizzard didn't get any worse she'd be all right. All she had to do was find the railway tracks.

A few minutes later she saw a tall tower of smoke rising far ahead, and again she stopped and looked at it curiously. For a brief moment she thought of forest fires, but then quickly dismissed the idea. This high up the forests were far too sparse, and in any case, forest fires don't start in the middle of a blinding snow storm.

Not once did she connect Frank with either the explosion or the fire. She tried not to think of Frank at all, but of course that was impossible. It was strange, but in her mind it was almost as though Frank were already dead.

She hadn't stopped loving him; she didn't think she ever would. But he no longer seemed real, no longer seemed to be a man whom she had known and loved and held dear.

The Frank who had left the house this morning and who was out here somewhere in the bleak hills, this Frank was a man that she really had never known at all. That other Frank, the man with whom she had fallen in love, was another man altogether. No—he wasn't really another man. He was a man who had never really existed, one whom she had made up.

At four o'clock Tina reached the last rise, and when she came to its summit she halted and looked down the long slope leading to the canyon beneath the trestle.

It was several minutes before the full impact of the scene below really hit Tina. The remains of the wooden caboose were still burning vividly and she was able to make out the wreckage of the locomotive were it lay crushed and broken.

Her eyes finally went up and she saw the ends of the broken trestle hanging out over each side of the gorge. She was still ignorant of what had happened, but she knew that there had been a train wreck and that the engine and at least two cars had fallen into the canyon. At the same time she realized the significance of that great explosion which had reached her ears.

The color left her face and she shuddered. It was then that all thoughts of Frank, of Frank and herself and those others at the lodge, left her mind. Once more she was Tina Bennet a trained nurse.

Somewhere down there in that wreckage there might still be life. She quickly began the long glide down the slope.

It wasn't until she'd almost reached the overturned money car that she noticed the smoldering remains of the snowmobile. It was a moment before she recognized the vehicle, believing it at first to be a piece of scattered wreckage from the train. She swerved toward it and it was then she saw the body in the snow.

A quick gasp escaped her and she went over and bent down. She recognized Stanley, and knew that he was dead. She was starting to her feet, fear and horror in her face, when she saw Frank.

He was trudging through the heavy snow, leaving the wrecked money car. He was bareheaded and without gloves and he had lost the dark glasses. She stood then, dumb and shocked with horror as he came toward her, and at last stood in front of her and looked into her face.

She saw the blind, vacant expression in his eyes, and she didn't think he recognized her. But then he reached out and he touched her and he spoke.

"They're all dead," he said. "All of them. Dead. We've got to go now, Tina."

His voice was soft and unhurried; she knew he was no longer sane.

It was strange, but in all of that scene of horror and bloodshed, the one thing she noticed was the thin stream of blood coming from the corner of his mouth and channeling down his chin. That and the fact that he'd lost his hat and his gloves and his dark glasses.

"Frank," she said. "Oh, God, Frank. What happened? What..."

It was as though he didn't hear her at all.

"The money's still in the safe," he said, speaking in that odd, impersonal monotone. "In the safe and there's no way at all to get it. Joe's gone and Stanley's gone and there's no way to get the money."

She leaned forward and took him by the arms and shook him.

"Frank," she said. "Frank—what happened? You came from the train. Is anyone ..."

"They're all dead," he said. "Joe and Stanley are gone, and they're all dead."

He looked at her and it was as though he were seeing right through her. He pulled his arms away and turned and went over to where the pair of skis lay in the snow. Leaning down, he began to strap them to his feet.

For a moment she watched him, and then she turned back toward the train. She saw Cal Treacher's body in the snow a few yards away and she went over and knelt down. She saw the rifle lying at his side and she saw his wounds, and she knew he hadn't been killed in the train wreck.

Standing up, she looked once more at the shambles in front of her and then she slowly turned and walked back to Frank.

He had secured the skis and was standing again.

"We've got to go now, Tina," he said.

Without another word he slowly started up the slope of the hill.

For a moment she hesitated, and then she heard a cry come from far up the valley. It wasn't a cry of alarm, but rather a long hail. Dully, in the back of her mind, she realized that someone was coming from the opposite direction. She hesitated for a second or so, and then turned and quickened her pace as she hurried to catch up with Frank.

Although he didn't look at her, he seemed to know she was with him. He was coughing now at regular intervals and between coughs he mumbled under his breath. After a few minutes he stopped and turned toward her.

"I've lost my glasses," he said. "There's something wrong with my eyes, and I can't see without them. Everything seems blurred."

"I know, Frank," Tina said.

"You must help me," he said. "We must get back to the lodge. We must get back and get the guns."

His eyes focused on her then and she realized that she had been wrong. He wasn't in a state of shock; he knew what he was saying and what he was doing.

"The guns," he said. "You heard that cry—back there in the canyon. Someone was coming. We must get back and get the guns."

For a moment she wanted to scream out at him, to reach for him and to strike him and to cry the words in his face. She wanted to tell him that he was insane, stark mad.

Back to the lodge? And what was there? Guns and more bloodshed? Did he actually think he had a chance? Did he believe he could still go on running and killing?

But then she merely looked away from him and when she spoke her voice was calm and controlled.

"All right, Frank," she said. "All right. We'll go back."

"You'll have to lead the way," he said. "Don't get too far ahead. I can hardly see."

"I'll lead."

She started out again, this time stepping in front of him and keeping her eyes on the ground where she could see the traces of the tracks she had left on her way out from the lodge to the canyon. It was still snowing, but the wind had died a little and she hurried on, knowing that soon the last twin marks of her skis would be lost.

The route was familiar now and although it was rapidly getting dark, she knew exactly where they were. It wouldn't be long now.

At last she came to it—the stunted pine stump. Seeing it there up ahead brought back vividly the memories of that trip they had made last Tuesday when they had gone out together on their sightseeing trip. She even remembered the words: *You must be careful, very careful, when you come to it. It marks the edge of the precipice.*

She stopped and waited until he'd caught up to her.

His head was covered with snow and frost had formed on his eyebrows under the white forehead. His large dark eyes stared into her own but she sensed that he wasn't really seeing her. There was a rim of dried blood around his blue lips when he opened them to speak.

"Which way, Tina?" he asked. "Which way?"

This time the tears did come to her eyes, and in spite of every effort at control the sobs shook her. Yes, which way?

"Stop it, Tina," he said. "Stop it and tell me the way. Everything has faded now and you must tell me the way to go."

She lifted her face then and looked at him for a long moment. Then she took him very gently by the arm.

"This way, Frank," she said. "Straight ahead. We'll be home soon now."

He nodded and started out and she guided him as they approached the crest of the hill. For a second then she hesitated. He took another step and for a brief moment he too seemed to hesitate, silhouetted there in the blinding snow, on the lip of the great precipice.

And then he was gone.

When Trooper Upton reached her half an hour later she was over by the pine stump, kneeling in the snow. She was just kneeling there motionless, the tears coursing down her cheeks and falling to the ground where they burned tiny deep wells in the soft white snow.

THE END